SHOTGUN JOHNNY

LOOK FOR THESE EXCITING WESTERN SERIES FROM BEST-SELLING AUTHORS WILLIAM W. JOHNSTONE AND J.A. JOHNSTONE

The Mountain Man

Luke Jensen: Bounty Hunter

Brannigan's Land

The Jensen Brand

Smoke Jensen: The Early Years

Preacher and MacCallister

Fort Misery

The Fighting O'Neils

Perley Gates

MacCoole and Boone

Guns of the Vigilantes

Shotgun Johnny

The Chuckwagon Trail

The Jackals

The Slash and Pecos Westerns

The Texas Moonshiners

Stoneface Finnegan Westerns

Ben Savage: Saloon Ranger

The Buck Trammel Westerns

The Death and Texas Westerns

The Hunter Buchanon Westerns

Will Tanner: US Deputy Marshal

Old Cowboys Never Die

Go West, Young Man

Published by Kensington Publishing Corp.

SHOTGUN JOHNNY

WILLIAM W. JOHNSTONE
AND J. A. JOHNSTONE

PINNACLE BOOKS
Kensington Publishing Corp.
www.kensingtonbooks.com

PINNACLE BOOKS are published by

Kensington Publishing Corp.
119 West 40th Street
New York, NY 10018

PUBLISHER'S NOTE: Following the death of William W. Johnstone, the Johnstone family is working with a carefully selected writer to organize and complete Mr. Johnstone's outlines and many unfinished manuscripts to create additional novels in all of his series like The Last Gunfighter, Mountain Man, and Eagles, among others. This novel was inspired by Mr. Johnstone's superb storytelling.

First printing: February 2020
ISBN-13: 978-0-7860-4849-6
ISBN-13: 978-0-7860-4852-6 (eBook)

10 9 8 7 6 5 4 3 2

Printed in the United States of America

CHAPTER 1

"Ouch!" said "Rocky Mountain" Vernon Wade.

"What'd you do?" asked his partner, Pete Devries, with a snort of laughter.

"Burned myself." Wade winced as he shifted his hot coffee cup in his hands. "Think it's funny?"

Devries shrugged and sipped from his own hot cup. "Yeah, I guess so."

"Why is my burning my hand so funny to you, Pete?" Wade asked, glaring across a corner of their low fire at his partner, Devries.

"Oh, hell, I don't know," Devries said. He was tall and sandy-haired, and the brim of his Boss of the Plains Stetson was pulled low over his gray-blue eyes. "I reckon it was funny cause you otherwise act so tough. Forget it, Vernon. Stand down. I just chuckled at somethin' I thought was funny, that's all. I didn't mean to give offense."

"You did give offense."

"Well, then, for that I apologize."

"I am tough, Pete." Wade glared darkly. "And don't you forget it."

"Okay, I won't forget it." Devries looked off into the darkness of the Sierra Nevada Mountain night.

"There you go again, laughin'."

Devries looked back at Wade, who was dark and solidly built with a thick beard he hardly ever washed and certainly never ran a comb through. On a previous bullion run he'd pulled a tick out of it the size of a sewing thimble but only because Devries had noticed it and mentioned it. Otherwise, it might still be there, sucking blood out of the humorless killer's cheek.

"What'd you laugh at that time, Pete?" Wade wanted to know.

"Oh, hell, Vernon!"

"Stop callin' me Vernon, Pete. Folks call me Rocky Mountain or nothin' at all. Folks call me Vernon only when they want to disrespect me, an' you don't want to do that, Pete. You really don't want to do that!"

"All right, all right, Vern . . . er, I mean, *Rocky Mountain.* I apologize for callin' you Vernon and for any and all other sundry ways I might have given offense during our time workin' together!"

"In case you're at all interested in anything except snickerin' like some twin-braided schoolgirl, I jerked with a start because I got distracted by a sound I heard out there." Wade pointed his chin to indicate the heavy darkness beyond the flickering orange light of the fire. "And, while I was silently opinin' on the source of the sound and the possible nature of the threat, if the sound's origin is in fact a threat, I let the cup tip a little too far to one side. So I was, in fact, reactin' as much to the sound as to the hot coffee washin' onto my fingers."

"Well, now that we got *that* all straightened out,"

Devries said, trying very hard not to give another wry snort, "what sound did you hear or think you heard?"

"I heard it, all right." Wade set his cup on a rock ringing the fire. He grabbed his Henry repeating rifle, rose from where he'd been sitting back against the woolly underside of his saddle, and walked over to stand by a tall fir tree at the edge of the encampment. One of the three horses, tied to a picket line nearby, gave a low whicker. "I got the hearin' of a desert jackrabbit, an' I heard somethin', all right. I'm just not sure what it was."

"Why don't you take a guess?"

Again, Wade turned a dull, hateful stare at his partner. "You don't believe me? Or you think I'm just actin' like some fearful old widder woman, hearin' things?"

Devries looked at the Henry. Wade held the sixteen-shot repeater in his right hand, partly aimed, threateningly, in Devries's direction. That was no accident. Wade wanted Devries to feel the threat. Devries knew that it was entirely likely that Rocky Mountain Vernon Wade would kill him for no more reason than because he felt Devries had insulted him, which Devries supposed he had, though he'd mostly just been funning around.

Before they'd started working together, hauling bullion down out of the mountains from the Reverend's Temptation Gold Mine to the bank in Hallelujah Junction, Devries had heard that Wade was thin-skinned and hot-tempered. He'd also heard that Wade had killed men for little more reason than he'd taken offense at how they'd glanced at him, or for something someone had said in passing likely not even meant as an insult.

Now Devries realized those stories were true, and he made a mental note to tread a little more cautiously from here on . . .

"No, no, Vern . . . er, I mean, Rocky Mountain!" Devries said. "Will you please get your shorts out of the twist they seem to be in? I do not think you were acting like no widder woman. I believe that you in fact heard something, and I was just thinking that if you can't pinpoint exactly what that something was, maybe you could just opine aloud on it."

Wade studied him skeptically from over his shoulder.

Devries's heart quickened. Jesus, he did not need this. Life was too short to be guarding gold with some sorehead with a hair trigger. And as loco as an owl in a lightning storm to boot!

Wade turned his head forward suddenly, sucking a sharp, shallow breath. "There it was again."

Devries pricked his ears. All he could hear was the snapping and crackling of their low fire and the infrequent stomps and shifts of the two horses and pack mule picketed twenty feet away. "I didn't hear anything."

"Well, I heard it."

Devries set down his coffee and rose from the log he'd been sitting on. He grabbed his Winchester and walked over to stand near Wade. Devries stared out into the darkness beyond their camp here in Henry's Hollow, not far from the South Fork of the Avalanche River and Grizzly Falls. He held his breath as he listened, squinting into the darkness, blinking, waiting for his eyes to adjust to the lack of light over here.

Normally, only fools and tinhorns would build a

fire when they thought there was a chance they were being stalked. But neither Devries nor Wade had thought anyone would be fool enough to shadow them—two gunmen of significant reputations in this neck of California and Nevada. No man was fool enough to think they could swipe the bullion out from under Pete Devries and Rocky Mountain Vernon Wade.

Devries had thought so before, and, not hearing anything except the hooting of a distant owl and the soft scuttles of some burrowing creatures, he still thought so.

Maybe Wade was not only crazy. Maybe he was like some fearful old "widder" woman—hearing things.

Best not allude to the possibility, Devries silently admonished himself. Or at least do so in a round-about way . . .

"Hard to believe anyone would fool with us, Rocky Mountain," he said softly, staring into the darkness. "I mean you alone carry one hell of a reputation on them broad shoulders of yours. How many men have you killed, anyway?"

"I stopped countin' when I was twelve."

Devries snapped a disbelieving look at the big man standing to his right.

Wade felt it was his turn to snort. He turned to Devries with a crooked smile inside his black beard. "Just foolin' with ya, Peter. I think I stopped countin' when I was thirteen and a half." His smile grew wider.

Devries smiled then, too, thinking it was all right since Wade had made a joke.

Was it a joke?

Not that Devries was all that impressed or afraid of Vernon Wade. Devries had been a gunslinger and regulator of some renown for half a dozen years, before he'd ended up in the Texas pen for killing a barman in Nacogdoches. His attorney had gotten him out early when he'd discovered that the prosecutor had bought guilty verdict votes from three jury members. Devries hadn't been out of the pen for more than two days before he'd broken into the prosecutor's home one night and slit the man's throat while the man had been sound asleep beside his wife, who'd woken up screaming when she'd heard her husband choking on his own blood.

In other words, Devries's past was as impressive as Vernon Wade's. Pete just wasn't the blowhard Vernon was. Yes, *Vernon.* Devries might call the man "Rocky Mountain" to his face, just to keep things civil between them, but in his own mind he'd forever know him as *Vernon.* Or maybe even Ver*nie.* The only reason Pete didn't put a bullet through the blowhard's left ear right here and now was because this bullion run they were on, from the Reverend's Temptation to Hallelujah Junction, was one of the most perilous runs in all the Sierra Nevadas. The Temptation was a rich mine, and every owlhoot in California and Nevada knew it. There might be a handful just stupid enough to make a play for the gold, maybe not knowing who was guarding it.

The way Devries saw it, four eyes were better than two. Best to keep the peace.

Besides, Devries didn't want to ruffle the feathers of his comely employer, Miss Sheila Bonner, the young lady who'd taken over the Bank & Trust in Hallelujah Junction from her father, who'd also owned the Reverend's Temptation Mine. Miss Bonner was quite the looker, maybe the prettiest woman Devries had ever laid eyes on. She filled out her fine, if overly conservative, frocks just the way a dress was meant to be filled out. Pete was figuring to make a play for the woman. Not to marry, of course. Devries was not the apron-strings sort. But he purely would like to see what Miss Bonner looked like under all them fancy trappings, and, most of all, how she'd treat a fella after the lamps were turned down in her deceased father's stylish digs on a nice shady lot in Hallelujah Junction.

Devries didn't want to do anything that might spoil his prospects for a conquest. Shooting his partner, he supposed, might do just that. He'd put up with only so much, however. He could always shoot dim-witted Vern*ie*, and blame it on a bushwhacking owlhoot making a play for the bullion.

He stifled a laugh then jumped with a little start when Wade leaned toward him and said quietly, "I'm gonna wander on over this way. What I heard came from over there. You head that way. We'll circle around, check it out."

Devries's hackles rose a little at being given orders by one so cow-stupid not to mention ugly and with the hygiene of a hyena, but what the hell? "All right," he said, rolling his eyes. He still hadn't heard anything and was beginning to believe his partner really was as jumpy as that "widder" woman.

Vernie strode into the darkness to Devries's right. Devries stood looking around and listening a while longer. When he still hadn't heard a damn thing except the soft crunch of Vernie's boots in the dead leaves and pine needles, he indulged in another acidic snort then moved out into the darkness to his left.

"Big dummy," he muttered under his breath, and chuckled.

He stepped over a log, pushed through some shrubs, and stopped to look around and listen again.

Nothing.

He turned to his left and headed along the camp's eastern periphery, maybe ten feet beyond the reach of the fire's dwindling umber glow. When he was off the camp's northeastern corner, exactly opposite from where he and Vernie had separated, he stopped and listened again.

Not a damn thing. Hell, even the owl had stopped hooting.

Pete yawned, raked a hand down his face. They'd had a long day on the trail in the high-altitude wind and burning sunshine. He was tired, wind- and sun-burned, and he was ready to roll into his soogan. They'd rig up the horses and pack mule and set out again on the trail that led down out of the mountains soon after first light.

He turned to look back over his left shoulder, across the encampment toward where Vernie must be stumbling around in the darkness, chasing the shadows of ghosts. Pete had just opened his mouth to call out to his partner, when Wade himself yelled suddenly, "Stop! Stop! I see you, dammit! Stop or I'll shoot!"

Wade's Henry thundered—a loud booming report that made Devries leap with a start, his heels coming up off the ground.

He jerked again when the Henry spoke again . . . again . . . and again.

The sound of running footsteps sounded on the far side of the camp, maybe two hundred feet away, beyond the horses that were nickering and prancing around in fear, the mule doing the same, braying softly, all three tugging on their picket line.

"What is it?" Devries yelled, his heart pounding. "What do you see, Vern . . . I mean, *Rocky Mountain*?"

The running footsteps stopped suddenly.

Wade said something too softly, or maybe he was too far away, for Devries to hear.

Pete did hear the sudden gasp, however. It was loud as gasps go and it was followed by what sounded like a strangling sigh. The sigh was followed by a shrill, "Ahh . . . ohhh . . . ohhhh, *gawd!* Oh, you dirty, low-down . . ."

There was a light thump.

"What is it, Wade?"

Devries ran toward the sound of the commotion. He sprinted through the weak light thrown by the fire and then out of the light again and into the darkness near the whickering, skitter-hopping horses and mule. A deadfall pulled his right foot out from under him, and he hit the ground hard.

He lifted his head, sweating, his heart thundering in his ears. "What is it, Rocky Mountain?"

He stared into the darkness, breathing hard from the short run and the fear that verged on panic.

Footsteps rose on his left. Devries whipped his head in that direction. Someone was moving toward him, taking heavy, lunging strides. He saw the man's thick shadow.

"Wade?" he called. "Rocky Mountain, that you?"

No reply except for the heavy, lunging steps. The

thick man's shadow moved through the forest, crouched slightly forward.

"Wade?" he called again, panic a living beast inside of him.

He looked around quickly, not hearing anything but the big man's approach. Still, he had the sense that he was surrounded and that men were tightening their positions around him.

He turned again toward the camp. The light from the fire began to reach the approaching man. Devries swung around from the darkness and, squeezing his cocked Winchester in both hands, hurried back into the camp just as the thick figure stepped up to the fire on the camp's opposite side.

Devries stopped.

"Rocky Mountain?"

Vernon Wade stood with his knees bent. He was crouched forward, chin dipped toward his chest, his arms crossed on his belly. Slowly, Wade lifted his head. He wasn't wearing his hat. His shaggy, unwashed hair hung in his eyes, which flashed in the fire's umber light. His gaze found Devries gaping at him from the other side of the fire.

"Th-they're . . . they're . . . here," Wade said in a strangled voice.

Devries sucked in a breath when he saw what appeared to be blood—what else could it be?—oozing out from between his partner's crossed arms. Blood and Vernon Wade's innards.

Devries shuddered as though racked with a violent chill. Cold sweat pasted his shirt under his leather jacket against his back.

"Who's here, Rocky Mountain?"

"Oh . . . oh, *gawd*!" Wade sobbed, dropping to his

knees. He lifted his head and stretched his lips back from his teeth. "*They killed me!*"

His arms fell to his sides. As they did, the guts he was trying to hold inside him plopped onto the ground before him. He fell face forward and lay across his bowels, shuddering as he died.

Devries stared down at the big, dark lump of his dead partner. "Who killed you, Rocky Mountain?" he whispered, rolling his eyes around, trying to peer around to all sides at once.

He glanced toward where he and Wade had placed the panniers filled with bullion from the Reverend's Temptation, between their two saddles, one on each side of the fire. Devries blinked his eyes as if to clear them.

The panniers were gone.

Again, his poor abused heart gave a violent kick against the backside of his sternum.

Someone laughed behind him. It was a high, devilish squeal. It was followed by the crunching of running feet.

Devries whipped around, raised his Winchester, and fired.

"Who are you?" he shouted, ejecting the spent shell from the Winchester's breech and seating a fresh one in the action.

He fired again. Again. The rocketing blasts shattered the night's heavy silence and made his ears ring.

More squealing laughter, like the laughter of a devilish boy pulling a prank, rose on his right. It mingled with the laughter of what sounded like a woman.

Devries slid the rifle in that direction, cocking it, the spent shell pinging onto the ground behind him.

The rifle leaped and roared in his hands, flames stabbing from the barrel.

More laughter—this time on Devries's left.

Pete fired.

He fired until he had no more cartridges left in the Winchester's magazine. He winced when he heard the ping of the hammer dropping benignly against the firing pin.

He stared through his wafting powder smoke into the darkness around him.

No more laughter now. No more running footsteps. No more sounds of any kind. Not even the breeze.

The horses and mule must have pulled free of their picket line and hightailed it, for he did not see their bulky silhouettes on his left, though in his anxious shooting he hadn't heard them bolt.

The empty rifle shook in Devries's hands.

He dropped it as though it were a hot potato. It plopped onto the ground at his feet.

He reached across his belly with his right hand and pulled the big, top-break Russian .44 positioned for the cross-draw on his left hip. His hand was shaking so badly that he had trouble unsnapping the keeper thong from over the hammer, raising the heavy pistol, and cocking it.

"Show yourselves!" he screamed. "Show yourselves, you devils!"

His own echo washed over him, further chilling him. It sounded like the echoing cry of a terrified old widder woman.

A man's voice said casually behind him, "You boys sure can cook a good pot of coffee."

Devries whipped around so quickly that he almost fell.

He swung the big Russian around, as well, and aimed toward the fire. The blaze had been built up a little so that the light shone on the face of the man crouched over the opposite side of it. The man held a steaming tin cup in his gloved hands.

Devries moved slowly toward the fire. His heart was like a giant metronome in his chest, the pendulum assaulting his heart like a sharpened steel blade.

Devries stopped about ten feet away from the fire, staring aghast at the man hunkered there on the other side of the flames, on his haunches. He had a devil's grinning face with high, tapering cheeks obscured beneath a thick, sandy beard, and wicked slits for eyes. Coarse, sandy blond hair poked out from beneath the battered Stetson stuffed down on his head. He wore a buckskin coat with a fox-fur collar. A Colt's revolving rifle leaned against the log to his right, within easy reach.

The man smiled his devil's smile at Devries. He raised his coffee to his lips, blew on it, and sipped. Swallowing, he straightened to his full height, which was maybe six feet, if that. He was not a tall man. But, then, Harry Seville had never needed to be.

What Seville lacked for in height, he made up for in pure cunning and blackhearted meanness and storied savagery.

Footsteps sounded around Devries. Squeezing the big Russian in his hands, he swung the pistol from right to left then back again, that metronome in his chest fairly shredding his heart. Men stepped into the firelight around him by ones and two and threes and fours . . . until well over a dozen men aiming rifles or pistols at him surrounded him, grinning beneath the brims of their battered hats.

Make that over a dozen men and one woman, a big one who looked very much like a man except she wore a long, black skirt. She was laughing beneath the round, wide crown of her man's felt hat.

"Ah," Devries heard himself say in a small, defeated voice. "Ah . . . hell . . ."

The big man laughed heartily, his devil's eyes slitting so much that they were nearly closed. The other men laughed, as well. They laughed and elbowed each other and pointed out the object of their mockery. They snorted and brushed fists across their noses and poked their hat brims back off their foreheads.

Devries had just begun to feel warm liquid trickling down his leg before a hand slugged his hat from his head from behind then grabbed a fistful of his hair. Pete cried out as the brusque hand pulled his head back by his hair until he found himself staring up at a big, dark man towering over him from behind. Devries tried to raise the barrel of the Russian, but then he felt an icy line drawn across his throat, and all strength left him at once.

He sank to the ground, gasping, lifting his hands to his neck to try to remove the cold noose that had been drawn taut around him. His fingers touched only the oily slickness of blood.

There was no noose. His throat had been cut.

Lying on his back, Devries stared up from the ground at the man who'd killed him. He was a tall, broad-shouldered gent in a bearskin coat and a bullet-shaped black hat from beneath which twin black braids trailed down over the front of his broad shoulders.

Seville and his half-breed Sioux partner, Louis Raised-By-Wolves. He knew their dastardly reputations.

Devries had done some lousy things on this earth, but he didn't believe he'd ever committed an atrocity horrible enough to warrant the last thing he saw on this side of the sod be Louis Raised-By-Wolves staring down at him, chuckling at him and licking Devries's own blood from the blade of his bowie knife as though it were the sweetest nectar he'd ever tasted.

CHAPTER 2

"You have such a lovely body, Miss Sheila, for the life of me I can't understand why no man has yet staked a claim on you!" intoned Verna Godfrey early the next morning in Hallelujah Junction.

Sheila Bonner stood holding her breath while the maid laced up the back of her blue silk whalebone corset. She said in a somewhat pinched voice and with a vaguely ironic air that was no doubt lost on Verna, "I don't know, Verna. I guess men are smarter than we give them credit for."

"Oh, that's just silly. No *smart* man would pass up such a beauty. They're all imbeciles!"

"Most men feel threatened by professional women . . . and women who don't put up with their blather. Wrap that into one female package, Verna, and you get an old maid."

"Shame. Just a shame," Verna said with an exasperated sigh, sadly shaking her head as she stared into the looking glass of Sheila's recently deceased father's stout English shaving stand. It was the only large looking glass in the crisp, brick, Victorian-style house that Sheila's father had built soon after the mining camp of Hallelujah Junction had boomed into a town of considerable wealth and distinction, at least by remote Sierra Nevada Mountain standards.

The young woman standing half-naked in the looking glass, staring back at her own image, was one of considerable wealth and distinction, as well. The wealth might be somewhat precarious, given her father's recent death and some of the risky business decisions he'd made preceding it, as well as the temperamental boomtown economy, but there was no questioning the young woman's attractiveness. The dark brown of her almond-shaped eyes was exquisitely complemented by the rich chestnut sheen of her long, thick hair, which Verna had spent nearly the entire last quarter-hour brushing out so that it flowed down Sheila's slender back like the thick mane of a blooded mare. The young woman's subtly heart-shaped face with its long dark lashes, pert nose, gently tapering cheeks, and strong jawline, might have been carved out of ivory with the precise chisel-work of the most delicate of carvers.

Her bosoms, while not overlarge, were pert, firm, and perfectly shaped.

Looking down in that direction, unable to not feel a little pride at the attributes God had found her worthy of owning, Sheila said with a wry snort, "Men *are* smarter than we women give them credit for. The proof is in the pudding—er, the corset, I should say."

Still tightening the laces against Sheila's back, Verna met her gaze in the looking glass and frowned. "What on earth do you mean, dear?"

"Who else but a man would invent such a draconian and demeaning contraption as the whalebone corset? And who but a woman, foolish in our need to please said men right down to wearing the most uncomfortable contraptions invented since the Middle Ages' instruments of diabolical torture, would be harebrained enough to wear them?"

Verna stared at Sheila in the mirror, the old woman's frosty blue eyes opaque with distressed incomprehension. "Oh, dear . . . how you do go on!" She laughed heartily, causing her sagging jowls to quiver. "I declare, you do so remind me of your father sometimes in the way you put words together. Just like Mister Bonner, I often can't understand but maybe two or three words you throw out at a time!"

The older woman laughed and shook her head as, finished tying the corset, she lowered her hands to her sides. "Oh, dear . . ." She glanced around Joe Bonner's sparsely but tastefully furnished bedroom with its canopied, four-poster bed, which was where the two women were standing for the use of the dead man's mirror. "I do so miss the mister so . . ." She turned back to regard Sheila tragically in the looking glass. "I'm so sorry, dear! How utterly heartless of me to mention—"

Turning, Sheila took the old woman's thick wrists in her hands, smiling gently at her, caressing her hands with her thumbs. "How heartless of you to remember my father? Nonsense, Verna. It warms my heart to know how much you cared for him."

"Oh, but it's so soon . . ." The housekeeper turned her head to gaze out the window to her left, which nearly as perfectly as a picture framed Martin Bonner's grave set back in a small stand of young spruces and marked off from the rest of the yard by a black, wrought-iron fence. The grave itself was a firm young mound covered with rocks and adorned with the flowers Sheila had laid atop it only yesterday, having laid a fresh spray of hollyhocks on the grave every morning since her father's funeral the previous week.

Martin Bonner had been stricken with a series of small but debilitating strokes over the past year, due in no small part, the local doctor had opined, to the financial strain Bonner had been feeling for the past eighteen months at the bank he'd owned, the Hallelujah Bank & Trust. The beginnings of that strain had corresponded with the first of several robberies of the gold bullion Bonner transported, by independent contractors, out of the mountains every month from the Reverend's Temptation Gold Mine, which he also owned, at the base of Grizzly Ridge, on the east side of the Sierra Nevadas.

With each succeeding robbery and the loss of over two hundred thousand dollars in bullion, the poor man's health had deteriorated until, unable to ignore his wretched state any longer, he'd finally written a letter to his daughter, Sheila, who'd been working as an accountant for her uncle, Martin's younger brother, in Philadelphia. Martin had moved to California alone after his wife, Margaret, had died back east, leaving Sheila with his brother, John. Martin had not believed the Wild West a place for a young lady of Sheila's intellectual gifts—especially a daughter he so desperately wanted to see wedded. However, knowing that if anyone could keep the bank on its feet, Sheila could, he'd requested his only daughter's assistance until his health improved.

"It's never too soon to start keeping a man's memory alive, Verna," Sheila said, squeezing the old woman's thick, work-toughened hands in her own. "Especially a man as good as my father was."

"I know, child, but—"

"I only wish I'd gotten here sooner, so that I could have spent more time with him when he was still well enough to know who I was." By the time Sheila had reached Hallelujah Junction, Martin Bonner had been bedridden and nearly unable to speak. Only two days after Sheila had arrived, the old man had died, frighteningly frail and weak, in her arms as she'd sobbed against his shoulder.

"What a tragedy," Verna said, canting her head to gaze sadly at Sheila, a single tear rolling down her suety cheek. The older woman placed a gentle hand on Sheila's cheek, brushing Sheila's own tears away. "What a fine legacy you are to the mister, child. You're the spitting image, and you're a fine, fine young woman who needs a—"

Sheila quickly placed two fingers on the older woman's lips. "No more man-talk! From here on in, this is a man-free house, Verna—verbally as well as physically!"

"Oh, dear . . ."

"They aren't worth having around, most of 'em. In fact, I've met nary a one aside from my father and Uncle John who was worth the polish it took to shine his shoes, worth the wax in his mustache!"

Verna cupped a hand to her mouth. "Oh, oh . . . *dear*!"

Sheila laughed, sniffing back her tears. She walked to the window, gazing at Martin Bonner's grave, folding her arms on the two firm mounds pushed up by her whalebone-reinforced corset, like the chain mail of Roman warriors. "And what kind of a testament I am to my father's memory remains to be seen. If I can't turn his bank around, I'll be a pretty sorry one, I'm afraid. This *legacy*, as you call it, will be heading back East with her tail between her legs. So . . . what I need to do first off is make sure that no more of those bullion runs is robbed."

"You said you hired a couple of capable guards . . ." Verna said behind Sheila, her voice tentative and unconfident as always when discussing business matters.

Sheila sighed. "Let's just say they came . . . highly recommended. Not exactly the finest citizens, but then sometimes wolves are the best weapons to use against . . . well, wolves."

"Let's just hope they're the answer."

"Let's hope." Sheila turned suddenly from the window. "Speaking of wolves, my two are due down from the mountains today. And I have an early meeting with Mister Poindexter, so I'd best get a move on." She chuckled as she fairly ran out of her father's neat room and down the hall to her own, which she'd been too busy to bother furnishing with a mirror. "I've been lounging around this morning like a lady of leisure, which I certainly am not!"

In fact, she had a bank she was working overtime to try and get back on its feet, with the help of her father's vice-president, George Poindexter, a man around Sheila's father's age who, while long past his prime, was honest and genuine enough that Sheila, like her father, did not have the heart to let him go. Besides, the customers liked him, and it was a rare banker who was liked.

So far in Hallelujah Junction, Sheila was barely tolerated. The good citizens might have revered her father, but Sheila knew that she was seen as "uppity" and "foreign." She was also held in a special contempt reserved for women who had the gall to meddle in a man's world. To not only meddle, but to work *above* them, with the power to hire and fire.

Somehow, Sheila had a feeling the good citizens of Hallelujah Junction might have gone easier on her if she were ugly. She'd discovered in her twenty-six years of life that men as well as women seemed especially suspicious of a beautiful woman with power.

"I'll have your ham and eggs ready in five minutes!" Verna called from the hall.

"Just coffee, please, Verna," Sheila called as she rummaged through one of her steamer trunks, which she had not yet taken the time to fully unpack, for her day's attire.

"Oh, Miss Bonner, you can't start the day with only coffee!" protested the maid. "What would your father say?"

"Just coffee, please, Verna!"

Ten minutes later, her father's cracked leather valise tucked under her arm, Sheila stepped out of the house's front door and onto the brick porch with its crisp white rail supported by scrolled columns. She was decked out in an only slightly wrinkled caramel moleskin suit with a white Abbington blouse trimmed with delicate lace sewn vertically down the bosom and sleeve.

The blouse had a high collar and long barrel cuffs. Puff-top sleeves and a gathered back yoke helped give the chestnut-haired beauty the hourglass silhouette so valued by the era, despite the constant pinch she felt from having her womanly curves so torturously restrained. A wide, black silk belt encircled her slender waist, a black felt riding hat sat atop her head, and her feet were clad in tweed ankle boots with spats.

"In my next life, I'm coming back as a man," she grumbled, stepping carefully down the porch steps while pinching the long caramel skirt up above her ankles so she didn't trip and fall.

At the bottom of the porch steps, she stopped and glanced toward the long plot of hollyhocks growing along the white picket fence surrounding the yard shaded by several ponderosa pines and apple trees. Automatically, she started toward the flowers with the intention of picking a few for her father's grave, then stopped and shook her head.

"I'm sorry, Pa," Sheila said. "No time today. I'm late for a meeting. I'll make it up to you tomorrow, I promise." As she strode down the brick path toward the gate in the picket fence, she glanced over her shoulder toward the fresh grave at the rear of the house. Tears rolled down her cheeks. This would be the first morning she missed adorning her father's grave, and she knew with a pain of bitter anguish that it was probably not the last. "Wish me luck, Pa!" she called, her voice cracking with emotion.

She rubbed the tears from her face as she walked along California Avenue in the early morning quiet, the log shacks and shanties just now touched by the buttery glow of the rising sun poking its head above the high, stony eastern ridges. Smoke from breakfast fires, rising from tin pipes and brick chimneys, hazed before her, wafting gently against the deeper blue-green of the fir-clad ridges that hemmed in this small village set along the Paiute River in the Northern Paiute River Valley. The fresh air was still cool after the long mountain night, and tanged with pine as well as the mineral smell of the river that curved around the edge of the village in its wide, black bed.

Her father had loved this little town. He'd fallen in love with the romance of the West through books and magazines and had ventured here in search of a new life in the wake of Sheila's mother's passing. Sheila hoped she'd come to like it, as well. She didn't see much romance here, however. All she saw were a lot of drunken miners in their thick-soled boots and filthy dungarees, and the girls who worked the line, luring the men, fresh from their diggings after a hard day's work, into their squalid cribs, called "hog pens" in the parlance of the rough-and-tumble frontier, off backstreet alleys.

Oh, well. Once she had her father's accounts in order, and the bank back on its feet, she'd probably feel . . .

Sheila let the thought trail like morning vapor from her mind. She was approaching the bank, opening her valise to search for the bank keys while clomping along the rough wooden boardwalk on Paiute Street's north side. Now she slowed her pace, frowning as she stared ahead of her.

Two horses were tied to one of the two hitch rails fronting the bank. They were each carrying something sprawled across their backs, over their saddles. At first, Sheila thought dead deer or some other game animal were tied across the horse's backs, for there was a good deal of blood. She'd gotten used to

seeing dead deer, elk, bears, and moose as well as
birds of many kinds hauled into town in similar fash-
ion, to be sold to game merchants and grocers who'd
butcher them right out on the main street.

But, no. These horses weren't carrying game. It
took Sheila only one or two more seconds, after a
blink of her disbelieving eyes, to see that the horses
were each carrying a *man* sprawled across its saddle.

Sheila's heart kicked like a horse against her
breastbone.

Her lungs grew tight, her breath shallow. A shudder racked her.

Her mouth hanging half open, she strode ahead
slowly and moved to the edge of the boardwalk to
stare in wide-eyed horror at the man sprawled back
down across his saddle. The man's head hung down
over the big buckskin's belly. The man's broad, black-
bearded face was turned outward so that Sheila could
recognize one of the two bullion guards she'd hired
two months ago—Vernon Wade, or "Rocky Mountain," as he preferred to be called.

Wade's mouth hung wide open. His eyes were
open, as well. He seemed to be staring and screaming in silent horror at his agonized demise. His arms
hung back over his head so that his fingertips nearly
grazed the ground.

His belly was at the very top of the saddle, facing
the morning sky. The man's midsection had been
laid open by some savage instrument of destruction—
probably a knife—so that the man's entire middle
was coated in dark-red blood.

"Oh, God!" Sheila croaked, clamping a hand
over her mouth as she stumbled backward on the

walk's scarred boards. Her valise dropped from under her arm.

She swallowed several times, trying not to vomit. She would have vomited for sure if there'd been anything in her belly except coffee. Reluctantly, she turned her stricken gaze to the horse just beyond Rocky Mountain's buckskin. She moved heavily forward, dragging the heels of her shoes. She moved around past the drooping head of the buckskin and stared into the gap between the buckskin and the other horse, a roan.

Another man lay sprawled back-down across the roan's saddle. She knew he would be the second bullion guard she'd hired, Pete Devries, before her eyes raked across his face, which owned an expression similar to that of the man known as Rocky Mountain. What was dissimilar in Devries's condition from that of Rocky Mountain was that Devries's throat had been cut from ear to ear, the rent skin stretched back to reveal a wide gap of open flesh and shredded veins and arteries beneath.

CHAPTER 3

Again, Sheila clamped a hand over her mouth and stumbled backward against the bank's closed doors.

"Oh, sweet merciful Christ!" rose a man's voice to her left.

She turned her head to see a man in a black suit drop to his knees on the boardwalk only a few feet away from her, lower his head, and lose his breakfast right there on the boardwalk. That made Sheila heave, and again she thanked herself for not indulging in breakfast that morning, though her vice-president, George Poindexter, obviously had.

The Hallelujah Bank & Trust's vice-president raised his nearly bald head and looked in glassy-eyed terror at Sheila, running a sleeve of his broadcloth, swallowtail coat across his mouth fringed with a silver mustache and goatee. "Those are the . . . those are the . . ."

"Bullion guards," Sheila said, composing herself. "I know."

Kneeling there on the boardwalk, Poindexter turned to the men again. He swept his left arm up to his mouth to forestall another convulsion, then, lowering the arm, turned his bewildered gaze back to Sheila. "You tried," he said, raggedly, breathing as though he'd run a long way. "I think . . . we'd best close our doors."

Sheila turned her gaze back to where Pete Devries hung down across his saddle, staring in wide-eyed horror. She kept her eyes on the gaping wound, daring herself to look. She looked until her horror and revulsion retreated somewhat, making way for something else.

What?

Rage.

Compressing her lips, she turned again to the vice-president still on his knees to her left. "I'm not closing any doors. You can run, Mister Poindexter, if that's your way. My way, like my father's way, is to stand and fight until all of my weapons have been emptied and I myself am as dead as those two bullion guards."

"They're taunting you," Poindexter said, weakly. "Don't you see? The robbers . . . whoever did this . . . sent these men to town to laugh in your face, to tell you just how futile it is to . . ."

"If I don't haul that bullion down out of the mountains, the mine will fail and then the bank will fail, and that will be my father's legacy. Failure!" Sheila drew a calming breath. "I simply have to get that gold safely out of the mountains."

"But you need the right men to do it!"

"Correct."

Poindexter flung a hand out toward Wade and Devries. "You had the right men!"

"Obviously, I did not."

"Oh, good Lord, girl," Poindexter intoned, glancing

once more at the dead men. "You're gonna need an army! You're gonna have to *pay* an army! By the time you ship the bullion to the mint in San Francisco—why, you'll have nothing left!"

Just then a man's laughter sounded from the other side of the street.

Sheila turned to gaze across Hallelujah Junction's main thoroughfare toward the Black Widow Saloon, which sat to the right of the Silver Slipper Saloon, with a twenty-foot gap between the two log structures. The man's laughter had come from behind the Black Widow's louvred doors. The laughter grew louder, accompanied by the softer chuckling of a woman, until a man and a woman pushed out through the batwings to step out onto the front boardwalk.

The man—tall and red-haired and unshaven, and wearing a deputy U.S. marshal's sun-and-moon star pinned to his black shirt—had one arm draped around the neck of a young blond in a short red dress edged in black lace. As the man swung around, stumbling drunkenly while the blond helped hold him up, he said, "I told Schneider—I said, 'Burt, that rannie wasn't even armed!' And you know what he said?"

"No," said the blond as she and the red-haired man stepped off the end of the boardwalk, heading toward the Silver Slipper—"what'd Burt say?"

"He said, 'Well, hell—sure he's armed. Both his arms is hangin' right down by his sides. There wasn't any pistol in either hand, but he was armed, all right!'"

The red-haired man threw his head back and laughed as though at the funniest joke he'd ever heard. He and the blond mounted the boardwalk fronting the Silver Slipper, and he said, "Come on, darlin'—you can buy me a nightcap!"

He and the laughing blond stumbled through the Silver Slipper's batwings and disappeared into the watering hole's shadowy depths.

"Who was that?" Still kneeling, Poindexter was not in a position to see across the street.

"Marshal Wallace," Sheila said through gritted teeth, barely able to contain her fury, which was directed now toward Deputy U.S. Marshal Lyle Wallace, who rode through town from time to time, though the only thing he appeared to do was drink and carouse with Hallelujah Junction's just-as-useless town marshal, Jonah Flagg.

Poindexter cursed as he heaved himself to his feet, red-faced with anger. "Why in tarnation is that man not out preventing this from happening?" He indicated the two dead bullion guards with a swift sweep of his arm.

"That's what I intend to find out." Leaving her valise where she'd dropped it, Sheila stepped around Poindexter to move down off the boardwalk and into the street.

"What? Wait, now, Miss Bonner. Sheila! You can't go marching into a *saloon*!"

"Just watch me."

Sheila strode straight across the street toward the Silver Slipper. It was only a little after seven o'clock in the morning, but she could hear the low rumble of conversation and the clinking of glasses emanating from both the Slipper, as the saloon was locally called, as well as from the Black Widow. Like all of the other saloons and suds shops in Hallelujah

Junction—and there was at least one saloon or parlor house for every six men in the town, or so it seemed—both the Slipper and the Black Widow were open twenty-four hours a day, with brothels and private gambling dens occupying their second and third stories.

One man was passed out on the loafer's bench fronting the Silver Slipper. He lay on his back, legs crossed at the ankles, his dark-brown slouch hat tipped down over his eyes. An empty bottle sat on the boardwalk beneath the bench as well as a good many cigarette stubs. As Sheila mounted the walk and angled past the sleeping drunk, the man awakened suddenly, nudged his hat up off his forehead, and threw his arm out in front of her, blocking her way.

He blinked, spat to one side, and gazed blearily up at her. His lusty eyes raked her up and down, and his mouth shaped a goatish grin. "Heyyy, purty lady . . . spare a nickel fer a beer?"

Sheila pursed her lips and flared her nostrils, feeling the flames of fury climb higher into her cheeks. "Put your hand down, you lowly cur!"

"Ah, hell!" The unshaven man, who smelled like rancid whiskey sweat, looked truly heartbroken. "That ain't no way fer a purty lady to act . . ." he complained, dropping his arm.

Sheila marched past him and through the Slipper's swing doors.

She paused just inside the doors, which clattered into place behind her, and raked her gaze quickly around the saloon. Her gaze held on Lyle Wallace, who stood before a table in the middle of the room and around which a half-dozen men were playing poker under a billowing cloud of tobacco smoke.

One of the card players was Town Marshal Jonah Flagg. Wallace stood facing Flagg and jabbering on the way drunken men do, incoherently, while the blonde climbed from a chair onto Wallace's back, wrapping her arms and legs around his torso and resting her head on his shoulder as though on a pillow.

Flagg turned his head to gaze up at the sleepy blonde over his left shoulder, laughing and saying, "Annabelle, honey, you can't go to sleep. You promised you'd buy me a nightcap!"

Behind Sheila, the batwings clattered. She got another strong whiff of rancid whiskey sweat, and glanced to her left to see the old drunk from the loafer's bench now entering the saloon to crouch beside her, clutching his hat to his chest and holding out his dirty hand, palm up.

"Now, forgive me for oversteppin'," he said, badly slurring his words and blowing his sour breath in Sheila's face. "But you, darlin' . . . you purty l-lady . . . you look like a woman with not only m-means but a con-conscience . . ." He smiled beseechingly, truckling like a mutt begging for a bone.

He wasn't old, Sheila saw now. A hawk-faced but handsome man, he was maybe only a little older than she. It was just his drunken eyes that were old. He was old and used up before his time, and, like so many other men who populated this perdition, he was useless. A young, lazy, pathetic, useless drunk no better than a back-alley mongrel stealing scraps from trash heaps.

The rage in Sheila had been building like the pressure in an overheated locomotive. She fairly blew out her fittings now as she grabbed the scoundrel's

hat from his hands and whipped it across his face—
from right to left then back again.

The drunk gave a yowl and stumbled backward,
tripping over a chair and hitting the floor hard with
a loud thud, the chair falling on top of him. Sheila
bent toward him, threw his battered hat at him, and
shrieked, "Stay away from me, you gutless pile of
trash!"

The saloon had fallen deathly silent as soon as the
drunk had hit the floor. Now as he lay grunting and
moaning, Sheila turned away from him to see all eyes
in the place on her. Including the eyes of Town
Marshal Jonah Flagg and Deputy U.S. Marshal Lyle
Wallace. The blond doxy was regarding Sheila skeptically from her perch on Wallace's back, her blue
eyes giving Sheila the cool up and down.

Wallace's drunken gaze slid from Sheila to the
moaning drunk on the floor behind her. He jerked
his head around the room and said loudly, "Hey,
Johnny, I reckon you just got your hat handed to
you—didn't you, old buddy?"

All dozen men in the saloon erupted in loud,
drunken laughter.

Sheila focused her infuriated glare at Wallace and
then at Jonah Flagg, still sitting at the gambling
table, playing cards fanned out in his hand, a cigarette smoldering in one corner of his mouth, the ash
so long it just now broke off and dribbled into the
shot glass on the table before him. When the laughter died, and all eyes in the room had returned to
Sheila, lustily raking her up and down—fairly ogling
her in broad daylight, as so many were wont to do
without an ounce of shame!—she had to refrain
from screaming as she said, "Why aren't you two

so-called lawmen out there, doing your jobs?" She raised an arm and thrust an angry finger toward the street beyond the saloon's dirty front windows.

Wallace slid his gaze to Flagg then back to Sheila. He shrugged. "I don't know—'cause we're in here, I reckon."

The blonde on his back laughed then covered her mouth with her hand. Chuckles rose from the other men in the room, including Flagg, who slitted his eyes against the smoke rising from the cigarette. "How can we help you, Miss Bonner? Was Billy Jenkins peeping at you through your bedroom window again last night? I'll have a talk with him later, though, uh . . ." Flagg smiled around the cigarette clamped between his teeth and let his goatish gaze rake Sheila up and down. "Can't really blame him . . ."

Again, the men in the room chuckled or snickered devilishly.

The blonde on Wallace's back curled a disdainful nostril at Sheila.

"No, Billy Jenkins was not peeping at me again through my window last night. If either of you had been doing your jobs, by now you would know that my bullion guards are right now lying dead across the saddles of their horses tied right out there on the other side of the street!"

Wallace removed his hands from the blonde's legs, and she slid down his back to the floor. She slumped into a chair and crossed her legs beneath her short skirt, again giving Sheila the woolly eyeball. Wallace's smile dwindled from his lips as he looked from Sheila to a window flanking her. "You don't say."

"I do say. Both of my latest guards, Devries and Wade, are lying dead over their horses, the bullion gone." She paused, and her anger churned hotter as both lawmen stared at her dully. "I have been robbed again, Mister Wallace." She slid her gaze to the town marshal, adding, "*Mister Flagg!*"

"You don't say," Flagg said, purposely echoing Wallace. "Well, I'll be jiggered." He lay his cards facedown at the table and, plucking the quirley from between his lips, slid his chair back, and rose a little uncertainly no doubt due to all the forty-rod he'd consumed during the course of his all-night poker game. (Sheila would have loved to have had a job so free of worries that she could spend hour upon hours frittering her precious time away!)

Flagg turned to the man sitting to his left and said with mock menace, "Bill, if you take a peek at my cards, I'll tell Dora you were upstairs for a whole hour last night."

Bill Showalter, the middle-aged grocer in Hallelujah Junction, flushed from his neck to the bald crown of his skull. The other men laughed. The blonde squealed. Flagg stepped out from behind the table and walked to the front of the room to stare out the front window toward the two horses standing tied to the hitch rail fronting the bank on the street's other side. Several other drinkers had already risen to stare out the window or over the batwings toward the two horses carrying the dead men.

Flagg stopped, took a deep drag off his cigarette, and then blew the smoke against the dirty glass as he stared through it. "They hit ya again, did they? Well, I'll be damned."

"Yes, they hit me again, Marshal Flagg," Sheila said, her voice quavering with emotion as she stood glaring at the man's back and clenching her fists at her sides. "What do you plan on doing about it?"

"Me?" Flagg whipped an incredulous look at her. "Hell, my jurisdiction stops at the town limits. Now, I can keep the boys from ogling you through your bedroom window of a night, but as far as what goes on up in them mountains . . ." He slid his gaze, bright with mockery, to Wallace. "That's a federal job."

"I got the day off," Wallace said, plopping into a chair near the blonde. "I come up here to cart a prisoner of Flagg's back to Denver. Said prisoner has a judge and a hang rope waitin' on him, don't ya know. My orders are to get said prisoner back to Denver without delay. Er, uh . . . after my day off, of course."

He glanced at the blonde, then flushed a little sheepishly. The others around him chuckled.

"But just as soon as I've fulfilled my duty as required by law," Wallace continued, "I will return to Hallelujah Junction posthaste, and I'll try to pick up the killers' trail. Now, uh . . ." He smiled at Sheila. "Why don't you have a drink with me, Miss Bonner? The whiskey here in the Silver Slipper has been known to cure what ails you."

"Hey!" the blonde said, indignant, and slapped his arm with the back of her hand.

Sheila glared at the insipid, fleshy-faced, red-haired Wallace. She'd never been so angry. She could feel a vein throbbing in her neck. So much rage, fury, and desperation welled up in her that she was afraid she would burst into tears. She'd been robbed again, nearly twenty thousand dollars in gold bullion gone. Two more guards murdered. Sheila doubted she could recover from such a loss on top of so many others. Who else could she possibly find to carry the bullion out of the mountains, after so many others had been butchered by some maniacal gang out to get rich off of her?

But she couldn't cry about it. At least not yet. Not here. Oh, God—not here in front of these men who had such contempt for her . . .

She drew a deep breath and lifted her chin, and said, "No, I will not have a drink with you, Marshal Wallace. I don't drink with cowards."

She spoke the words softly, so that they'd cut as deeply as a razor-edged bowie. The effect shone on Wallace's face, which slackened first as the cuts made themselves felt, and then turned red.

The other men chuckled quietly or grinned silently, sliding their mocking gazes toward the deputy U.S. marshal.

Wallace filled up his lumpy chest, flared his nostrils, and slammed his fist onto the table before him, making glasses bounce and knocking a bottle over. "Now, wait just a minute!"

Ignoring him, trying to maintain a stony expression, Sheila swept her cool, casually incriminating gaze across the other men in the room. "If any of you are capable of going after the stolen bullion, I am prepared to make an offer of one thousand dollars for the gold's safe delivery to the Bank & Trust. I will pay fifty dollars for each robber you bring back to Marshal Flagg—dead or alive. If none of you here is up to the task, please spread the offer around. Good day, gentlemen."

With that, Sheila wheeled and marched back toward the batwings.

Gentlemen—ha!

There were no gentlemen anywhere in or even

near Hallelujah Junction. There were only spineless vermin, including the men who call themselves the law.

Sheila was halfway to the batwings when she heard footsteps thudding loudly behind her. She wheeled to see Wallace striding toward her, his face bunched with fury. "Just hold on, missy. You stop right there and apologize for—"

Just then a chair came hurling from Sheila's left toward her right. It slammed into Wallace's legs, clipping both feet out from beneath him. The lawman gave an indignant scream as he tumbled forward and fell over the chair. He hit the floor with a loud *bang!*

Wallace cursed as he kicked away the chair, rolled onto his butt, and grabbed his knee with both hands, his red face swollen with rage and pain. He jerked his head toward the chair-kicker. No one was more surprised than Sheila to see that the man who'd come to her rescue was none other than the sweaty, stinky drunk. He was still on the floor where he'd fallen after Sheila had battered him with his own hat. He lay on his side, cheek propped against the heel of his hand, legs crossed at his ankles.

He slid his gaze from the raging deputy U.S. marshal to Sheila, grinning up at her and winking one of his rheumy brown eyes, partly obscured by a wing of his disheveled, dark-brown hair to which dirt and sawdust clung.

Glaring at the drunk, Wallace slapped his hand over the revolver holstered on his right leg. "I oughta kill you for that, Johnny!"

Johnny smiled at the man, his cheeks dimpling. "Prob'ly. But you won't. Cause I ain't worth it, an' you know it, Lyle."

Sheila turned away with a frustrated groan, again clenching her fists at her sides. She pushed out through the batwings and stomped back across the street toward the bank. George Poindexter stood where she'd left him, waiting for her, regarding the enraged woman warily.

"Worthless!" she cried aloud. "No man in this whole town is worth the dynamite it would take to blow him to hell!"

CHAPTER 4

Johnny smiled up at the fleshy-faced, redheaded lawman just then sliding his Colt .44 from the holster strapped to his right leg. "You might be worth one, bullet, Johnny. Just one!"

"Okay, but only one," said Johnny Greenway. "So make it count, Lyle."

"Oh, I will, Johnny!" Wallace clicked the Colt's hammer back and aimed at Johnny's head.

Johnny continued to smile at the man, his cheek resting on the heel of his hand.

Wallace aimed down the Colt's barrel, one eye narrowed. Both dung-brown eyes were bright with fury. Johnny leaned up and forward, pressing his forehead to the end of the barrel. "There you go, Lyle. Now you can't miss."

"Don't kill that worthless bugger in here!" yelled Jip Luther, owner of the Silver Slipper, who was leaning forward over the mahogany bar, glaring down at where Wallace knelt aiming his Colt at Johnny's head. "He ain't worth the work of cleaning up the mess!"

That seemed to temper Wallace's fury. The lawman

depressed the revolver's hammer, slid the gun back into its holster, then heaved himself to his feet. Crouching forward, he grabbed the front of Johnny's grimy, puke- and liquor-stained shirt, and pulled him to his feet.

"Why, thank you, Lyle," Johnny said in his drunken slur. "I was thinkin' about gettin' up, but the climb just looked so damn steep."

"Shut up, you horse's ass!"

"All right, Lyle," Johnny said. "I can see you got your bloomers in a twist, so I'll hold my tongue."

"You insolent son of the devil!" Wallace whipped Johnny around and hurled him through the bat-wings. Johnny went through the doors at an angle and slammed up against an awning support post.

Laughing, he turned toward Lyle Wallace bulling through the door behind him, thick and stout on thick legs, his deputy U.S. marshal's badge flashing on his black shirt. Wallace stopped and raised his pistol, gritting his teeth in fury. "Here—maybe now you'll show a little respect for your betters!"

He slammed the revolver down, smashing the barrel against Johnny's left temple. Johnny grunted and spun around. He staggered out into the street, clutching his temple with both hands, feeling blood ooze between his fingers. He dropped to his knees, the pain biting him deep. Despite the agony, he heard himself laughing.

He tried to rise, but all the alcohol coursing through his system as well as the braining he'd just received rendered his legs to the consistency of wet noodles. He tried once more to gain his feet but plopped onto his chest, instead. He lay with his head propped on his arm, chuckling at his folly, which for some reason never ceased to amuse him of late.

Or maybe it was just the tangleleg . . .

He turned to shout back at Lyle, just then retreating into the saloon. "I'm surprised at you, Lyle. That was nothin' but a love tap, you harebrained weakling!"

"Johnny!" The familiar voice had sounded from somewhere nearby but it was hard to tell from where exactly, because of the bells of pain tolling in Johnny's ears.

"Johnny!" came the voice again, closer this time. Johnny opened his eyes to see a boot in the dirt to his left—a big, hobnailed, lace-up boot with cracked and worn brown leather and several small tears between the upper and the sole.

"Go 'way, Bear," Johnny grumbled. "Go 'way. Let me sleep."

"Oh, fer cryin' in the Queen's ale, get your ass up, you damn fool! You can't sleep in the street!"

"Go 'way, Bear!"

"Johnny, dammit, get your butt up!"

A big hand clamped around Johnny's left arm and pulled him into a half-sitting position. Johnny opened his eyes. His vision was blurry from all the booze and from the barrel of Lyle Wallace's hogleg. It clarified gradually, until Johnny was staring at the broad, horsey, bearded face of his friend Bear Musgrave, a big burly man in a knit cap and suspenders drawn up over his red flannel shirt.

"Bear, dammit, you're interruptin' a fella's snooze."

"I ain't gonna let you snooze in the street, you crazy polecat. We gotta get you back to the cabin, and we gotta get that tattoo in his your head sewed up before you bleed dry." Again, Bear pulled on Johnny's arm. "Come on, now—don't make me carry you!"

"Johnny!" This time it was a woman's voice.

"Ah, hell," Johnny complained. "How'd I get to be so pop'lar? I just wants to get a little shut-eye's all . . ."

He turned his head to see a young woman with long, pale blond hair and clad in a gauzy black wrap over white cotton pantaloons and a white chemise run toward him, a long black cheroot in her right hand. His sometime friend, sometime lover—if you could call it love—Lenore Dupont dropped to a knee beside Johnny, her red-rimmed, soft blue eyes creased with sadness as well as concern. "Oh, Johnny—what happened?"

"He done crawled Lyle Wallace's hump and got a tattoo fer his trouble," Bear told the young woman.

"Oh, Johnny!" Lenore exclaimed. Of course, her name wasn't Lenore Dupont. That was her made-up "working" name, for Lenore worked the line. Her real name sounded so German—or was it Norski?— that he couldn't have pronounced it even had he remembered it. She had a faint German or Norski brogue though Johnny thought she'd been born on this side of the ocean. Minnesota? Maybe Dakota.

Lenore gave a sudden start as Jonah Flagg pushed through the Sliver Slipper's batwings, dragging his boots drunkenly. He stopped at the edge of the board-walk and pointed an angry finger toward Johnny. "Get that drunk out of the street or I'm gonna lock him up!"

"That's what we're fixin' to do right now, Mar-shal," Bear called, giving a good-natured smile accompanied by a wave. "We'll have him out of the street in three jangles of a doxy's bell!"

"Make it *one* jangle, or I'm gonna turn the key on that useless pile of trash!"

"You got it, Marshal!" Bear said, still smiling. As Flagg turned and stumbled off in the direction of his boardinghouse, the former mountain man called to his back, "Have a good day, Marshal!"

"Go to hell!"

Bear turned to Johnny. "Gotta get you up, son. Get you back to the cabin."

"No, no," Lenore said, tugging on Johnny's opposite arm. "My place is closer. I'll tend that cut. The doctor won't do it, because he knows Johnny can't pay."

Bear glared at the young blond woman, her lusterless hair hanging in tangles about her shoulders. A green henna rinse streak ran through it. "He don't need no more of your so-called help, Lenore. The kinda help you offer is the kinda help that's gonna get him planted!"

"Go to hell, you ugly pig!" Lenore spat at him, her hair dancing wildly across her chemise. "Johnny loves me, and I love him!"

"Bull fritters!"

"Please, don't fight over me, you two." Johnny grinned. "There's enough of me to go around. But all I really want right now is just to lay my head down here and collect myself."

Before Johnny could drop his head down on his arm again, Bear said, "Oh, no you don't!"

Johnny cried out as the big bear of a man grabbed Johnny's left arm and, rising, pulled Johnny up and over Bear's right shoulder. "All right, Lenore," Bear said. "You win. Lead the way!"

Johnny sort of half slept as he rode belly down over his big friend's shoulder, as Bear followed Lenore down a side street and then down a cross street and then along a winding path through willow shrubs. Johnny would have passed out altogether if the braining Wallace had given him weren't grieving him so savagely.

Looking down, which was about the only place he could look in this uncomfortable position, he watched Bear's big boots follow Lenore's bare feet as they both splashed across a shallow stream, which would be the appropriately named Willow Creek, on the northern edge of Hallelujah Junction and along which several of the independent doxies kept their boxlike plywood-and-tarpaper cribs, which were scattered around without any civic planning whatever but occasionally adorned with small, rock-lined flower beds that never lived long for lack of tending.

Lenore opened the spindly door of her own quarters and made way for Bear, who crossed the single-room cabin in two strides and dropped Johnny onto Lenore's brass-framed bed as though he were dropping a hundred-pound sack of cracked corn into a wagon.

"*Oh!*" Johnny complained, half-sitting up and pressing the heels of his hands to his forehead. "Ohhh . . . that *hurt*! Thanks a lot, partner!"

Ignoring Johnny, Bear turned to Lenore, who was already ladling water out of a wooden bucket on the small plank counter that served as her kitchen. "I know it ain't gonna do me a damn bit of good to say this, but don't give him any more to drink. His liver's already swelled up to the size of a gourd!"

Lenore turned from her work to glare at the big man who dwarfed her. She thrust her arm toward the open door and narrowed her pale blue eyes that were as dull as her hair from lack of much of a diet except rotgut whiskey. "You have done your part, you big ugly dog. Get out!"

Bear glared back at her, then turned to Johnny. He shook his bearded head and said, "Go with God, son. Go with God."

He turned and ducked out through the door. His boots clomped back along the path, splashing through the creek.

Lenore looked at Johnny. "He is no friend of yours."

Johnny sighed and lay his head back on Lenore's musty pillow. "You got a bottle, honey?"

"Sure, I have a bottle, stupid." Lenore pulled an unlabeled bottle down from a shelf and turned toward Johnny. She plucked the cork from the bottle with her teeth and spit the cork onto the shack's scarred wooden floor. It landed on one of the several soiled undergarments strewn around nearly every inch of the little shack, which was gamy with the smell of the many sweaty men who'd passed through the rickety door. "The big man's right, though. Maybe you've had enough for one night, huh?"

Lenore turned and dumped a goodly portion of the Taos lightning into the bowl she'd filled with water from the bucket.

"Easy—easy, darlin'!" Johnny remonstrated her. "Don't waste good whiskey."

Lenore tossed a cloth into the water bowl, tucked

a small sewing pouch under one arm, then walked over to the bed with the bottle in one hand, the bowl in the other. She gave the bottle to Johnny and sat on the edge of the bed beside him, curling one bare leg beneath the other. She opened her arm to let the pouch drop onto the bed.

"Go easy."

"You go easy," Johnny said, tipping the bottle to his lips. "You ain't been tattooed by Lyle Wallace."

"Why'd he tattoo you?"

Johnny chuckled. "I'll be damned if I can remember."

Lenore sighed as she leaned toward him, dabbing the gash on his temple with her rag soaked in water and whiskey. "The trouble you get into."

"Tell me about it."

She frowned at him. "Does it hurt?"

Johnny lifted the bottle and took another deep pull. "Just a little now."

"Go easy on that stuff, Johnny," Lenore yelled at him angrily. "It's all I have, and you're gonna need more when I sew you closed!"

"Jesus, stop yellin', Lenore, honey!" Johnny yelled back at her. "I mean, it ain't like we're married!"

That amused him. He laughed then sucked a sharp breath through his teeth as pain stabbed through his brain like a rusty pigsticker.

"What's that supposed to mean?" she asked after a few minutes, continuing to slowly and deliberately clean the blood from the wound, frowning into his eyes as she worked.

"What's what supposed to mean?"

"You said it's not like we're married."

Johnny shrugged. He lay staring at the ceiling,

holding the bottle close against his side for security. It was like a child's stuffed animal. "Just a joke."

"Maybe it's not a joke."

He kept staring at the ceiling. "What do you mean?"

"Did you and your wife yell a lot?"

Johnny turned to her, scowling, the skin across his broad forehead and at the bridge of his nose deeply creased.

"All right, all right," Lenore said, exasperated. "Never mind! I know you told me you didn't want to talk about her!"

"That's right." Johnny took another pull from the bottle. "I don't."

"Go easy on that stuff! I bet you don't have any money for more—do you, idiot?"

"No, I don't."

"See!"

"I'm sorry. Here—take it!" He held the bottle up to her.

Lenore turned her mouth corners down as she dropped the rag into the bowl and set the bowl on the floor. "Never mind. You need it worse than I do. I will have some money soon."

"Someone comin'?"

Lenore nodded.

"Who?"

"I didn't ask him his name, idiot. He just grabbed me on the street and asked me if I was free at noon. I wouldn't know him from Adam. He better pay me first. If another cheap rannie tries to hornswoggle me, he'll get a knife in his guts for his trouble!"

Johnny lay staring up at the soot-streaked ceiling, trying to keep his mind blank as Lenore sterilized her sewing needle with a lucifer, threaded the needle with catgut, and went to work sewing the wound in his temple closed. That was the trick between bottles. It was an art, really. Keeping the mind blank when you didn't have any help from forty-rod. It was a delicate balance a man had to maintain to keep from stealing a gun and blowing his brains out.

"Does it hurt?" she asked as she drew the first suture taut.

"It does and it doesn't. I like it."

"You like it?" Lenore laughed.

"Yeah, I like it," Johnny said, staring at the ceiling. Physical pain took his mind off other things that hurt worse. He didn't bother telling Lenore about it. She wouldn't understand, though she'd withstood as much injury as Johnny had. In fact, she withstood it every day of her wretched life. He didn't know what kept her from hanging herself or throwing herself in front of one of the three-ton ore or timber drays that passed through town daily.

"I think we should get married, Johnny."

Johnny turned to her and laughed. "You do, do you?"

Lenore shrugged as she drew another suture taut. "Why not? We like each other, don't we? At least we have that. We like to spend time together."

"We like to spend time together *drinkin'*, darlin'."

"That's more than what most people have!"

"Good point, but I don't think it's much to base a marriage on."

"Stop laughing at me."

"I'm not laughing. I'm smiling."

"You're laughing at me, Johnny." Lenore cut the catgut and turned to him. She placed a hand on his cheek and canted her head to one side, making a sad, lonely, desperate expression. "You care about me—don't you, Johnny?"

Johnny stared up at her for a long time before he slid a lock of her lank hair back from her cheek. "To tell you the truth, darlin', I don't rightly know."

"You like to make love to me."

Johnny thought long and hard about that. If he were honest with her, he would say that he really couldn't remember ever making love with her. He knew they had. At least, some might call it love in a pinch. But he really couldn't remember, so soaked in whiskey had been his brain.

He couldn't tell her that though. Not even he was low enough to be that honest.

"Sure, darlin'," he said, smiling. "Sure, I do."

CHAPTER 5

"I don't know how we can survive this," said George Poindexter later that evening, after he and Sheila Bonner had long since closed the bank's doors for the day.

He sipped from the glass of brandy in his hand, then set the goblet down on the edge of Sheila's desk and sighed. "Five holdups over the past year. Over two hundred thousand dollars in bullion gone. Vanished. Just like it evaporated."

"It didn't evaporate. It was stolen," Sheila said, bitterly.

"Oh, yes. I know."

"I have to survive, Mister Poindexter." Sheila sat back in what she still considered her father's high-backed, quilted leather swivel chair, running a finger along the rim of her own glass. "I have no choice in the matter. This bank and the mine are all I have."

"Surely you can return . . ."

"East?" Sheila shook her head. "That's not an option for me. You see, I have my father's stubborn streak. I refuse to fail. Besides, I have nothing to return to. My Uncle John plans to retire next year, so I would have no job. As a woman, finding a similar position would be nearly impossible, and I'm afraid I'm not cut out to work in a laundry or clean hotel rooms."

Poindexter smiled across the large oak desk at her. "You could find a man. Settle down." His eyes flicked unconsciously to the bodice of her powder-blue frock. "A young lady with your beauty, Sheila . . ."

She flinched at the notion of turning her fate over to a man. Or to anyone. Like her father, Sheila Bonner had been born with a steely independence and a near-desperate need to push boundaries and challenge society's norms. She would marry someday, if she ever found a man she deemed worthy. (She herself knew that her standards were often impossibly high.) But she wouldn't marry out of fear or because she needed a man to provide for her. She'd rather go bankrupt here in Hallelujah Junction and be put out on the street to make her way with all the other . . .

She dismissed the thought. No, she wouldn't want to be forced into the kind of livelihoods so many women on the frontier were forced into. Selling their bodies, their souls, for money. No, that she would not do. If her life came to that, she would end it by her own hand.

"I'm going to make it work, Mister Poindexter. For me, you, and our five employees here at the bank, and for Mister Nolan and the dozen men who work at the mine. Like you, the bulk of them have families to provide for. The cost of going out of business is too high. And I don't mean only the monetary cost."

The Bank & Trust's vice-president gave a rueful sigh, dropping a hand onto the arm of his chair.

"Please, Sheila . . . we've known each other for nearly five months. Surely that's long enough that you can now call me George. I work *under* you, after all." He smiled a little weakly at the notion, then sipped from his glass to cover it. As he did, the pinky ring on his right finger glinted in the light from the green-shaded Tiffany lamp.

Sheila wasn't offended by the man's attitude toward her. She liked George Poindexter. What's more, she trusted him, because her father had trusted him. He and Joe Bonner had met here in Hallelujah Junction when they'd first come into the Sierra Nevadas, following the miners, to seek their own El Dorados.

Poindexter had been an attorney for a now-defunct mine, while Joe Bonner had been an investor, his pockets full of cash, who'd bought the Reverend's Temptation when he'd heard back east that it had gone up for sale. Bosom buddies from their very first meeting in a Hallelujah Junction gambling den, they partnered up to establish the first bank in town, the Bank & Trust. They'd worked together well. They'd admired and respected each other, had formed a lasting bond. Sheila had always trusted her father's instincts concerning the character of others, more so than she did her own.

She tended not to trust anyone.

No, she took no umbrage with George's outdated opinions regarding male-female relations. Like her father, he was from another time. It wasn't easy for any man—especially a man on the frontier—to be in the employ of one of the so-called fairer sex. Generally, George wore the indignity about as well as any man could.

Besides, he had his own problems, not the least of which was his pushchair-bound wife, Claudia, as well as his own financial insecurities due to the current trouble with the bullion thefts. Sheila's trouble was Poindexter's trouble, and vice versa. Just like Poindexter and her father, they were in it together, for good or bad.

"I am bound and determined to keep the bank and the mine open, George. Somehow, I have to find a way to get the bullion safely down to Hallelujah Junction from the mine."

Poindexter grimaced and dropped his free hand again onto the chair arm. "Without the money from the bullion—"

"Without the money from the bullion, I can't pay the miners, and, with business being what it is here in Hallelujah Junction, I can't keep the bank open, either. The bank can't stand on its own two feet. My father was only too aware of that. That's why when he first came out here, he opened the bank only *after* he'd purchased the mine, knowing that one needed the other."

Poindexter filled his lungs up, puffing out his red-splotched cheeks that contrasted with the deep white of his curly muttonchops and spade beard, and cast his fateful gaze at the brandy he slowly swirled in his glass. "We both had such high hopes for Hallelujah Junction. We thought it would be the next Virginia City. The preliminary assays all looked so promising."

The problem was, much of the gold already taken out of the mountains around Hallelujah Junction had been high-grade stuff. Unfortunately, those deposits had played out quickly. The miners up at the Reverend's Temptation were still plundering good color out of Grizzly Ridge, but if Sheila couldn't get the bullion safely down to the bank and then loaded aboard a stagecoach headed for the U.S. Mint in San Francisco, she was only paying the miners to mine the gold that the gold thieves robbed.

It was a losing proposition. A sure way to go bankrupt.

If things kept going the way they were, Sheila wouldn't have any money left to pay the miners at all, and she'd have to close the mine as well as the bank that depended on it so heavily. The mine was her greatest asset, but she couldn't even sell it under these conditions.

"If only we'd been insured," Poindexter commented.

"Yes, if only . . ." Sheila rose from her father's chair and strode to a window that looked out onto the dark night relieved by a sickle moon silvering the tin roofs of a couple of whores' cribs situated haphazardly behind the bank. In the nearest crib, shadows moved behind the thin curtains of a dimly lit window. The shadows rose and fell in primal consort with one another.

Feeling a strange warmth pool in her belly, Sheila turned abruptly from the window, squeezing the brandy goblet in both hands. Flushing, she stared down at her drink. Poindexter must have seen her reaction. He said in a concerned tone, "Are you all right, Sheila? You don't look well."

She shook her head. "No." She chuckled, half to herself, amused by her strange reaction to another woman's lovemaking. If you could call it that, which of course you could not. There was no love involved, only the exchange of scrip or specie. "I'm fine. It's just been a long day is all. But as you were saying about the insurance . . . or lack thereof," she added drolly. "No company will insure the bullion run from the mine. From the bank to San Francisco, sure. But not from the mine to the town. It's too remote. The risks too high. That's one thing I guess my father didn't take into consideration."

"The bullion run, you mean . . ."

"The bullion run made perilous due to the particular savagery of the brand of man—present company excluded, of course, George—who resides in these remote environs. The general lawlessness of the location, not to mention the *cowardice* of the law—or the men who have the gall to call themselves the *law* in and around Hallelujah Junction."

Again, the fragile smile came to Poindexter's plump, red cheeks. "You mean Flagg and Wallace."

"You bet I do." Again, fury burned inside of Sheila. She threw back the rest of her brandy to soothe her nerves, then stepped forward to set the glass back down on the desk with more vigor than she'd intended. A fine crack appeared in the side.

She looked down at the crack, ran her thumb absently along the fissure. She glanced at Poindexter, who studied her with a dubious expression. Again, Sheila blushed. She bit her lip, pondering the situation.

"Well, five robberies over the course of just over a year is averaging a devastating holdup nearly every other month," Poindexter reminded her. "Unless we can get the bullion down from the mine with no more holdups . . . I mean, we couldn't afford the *last* holdup. And you know as well as I do, from going over our accounts all day, that we're simply in trouble here. Deep in trouble. The situation at present is unsustainable."

Sheila splashed more brandy into her cracked glass, then slid the decanter across the desk toward Poindexter. "And the miners are due to be paid in two weeks."

"That will clean us out, I'm afraid. We won't have enough cash to cover the bank accounts."

"The next bullion run must make it through." Sheila pursed her lips and shook her head in frustration. "I need an army, and I can't afford an army."

"There you have it," Poindexter said. "It's a real pickle, Sheila. I'm sorry."

"We'll have to haul more bullion down from the mine in three weeks . . ."

"And we have no one for the job."

Sheila walked over to a potted plant that had been healthy when she'd first arrived but that was now dying for lack of watering. Not only was she killing her father's business, she was killing his plants, as well. She poked a finger into the dry dirt at the ivy's base, then absently ran her finger and thumb together, staring at the parched dirt sifting down to the carpeted floor around her expensive tweed ankle boots that suddenly seemed so frivolous. "Maybe we do."

Poindexter arched a surprised brow. "Pray tell."

"Over lunch I sent out a telegram. To a man named Willeford. He's a professional private detective who specializes in just such dilemmas as ours. He's right here in California—Sacramento, to be exact—and he comes highly recommended by several of my father's

West Coast business connections. Willeford works with a small crew I'm hoping we can afford. I expect to hear from him tomorrow.

"With luck, he'll be able to make the next run for us. With even more luck, the Pinkertons will be able to run the thieving killers to ground and recover *all* of the stolen bullion. I'm betting those devils are still up there in the mountains"—she jerked her chin to indicate the high country beyond the town—"haunting the trails, waiting for more loot, and that they haven't spent any of the loot they've already robbed yet. I think they're going to try to grab everything they can from us, and when they've ruined us, they'll light out for Mexico or God knows where."

"Wouldn't that be nice?" Poindexter smiled. "I mean," he quickly amended, "wouldn't it be nice if they had it all piled up somewhere . . . unspent?" He chuckled.

"It would be nice, indeed." Sheila chose to be confident. It was hard, but what other choice did she have? Being sour didn't make a hard situation easier. She turned, brushed the dirt from her finger onto her skirt, lifted her glass, and smiled at the older, pudgy-faced man on the other side of her father's desk. (No, *her* desk!) "Cheers, Mister . . . uh, I mean, George."

Poindexter chuckled. "Old habits die hard." He rose heavily from his chair and clinked his glass against Sheila's. He tossed back his brandy, set the glass on the desk, then reached for his bowler hat. "I'd best head home. It's been a long day."

"Frightfully long." Sheila gasped and covered her mouth with her hand. "Oh, good Lord—how thoughtless of me. Claudia's been home alone all day long!"

"No, no—now, that's not true," Poindexter said as he walked out of the office and pulled his black swallowtail off a coatrack. "I told her at noon when I went home for lunch that it might be a long day. On the way back to the bank, I stopped at the Crowley place, and asked Edna to check on Claudia from time to time. Edna was only too happy to do so."

Sheila grabbed her hat and valise, blew out the green Tiffany lamp on her father's desk, and followed Poindexter across the nearly dark bank, past the two tellers' cages, to the front door. She blew out the last two lamps then followed the vice-president outside, pausing to lock the door behind her.

Turning back to him, she said, "I'm so sorry, George. I'm thoughtless!"

Still smiling, Poindexter leaned close to her and placed a hand on her forearm. "Not at all. You have only *too* many thoughts on your mind these days. Besides, like I said, Edna Crowley has stopped in several times to check on Claudia. I'm sure everything is fine, or I'd know about it by now."

"She probably has supper waiting for you."

"I doubt it." Poindexter pulled his mouth corners down and gave his head a single, dark shake. "She's really not up to cooking supper . . . or doing much of anything around the house anymore, poor gal."

"Oh, no. I'm sorry, George. She's taken a turn for the worse?"

Poindexter nodded. "'Fraid so. The specialist I took her to in Sacramento said the tumor is growing and pressing up hard against her spine. That's why she lost the use of her legs in the first place, and now, I'm afraid it's caused her to be in fairly severe pain. It's almost too much for her to sit up in her chair anymore."

"Isn't there anything they can do?"

"There's a surgery—an expensive one—but the doctors think it's too risky. Claudia doesn't want to go through with it. She's afraid it'll kill her. About all she can do is take the laudanum they prescribed and pray for a miracle. And that she does. She prays and prays and prays. You know what a devout lady she is."

"At least she has that."

"Yes, it gives her hope."

"I'm so sorry, George."

"Nothing to be done, I'm afraid," Poindexter said, giving Sheila's forearm another gentle, reassuring squeeze. "Don't you worry about me and Claudia now. You have enough on your plate the way it—"

Poindexter clipped the sentence when boots thudded and scraped on the boardwalk to his right, Sheila's left. There was a loud thump and the crash of breaking glass. Sheila whipped her head around to see a man on his hands and knees ten feet away from her and Poindexter, at the end of the boardwalk.

Chapter 6

The man on the boardwalk groaned and cursed, slurring his words.

Sheila could smell the sour odor of both the man and the pool of whiskey from the broken bottle and knew who he was even before he lifted his head. The drunk she'd seen earlier lying on the loafer's bench out front of the Silver Slipper. He'd kicked that chair out in front of Lyle Wallace, and Sheila winced now as she saw the long, sutured gash on his temple, half-exposed by a wing of his thick, dark-brown hair.

That chair stunt had cost him dearly. No telling what Wallace might have done to her if the drunkard hadn't intervened.

Gazing up at her and Poindexter, the drunkard gave a sheepish smile. "Misjudged that step, reckon. These boardwalks seem to be gettin' higher an' higher every dang day!"

"I highly doubt that," Poindexter said. "It's just that you're getting drunker and drunker."

"That it?" The drunk––what had the others called him? Johnny?––looked down at the smashed bottle glinting in the light of several near oil pots, and gained a pained expression. "Ah, now . . . dammit. That grieves me—purely, it does!" He dipped a finger into the whiskey then stuck the finger in his mouth, sucking the whiskey from its tip.

Sheila gave a repelled groan. Poindexter gave a caustic chuff. "Oh, Johnny!"

Johnny looked up at Sheila and Poindexter scowling down at him. He smiled, grabbed his black slouch hat from where it had fallen just ahead of him, and heaved himself uncertainly to his feet. He staggered up to Sheila and Poindexter, holding his hat out before him. "Alms for the poor? Alms for the poor?" He smiled broadly. "Drinkee for the drunk . . . ?"

"Go to hell, Johnny!" Poindexter castigated the young drunkard, slamming one of his half-boots down hard on the boardwalk. "Why don't you find a pile of hay and sleep it off? You're just embarrassing yourself out here! Good God, man—you used to be somebody!"

Ignoring Poindexter's remarks, seemingly unflappable in his inebriation, Johnny slid his hat toward Sheila. "How 'bout you, purty li'l lassy? Help er fella out? I sure could do . . ."

He let his voice trail off to silence. He blinked, scowled, ridging his brows as he studied Sheila closely, staring right into her eyes.

"Johnny, for goodness sakes," Poindexter objected. "Do I have to fetch Flagg?"

Sheila flushed with embarrassment under the drunkard's scrutiny. She glanced at Poindexter, then turned back to the man in his late twenties, early thirties studying her as though he thought he knew her but couldn't quite place her.

"What is it?" she asked him. "Why are you—?"

"It's you."

Sheila scowled at him. "Yes. Yes, it's me. From the Silver Slipper. I suppose you think I should give you money because you kicked that chair into Lyle Wallace. Even if I were in a position to dole out money to a drunk too lazy to get a job and support himself— when there is obviously nothing physically wrong with you—I would *not*! What kind of man staggers around drunk all day, begging money off strangers?"

Johnny drew his head back a little, as though against the sting of her harsh retort. Suddenly, his dimple-cheeked smile returned, and he said, "What kind of man does that? Well, let me answer very clear to ya, ma'am. *This* kind of man does that." He thumbed himself in the chest, his movements awkwardly exaggerated. "Johnny Greenway."

He gave a cordial but drunkenly uncertain bow, shifting his weight from boot to boot to keep from falling. "Pleased to make your acquaintance . . . whoever in hell you are, Miss Uppity Bloomers!"

He nodded once, placed his hat on his head, not quite getting it straight, then clapped his hands together. He stumbled wide around Sheila and Poindexter and staggered off down the boardwalk, throwing his arms out for balance, almost falling at times.

Sheila watched him go, shaking her head in reproof. "What a waste," she said. "A young, able-bodied man . . ."

"And a handsome one."

Sheila turned to see Poindexter studying her closely, a vague, knowing smile on his red lips inside his silver goatee. "What did you say?"

Poindexter nodded in the direction the young man was retreating into the darkness beyond the guttering light of the oil pots. "Greenway. A handsome man—wouldn't you say?"

Sheila shrugged. "Yes . . . yes, I suppose he is—now that I think of it. I guess I didn't really notice." But she had noticed. She wasn't sure why she'd felt the need to lie. Slowly, unconsciously, she crossed her arms on her chest, as though chilled.

Poindexter stared after where the man had drifted off into the night, probably stumbling over the threshold of yet another smoky watering hole to cadge drinks off the clientele. "Hard to imagine it now, but he was a good man at one time. A lawman—one of the best in California and Nevada."

"Really?" Sheila asked in astonishment. "What kind of lawman?"

"Deputy U.S. marshal."

"Certainly not!" Sheila laughed in disbelief. *"That* man?"

"That man. That's right. Johnny Greenway lived in Carson City with his wife and son. His given name is Juan Beristain. Came from a Basque family in these parts. Hot-blooded people, easily riled. A mix of French and Spanish blood from the Pyrenees Mountains in Europe. The Beristains were sheepherders that got crossways with the cattlemen. Anyway, Johnny had quite the reputation as a lawman. Unfortunately, that reputation reared up and bit him one night when the friends and family of two men he sent to the Nevada Territorial Pen invaded his house, beat him nearly to death, and raped and killed his wife and murdered his young son with a shotgun. They left

Johnny for dead. Only, he wasn't dead. He hunted those men down, clear to the east end of Nevada, catching them all along the way, all thirteen, and giving most of them their own special necktie parties."

"Necktie parties?"

Poindexter used his hands to indicate a noose around his neck. He stuck out his tongue in a grisly pantomime of a man being hanged. He chuckled.

"Oh, Lord . . ."

"The chief marshal fired him, of course. There were witnesses. Johnny's lucky he didn't go to jail or face an executioner. Several of those men gave themselves up to him, and he hanged them from the nearest tree, anyway. Not a trace of due process." Poindexter wagged his head, pooching out his lips. "Can't blame him, I suppose, after what those killers did to his family. Frontier justice, and all that. It's how things are done out here. But we expect more from lawmen, of course. Johnny went crazy, some say, and his sanity hasn't been seen since. I'd feel sorry for him if he didn't make such a spectacle of himself!"

"What brought him to Hallelujah Junction?"

"He came here a little over a year ago in a prospector's wagon. He was going to hunt for gold, like all the other men still pouring into these mountains. Only, the memories were too much for him, I guess, and he took to drink and fallen women. So . . . there he is now. A shadow of his former self. A shell of a man. He'll likely be dead soon. Some would say the sooner the better for his own sake. Why live like that—a slave to the bottle? Begging for money, humiliating yourself for drinks."

Sheila shook her head. "What a shame."

"Indeed." Poindexter shuddered with a sudden chill. The night at this altitude, nearly eight thousand feet above sea level, got cold even now in late summer. "Well, I'd best get back home, relieve Edna Crawley of her duties with Claudia."

"Yes, yes—thank you for staying late, George. Feel free to spend a little extra time at home tomorrow morning. My way of making at least part of this day up to poor Claudia."

"All right, I'll do that." Poindexter lifted his bowler hat, winked, and started to turn away. He stopped and turned back to Sheila. "What am I thinking? It's dark out here. I'll see you home, Sheila."

"No, I wouldn't think of it. I'll be fine. You go home to your ailing wife, George."

"Are you sure? Your father's house is a good half mile's walk, and it's awfully dark."

"The walk will do me good, and I'm not one bit afraid of the dark. I'm a capable woman."

Poindexter chuckled. "Indeed, you are. All right, then. Good night, Sheila."

"Good night, George."

He turned around and walked along the street in the direction of his house.

Sheila turned and walked in the opposite direction, retracing her route from early that morning, when she'd come to work to find the dead bullion guards waiting for her in front of the bank. She turned down the side street that led to her father's house—now *her* house—and found herself in heavy darkness only partly relieved by the sickle moon tumbling down the western sky.

There were only a few widely scattered log cabins,

small frame houses, and a barn and stock pen out
this way. Ponderosa pines pushed up close to the dirt
street she was walking along, keeping her eyes on
the path before her, watching for hidden obstacles.
The night breeze made a soft rushing sound in the
tops of the pines. An owl hooted and a coyote yam-
mered mournfully in the far distance, probably
standing sentinel atop some stony mountain crag
overlooking the town.

Just after she passed the log barn and stable owned
by a German dairy farmer, Sheila stopped suddenly,
her heart quickening. She turned her head sharply
right, opposite the side of the trail from the barn.
She'd heard something.

What?

The crunch of a twig under a stealthy boot, perhaps . . .

Sheila probed the darkness with her gaze. All she
could see were the dark, columnar shadows of the
pines, a few of the boughs nodding in the breeze.
She looked behind her, then ahead, feeling her pulse
in her fingertips.

Finally, she continued walking, increasing her
pace. She could see her house now in the shadows
ahead and off the trail's right side in a slight clearing
in the forest. It was dark. Too dark. Verna Godfrey
would have long since left the house and gone back
to her own in Hallelujah Junction. Sheila wished
she'd had her leave a lamp burning in a window.

She felt very alone and vulnerable out here. She'd
never walked home this late at night. Maybe she
should have taken Poindexter up on his offer to
accompany her . . .

Another sound. On her left this time.

Sheila gasped as she stopped once again, her heart beating even faster.

"Hello?" she called into the darkness. "Is someone there?"

Nothing but trees over there. At least, as far as she could tell. The moonlight barely penetrated. An old prospector's cabin sat back in the woods maybe a hundred yards from the trace Sheila was on. Otherwise, there were no other houses. Her father, enjoying his privacy, had built his house beyond the very edge of Hallelujah Junction.

Sheila didn't think the old cabin was occupied. No one else should be out here this time of the night. But she sensed someone's presence. She felt eyes on her, boring holes into her . . .

"Who's out there?" she called, putting some steel into her voice.

The only response was the faint rush of the wind in the treetops.

Sheila turned her head forward again and hurried up the path, quickening her pace. Her house was within fifty yards now and growing closer with every step.

Sheila angled off the trace's right side. It dead-ended just ahead, at the base of a mountain wall. All that was out here was her own house, whose shadow loomed in the darkness, silently beckoning beyond the white picket fence that shone pale in the darkness.

She gained the fence and fumbled with the gate latch. She glanced over her shoulder. She didn't see anyone back there but in her mind, someone was stealing up on her from behind . . .

Hurry, Sheila! Get inside!

"Ow, dammit!" she cried when she got her finger caught in the latch.

She pulled her hand away from the gate, leaving the gate yawning behind her, rocking and creaking on its hinges, and strode quickly, half-running, along the flagstone walk. She reached into her valise and withdrew her house keys. She was almost home!

She started up the five wooden porch steps. The heels of her ankle boots sounded inordinately loud in the quiet night, further rattling her nerves.

A dark figure moved in the darkness atop the veranda.

Sheila cried out and stopped, tripping on a riser and nearly falling, dropping her keys with a loud, jangling thud.

A tall, broad-shouldered man stepped out from the veranda's shadows. He stopped at the edge of the steps to tower over her. He moved his hand out to one side, toward the ceiling support post to his right, and there was a *scritch*ing sound. In his hand, a match flamed to life. He lifted the flame.

Its fluttering red glow revealed the broad ugly face of Deputy U.S. Marshal Lyle Wallace.

CHAPTER 7

"You!" Sheila cried, down on one knee. She'd dropped her valise on top of her keys. She stared up in exasperation at Wallace. "What the hell do you think you're doing here?"

"Nice evenin'," Wallace said, waving out the match and blowing the smoke at Sheila. He drew deep on the cigarette dangling from between his lips then blew more smoke over her head.

Sheila heaved herself to her feet, trying to suppress her trembling. "I asked you a question, Marshal. What are you doing here?"

"Thought we'd have a drink."

"What?"

Wallace laughed. She could smell the sour stench of beer on his breath mixing with the peppery aroma of the tobacco. "Why not? You're alone, ain't ya? Don't got a man. You must be lonely—a purty young woman livin' alone out here in this fancy house, all this room to move around in. Right lonely, I'd think."

"Get out of here!"

"One drink."

"No! Leave here, Marshal. You are trespassing on private property."

Wallace chuckled. He doffed his hat and batted it absently against his thigh. "Well, now—ain't you the ungrateful one? I came over to tell you that I lined up a posse. Several of the fellas and I are gonna go out looking for them bullion robbers of yours. First thing tomorrow morning."

"Tomorrow? Don't you think the robbers' trail might be a little cold by tomorrow?"

Again, Wallace chuckled but this time with less humor than before. "Yessir, I don't recollect ever meetin' up with a woman less grateful. Or less friendly." He set his hat on his hand, pulled it down tight atop his cap of curly red hair. "Most single women would invite most single men in for a drink, as a gesture of gratefulness."

"It's not that I'm not grateful," Sheila lied. "But you are just doing your job—aren't you, Marshal? I mean, isn't forming a posse and going after the thieves *your job*?"

Wallace scowled darkly down at her from beneath the brim of his hat. The cigarette smoldered in his right hand, which he held down low over the re-volver holstered on that leg. He lifted the cigarette to his lips as he continued staring with silent menace at Sheila and took a long drag, making the coal glow red for a long time.

He drew the smoke deep into his lungs then let it dribble slowly out through his nostrils. He blew the last of it out through his mouth then dropped almost casually down the steps.

Sheila felt herself inwardly shriveling against the big, threatening man before her, but she refused to yield her position. This was her house, after all. He had no place here.

He stood staring down at her again, close enough now that she could smell his body odor mixing with the beer and tobacco smoke on his breath. His lumpy chest rose and fell heavily as he breathed, and his bulging potbelly expanded and contracted behind the black shirt he wore beneath a brown leather jacket.

He reached out suddenly and grabbed her right wrist. She gasped and tried to pull her hand free, but he tightened his grip and drew her toward him. He pushed his face down close to hers, and for a second she thought he was going to try to kiss her.

Instead, he held his face just inches from hers and, hardening his jaws and flaring his nostrils, said, "I don't like your attitude, Miss Bonner." He gritted his teeth as he squeezed her wrist even harder, and twisted it.

"Ow!" Sheila said, gritting her own teeth against the grinding pain.

"People around here—they try to get along," Wallace said tightly, blowing his sour beer breath against Sheila's lips. "We don't cotton to uppity folks around here. Especially uppity women. Women who hold their noses up high, like they're too good to look anyone in the eye. Like their bloomers is starched so stiff they walk around like they got a pole up their behind!"

"You're hurting me, Marshal!" Sheila grated out, one knee buckling against the wrenching he was giving her wrist, drawing it up between them and back, squeezing.

"I don't like what you did in the Slipper earlier.

That chafed me raw, Miss Bonner. You ain't been around here long enough, and you ain't given me enough *attention*—if you get my drift—to go dressin' me down in front of my friends!"

"I'm sorry if you were offended, but you can imagine how *I* felt, Marshal!"

Ignoring her, Wallace said, "Now, I'm gonna lead me a posse after them thieves tomorrow. I'm gonna do everything I can to get that gold back for you. And when I get back to town, I'm gonna expect you to treat me better. See? You get my drift?"

Sheila grunted as Wallace jerked her wrist again, squeezing, grinding the fragile bones. "If you think I'm going to—"

"I think you're gonna get all gussied up in somethin' nice. Not in one o' them old-ladies' dresses you always wear, but somethin' that flatters your purty figure a little better. Yeah, yeah . . . you're gonna get all nice an' fresh an' purty . . . show a little of your purty flesh . . . and you an' me are gonna go out to the Sierra Nevada Hotel an' have us a few drinks and a nice supper together. After that . . ." Wallace chuckled goatishly. "After that, well . . . we'll just see how happy you are to have your bullion back . . ."

"Ow! Let go of me, damn you!"

"There!"

Wallace released her hand and straightened, smiling maniacally down at her. "See—I can be nice when you treat me nice. Which I know you're gonna do. See—I'm a big man in this town, Miss Bonner. I don't live here, but I pass through here often enough that I've made a few friends. You? You're new here. And you have a reputation for bein' a mite uppity. If you want to hear it plain—no one really likes you. Oh, the men like *lookin'* at you, but they don't really like you. No one likes a high-headed woman.

"So if you think you're gonna go runnin' to Flagg and complain about what happened here tonight— you an' me just havin' us a reasonable chat over important matters—you got another think comin'. No one's gonna take your word over mine. Besides, that . . . somethin' bad might happen. Somethin' that makes your wrist feel like nothin' more than a bit lip. You understand?"

Still on one knee, massaging her injured wrist, Sheila glared up at him, her jaws taut. Tears dribbled down her cheeks. She didn't want them to. She didn't want to give this bully the satisfaction of knowing he'd frightened her, but he had, and she couldn't stop the tears of rage and terror.

She did not sob, however. No, she would not do that.

Wallace lifted the cigarette to his lips, took a drag. He blew the smoke down at Sheila and said, "I asked you a question. Do you understand what I just told you?"

Sheila knew she had no choice but to answer him. She just wanted to make him leave and she knew the only way to do that was to swallow her pride and to say, "Yes. I understand." She licked her lips, swallowed. Her taut voice trembled as she said, "Now get the hell out of my yard."

"I still don't like your tone," Wallace said with menace, giving his head another reproving wag. "But I reckon we can work on that in the future. We'll have plenty of time." Stepping around her, he dropped down the porch steps and into the yard, tipping his hat to her. "Good night, now, Miss Sheila. Be seein' you again soon."

He started toward the fence gate, then stopped and turned back to her. "Oh, I seen a nice little, low-cut frock in Mrs. MacLean's store window uptown this mornin'. Looks pricey, but you can afford it. I sure would admire to see you in it when I get back."

He cast Sheila a lascivious wink, chuckling, then poked the cigarette into his mouth and strode down the flagstone path and through the gate in the picket fence. Sitting on the steps, clutching her injured right wrist in her left hand, Sheila watched his shadow dwindle into the night.

It took her heart a long time to stop beating like that of a terrified bird.

George Poindexter stopped for a leisurely beer at the Gold Nugget before dropping a nickel onto the bar, donning his hat, winking at the barman, O'Grady, then strolling back out through the batwings and into the night. This is how it was going to be every night soon. He'd stop for a beer after work. Hell, he might stop for three beers and a steak and a big plate of beans . . .

After that, he might stop at one of the hurdy-gurdy houses along the river for a shot and a frolic. Not at the seedier places, but at the higher-end place owned by the former dancer, Lola Neal, who'd grown to fame in Deadwood and Leadville, and who still looked pretty darn good for her years. What George wouldn't give for a frolic. But not yet. No, not yet. Folks would talk. Gossip spread through a town the size of Hallelujah Junction like a wildfire.

He tramped on home along Third Avenue, turned right beyond the mercantile, and strolled along the stone path winding gently between tall firs and spruces. Stars seemed to hang like glitter in the evergreen boughs. He smiled at the serenity of such a view, unable to remember when last he'd taken the time to appreciate such a thing as the stars in the pine branches.

He climbed the porch steps of his small, neat, two-story house flanked by Claudia's rose garden and by a buggy shed and a stable. He unlocked the door and stepped into the foyer, doffing his hat and hanging it from the tree in the corner on his left, opposite the cabinet clock that had belonged to Claudia's parents and whose monotonous, droll ticking had greeted George for the past four years that he and Claudia had lived here, having followed their dreams out from Ohio.

Well, George's dream, at least. The dream of frontier gold.

The clock would be one of the first things to go. He'd lift the heavy bugger himself, drag it out the back door, and heave it into the ravine through which Eagle Creek meandered.

He smiled at the thought, but the smile drew taut when a reedy voice sounded from above, "Georgeyyy . . . ?"

"Oh, dear," Poindexter muttered. Stepping up to the bottom of the stairs that angled up into the second story, he grabbed the ball atop the newel post to his left and called, "I'm home, dear."

Silence.

Then, in the same week, raspy tone: "Georgeyyy . . . ?"

Poindexter drew a deep, calming breath and said, "Coming, dear."

He climbed the dark stairwell lit by starlight angling through a window at the top of the stairs. He strode down the hall padded by a carpet runner, heading toward the light at the hall's other end. The light shone through the long, vertical, eight-inch gap between Claudia's door and the frame.

He approached the door and nudged it open. Claudia lay in the big, canopied bed before him. This was the guest room into which he'd moved Claudia several months ago, telling her she'd be better off in here, as he'd be working in bed at night and he didn't want to interrupt her badly needed sleep. In truth, her illness had repelled him—the way she moaned in her sleep from the pain at times, and from her raspy breathing.

"I'm home, dear," Poindexter said.

Claudia turned her haggard face framed by her long, coarse, colorless hair, and gazed up at him through her little gray eyes, opaque with constant pain, and said, "Wh-where . . . where have you been, George?"

"I'm so sorry, Claudia, dear," Poindexter said, sitting on the edge of the bed. He smiled gently down at his ill wife and patted her head as though he were petting a dog. "I had to work unexpectedly late this evening. Have you been terribly uncomfortable?"

"Well, yes . . ." She winced and squeezed her eyes closed against the pain that lanced through her repeatedly. "Yes, I've . . . I've been in awful pain. I ran out of laudanum up here. The bottle's downstairs, I believe."

Poindexter frowned. "Didn't Edna stop in around

noon? I asked her yesterday to come over and check on you," he lied. "I was very precise in informing her that I would be working late this evening."

"No . . . no, she didn't. She must have forgotten, poor dear. Oh, I shouldn't complain. She's helped so much . . ."

"If Edna didn't come over, you must not have gotten any lunch."

"No, no. I tried to make it downstairs, to make a sandwich, but I just couldn't do it on my own. I couldn't even crawl out of bed."

"You poor thing, Claudia. I feel so ashamed!"

"It's not your fault, dear George." Claudia reached up and placed a clawlike, powder-white hand against his cheek. "You've been so overburdened yourself, between my illness and Martin dying, and his worthless daughter coming here to complicate matters with her incompetence, and to make more work for you!"

"Nonsense. I should have come home at noon and checked on you myself."

"Don't worry about that now, dear. I'm sure after I've had the surgery, I'll be able to fend for myself again, and not be such a burden to you and the others. Oh, I just hate what I've become! How do you stand me?"

"Enough of that." Poindexter pulled the covers down to reveal Claudia's pale, shriveled legs beneath the hem of her nightgown, webbed with dark blue varicose veins. "Let's get you downstairs. You need to move around a little. I'll get a fire going, and you can eat in front of the hearth. First, though, we'll get some laudanum into you."

"Yes, yes—I suppose I should get up or I'll open my bedsores again."

"You certainly might, and we don't want to deal with those again." Poindexter certainly didn't want to deal with the bedsores again. The smell had been awful, and, as per the local doctor's orders, he'd had to treat and wrap them twice a day.

He grunted now as he eased Claudia into her high-backed wooden pushchair, though she hardly weighed anything at all anymore. Her sickly body, which stank of camphor and disease, repelled him. Still, he pasted an administering smile on his face. "There, now. We'll just take you downstairs and get you all fixed up," he said, wheeling her stiff, nearly weightless body around the bed toward the open door.

Claudia flung out her spidery hand. "Oh, George, my afghan. Please, it's chilly."

"Certainly, certainly."

Poindexter pulled an afghan off the trunk at the foot of the bed and draped it around her shoulders. "Oh, not that one! That's the last one of my mother's. The one on the chair."

"Of course, of course." Poindexter removed the afghan from her shoulders, folded it neatly, lay it back down on the trunk, and retrieved the one from the chair. He wrapped it around Claudia's shoulders.

"Yes, that's the one," she said with a pleased sigh.

Poindexter wheeled her through the door and into the hall.

"I'm so sorry to be such a burden, George," she said, her voice shaking as the wheels drummed softly along the carpet runner.

"Nonsense, my dear."

"No, not nonsense. You're a dear, sweet man to tend me so selflessly . . ."

The mouth of the stairs yawned toward Poindexter, moving up closer and closer. It looked like a deep dark pit there where the stairs curved sharply to the left as they dropped toward the first story.

Closer and closer the stair mouth came, opening like the jaws of freedom . . .

Poindexter's heart raced. Suddenly, he was sweating as though he'd run a long distance in the summer sun. He gripped the pushchair's wooden handles in both hands until they creaked, splintering . . .

Closer and closer . . .

Poindexter's heart hiccupped.

No, not yet, you fool, a voice shouted inside his head. *Not yet. You have to wait, you fool. Now is not the right—*

"Oh, George, stop!" Claudia cried.

Too late.

He couldn't have stopped even if he'd wanted to, for the chair's front wheels had already dropped over the first step.

Poindexter gave a grunt as he heaved the chair forward with all his might . . . and let it go . . .

CHAPTER 8

Several weeks later, pain in his right thigh woke Johnny Greenway with a startled, "Ouch!"

He opened his eyes to see a man stumbling to his left and dropping to a knee. The man had obviously tripped over Johnny, who lay slumped in a Hallelujah Junction alley, between discarded packing crates and half-buried in the old newspapers he'd drawn over himself to keep out the previous night's chill.

"Watch where you goin', amigo!" Johnny admonished the man. "I'm tryin' to get a little shut-eye over here!"

The man who'd tripped over him cursed and, down on one knee, glared at Johnny. "Damn drunk! What're you doin' out here?"

"*Shhhh!*" said another man, to the right of the first one. "Keep it down, Rance, ya damn idiot!"

Rance walked over to Johnny. He was holding a double-barreled shotgun—a ten-gauge—in both his black-gloved hands. He was dressed nearly all in black including a black duster. He looked like a dandy, maybe a card sharp, but something told Johnny he was neither. Long mustaches hung down over both sides of his mouth. His dark eyes were savage, and he wore a twisted white knife scar on the nub of his dimpled chin.

"Worthless piece of trash," he bit out at Johnny, who was, indeed, half-buried under trash. "I oughta blow your lights out for ya."

He angled the shotgun's barrel down toward Johnny.

Johnny leaned forward, smiling, and pressed his head up close to the end of the shotgun. "Go ahead," he said. "I been needin' me some peace an' quiet."

"Maybe I just will," Rance said, tensing his jaws and flexing his hands around the ten-gauge.

"Rance, dammit!" ordered the other man, who was kneeling behind some stacked packing crates at the alley mouth fronting the brightly sunlit main street. "Ignore him. He's a no-good drunk, fer chrissakes. We got bigger fish to fry!"

Rance continued to gaze down at Johnny grinning annoyingly up at him, not one bit afraid of the Greener in the man's hands.

"Here she comes! I heard she's the only one who can open the safe!"

That spun Rance around. He took a knee behind a rain barrel straight out from Johnny, maybe ten feet away. He peered over the rain barrel into the street.

Blinking the cobwebs from his eyes, Johnny sat up a little and stretched his gaze over Rance's right shoulder, peering beyond him into the street.

She?

He blinked again to clear his vision, wincing at the sharp throbbing behind his left eye. Gradually, as his vision clarified and he continued to stare into the street, gritting his teeth against the assault on his tender brain by the harsh, high-country sunlight, the woman from the bank swam into view.

The pretty brunette with a heart-shaped face that had no doubt shredded many a male heart was walking along the boardwalks on the street's far side, heading from Johnny's right to his left. She was heading toward the bank. Judging by the light, it was midday, and she must have left the bank to fetch the mail, for she was holding a bundle of envelopes and a brown-paper parcel tied with string in her arms.

She was heading for the bank nearly directly across the street from where the two men with shotguns knelt and Johnny slumped, peering over Rance's shoulder.

As the young lady whose name Johnny had forgotten, though not her lovely face and figure, worked her way through the midday foot traffic, then disappeared through the bank's front door, the door closing behind her and the sunlight glinting off the shaded glass, Johnny's heart quickened.

Rance and the other man turned to each other and grinned. "Real looker," Rance said.

"We'll take her when we go," said the other man. "That'll keep a posse off our backs."

"Keep the loneliness off our backs, too . . . later this evenin' around the fire," Rance added, grinning seedily.

The other man, also smiling, winked his complicity in the intended rape.

"Is it time?" he asked.

"Lemme check."

As Rance reached into a vest pocket for a timepiece, Johnny found himself scuttling up low behind the man. The other man turned his head sharply toward Johnny and said, "Hey, what're you—?"

Before he could finish, Johnny found himself—and he was just as surprised by his actions as Rance's partner was—jerking a long-barreled Colt revolver from the holster tied down on Rance's right thigh. He raised the gun above his right shoulder and swept it down, smashing the barrel soundly and with a dull thud against the high crown of Rance's hat. The crown was instantly not as high as before, and it showed the long, narrow dent made by the Colt's heavy steel barrel.

Rance dropped like a poleaxed bull.

His partner stared in hang-jawed exasperation at the unfortunate and unlikely turn of events. He was just starting to leap to his feet, raising his shotgun, when Johnny swung the Colt toward him, clicking the hammer back, and drilled a neat, round, quarter-sized hole through the middle of the man's freckled forehead, beneath the crown of his tan Stetson.

The Colt's thunderous report vaulted out over the street and echoed inside the timber-rimmed canyon in which Hallelujah Junction nestled.

There were a good many folks on the street, either walking or riding horses or riding in wagons. All heads swung toward the alley mouth in which Johnny had just thrown Rance's partner back against a building wall painted with blood and brains from the man's ruined skull. A collective gasp lifted from the onlookers, many of whom were now frozen in place.

"*What the hell . . . ?*"

The query had come from the far side of the store on Johnny's left, where, he now assumed, more bank robbers were huddled, waiting for the appointed time they would all make a move at once. Johnny didn't think these thoughts as much as he knew them deep inside his former lawman's soul, surprised that that lawman hadn't been totally obliterated by all the barrels of whiskey he'd consumed over the past many months.

A rifle cracked, the report also thundering out over the street. A quarter second earlier, Johnny had seen the rifleman step out from the alley to the left of the bank and extend a Winchester toward him. Now the bullet curled the air off his right cheek and smacked into the chest of Rance's partner, who was still standing against the building to Johnny's right, his knees slowly buckling, his butt sagging.

The man had dropped his shotgun. It lay on the ground near his shaking boots.

Rance had dropped his ten-gauge, as well.

As shouting and more gunfire erupted in the street, Johnny shoved the Colt down behind the waistband of his patched and filthy whipcord trousers and scooped Rance's ten-gauge off the ground. He grabbed the shotgun of Rance's partner, as well, and as the shooting continued, several bullets screeching past him to hammer the side of the building now on his right, he strode quickly down the alley toward its rear.

Gripping each shotgun in each hand, he eared back a rabbit-ear hammer of each.

At the rear of the building on his right, he turned sharply and walked along the building's back wall. At the far corner, he turned right again, and, gazing up past the building toward the street, raised both shotguns and tripped the cocked trigger of each.

The twin, dynamite-like explosions filled the alley, reverberating violently off the brick walls abutting it on either side.

Two men had been striding quickly toward Johnny, also holding shotguns. One was a tall blond in a green bowler hat to match his green and brown three-piece suit. The other was a long-faced Indian in a calico shirt under a brown vest. They'd stopped when they'd seen Johnny, eyes widening in surprise. They'd started to raise their shotguns too late, for now those shotguns went leaping out of their hands as both of Johnny's fist-sized wads of double-ought buckshot ripped through each man at nearly the same time, picking them up and hurling them straight back toward the main street, screaming.

They hit the ground and rolled, no longer screaming, for they'd died while they'd still been airborne.

Johnny continued walking straight up through the alley, barely aware of how calm he felt, of how slowly his heart was beating. In his strong hands at the ends of his strong arms, accustomed to the weight and recoil of a ten-gauge Greener, formerly his weapon of choice, he cocked the weapons once more, engaging each double-barreled popper's second barrel.

Ahead, the street had cleared, men and women dashing toward the safety of doorways or the breaks between buildings. Dust wafted in the wakes of running feet, galloping hooves, and churning wheels.

No, it hadn't quite cleared. Three men were running toward Johnny—one from the opposite side of the street straight ahead of him, and two from his right, from where they'd variously positioned themselves, probably to give cover to their accomplices leaving the bank with the stolen loot.

Two were firing rifles while the one straight out ahead of Johnny—a black man with a black hat and a red kerchief knotted around his throat—triggered a revolver.

Johnny stopped and raised the shotgun in his left hand.

The black man stopped halfway across the street, his black eyes widening until they were ringed entirely in white. "No, no!" he screamed, raising a gloved hand palm out. *"Wait!"*

Johnny calmly squeezed the eyelash trigger and blew the black man into Eternity.

He dropped the empty shotgun and took the second one in both his hands. The two riflemen approached Johnny on his right, running straight down the middle of the street, furiously triggering their carbines. Most of their bullets flew wide around and over Johnny, thumping into the shop flanking him, two grinding into the street around his boots.

One carved a hot line across the outside of his left thigh. Johnny didn't even wince.

Instinctively turned sideways to make himself as small a target as possible, he leveled the shotgun at his two assailants, who were within fifteen yards now and still coming, cursing loudly as they fired hastily and missed.

Johnny squeezed the flat, curled trigger, feeling the pleasant, resolute punch of the gun's butt plate against his side. Flames and smoke roiled from the large, round maw. Johnny smiled in satisfaction as both men, running only inches apart, screamed as the steel buckshot tore into them, shredding their shirts and vests and faces. They dropped in mid-stride and rolled, screaming and clawing at their torsos as though to ward off a horde of enraged bees stinging them savagely.

Johnny dropped the empty, smoking shotgun.

He clamped his hand around the ivory grips of the Colt revolver, pulled it out of his pants, and cocked it. He polished off both screaming, buckshot-peppered would-be robbers with a single shot apiece.

He raised the Colt's barrel when the front door of the bank opened and a man came running out. He had a curly mop of blond hair, and he wore a Prince Albert summer-weight coat over a paisley vest, a ruffled silk shirt, and black ribbon tie. He held a carpetbag in one hand and a long-barreled Smith & Wesson revolver in his other hand. As two more people emerged from the bank behind him, he leveled both pistols at Johnny, who dispatched the blond with a single shot from the Colt.

The blond dropped the carpetbag as he stumbled backward, and fired the Smithy into the street just before he folded up like a barlow knife, hitting the ground with a thud.

"Stop right there, you son of a buck!" shouted the second man who'd emerged from the bank.

There were two people there, all right. One was a man dressed similarly to the man Johnny had just dispatched, only with dark hair, a gray-flecked mustache, and a bolo tie. He had a hard, chiseled face and hard brown eyes to match, set beneath a rigid, dark-brown brow. He held the pretty brunette owner of the bank before him.

Her almond-shaped brown eyes were wide and shiny with fear as the man behind her held a silver-chased cocked Colt to her head, just beneath her right ear, which her pinned-up hair revealed. A light-brown earring that complemented the nut-brown of her eyes dangled from each pale earlobe.

She wore a peach-colored suit with a lace-edged white shirtwaist that bulged nicely right where it should have.

The hard-faced man glanced around quickly, his eyes darting to his dead cohorts lying in growing blood pools around him. Apparently satisfied that Johnny was the only living man on the street, he turned his full attention to him. "You clean up right well, you wild dog!"

"Thanks," Johnny said. "And you're next."

"I'll kill her!"

"And I'll kill you," Johnny said, calmly extending his own Colt at him, centering his sights on the man's left eye.

"She'll die before I fall!" the man screamed, fear and exasperation flashing in his otherwise flinty eyes.

The brunette opened her mouth and closed her eyes as though praying for calm while awaiting the bullet.

"You got it, hero?" the robber snarled at Johnny, stretching his lips back from his large teeth. "She dies if you don't put that gun down!"

"Let her go, and I'll let you ride out of here."

"Put the gun down!"

"Let her go, and I'll let you ride out of here." Johnny glanced toward several horses standing in the street to his right, in various positions, reins dangling. He assumed that one of the men he'd killed had been holding the robbers' horses. Now they'd scattered. Some had fled, some remained nearby.

The robber glanced at the horses. His eyes were vaguely thoughtful. He fidgeted, thinking through his options. Johnny had called his bluff, and the robber knew it. If he killed the woman, he'd be dead a second later. If he tried to kill Johnny, he'd also be dead. The only thing he could do was take Johnny's advice.

He licked his lips and studied Johnny closely.

"I got your word on that?"

"You do. Take the money and go. It's not worth her life."

"Hell, we didn't get but a hundred dollars!" the robber yelled at Sheila, flaring his nostrils and flashing his eyes in anger.

He threw her forward. Johnny pulled her behind him.

The man kept his gun on Johnny and the woman as he sidestepped toward the horses. "You gave me your word!" he shouted, backing away now toward where a fox-red gelding stood several yards away, eyeing the men and the woman warily, twitching its ears.

"I lied," Johnny said, calmly. He smiled.

Still backing toward the horse, the robber frowned. "What?"

Johnny extended the Colt. The robber's eyes widened in horror. He stopped and started to steady his own gun on Johnny. Johnny's Colt bucked and roared.

"*Oh!*" the brunette said, flanking Johnny. She cupped both hands over her mouth.

The bullet punched through the dead center of the robber's chest. It sent him stumbling backward. He dropped his pistol. His eyes rolled back in his head. He tripped over his spurs and fell in the street.

He arched his back, writhing, grinding his spurs in the dirt.

He gave a gurgling groan, and then his muscles relaxed and he lay slack in the street, dead as a post.

Johnny looked at the smoking Colt in his hand. It was as though he noticed it now for the first time. He brought it in closer to his body, stared down at it.

He became aware of voices around him, of town folks moving out from where they'd taken cover, staring down in shock and amazement at the dead men piled up in the street fronting the bank. Several dogs appeared as though from nowhere to sniff the dead men, one lifting his leg on one.

Johnny removed his gaze from the still-smoking Colt in his hand to see the brunette staring at him from three feet away. Her eyes probed his as though reaching deep inside him, plumbing his depths.

Johnny held her gaze for several seconds.

Then his customary smile returned to his lips. He dropped the gun in the street.

"Whew!" he said. "That's the most work I've done in a month of Sundays." He extended his hand to her, palm up. "You couldn't spare some jingle for a bottle—could you, ma'am?"

She studied him a moment longer. Then she blinked, turned away, and without saying a word, walked back into the bank, leaving Johnny standing amidst the astonished crowd gathering around him.

CHAPTER 9

Several days later, Sheila reined her sorrel filly off the main trail leading west out of Hallelujah Junction and onto a narrow right fork.

She rode over a mountain shoulder, the air rife with the refreshing tang of pine and the smell of the sun-soaked pine needles, moldering aspen leaves, and the heavy black dirt of the forest floor. She pulled her tan felt hat down against the glaring sun angling through the aspens, pines, spruces, and tamaracks, then dropped down the slope and into the open. She crossed a creek nearly hidden in deep green grass, willows, and purple mountain sage via a wooden bridge, the sorrel's shod hooves clomping over the worn gray half logs.

On the far side of the bridge Sheila passed through more trees offering ink-black shade contrasting sharply with the bright, early afternoon sunlight, then entered a sun-splashed clearing gleaming like jade. Here she reined the frisky sorrel to a stop. The young horse champed its bit playfully and shifted restlessly on its feet, wanting to keep moving.

Sheila leaned forward to pat the mount's right

wither as she inspected the humble log cabin set in the forest in front of her, saying, "We're going to stop here for a bit, girl."

The cabin was small, with a covered front stoop. Its peaked brush roof was as green as the glen around it, contrasting sharply with the dark color of the ancient logs comprising the shack.

A pair of snowshoes, a corrugated tin washtub, and several skins and animal horns were tacked to the front wall and the square-hewn awning support posts. A liver-colored cat moved out from the shade beneath a hide-bottom chair to lean up against the porch rail, arching its back and curling its tail in cautious curiosity of the stranger's sudden presence.

"Who's there?" a man called from inside the shack.

Sheila rose up in her stirrups to call, "It's Miss Bonner. Miss Sheila Bonner." She paused, angling her head this way and that, trying to peer into the shack through its door, which was propped open with a stone jug. She could see nothing inside but shadows. "From the bank," she added in afterthought, feeling the need to further elaborate: "The Bank & Trust in Hallelujah Junct—"

She stopped when a large figure appeared in the open doorway, nearly filling it. In fact, he had to duck his head to poke it out through the low door. He stepped forward, the rest of his large, bulky body following his head out onto the stoop. He was a burly, bearded, nearly bald man with a belly like half a rain barrel, and clad entirely in smoke-stained buckskins. Snakeskin suspenders held up his trousers, the cuffs of which were tucked down into high-topped, lace-up boots.

"I got no accounts with you," said the big man in

his deep, raspy voice, his close-set, lake-blue eyes cast with suspicion. "No loan, neither. I stay away from banks. Any extry jingle I've ever had I buried. I don't trust banks"—he offered a somewhat playful smile—"no more'n they'd trust me . . ."

The man's sudden tempering of tone was a relief to Sheila. She'd hesitated to ride out here, knowing that most Western men, especially those who chose to live out in the "tall and uncut," as the backcountry was called in the parlance of the frontier, are in the main eccentric loners mistrustful of others, especially women and banks. Sheila thought it entirely possible that she—not only a woman but a woman who owned a bank—might be shot off her horse before being invited to dismount of her own volition.

So far, so good. The big man before her had a pistol wedged behind his large, black belt, over his bulging belly, but he had none in either hand.

"Mister Musgrave?" she called, holding a gloved hand to her hat brim to additionally shade her eyes. "Bear Musgrave?"

"That's right."

"I was told by a Miss Lenore Dupont that I could find Mister Greenway here."

"Yeah, well . . ." Musgrave smiled crookedly. "They had 'em a fallin'-out—Mister Greenway and Miss Dupont—don't ya know."

"He's here, then."

"I reckon you might say that."

"I'd like to have a word with him."

Musgrave leaned back to peer into the cabin. Straightening and turning his head forward again, he gave another guilty smile. "I'm afraid Mister

Greenway ain't receiving visitors at this time. Maybe some other time, Miss Bonner."

He started to turn back into the cabin but stopped when Sheila said, "Won't you please rouse him for me? I've brought him something."

The big man furled a skeptical brow liberally flecked with gray. "Brought him somethin' . . ."

"Both of you, in fact." Sheila swung her right leg over the sorrel's rump, dismounting. She smoothed the lime green pleats of her riding skirt, slitted for straddling a regular saddle instead of a horrid and impractical not to mention grossly uncomfortable side saddle, and unbuckled a flap of a saddlebag pouch. She reached into the pouch and withdrew a small burlap bundle.

"What you got there?" Musgrave asked, his deep voice pitched with caution.

Sheila drew a deep, guilty breath as she flung aside the burlap then held up a labeled bottle by its neck. "A bottle of good whiskey. Would you please rouse Mister Greenway? Inform him that I have a bottle of very good whiskey which I will bestow upon him in exchange for two words."

"Two words." The big man fingered his long, tangled, gray-brown beard, narrowing one speculative eye at the bottle. He gave another wry grin, his blues sparkling, and said, "Hell, you can talk to me all day for a bottle of Four Oaks."

Sheila gave a strained smile.

"All right, all right." Musgrave beckoned with his arm, then stepped back inside the cabin. "Hey, Johnny," he said as Sheila led the sorrel up to the hitchrack fronting the porch. "Johnny, a woman's here to see ya. The purty one from the bank."

Sheila tied the sorrel to the worn rack then, cradling the bottle like a baby in the crook of her arm clad in the sleeve of a crisp tweed riding coat that had accrued a layer of dust on the trail out from town, she mounted the porch, stopped just outside the cabin, and leaned forward to peer inside. Musgrave turned to her and said, "Johnny—he don't show much life till three, four o'clock in the afternoon."

"I see." What she saw was a man lying belly down and covered with a ratty wildcat hide on a cot in the room's far rear corner. He was snoring, but the snores were muffled by the pillow his face was buried in. Two bare feet stuck out from the bottom of the hide, beneath the red bottoms of wash-worn long handles. She turned to Musgrave. "May I come in?"

"Sure, sure." The big man was eyeing the bottle cradled in her arm. "Be careful, though. It ain't really fit for a lady in here." He ran a fist across his mouth and stepped back, nervously rubbing his big, thick, dirty-nailed hands on his shirt. "Don't recollect any that ever been in here before, matter of fact."

As Sheila entered, she glanced around, mildly impressed. The cabin was cluttered with tack and prospecting and trapping paraphernalia, and many other things whose use Sheila couldn't fathom, but everything appeared to be in its own pile, at least. And relatively clean. There was a kitchen with a small stove and a square eating table to the right. Shelves with airtight tins and neatly arranged cooking utensils. On the table a hand of solitaire had been laid out, near a cigarette smoldering in an ashtray, and a stone mug of what appeared to be coffee steaming near the cigarette.

The living area was to the right, two cots at the rear, abutting opposite walls.

Feeling as self-conscious and awkward as she thought she'd likely feel upon entering a bear's den, with the bear still hibernating inside, Sheila stole slowly forward. Her riding boots thudded loudly on the worn wooden floor then not so loudly when she trod across one of the several dusty animal-skin rugs. The cabin smelled of the gaminess of those rugs and of the coffee Musgrave must have recently brewed, and woodsmoke, cigarette smoke, man sweat, leather, sour wool, and liquor.

All in all, they were not uninviting smells. At least, she didn't find them so.

Sheila stopped about eight feet from the cot, near a ceiling support post, and cleared her throat. "Mister Greenway?"

The unconscious man's only reply was more slow, leisurely, deeply slumbering snores.

Sheila cleared her throat again and raised her voice a little louder. "Mister, um . . . Mister Greenway? I'd like to chat with you, please."

The snores faltered before resuming.

Sheila drew a deep breath, stepped forward, and said again, louder, "Please . . . Mister Greenway? It's Sheila Bonner from the Bank & Trust . . . ?"

"Oh, hell." Musgrave pulled a tin pot off a nail in the wall. He grabbed a big metal spoon off a shelf beneath the dry sink then brushed past Sheila on his way to the cot. Holding the pot maybe one foot above the sleeping man's head, he rapped the spoon against it over and over again.

The racket made Sheila's ears hurt, so it must have sounded like multiple explosions above the sleeping man's head. Still, it wasn't until the fifth or sixth rap that Mister Greenway rolled onto his back, the wild-cat skin sliding off most of him as he raised his knees and covered his ears with his hands.

He glared up at the big man, bellowing, "*Stop! Stop! Stop that infernal racket, Bear! You gone as loco as a peach orchard sow!*"

Bear stopped beating the spoon against the pot. He canted his head to indicate Sheila. With ironic quietness and in a phony British accent, he said, "A visitor has come fer tea, Lord Greenway. A purty one." He winked at Sheila but not in a lewd way.

He turned and walked back toward the kitchen, giving Sheila a dry smile and saying, "Good luck."

He dropped the pot and the spoon on the table. "If he goes to sleep again, let me know." He disappeared out the open door and called, "Here, Louie-Louie-Louie-Louie!"

Sheila turned to the man on the cot. Greenway was sitting up, leaning back against his elbows, his knees partly raised and spread so that he could look at her between them. He studied her for a time, blinking, looking befuddled, addled. His brown eyes were set wide to either side of his long, aquiline nose that gave him a decidedly raptorial look. He stared at her as though an eagle regarding possible prey.

Still, as she'd noted before, he was not unhand-some. There was something rather absorbing in his haunted, hawkish demeanor. He was like a priest undergoing a severe spiritual crisis, yet there was also something of the outlaw in him, which tempered his attractiveness with a danger that made Sheila feel the need to stay well back from him. He was a man whose actions were unpredictable, possibly even to himself.

His ears were probably still ringing from the big man's din. His unshaven face was pale and splotchy, his thick hair hanging down over one eye. He resembled men she'd seen suffering from consumption.

He blinked again, hacked up phlegm, spit it expertly into a chamber pot on the floor beside the cot, and brushed his sleeve across his mouth. "What do you want?"

The bluntness of the question took her aback slightly, though it did not surprise her, coming from him.

"I'd . . . I'd like to have a word with you, Mister Greenway."

He shook his thick hair back from his left eye then rolled both eyes around, suspicious, as though looking for someone else in the cabin. "What'd I do?"

"Excuse me?"

Haltingly, as though he were sifting through the vague and muddled thoughts in his half-pickled brain for a memory of recent transgressions, he said again, more slowly, "What'd I do?"

"Nothing wrong, I assure you. At least, not to me. On the contrary, I've been remiss in not thanking you for what you did last week. You saved my life, Mister Greenway. And you also saved what little money the robbers would have taken from the bank. I can't afford to lose another dime."

Greenway shrugged, shook his head, and lowered his gaze, as though the whole thing embarrassed him. "Forget it. Now, if you'll forgive me, but I was up late—"

"I'd like to speak to you about an important matter, Mister Greenway," Sheila interrupted him.

"I no longer speak on important matters." Greenway started to roll onto his side, drawing the wildcat hide over him again, but stopped when Sheila held up the bottle.

"Please," she said. "Two minutes of your time. I brought a bottle of the good stuff. I was told you favor bourbon." She'd asked the bartender in the Silver Slipper what Greenway drank when he could afford to drink what he wanted.

"Four Oaks." He studied the bottle with a vague look of longing, like a man staring into a glen and remembering a past love. Guilt landed heavily on Sheila's shoulders. She was offering a dying man poison. She hadn't been able to come up with another way, however, to try and save his life. Her own life, as well. At least, her financial life . . .

"Let's sit at the table, shall we?"

He scowled at her, his eyes hardening on either side of his long, curved nose. "What's all this about, lady? You come in here like—"

"Please!" Feeling like a siren straight from hell, Sheila held up the bottle and gave it an enticing wag. "Let's sit at the table."

Greenway studied the bottle. He gave a little shiver, as though chilled, then cursed and flung the hide off himself. As he crawled off the creaking cot, chuffing his disapproval, Sheila walked into the kitchen area and set the bottle on the table. "Do you have any glasses?"

Greenway tramped barefoot into the kitchen, a little unsteady on his feet. He held the wildcat hide around his shoulders. He grabbed two tin cups off a shelf near the range and set them on the table. "The maid ain't been in to wash the crystal, so we'll have to settle for the set usually reserved for Bear's in-laws."

He gave a dry chuckle.

CHAPTER 10

Johnny Greenway, formerly Juan Beristain, sank into the chair Mister Musgrave had been sitting in. He was a long, broad-shouldered falcon in a man's body, sitting there regarding Sheila sitting in the chair across from him as though she were a mouse making a dash across a meadow and he was wondering if she was worth stretching his wings for.

At least, that's how this strange, brooding, dark man made her feel under his sullen, vaguely hateful gaze.

She doffed her hat and set it on the table. She straightened her hair. Greenway grabbed the bottle, uncorked it, and sniffed the lip.

"Four Oaks," he said, his mood seeming to instantly lighten. "Been a while."

He poured some into her cup. "Whoa, that's enough," she said with a wry laugh. "I have more work to do at the bank."

Greenway splashed a goodly portion of the whiskey into his own cup. Sitting sideways to the table, slumped back in his chair, he crossed his ankles out before him and swirled the whiskey in the cup, savoring it like a fine wine. "This ain't exactly proper, you know, Miss Bonner. Ridin' out unescorted to the cabin of two bachelor men."

"Yes, well, unfortunately I had no choice. Mister Poindexter would have accompanied me, I'm sure, but he's taken some time off to grieve for his wife."

"Oh?" Greenway sipped the liquor, rolled it around on his tongue for several seconds, then swallowed it, and sighed pleasantly. "What happened to his wife?"

"Took a fall down the stairs in their home. She's been invalided for quite some time. I feel as though I myself played a part in her death, as I kept poor Mister Poindexter at the bank longer than usual that day. He thought their neighbor was going to check on Mrs. Poindexter but apparently, she forgot to. His poor wife was probably trying to get downstairs for more laudanum. She was pushchair-bound and in terrible pain from a tumor."

"That's too bad." Greenway stared into his cup while running the tip of his index finger around on the rim.

"I heard what happened to you," Sheila said after a brief silence.

He looked up at her and a cold light entered his gaze. "I don't talk about that."

"All right. I didn't come here to talk about that."

"What did you come here for, risking your reputation an' all to visit the town drunk and his ne'er-do-well friend?"

"I came here to offer you a job."

Greenway stared at her blankly. "A job?"

"A job."

He chuckled. "Less'n you ain't heard, Miss Bonner, I'm the town drunk. I don't work. Oh, if I get desperate, I'll muck out a stall or two at one of the livery barns in Hallelujah Junction, empty a few spittoons in the Silver Slipper for shots of whiskey, run an errand for some muckety-muck, but mostly I just—"

"Yes, I know what you do, Mister Greenway. You've made that all too apparent. You drink and you grieve for your murdered wife and your boy."

Greenway pointed a finger at her and gazed at her sharply. "I told you—I don't talk about that."

Sheila drew a deep breath and sat back in her chair. She held his falcon's stare with a level one of her own. "I need a man to haul a load of bullion down from the Reverend's Temptation Mine to the Bank & Trust in Hallelujah Junction."

Greenway furled the skin above the bridge of his big nose slightly. He glanced over his shoulder, as though he thought she must have been speaking to someone else in the room. He looked under the table then returned his brightly ironic gaze to her. "Oh—you mean *me*!"

"I mean you, Mr. Greenway. I am prepared to offer you one hundred dollars for six days' work. It's two days up and three days down from the mine. Of course, that includes hazard pay, as you'll be guarding the bullion, which, as you may or may not know, has been the target of gold thieves of late."

He stared at her as though he'd found himself conversing with a crazy person. "You must really be desperate, havin' to offer the job to the town drunk!"

"After seeing how well you handled those would-be

bank robbers last week, I've come to believe you are exactly the man for the job. You may not think so, Mister Greenway, but I do. And Mister Poindexter does, too."

Greenway laughed. "That was an accident! Trust me—only an accident. I woke up from a three-day bender, and . . . and . . . hell, I don't know what happened." He did know what happened. He'd seen that she was in trouble, and he had a soft spot for her, as likely did every man in town despite her high-headedness. What man didn't have a soft spot for a gal who looked like she did?

Fortunately, while his brain might have forgotten his earlier life as a deputy U.S. marshal of some renown, his hands had not. No one had been more surprised than Johnny himself had been.

"That was no accident, Mister Greenway. The accident is what happened to you. Your run of bad luck and the drinking. That was the accident. Deep down you are still a man to be reckoned with. Why not act like it? Why not stop this sulking and killing yourself slowly with drink? Pull your boots back on, get back to work. The rest of us have to do it. Why are you so special?"

"I didn't say I was special." A forked vein in his forehead bulged, and his not unhandsome face flushed beneath his several-days' growth of beard stubble. "I ain't special—that's my problem. I'm weak. I couldn't handle what happened to my family, so I turned to drink and fallen women. No, no. I ain't special at all. I'm a privy rat, Miss Bonner."

"Isn't it convenient to think so?"

"You're wastin' your time here." Greenway lifted the cup to his lips and threw back the entire rest of the whiskey. "Thanks for the bottle, though. You can stop by any ole time if you bring a bottle." He let his raptorial gaze drift down her long, pale neck to the ample swell of her riding gown's bodice. "You can stop by any ole time . . . an' stay awhile."

A chill gripped her. It was tempered by a warming down low in her belly. An odd competition of feelings, indeed.

The former Juan Beristain lifted his eyes to hers, winked, and smiled the same lascivious smile men had been bestowing upon her for years. Only it was as phony as the rest of the human slime he was feigning to be.

"What?" Sheila asked, unfazed. She gave a defiant chuckle. "Am I supposed to run screaming out of here now?"

"Maybe you'd better. You stay much longer, sitting there looking as good as you do, I might just lock the door and prove to you what a mistake you made in riding out here."

"Go ahead."

Her response surprised him, as it had surprised her. He widened his eyes at her.

"You heard me. Go ahead. Close the door and force me. You're a big man, Mister Greenway. Bigger than I realized. When I first saw you, you seemed so small. But you're not a small man. There would be little I could do to stop you from doing anything you wanted to me."

Against her will, the thought excited her.

Greenway stared that falcon stare at her, his sallow cheeks turning red. Finally, he lowered his gaze, picked up the bottle, and poured more whiskey into his cup. "You've worn out your welcome now, ma'am. I got better things to do than sit here chinnin' with some high-hatted harpy from the bank."

"All right." Sheila nodded slowly. "You've convinced me. I guess you have sunk too low to ever climb out of your quicksand of self-pity." She rose and snatched her hat off the table.

"It ain't self-pity," he protested, gritting his teeth but staring at the table. "I lost everything!"

"Everybody loses everything, Mister Greenway. I'd have figured you a wise-enough man to realize that. Yes, we all lose everything. Sometimes more than once. What decides our measure is what we do to get it back."

Sheila turned to the door.

"Yeah, well, you know my measure, now, don't you?" he barked at her, fuming, holding his whiskey cup so tightly that his knuckles were white.

Softly, Sheila said, "Yes, I do."

"Just stay away from me!" he yelled as she stepped out through the open door and onto the front stoop. "Just stay away—you hear?"

Sheila stopped and looked to her right. The big burly man, Musgrave, sat on the hide-bottom chair. The liver-colored puss lay on his lap. Slowly, the big man stroked the cat with his large hand. Sheila could hear the rhythmic purring from seven feet away.

Musgrave looked up at her guiltily. Keeping his voice low, he canted his head toward the door and said, "That . . . that in there?" He wrinkled his nose and shook his head. "That ain't Johnny Greenway."

"No?" Sheila arched a brow. "I think you're wrong, Mister Musgrave. I've changed my mind about him.

I think that in there . . . whatever *that* is . . . is exactly Johnny Greenway."

She stepped down off the stoop, untied her reins from the rack, mounted up, and rode away.

When he'd heard the thuds of her horse's hooves recede into the distance, until all he could hear from the porch was the purring of Musgrave's cat, Johnny called, "Get in here and drink with me, you old scalawag!"

"Go to hell!"

Johnny hadn't expected the harsh retort. He climbed to his feet, again unsteadily, for he'd had enough of the Four Oaks that he was drunk again, and picked up the bottle in one hand, his cup in the other hand. Letting the wildcat hide tumble off his shoulders, he made his way to the doorway. He ducked his head through the low opening and looked over at where Bear sat with his cat, Louie.

"Who the hell crawled your hump?"

"You."

"Why?"

"I think you should've accepted her offer."

Johnny looked incredulous. "You, too?"

"Yeah, me, too!"

Johnny stepped through the door and leaned back against the frame. "You know"—he shook his head—"you know that ain't possible."

Bear looked him up and down. He looked like he'd just taken a big bite out of a lemon. "No, I guess it ain't." He turned and spat a wad of phlegm over the porch rail and shook his head in disgust.

Johnny held out the bottle. "Take a pull off that. Good stuff. It'll make you feel less colicky about ole Johnny."

"Go to hell, ole Johnny," Bear said, staring out at the green grass and the sparkling pines at the edge of the sun-soaked clearing.

"Come on!" Johnny shook the bottle. "Drink with me, you old son of a buck!"

"I ain't drinkin' today. I ain't in no mood for you or the liquor."

"It's Four Oaks."

"I don't care how many oaks it is."

Johnny was exasperated. Heartbroken, even. "What's the matter with you? It's Four Oaks!"

"I told you—I don't care how many—"

"Ah, hell!" Johnny turned back into the cabin.

Bear could hear him stomping around in there, cussing, pausing to take occasional pulls from the bottle. Finally, Johnny came back outside clad in only his red long handles, boots, and hat. He had a green scarf knotted around his neck. He held the bottle in his right hand. He stomped down off the porch and into the yard.

Bear gave a caustic laugh. "Where in the hell you think you're goin'?"

"To find somebody who'll drink with me!" Johnny said without turning around or even glancing behind.

Bear laughed again. "Dressed like that?"

"Yep!"

"And you're walkin'?"

"How the hell else am I supposed to get where I'm

goin'?" He'd sold his horse three months ago for liquor money.

"It's two miles to town, you fool! You wouldn't make it even *without* a storm comin' on. Look up!"

Johnny glanced at the sky. Plum-colored clouds were rolling down from the high peaks to the west, their dark bellies pregnant with rain. "A little rain never hurt anyone!" Johnny said, stretching his stride.

"You cork-headed fool," Bear called behind him, the laughter gone from his voice now. "You'll drown when the arroyos flood!"

"Go to hell!"

"Have it your way, ya dunderheaded peckerwood!"

"Hah!" Johnny laughed. "Look who's talkin'!"

He strode into the woods, following the meandering horse trail in the direction of Hallelujah Junction. As he walked, he paused every now and then to take a pull from the bottle.

Wary of finishing the bottle before he got where he was going, he soon started counting his steps, making the rule that he could only take a small sip after every fifty steps. He knew himself well enough to know that if he didn't take this precaution, he'd have drunk all the whiskey before he'd gotten to town.

Somewhere between the town and the cabin, he'd half-consciously decided to share the Four Oaks with his only other friend in the world—Lenore Dupont. Johnny didn't know if she'd have him back in her crib, or even if it were possible for her to do so—she might be entertaining—but he didn't want to drink alone. Sometimes he did, but now he didn't. He wanted to share the splendid gift of the Four Oaks with someone else, and the only other person he was friendly with these days in Hallelujah Junction, or elsewhere, for that matter, was his good pal and sometimes lover, Lenore.

She might still be mad at him. He'd acted like a fool the last time they were together. He couldn't remember exactly what he'd said or done, but he knew himself well enough to know that it was likely something pretty stupid, and that Lenore hadn't deserved his ire. It had been the whiskey talking.

The whiskey did a lot of talking for him these days. Just one of the downsides to being drunk all the time. Not too high a price to pay, however, for the hazy bliss it otherwise made of his life, blotting out his memories as though they weren't really scuttling around, secret as church mice, inside his head.

Memories.

Damn—it was almost like he'd invited the mice to play in the daylight.

"No," he said aloud, walking unsteadily, following a bend in the trail, only vaguely aware of a cold mountain rain pelting him, of thunder crackling and wind blowing, lightning glinting in the thrashing boughs around him. "No . . . no . . . *no!*"

Each time he said "no," however, an image fired in his brain much the same way the lightning was forking and streaking across the sky around him.

The front door of his home in Carson City explodes inward, several armed men rush through it, one after another . . .

"No!"

Lisa screams and her blond hair flies as she swings

around from the dishes she's returning to their shelves in the kitchen . . .

"No!"

Johnny tosses away the newspaper he's been reading in his elkhorn rocker and reaches for the shotgun leaning against the wall behind him. Too late. Three men rush him, grab him, bull him back against the wall by the fireplace . . .

"No! No, dammit!"

"Daddy!" David screams. He's been lying on the floor in front of the fireplace, reading and penciling away on his schoolwork. As the boy leaps to his feet, a shotgun explodes, and Johnny watches in horror as his son is blown back onto the kitchen table, howling.

"Nooooo! Oh, God—noooooooooooo!"

Johnny doesn't feel the fists hammering his face, the boots being rammed into his belly and ribs and hips and legs. Instead, he's trying in vain to get to Lisa, who's being ravaged by four men on the kitchen floor. She screams as she's beaten, her clothes ripped off her body and tossed aside like newspapers being swept away in the wind . . .

"Lenore!" Johnny screamed, trying to drown out the screams of his wife and his boy in his head. *"Lenorrrr!"*

He fell to his knees outside the crude frame shanty. The screams in his head faded as he became aware of the world around him.

Sure enough, Lenore's shanty was only a few feet away. The rain rushed down on it, large drops pelting it at a wind-driven slant. Water streamed from its corrugated tin roof. Thunder exploded like vast boulders being hurled together by ancient gods. Lightning slashed down out of a sky the color of dirty wool.

The rain-sodden earth trembled beneath Johnny. He realized all at once that he was nearly entirely covered in mud. Somehow, he'd made it to Lenore's place from Bear's cabin. How much time had passed, he had no idea. He must have waded across several flooded arroyos. He was breathless, bleeding from several cuts and abrasions. Tears streamed down his cheeks to mix with the mud and the rain.

He looked at his right hand. He was still holding the bottle. Only, it was empty now save for a few inches of what appeared to be muddy water. He dropped it, looked up at the shanty.

"Lenore!" he bellowed, terrified that the awful sounds of that horrible night would return if he didn't see Lenore soon. If she didn't help him further drown the din of savage, bloody murder . . .

He doubted she could hear him above the hammering, high-country storm, however. He hoped to hell she wasn't entertaining. He needed to see her . . .

He heaved himself to his feet and went slopping through the muddy yard to the front door. He banged on the door.

"Lenore! It's Johnny!"

He banged again.

No response.

Finally, he opened the door. She hardly ever locked it, and it wasn't locked now.

"Lenore?" He could barely hear his voice beneath the drumming of the rain on the roof.

The room before him was dark. The pent-up air was fetid, sickly. Johnny couldn't see much of anything before him, but he sensed something was wrong.

Lightning flashed, for an instant lighting up the room and revealing what appeared to be a body on the floor by the bed.

"Lenore?" Johnny moved forward, tripping over scattered debris on the floor, most of which was clothing. He kicked a bottle, heard it rolling up against the wall to his right.

He called out to Lenore again and again, as he made his way to the bed. The only response was the storm—the thunder and lightning and the rain hammering the tin roof. He knelt beside her, the intermittent lightning flashes revealing her lying naked, limbs splayed.

"Lenore, honey—what's wrong?" Johnny said. "What happened, honey? You fall out of bed?" He shook her gently, trying to wake her. "Lenore? Honey? Lenore?"

She did not respond. Her flesh felt cold.

Fear gripped Johnny.

He rose, made his way to where a lantern sat on a dresser. Somehow, he managed to fumble a match out of a box, to lift the mantle, and light the wick, spreading a weak glow against the room's murky darkness. The wind through the door made the flame flicker wildly.

Tripping over more debris, including another bottle, Johnny returned to Lenore's side, dropping to both knees beside her. In the flickering light and shunting shadows, she stared up at him through glassy, unblinking eyes.

"Lenore?" Johnny placed his hands on her shoulders, gently shook her. Her head wobbled as though her neck were broken. "Lenore? Lenore, honey, wake up now, honey . . ." He could hear the desperation in his own voice. "Lenore? Lenore . . ."

He slid his arms beneath her, picked her up off the floor, and lay her on the bed. As he did, he knocked more bottles to the floor. There was another bottle on the bed along with the fetor of puke and urine.

Johnny continued to call out to her, to shake her more and more violently, terror making his voice quaver and causing tears to run down his cheeks.

He looked at the bottle that lay on his side to the right of her head with its tangle of greasy, matted hair wet with sweat, spilled whiskey, and vomit. He lifted the bottle and looked at the brown, unlabeled glass in the lamplight. He looked at the others on the bed and on the floor. He counted five.

Five empty bottles . . .

"Oh, Lenore," Johnny said through his tears, caressing her cold cheeks with his fingers, sobbing. "Why, Lenore? Why? Why'd you'd do it? Why'd you wanna leave your pal, Johnny?"

He lowered his head to her belly and lay bawling against her unmoving body, grief and rage and terror turning him into a quivering pile of boneless flesh there on the sour bed. After a time, it wasn't so much Lenore he was grieving for. It was himself. For the pathetic pageantry he'd made of his own life. With a third, disembodied eye, he caught a long, hard view of himself kneeling there in the dead doxy's foul crib, clad only in long handles that were glued to his body by rain and mud and liquor sweat and tears.

Finally, he lifted his head. He grabbed one of the bottles and threw it against the front wall, beside the open door through which the storm raged. The bottle shattered.

"No!" he bellowed into the wind. *"Nooo!"*

He rose heavily, his jaws set hard now. His face was a mask of defiance. He tripped back over to the door.

He slammed it and stood staring at it for a long time.

"*No!*" he cried. He pounded his fists against his temples. "No! No! No! No! *Enough!*"

He stepped back against the wall. He slid down the wall to his butt. He sat there on the floor against the wall, clutching himself, bracing himself for the approaching storm that he knew would make the one outside seem like a low-country sprinkle.

CHAPTER 11

Four days later, Bear Musgrave was sitting on his cabin's front stoop. He had a mug of coffee on the porch rail before him and Louie on his lap. He stopped stroking the cat as something came into view on the trail before him.

A man on foot was just then coming out of the forest and into the sun-splashed clearing.

Bear leaned forward, about to rise to retrieve his pistol from inside, but he stayed put as he squinted off along the trail. The man approaching the cabin was dressed in little more than long handles and boots. He wore no hat. He was tall and dark. His dark brown hair hung in tangles around his gaunt cheeks and hawk nose.

Bear leaned back in the chair as the man shambled up to the cabin.

"Well, well, well," Bear said. "Look what the cat dragged in. Only . . . not even Louie would drag you in. You look like you tussled with six bobcats in a locked stable."

Johnny stopped on the stoop's bottom step, grabbed an awning post for support, and canted his head, squinting, a wing of his dirty, badly mussed hair hanging over one eye. He didn't say anything.

"You lost weight," Bear told him.

"Have I?"

"I figured you for dead. I saddled up ole Bronco and went lookin' for you, after the storm, but found neither hide nor hair. Figured you got washed down one of the arroyos."

"Wished I had, more than a time or two."

"What's with you?" Bear studied him closely. Johnny looked old, pasty, filthy, and washed out, but his eyes were clear. At least, clearer than what had become normal over the past two years. He stood straighter than he normally did, as well. Come to think of it, when he'd been walking along the trail, he hadn't been stumbling over his boot toes. "I'll be hanged if you ain't sober. Just comin' off a drunk? I don't got no whiskey."

"I dried out."

"You *what?*"

"I come for the Twins."

"Nah." Bear looked at him askance. "I told you I'd hold the Twins for you—"

"Until I got sober again."

"Yeah, but—"

"Lenore's dead."

Bear didn't look surprised. He just looked at Johnny, pulling his mouth corners down and nodding slowly, grimly.

"I'm done, Bear. I dried out. I locked myself in Lenore's cabin. Damn near killed me. I went through it all. Snakes was crawlin' all over me, and there was a wild boar trying to chew its way out from inside me. I must've lost a couple gallons of raw whiskey sweat.

But when I woke up this mornin', I was alive. An' the snakes had cleared out, along with the spiders and the green-horned demons with their pitchforks."

Johnny held out his right hand. It quivered slightly. "I was steady enough to chisel her out a head-stone, Lenore." The work had helped distract him from his jangled nerves.

Bear fingered his long beard, pensive. "Is it gonna last?"

"It better."

"You wantin' the Twins—does that mean . . . ?"

"I'm accepting the lady's job."

"I'll be damned." Bear eyed him skeptically then set Louie on the floor and grudgingly heaved himself to his feet. He walked down off the porch steps and stood in front of Johnny, again eyeing him closely. "You're really done with the bottle?"

"I'm done, Bear."

"You sure?"

"I'm sure. I'm ready get back to work."

"If you go back to drinkin', and you shoot up the town with the Twins, I'm gonna . . ." He raised his clenched fist.

Johnny gave a wan smile. "I'd want you to."

"Come on, then."

Bear turned and walked around the cabin. Johnny followed him, drawing deep, even breaths. After four days of abstaining, and of gutting out the violent convulsions that had been his body's reaction to the sudden lack of the alcohol it had become so addicted to, the shakes still gripped him from time to time though not nearly as violently as they had even yesterday.

Johnny followed Bear out behind the woodshed flanking the cabin. There was a root cellar out here, Johnny saw for the first time, its doors cracked and rotting. Bear reached down and pulled up one of the doors by its steel ring.

"Help me here," he said through a grunt.

Johnny took the door and lay it back against the ground.

Bear stepped down into the cellar, which had been dug roughly six feet into the earth. The wooden steps creaked precariously under the big man's weight.

"I didn't know this was out here," Johnny said.

"No, I know you didn't." Bear smiled up at him, meaningfully. He'd hidden the Twins well, knowing how much damage Johnny could have done with them if he'd gotten his hands on them while drunk. It was just after Johnny had gone on his first bender in Hallelujah Junction that Johnny had turned the Twins over to Bear for safekeeping, knowing that under the influence of all the busthead he'd been drinking, he couldn't trust himself.

He and the Twins could lay waste to the whole town, maybe half of the county . . .

The air wafting up against Johnny from the cellar was rife with the smell of mold and rotten root vegetables. Bear crouched to scoop a burlap bundle off the cellar floor. He raised his arms, handing the bundle up through the door to Johnny, who knelt on one knee, accepting the package.

While Bear climbed up the creaking steps, huffing and puffing, Johnny laid the bundle out on the ground. He reached inside and pulled out one of the Twins, placing it on a bed of nearby ferns. When he'd removed the other Twin from the bag, he set it down beside the first one, and knelt there, admiring both Twins lying side by side.

The sawed-off, double-barreled shotguns, manufactured by the William Parkhurst Company in Belgium, were in the same fine condition Johnny had always kept them in. Their stocks still gleamed from the oil he'd rubbed into them religiously several times a week, and the wheat scrolling on the receivers set them apart from more common bird guns.

Johnny had won both pretty, savage poppers in a poker game in a Virginia City gambling den just before he'd been awarded a deputy U.S. marshal's commission six years ago, after he'd pulled stints as town marshal and deputy sheriff in towns and counties across Nevada. He'd always preferred a ten-gauge shotgun to a pistol. That might have been partly due to the fact that his foster father, Joe Greenway, had given him a pretty ten-gauge the same year Johnny had gone to live with the old rancher and his segundo, Old Marcel, at the Maggie Creek Ranch. Johnny had taken instantly to the big popper, and become proficient at bird hunting in the mountains with the large-bore scattergun, which he'd far preferred over a revolver. He'd used a rifle when he'd needed to, but his heart lay with the ten-gauge.

When he'd pinned a badge to his shirt, he'd preferred shotguns because they caused far more damage than even a Colt .45. What's more, most outlaws tended to respect the ten-gauges more than they did a handgun—with good cause. One round from a ten-gauge could blow a pumpkin-sized hole through a man. Of course, you had to get close to do so, but pistols were for close-up work, as well.

After his stint as a brash and decorated young cavalry lieutenant in the Plains Indian Wars, Johnny had come back to Nevada and worked as a lawman in some of the most remote and savage territory on the western frontier—namely, his home country of northern California and southwestern Nevada. (He'd been born into a family of Basque sheepherders, but when cattle ranchers had killed his parents and older brother when he was ten years old, he'd been adopted by one of the few sympathetic cattle ranchers, Joe Greenway, whose surname Johnny had taken.) Working alone as a lawman in such savage country, where outlaws outnumbered lawmen one hundred to one, a man of the law came to value a weapon that caused even the most cutthroat of curly wolves to squirt down their legs.

Such weapons were the Twins.

"Thanks for holding 'em for me, Bear," Johnny said as he reached inside the bag once more.

This time he withdrew the shell belt and two holsters he'd had custom-made in Elko for the pretty poppers. The black leather holsters were modified Colt .45 scabbards, only much wider and a few inches longer, with thinner, more pliable leather, and with open toes. Keeper thongs over the hammers secured both shotguns in place, and when the thongs were released, the top of the holster opened wide to assure a smooth, nearly effortless draw.

Johnny strapped the belt around his waist and slid each of the Twins into its corresponding holster. He tied each leg thong, securing the holsters to his thighs. He drew both guns, and with a single movement of his thumbs, clicked all four rabbit ear hammers back at once.

"Looks like you still got it," Bear said. "I reckon you'll find out for sure if you haul that bullion for the purty princess from the bank. That bullion gets hit as much as it don't. I don't know how she stays in business."

Johnny holstered the weapons then drew them again. He winced and shook his head. "I'm rusty. I'll practice along the trail."

Bear crouched to scoop the bag off the ground. He tossed it at Johnny, who caught it against his chest. "You forgot somethin'."

"Huh?"

"Look inside."

Johnny frowned.

"Look inside," Bear repeated.

Johnny gave him a mock suspicious look. "You didn't put a baby rattler in there, did ya?"

"Will ya look *inside*?"

"All right, all right."

Johnny poked his right hand into the bag. He frowned at Bear as he pulled out a small roll of silver certificates held together with a rubber band. "What's this?"

"Remember that stake you won off that gambler from Reno several months back?"

"You mean that half-breed who was drunker than I was?"

"Yeah, that's the one."

"What about him?"

"That's part of your winnings."

Still, Johnny frowned at the burly man.

Bear continued with, "That night after you come back with your pockets filled, greenbacks stickin' out of every one and even your boots and out from under your hat, I knew your newfound wealth wouldn't last long. So while you slept, I scavenged fifty dollars off your snorin' carcass an' tucked it into the sack. Figured that if you came out of your, uh . . . uh . . . period of *stompin' with your tail up*, let's call it . . . you'd need a stake to get you back on your feet. I figured if I didn't grab some money out of the poke, you'd just spend it on cheap whores and more busthead. I knew you wouldn't even realize it was gone."

"I'll be damned." Johnny smiled as he brushed his fingers over the roll. "There's fifty dollars here?"

Bear chuckled.

"I'll be damned." Tears glazed Johnny's eyes. "I . . . I don't know what to say. I need to get my horse back, if ole Nordekker hasn't already sold him, that is."

"Ah, hell, Riley Nordekker don't have your hoss!"

Johnny's incredulity grew. "Huh?"

"You sold ole Ghost for twenty-five dollars. Or tried to. That horse is worth eight times that much! I ran ole Riley down and paid him the thirty-five dollars out of my own poke. He had no use for that wild-assed hayburner of yours, an' he knew it. Why, Ghost would've killed him! Hell, Ghost's been out in the corral ever since that night. The Johnson kid comes by every now and then to ride the green out of him. You'd know that if—well, you know good an' well why you don't know that."

Johnny stared down at the roll of certificates in his hand. "Because I been three sheets to the wind."

"There you have it." Bear smiled. "But you're sober now, and that's the main thing."

Johnny looked at his old friend in shock and exasperation, lower jaw hanging. "You mean Ghost is in the corral yonder?" The corral was set off to the west of the cabin, flanking it, out of sight from the front. Johnny hadn't been back there since he'd started "stomping with his tail up," as Bear had so discreetly called it.

"He's been back there keepin' Bronco company."

Johnny shook his head as he continued staring at his old friend in astonishment. "Why, Bear?"

"Why what?"

"Why've you been so good to this no-good son of Satan?"

"Ah, hell," Bear said, chuckling. "I knew you'd come around eventual-like. You just got a big dose of wild-assed Basque in ya, that's all. Your pa did, too. Ole Joseba an' me did some stompin' when you were still knee-high to a porcupine. I knew other Basques just like your pa when I was still trappin' in the mountains, and those folks would start their Christmas celebration the day after the Fourth of July. Hah! But that wild in you was tamed down a little by ole Joe Greenway. Hell, in one month, Joe'd have a wild savage fresh out of the wilderness readin' that fella, what's his name . . . ?"

"Shakespeare," Johnny said, grinning, remembering his now-deceased foster father's love for reading Shakespeare plays and sonnets while sipping picon punch during long, cold winters on the ranch, in front of a popping fire in his massive fieldstone hearth. The punch was Old Joe's favorite busthead—a drink developed by immigrant Basque sheepherders from a bitter orange liqueur and brandy. Legend had it the drink helped keep the old shepherds warm on winter nights crouched around their dried sheep-dip fires.

"Shakespeare—that's the fella!" Bear said. He chuckled some more then looked Johnny up and down, his broad face suddenly acquiring a dubious expression. "You know—the Twins would look a whole lot better if they were strapped over somethin' a little nattier'n them long handles."

Johnny looked down at himself. He chuckled. He was still wearing his long handles, one knee poking through. His muddy socks showed between the soles and uppers of his muddy boots. "I reckon I better not waltz into the Bank & Trust dressed like this. I got me a feelin' Princess Bonner might reconsider the job offer."

"Yeah, I got that same feelin'."

Johnny looked at the roll of bills in his hand, and grinned. "I think it's time for a new wardrobe."

"I'd allow it's time for a new wardrobe. Perhaps a bath first?"

"Well, I just had several the other night . . . in three or four arroyos between here and Hallelujah Junction. But I reckon one more proper one, with clean water, couldn't hurt."

Bear laughed. "It wouldn't kill ya, anyways."

"Come on," Johnny said. "Let's saddle our hayburners and head to town. I'm so hungry my belly's thinkin' my throat's been cut. Then—baths and shaves all around! Johnny's flush, an' he's buyin'!"

"Shaves?" Following Johnny in the direction of the corral, Bear tugged on his beard, glowering. "Let's not get carried away, now, Shotgun Johnny!"

CHAPTER 12

Two hours later, as they stepped out of Lo Pan's Café on the corner of Paiute and Third Street, beside Madame Coignard's brothel, which was quiet at this hour in the midafternoon, Bear turned to Johnny and said, "How you feelin'?"

The burly man stuffed his old blue knit cap onto his nearly bald head. He rolled a sharpened matchstick around between his well-furred lips as he scrutinized the taller, hawk-beaked, younger man.

"A little shaky, but I'll get my pluck back soon."

"You should've eaten more."

Johnny had managed to get down only half his steak, one strip of bacon, and a couple bites of beans and potatoes. He'd enjoyed two cups of coffee with cream, however. "Quit wet-nursin' me. I got down as much as I could."

"At least you look better." Bear stepped back and looked Johnny up and down several times, whistling his approval. "I'll be hanged if you didn't clean up right well—yessir! You almost look like a proper gentleman."

After a long soak in one of the Swedish bathman's

copper tubs, and a shave and a haircut, Johnny and
Bear—who'd taken a bath but had taken only a trim
on his beard and what little of his hair remained—
had gone over to a male clothier's shop owned by a
taciturn German. Johnny had outfitted himself in
the same sort of attire he'd been accustomed to
when he'd ridden for the law.

He'd picked out a plain white cotton shirt, a black
leather vest, a black frock coat, and black whipcord
trousers. He'd also pulled on a pair of brown leather
Texas-style riding boots and a crisp, black felt
slouch hat to replace the one he'd lost on one of his
drunken debauches. He wore the new duds, which,
while not fancy, were the proper yet comfortable
attire of a respectable workingman, over a fresh new
pair of cream cotton long handles and white wool
socks.

He trimmed the outfit with a bit of color in the
form of a red silk neckerchief drooping like a mare's
tail down his chest. His Basque people had always
favored brightly colored cottons and wools to add
some color to an otherwise drab and grueling exis-
tence, so Johnny supposed the neckerchief was a
semiconscious nod to his lineage.

His people were hard workers, and Johnny hoped
he'd be working again soon. He'd know in a few
minutes.

"Yessir, I bet most of Hallelujah Junction ain't
gonna recognize you," Bear said, giving Johnny another slow, admiring up and down. "They might
even mistake you for a proper gentleman, in fact.
Wouldn't that be a joke?"

"Yeah, well, the joke would be on them," Johnny
said, lifting his hat to run a hand through his freshly

shorn hair. He'd instructed the barber, a Mexican named Rodriguez, to crop it short but to leave an inch or so of his sideburns. Lisa had always said he looked good with the sideburns, so he'd worn them until, of course, in his prolonged state of near-constant inebriation, they'd grown into his untrimmed beard.

Lisa . . .

No, he thought. *Don't think about her now. You'll only return to the bottle if you do that, and you'll continue to befoul her memory with your drunkenness. Both hers and David's. Now it's time for you to get your life back, to be the man they'd be proud of again.*

He found himself staring toward the bank two blocks along the sun-washed street on his right.

"Well, what you waitin' for?" Bear said. "Go on over there, get down on your knees, and beg the princess to give you that job."

Johnny started walking along the boardwalk in the direction of the bank. "Come on."

"I'll wait over at—"

"Come on."

"What?" Bear said, scowling at him. "You need me to hold your hand?"

Johnny snorted as he glanced over his shoulder at the older man. "You do, an' you'll get a black eye for your effort. Make that two." He beckoned. "Come on. You're comin' with me, you old scoundrel."

"Aw, fer Pete's sakes!" Bear groused. Cursing and grunting, he walked along beside Johnny.

A few minutes later, Johnny drew a deep, calming breath and pushed through the bank's front door.

"I'll wait out here," Bear said behind him.

"Get your ass in here," Johnny said, and stepped

into the Bank & Trust's cool, quiet shadows, the air smelling of crisp currency and varnished wood.

There were only two customers—two middle-aged ladies in simple housedresses, likely miners' wives—standing at one of the two teller's cages, to Johnny's left. As Johnny's eyes adjusted to the bank's dim interior, he saw Miss Bonner crouched over a desk about ten feet away from him, beyond a low wooden railing separating the bank's lobby from its office area, most of which appeared open.

A man sat at the desk over which Miss Bonner crouched. That was the vice-president, Johnny believed. He didn't know the man's name, though apparently the man was well aware of him, for he'd called him by name the other night—as far as Johnny could remember through the alcohol haze hanging over him like a dirty cloud. The man was older, gray, and with the pale, soft flesh of an indoor man.

He and Miss Bonner were conversing in low tones as they both studied a large, open book on the desk before them. Hearing Johnny and Bear enter the bank, Miss Bonner glanced toward them, glanced away, then returned her eyes to Johnny. She looked him over subtly, then, apparently approving of what she saw, she smiled and nodded, a faint flush rising into her perfectly curved cheeks.

She returned her attention to the book on the desk and resumed her quiet conversation with the elderly vice-president.

Johnny frowned. Had she dismissed him? Maybe she'd already hired a bullion guard.

Bear elbowed him, jerked his chin toward the woman.

Johnny winced, reluctant.

Bear leaned his head toward Johnny's shoulder and said under his breath, "You fought red-skinned savages for three years durin' the Injun Wars an' took down some of the nastiest cutthroats in the West. You're afraid of a purty *skirt*?"

Bear's bearded mouth twitched an ironic grin. He jerked his chin toward Miss Bonner again, cajolingly.

"All right."

Johnny removed his hat and strode forward. He pushed through the door in the wooden rail and stepped up to the desk. As he did, his long shadow passed over the desk, and both Miss Bonner and the vice-president looked up at him.

Straightening, Miss Bonner smiled pleasantly up at him. "Hello."

"H-Hello."

"Is there something either Mister Poindexter or I can help you with?"

Again, Johnny hesitated. "I, uh . . . I'm—"

"Oh, my goodness!" the young woman said suddenly, her face turning ashen as she stared up at Johnny in shock. She sagged back against the desk. "It's . . . it's . . . it's you. Mister Greenway!"

"Yeah," Johnny said slowly, his heart lightening a bit when he realized that she hadn't dismissed him earlier. She merely hadn't recognized him, being freshly shaved and wearing a new suit of clothes and all . . .

"*Who?*" asked the man she'd called Poindexter, scowling curiously up at Johnny. Then the realization must have come to him, too—all at once. He fairly leaped up from his chair to stare bewilderedly at the tall, dark man standing on the other side of the desk from him. "Oh, dear! I didn't . . . I didn't . . ."

"I didn't recognize him, either." Sheila looked Johnny up and down, and a flush drove the pale from her cheeks. "I must say, Mister Greenway, you clean up well." She gave an embarrassed chuckle.

Bear snorted back where he stood against the front wall, holding his knit cap in his hands. When Johnny glanced at him, he looked away and whistled raspily, with feigned casualness.

"How tall are you?" Sheila asked, frowning up at Johnny.

"Around six-four, ma'am."

"Funny," she said. "You seemed shorter. Much shorter . . . before . . ."

"I felt shorter before, ma'am." Johnny cleared his throat. "I'm here to tell you I've changed my mind about the bullion job. Guarding it, I mean. I'd like to accept your generous offer. If it's still on the table, I mean."

Sheila shared a glance with Poindexter then turned back to Johnny. "It is."

"Now, Sheila," Poindexter said. "I told you I have a man in mind for the job. Besides, I don't think you want to rush into any agreement with this man, regarding the bullion. I mean, he's . . . he's—"

"Are you sober, Mister Greenway?" Sheila asked.

"Forevermore," Johnny said, slowly turning his hat in his hands, nervously kneading the brim edge with his fingers.

"Hmm."

"Like I said, Sheila," Poindexter said, chuckling edgily and regarding Johnny dubiously from behind his round, steel-framed spectacles, "I think Mister Greenway has showed you his true colors. He may be sober now, but I don't . . . I don't think you can take a chance on his *staying* sober."

"She can, Mister Poindexter," Johnny told him assuredly. Turning back to Sheila, he said, "You have my word I will not take another drink. Not ever. I'm done with the busthead. I want my old life back. I can't go back to lawdogging, but I can guard your gold. I'll get it down here from the mine. I give you my word on that, Miss Bonner."

Sheila studied him through narrowed eyes, turning her head slightly to one side. Absently, she fingered the lace edge of her bodice, her chest rising and falling heavily. Slowly, she nodded.

"Sheila, please," Poindexter said, softly but with no little amount of urging. "I think we should think about this. You know I have a line on a very capable man who—"

"I have thought about it, Mister Poindexter," Sheila said, keeping her gaze on the tall, falcon-faced, darkly handsome man standing before her with two sawed-off shotguns strapped to his lean hips. "My California detective, otherwise engaged at the moment, can't arrive here until the end of the summer. I can't wait that long. I have to get the next load of bullion down from the mine and off to the U.S. Mint in San Francisco as soon as possible.

"The job is yours, Mister Greenway. I take it my original offer is still agreeable to you? One hundred dollars. Half up front, the other half after you've safely delivered the gold. You supply your own horse, of course. I'll supply the two packhorses you'll need for hauling the bullion."

"I'd like to amend the agreement to include my partner, Bear Musgrave."

"What?" both Sheila and Bear said at the same time.

Johnny said, "Bear knows the northern Sierras better than almost anyone alive today. He hunted and trapped in those peaks for thirty years. I'll need to be nimble as I start down from the Reverend's Temptation. That means I'll likely need to take alternate routes to keep the curly wolves off my trail or at the very least guessing about which trail I've taken."

"Hold on, hold on," Bear said, walking slowly forward. "I didn't agree to no guidin' job."

"Hold your tongue, old man. You need a job, and I need a guide."

"I still got me a stake from that nugget I found on—"

"Hush!" Johnny knew the stake from Bear's last gold digging was running low. He'd seen how the man scrimped when it came to cooking. Bear hardly ever went out anymore, because he didn't have the money. Besides, Johnny knew that Bear's true home was up amongst those lofty, fir-clad crags and sparkling cold mountain lakes. The old mountain man didn't fit here in town. He was too stove up for hunting or trapping, but he could still ride a horse, and that's all he would need to do as Johnny's guide.

"This is absolutely preposterous," Poindexter laughed in exasperation. "Why, these two are nothing but—"

"My guard and his guide," Sheila said. To Bear, she said, "I can offer you seventy-five dollars for the run, Mister Musgrave. Half up front. You both must provide for your own provisions." She paused then studied each man briefly in turn. "Agreed?"

Johnny arched a brow at Bear, who now stood to his left.

Bear tapped his fingers on the soiled cap in his hands. A flush rose in his cheeks at the prospect of riding back up into his beloved mountains again, of sleeping out under the stars, the wolves and coyotes howling him to sleep beside a crackling pine fire. He almost smiled but stopped himself in time.

Instead, he pulled his mouth corners down and turned to Sheila with a fateful sigh. "I reckon I'd better do it. The kid would just get lost up there on his own."

Johnny turned to Sheila and extended his hand. She nodded and shook his hand before shaking Bear's hand, too.

"Is tomorrow morning too early to start for the mine?" she asked.

"Tomorrow morning is just fine, Miss Bonner," Johnny said, glancing at Bear, who shrugged.

"All right, then. Meet me here at seven. I will have your pay and my two packhorses waiting in front of the bank."

"You got it," Johnny said.

He glanced at Poindexter, who stood scowling at him and Bear but was no longer voicing his objections. Vaguely, Johnny wondered why the man had his shorts in such a twist. Had Johnny done something to offend the man when he'd been drunk?

Yeah, that was probably it. Oh, well. After the two years he'd run off his leash, burning bridges, most folks in Hallelujah Junction would be slow to bank their trust in Johnny Greenway again. He was just glad Sheila Bonner wasn't one of them.

"Good day, then, Miss Bonner," Johnny said with a cordial dip of his chin.

Again, a lovely flush rose in the woman's cheeks. She entwined her hands as she smiled then shyly lowered her gaze to the desk. "Good day, gentlemen."

Johnny and Bear pushed back through the gate in the low fence and tramped across the bank to the door. Once outside, Bear chuckled.

"What is it?" Johnny asked.

"She don't like it one bit," Bear said, stuffing his blue wool cap onto his nearly bald head, "but the purty li'l princess has taken a mighty keen shine to you, you handsome devil."

"What?" Johnny was incredulous. "You're addle-pated, old man. Women of her station don't mix with men of mine, an' you know it."

Chuckling and shaking his head, he stepped off the boardwalk and headed for the livery barn.

Hurrying to keep up, Bear said, "Yeah—that's what's got her bloomers in such a knot!"

CHAPTER 13

"Come on, horse—step it up there, step it up there!" George Poindexter urged the gelding in the traces of his covered, two-seater buggy. He cracked the whip over the Morgan's back, and the horse lunged forward against its harness.

The horse shook its head. It was dark out here this evening, and the horse knew better than its driver the perils of a two-track mountain trail under cover of darkness. Only a sliver of moon rose over the steep southeastern ridge, making the shadows even darker in contrast to the sparse wash of pearl light barely penetrating the forest.

Poindexter's practical sense of caution was compromised by his fear of being out in these mountains at night. He wanted to do what he'd come out here to do—which could only be done at night, so no one saw him—and get back to town as soon as possible.

Desperate men haunted these trails, men who'd spent everything they'd had to come out from the East and Midwest to plunder the gold and silver gulches of the Sierra Nevadas. All too many found that their dreams of easy wealth had been just that—

dreams. A goodly number of these desperate men took to the trails to rob other men of their own hard-earned currency, to kill them so there would be no witness to their crimes, and leave them dead and bloody beside the trail.

The notion made Poindexter shudder inside his heavy coat, but he had too little imagination, not to mention self-awareness, to reflect on the irony of his own situation.

Not only did the fear of being robbed and murdered weigh heavy on the banker's shoulders, but the cabins that slid up along the trail from time to time, just as several were doing now as he dipped into yet another gold gulch, repelled him with their squalor. From one such cabin passing on his right came the tooth-gnashing din of an off-key fiddle and the laughter of drunken men and no-doubt-fallen women. Poindexter could smell the reek of home-brewed forty-rod as well as cheap tobacco and man sweat issuing from the cabin's propped-open front door.

Beyond the door he saw several men and gaudily dressed women dancing way too close together. At least one man was groping one of the women, who wasn't protesting. Several more men were huddled on the cabin's front stoop, silhouetted against the lamplit doorway. They were smoking and passing a jug and speaking boisterously and laughing, no doubt at bawdy jokes.

"Hey, look," said one of the men, raising his voice above the din, "someone's comin'."

Poindexter saw several heads turn toward him. He raised the collar of his black fustian and hunched low, hoping no one recognized him. He doubted they would. One good thing about so dark a night was that he'd pass along the trail just as he intended, in anonymity.

No one must know that he was out there. That would only draw dearly unwanted suspicion.

He whipped the reins over the Morgan's back and passed on down the trail.

He climbed yet another hill and then pulled off the trail's right side, onto a secondary trail. A minute later, the pale lights of windows shone in the darkness. A minute after that, Poindexter pulled the Morgan up to a hitchrack fronting yet another one of these small, seedy little mining shacks. From a small lean-to stable and corral to the left of the shack, a horse whinnied sharply.

The Morgan lifted its head and returned the greeting.

A man stepped quickly out of the cabin's door. He disappeared just as quickly to the left of the door, the darkness concealing him. His presence was made known, however, by the sharp, decisive rasp of a rifle being cocked.

In Spanish-accented English and with no little tone of menace, a voice said, "Who goes there?"

Poindexter set the wagon's brake. "It's Poindexter, Zambada. Point your rifle in another direction, please."

For a long moment, silence. Then the Mexican, Sevando Zambada, depressed his rifle's hammer with an audible click.

The short, stout, mustached man stepped languidly back into the light issuing out through the two front windows and through the long rectangle of the partly open door. "Welcome, señor," he said, grinning, holding his rifle low in his right hand. In his left hand, a brown-paper cigarette smoldered. "You've come slumming again, I see. Tell me—what brings you here to commune with we unwashed dogs of the countryside?"

"I'm coming in," the banker said with a grunt as he stepped heavily down from the buggy.

"Mi casa, tu casa."

Poindexter ran a hand along the Morgan's left wither. "Stay now, horse."

Still puffing from his climb down from the buggy, the banker stepped up onto the small, low stoop fronting the cabin and to the left side of which stood the stocky Mexican. Servando Zambada was staring off into the night, his muddy black eyes flicking this way and that with caution.

"What is it?" the banker asked.

"Are you sure you weren't followed, señor?"

"No one sees me leaving town. I make sure of that."

"How sure are you?"

Poindexter drew a deep, exasperated breath. "I am not a fool, Zambada. I know the price to be paid for mucking up!"

Zambada returned his liquid dark gaze to the older man. "Not a fool, huh? Oh, that's right. You're a banker." A mocking grin pulled at his mouth mantled by a thick, dark-brown mustache.

Poindexter gave another maddened sigh and stepped into the cabin, doffing his hat out of habit, though surely such formalities were not recognized here. "Where is Butler?"

"He retired early this evening," Zambada said, coming in behind the banker and setting his rifle on the cluttered table to the right of the door. "The boredom of this place . . . all the waiting around . . . is affecting his mind, I think. Makes him tired."

"Makes him drunk is more like it," Poindexter said, setting his hat on the table and pulling out a chair. He glanced around at the squalor and, repressing a wince, said, "You wouldn't happen to have a shot of something decent, would you? Preferably from a labeled bottle?"

"We are fresh out of French brandy, señor. My apologies. However . . ." Zambada was looking around at the cluttered shelves flanking the table and a stove in which a fire burned quietly, warding off the mountain chill. He whistled as he perused the mess of empty bottles, airtight tins, dirty plates, and food scraps, then said, "Uh-hah!" He pulled a bottle off a low shelf and held it up. "Look—it even has a label, señor!"

The label was badly faded, even partly torn away. Poindexter had no doubt that whatever the murky substance was that resided behind it had been put there after the bottle's original contents, corresponding to the label, had long since been guzzled. Still, his nerves were shot, and it was a chilly night.

"It'll do."

Chuckling, Zambada plucked a dirty glass off a shelf, blew dust out of it, popped the cork from the bottle, and poured the no-doubt foul and toxic substance into the glass. He looked at the banker. "I am very sorry for your loss, señor. I heard about your wife."

Poindexter's cheeks warmed. He frowned. "You . . . heard . . . ?"

Zambada nodded as though with concern. "Sí, sí. A fall down the stairs, was it not? In your casa?"

"How did you hear about that way out here?"

"News travels fast. All news. Even way out here. Especially news involving such an important man as yourself, Señor Poindexter." Zambada set the glass down before the banker, who'd slacked into a chair facing where the Mexican had obviously been sitting to face the front windows. Apparently, he'd been sharpening four knives of various styles with a whetstone and drinking from his own glass and bottle. The knives were laid out in a neat line on the table, according to size, near the glass and the bottle. "I hope she went quickly . . . did not suffer terribly."

Poindexter's cheeks grew warmer as he stared down at his drink. "No, no. She didn't suffer."

"She had not been well, I hear?"

"No, she hadn't been well." Poindexter glanced up at the Mexican grinning down at him. "Thank you so much for your concern, Servando. It warms my heart—surely it does."

"Having been relieved of such a weight around your neck probably warms your banker's heart, too, eh? One of the few things that can accomplish that difficult task, no doubt." The Mexican chuckled through his discolored teeth.

Poindexter glared up at the man, hardening his jaws. Who did this bean-eater think he was?

"Now, then," Zambada said, lifting a foot onto his

chair, resting his arm on his knee, and taking a drag off his cigarette. "To what do we owe the pleasure?"

Poindexter held up a finger clad in a thin, black leather glove. He threw back half of the whiskey—or whatever in hell it was—then set the glass back down on the table. He swallowed the substance quickly, not wanting it to linger too long on his tongue.

He arched a brow as he regarded the glass with unexpected appreciation. "Hmm." Not half bad. Of course, it wouldn't be anything he'd order if he were in anything but a pinch, but it didn't burn a hole through his insides, anyway, or cause him to go blind. So far . . .

He opened his mouth to speak but closed it when a man stepped through a curtained doorway flanking Zambada. It was the Mexican's partner, Walt Butler. Butler was a tall, dull-eyed American with dark blond hair and an untrimmed mustache and goatee. He wore only a pair of denim trousers and a long-handle top. He was barefoot. He had a horn-gripped, long-barreled pistol poked down behind the waistband of his pants.

He brushed a thick wing of his hair back off his forehead as he stepped into the cabin's main room, looking bleary-eyed, smacking his lips. He squinted sleepily at the banker, hacked phlegm onto the floor, then slid his gaze to the Mexican and said, "What's goin' on?"

"We are entertaining," said Zambada in his not-so-vaguely mocking tone, smirking, keeping his muddy eyes on Poindexter. "I was just telling the banker that if we'd known he was coming, we would have cleaned up the place and broken out the good china."

Ignoring Zambada's mockery, Poindexter shifted

his gaze from Butler to the Mexican, saying, "She's sending a man up for the gold tomorrow morning. Two men, in fact."

"About time," Butler said, standing near a corner of the table, off the banker's right elbow. "I'm so tired of waiting around here in this cabin, surrounded by these mining squareheads, I've been about to go screaming off over the next ridge."

Poindexter scowled up at the tall man. "You're being paid very well. Seville and Raised-By-Wolves worked out a plum deal for all of you."

"And you, too—eh, old man?" said Butler.

"Well, I am the one who arranged this whole venture, am I not? Yes, I think twenty percent for me is the very least I am due. I would have thought half, but . . ."

"But you're not doing any of the blood work, are you?"

These two vermin were really getting under Poindexter's collar. "Well, if I could do that, I wouldn't need you . . . you . . ."

"Careful, señor," cautioned Zambada. "You are a man far from your element out here. I would think you would want to be on your best behavior."

He glanced down at the razor-edged knives laid out neatly before him, forming a slight arc near his shot glass and bottle. He drew on his cigarette then, blowing the smoke out through his mouth and nostrils, said, "If you offend me, you might just return to Hallelujah Junction with only one ear. The other ear might be nailed to the wall there, as a totem, if you will, to politeness and civility."

He grinned again through his teeth.

Butler chuckled. "All right, you said your piece,

Poindexter. We'll ride up and pass the word to Seville and that rock-worshipper, Raised-By-Wolves, at first light."

"Hold on, hold on," Poindexter said, feeling both ears burn at the Mexican's threat. "There's more you should know. She hired two men again."

"So?" Butler said. "It don't matter how many she hires. She'd have to have a whole army to make the dozen of us break a sweat!"

"Be that as it may, I think you should know that she's hired Shotgun Johnny this time. Johnny Greenway, formerly Juan Beristain. And his old mountain man friend, Bear Musgrave. Now, I know Musgrave will be no challenge, but—"

"Who is Shotgun Johnny?" Zambada asked.

"The town drunk!" laughed Butler. "Basque stock. What'd she go and make a fool move like that one for?"

"She thinks he deserves a second chance," Poindexter said. "After all, he did save her life last week, when a gang of unfortunates decided to make a try for the bank. Johnny came out of his stupor long enough to intervene. He left eight men dead on Paiute Street."

"One man stood alone against eight?" asked the Mexican. "And killed them *all*?"

"Luck," Butler said. "That's all it was. I heard about that, too. So he took down eight raggedy-heeled former rock breakers." He shrugged.

"No, they weren't prospectors. It was a gang led by Max Langdon."

"I heard Max was gettin' up there in years," Butler said.

"I just thought you should know." Poindexter threw back the rest of his whiskey. "Shotgun Johnny was a formidable lawman in his time. And to me it looks like he might be back on his feet and with at least some of his former pluck."

Zambada looked at Butler, eyebrows raised in wary speculation.

"He's one man," Butler said, waving a hand dismissively. "We won't have no problem."

"All right, all right." The banker held up his hands in supplication. "I just wanted you to have all the information at your disposal." He slid his chair back and rose with a grunt, glancing edgily down at the sharp knives laid out in an arc on the other side of the table. "I will take my leave."

Again, the curtain over the rear doorway was thrust aside. This time, a girl stepped through it. She was clad in only a sheet that didn't cover even half of her. She frowned at Poindexter and said, "Hey, you work at the bank. What're you . . ." She glanced at the other two men curiously. "What's he doing out here?"

Rage burned like a blue fire through Poindexter. He glanced between the American and the Mexican, hardening his jaw and raging, "You fools! You know the rules—no girls!" He pressed the heels of his hands to his temples. "Oh, you bloody fools!"

"Take it easy, señor," said Zambada, holding up a placating hand. "You are going to make yourself sick."

"What's he doing here?" the girl asked again from the doorway, frowning curiously at the three men gathered around the table.

"I am already sick!" Poindexter told Zambada. He

thrust his arm out, gesturing at the girl. "This makes me very sick indeed! This . . . *she* . . . could ruin everything!"

Butler sighed and looked over his shoulder at the girl. "Honey, now, didn't I tell you to stay in the bedroom?"

"I'm hungry," the girl whined, shifting the sheet around on her pale, willowy body. "I thought you might have somethin' to eat out here, Walt."

Still glaring from Zambada to Butler and back again, Poindexter said, "You knew the rules. I made them very clear. No one else was to visit this cabin. Just the two of you. No one else could see me out here!" He thrust his enraged finger at the girl. "She knows who I am, and she'll blab it all over town!"

"Hey, what's your problem, mister?" the girl said, indignant.

"How was we supposed to know you'd be coming out here tonight?" said Butler. "Hell, it's been so damn long since our last job, we was beginning the think you forgot about us. A fella gets lonely, Poindexter!"

The banker only glared at him and then at Zambada.

The Mexican laughed. "Not to worry, señor. Not to worry. It was a minor mistake. It could happen to any red-blooded man, no?" He picked up one of the knives from the table. "You go now. Relax. Have a drink in town. Rest assured the problem has already been solved."

"What's going on?" the girl said, taking a tentative step farther into the room, canting her head as though to see what the Mexican was holding. Her pale, doll-like face had acquired a worried look.

"Go back to bed, honey," Butler said, keeping his

eyes on Poindexter. "Just go back to bed. I'll be right there. I'll explain everything."

"Wait," the girl said. "I want to know—"

"Go back to bed!" all three men shouted at her in unison.

She gave a frightened cry then wheeled and pushed back through the curtained doorway.

The Mexican smiled again at the banker. "You worry too much, señor." He held up the obsidian-handled stiletto. He turned it gently, letting the lamplight glint off the freshly sharpened blade. "The problem will be very easily solved." He jerked his chin at the door. "Go, now. Go back to town. Have a drink. The problem will have been solved even before you reach the main trail. Tomorrow, mi amigo and I will ride up and inform Seville of the new job."

"Oh, and, uh . . . sorry about your wife," Butler added with a taunting grin. "A tumble down the stairs? Tsk, tsk. That's rough!"

Zambada snickered through his teeth.

Poindexter drew a deep, calming breath. "This job will be the last," he said. "I can't take any more of this, and neither can she—for two totally separate reasons. When this one's complete, have Seville and the Indian meet me at the mine, and we'll split up the gold."

He donned his hat, left the cabin, and climbed into the buggy. He was halfway back to the main trail when he heard a muffled scream. He flinched.

Then he gave a slow sigh of relief. "Utter fools."

CHAPTER 14

Johnny and Bear approached the Hallelujah Junction Bank & Trust one minute before seven o'clock the next morning.

The sun was just then sliding the top of its lemon head into the V-notch between two rugged southeastern ridges. A couple of shopkeepers were out either cleaning their front windows or sweeping off the stoops fronting their stores, but most of the town was still quiet. Breakfast fires sent billowy smoke webs spiced with the savory aromas of bacon, ham, and fried potatoes into the still-cool morning air over Paiute Street.

Two mules and a sorrel filly were tied to one of the two hitchracks abutting the boardwalk running along the front of the Bank & Trust. The mules were solid, medium-sized beasts with short, strong legs—ideal for mountain packing. The horse was a fine filly with a blond mane and tail. The filly glanced behind her with a playful sparkle in her eyes when Johnny and Bear approached on their own mounts—a smoky cream gelding with a flaxen mane and tail and a beefy claybank, respectively.

The mules were outfitted with diamond-hitched pack frames to which empty canvas panniers were strapped. The horse had a bedroll and saddlebags strapped behind its saddle, and two canvas supply sacks hanging down over its withers, connected by a rope looped once around the horn.

Johnny and Bear glanced at each other curiously.

"Who do you suppose belongs to the filly?" the former mountain man asked.

"That's my horse." Sheila Bonner just then stepped out of the bank's front door. She glanced at Johnny and Bear sitting their horses beside the mules and the filly, and said matter-of-factly, "I've decided to ride with you."

She turned to lock the door behind her.

Again, Johnny and Bear shared a dubious glance.

"What do you mean?" Johnny asked her.

Sheila tried the door, making sure it was secure— the bank wouldn't open for another hour or so—then removed the key from the lock. "I mean I've decided to ride up to the mine with you. This is a very important run, under the circumstances, and I want to make sure it goes off without a hitch. I've left a note for Mister Poindexter, who . . . curiously . . . wasn't home last night when I called on him . . ." She added the last half of the sentence as though to herself.

She stepped into the street and dropped the bank key into one of the saddlebag pouches draped over the filly's back. "Besides, I need to speak to the mine superintendent up there. I was going to send a letter along with you fellows, but I've decided to discuss the matter in person. It involves a delay in his men being paid, what with me being as cash-strapped as I am due to all of the holdups. I have to ask Mister

Nolan to encourage his men to stay on despite the delay. I do, however, intend to compensate them for their wait."

Miss Bonner turned to face her gold guards, widening her brown eyes expectantly. She wore a dark brown wool-lined coat, fawn riding slacks, the cuffs tucked into the tops of her high brown riding boots. She wore black gloves on her delicate, fine-fingered hands. On her head was a brown felt hat with a braided rawhide band. Beneath the hat, she wore a red knit scarf angled down over her ears and tied in back. Her thick, lustrous chestnut hair hung forward over her left breast, gathered in a tail secured with a shiny silver clip.

"Are you men ready? I think I have everything I'll need for the journey." She glanced at her own saddle-bags, bedroll, and burlap pouches, and thoughtfully chewed her full bottom lip, considering her supplies.

Bear rubbed his chin and leaned forward against his saddle horn, chuckling. "Now, now—here, now, li'l miss . . . I don't think you understand . . ."

Rummaging around in one of her canvas bags, Sheila turned to look at him over her shoulder, both brows raised. "Understand what, Mister Musgrave?"

The former mountain man glanced at Johnny, who gave a wry chuff, and Johnny said, "You're a . . . a . . . well, you're a *proper lady*. And them mountains, see"—he gestured toward the rugged, dark peaks to the west as though to make sure she fully understood what peaks he was talking about—"ain't exactly a place for a lady. Not a proper one, anyways. No, ma'am." He extended his right hand and offered a gently tolerant smile. "You just hand over the letter, and I'll be more than happy to make sure Mister Nolan . . ."

"Oh, I see. So this is how it's going to be, eh?" Sheila had turned full around to face Johnny and Bear. A rosy flush had risen in her high-tapering, perfectly sculpted cheeks.

The men shared another dubiously conferring look.

"Uh . . . how what's gonna be?" Bear asked her, rubbing a gloved hand nervously on his trouser leg.

"Your attitudes toward me. They're going to be the typical oafish condescension and boorish super-ciliousness typical of all males everywhere when confronted by a *proper lady* having the gall to step beyond what they consider her seemly bounds."

Johnny and Bear shared another, extended look of silent consultation.

Johnny turned his gaze back to the young woman regarding them with wide, contemptuous eyes and said haltingly, "Ma'am, I'll be hanged if either of us could make out what you just said."

Sheila's eyes sparked, and she flared a nostril as she stomped one booted foot in the dirt and said, "It means I'm riding with you whether you like it or not, you cretins! Now . . ."

She turned and began to toe a stirrup but stopped when laughter rose from a corner of the bank, and a man said slowly and with no little tone of mockery, "Now, what in the hell do we have here?"

Johnny looked ahead to see Jonah Flagg standing on the boardwalk fronting the bank, off the bank's right-front corner. Flagg—wearing a denim jacket and his usual brown hat, his badge pinned to the jacket—laughed again and clapped his hands, then gestured to indicate Johnny and Bear sitting their mounts behind Sheila's filly. "These your two new bullion guards, Missy Sheila?"

Sheila had also turned to face the town marshal of Hallelujah Junction. Her voice still brittle with the anger she'd directed at Johnny and Bear, she said, "It's *Miss* Bonner to you, *Marshal* Flagg." She'd emphasized the "marshal" to highlight her disdain for the job the man was doing.

Flagg caught the rebuff right away. His smile became a glare as he said, "What's that supposed to mean—*Marshal* Flagg . . . ?"

"You know what it means." Sheila paused, glaring at the lawman. "Why haven't you ridden up into the mountains to look for Marshal Wallace? No one's heard from him or the posse he took with him since he left nearly a month ago."

"Wallace ain't my jurisdiction, an' you know it. My jurisdiction stops where the town stops. You just got your bloomers in a twist on account of how I wasn't there to bust up the little bank robbery. Like I done told you an' everyone else, I was out lookin' for the kids who stole Mrs. O'Brien's sows!"

Bear threw his head back and cast a wheezing laugh at the morning sky.

Flagg pointed at him, enraged, as he stepped down off the boardwalk and came around the two pack mules. "Shut up, you mouthy tub o' lard!"

"That's Dutch, Jonah! That's just Dutch!" To Johnny, Bear said, "He's still stickin' to his story that he was off chasin' Mrs. O'Brien's sows!"

"It's true, dammit! It's true, I tell you!"

"I heard it was true, Flagg," Bear said, still laughing despite the marshal's finger commanding him to stop. "But if I was you, I woulda lied and said I was holed up with a coupla doxies like you usually are. The sow story just made you an even a bigger laughin'stock than you already was!"

Bear slapped his thigh and roared again, pulling the edge of his blue wool cap down over his eyes as he howled.

Flagg cursed sharply and closed his hands over the walnut grips of his .45. "You shut up, you fat blustering old mossyhorn, or I'll blow you right out of your—"

"Take your hand off the gun, Flagg," Johnny told the lawman with menacing mildness. He stared down at the man, his eyes as threatening as his voice, though he kept his hands away from the two sawed-off ten-gauges holstered on his thighs. "I won't tell you again."

Flagg looked at him. He dipped his chin and narrowed his eyes in silent fury. He looked at the shotguns, then returned his gaze to Johnny's eyes beneath the brim of the new bullion guard's crisp black slouch hat.

Flagg pulled his hand away from his gun handles, reddening.

"Speakin' of pigs," he said, sneering, "you can paint a pig purty as you please. You can dress it all up in a brand-new outfit and strap shotguns around its waist, and put it on a fine cream hoss." He shook his head slowly, sneeringly. "But it's still a pig."

He turned to Sheila Bonner, who stood beside her filly, regarding the lawman with cold disdain. "He's gonna let you down, Missy Sheila. He mighta made a good showing last week, but it ain't had time to sink in yet. Bein' sober, I mean."

"Be quiet, Flagg," Sheila said.

"He's a drunk, ya see," Flagg said, keeping his taunting eyes on Johnny. "Deep down to his core. Yessir, when the chips are down . . . I mean way, way down, an' times is desperate . . . he'll go back to his own whore of choice—forty-rod."

"Shut up, Flagg!" Sheila yelled, balling her fists at her sides.

"You see," Flagg continued, staring at Johnny, "he's got him a big, deep pool of guilt inside him . . . on account of how he let what happened to his family that night because he had a few drinks in him . . ."

"Flagg!" Sheila shouted.

"Sure, sure," Flagg said, smiling now at Johnny and continuing slowly. "You see, rumor has it Shotgun Johnny was steppin' out on his wife . . . the lovely Lisa . . . an' he had a few drinks out with this other gal before he come home and—*ach! Christ!*"

Flagg had bolted backward and tripped over his left spur rowel. He dropped to a knee and held both his hands up, palms out, as though to shield himself from the imminent blast of the ten-gauge Shotgun Johnny had drawn quicker than greased lightning, cocked, and aimed at a slant down toward where Flagg now knelt in the street.

"Stop!" Flagg said, not as loudly as before, glancing up tentatively at the twin bores bearing down on him. He looked away and said again, "Stop! Stop it, now! Don't, dammit!"

"Johnny!"

Johnny heard his friend's voice as though from far away, as though from the far end of a long tunnel.

Johnny continued to stare down the double barrels of the ten-gauge at the cowering lawman's head. Johnny's left hand was shaking, making the shotgun flutter like a leaf in a chill breeze.

His finger was drawn taut against the ten-gauge's left trigger.

"Johnny!" Bear shouted. "Stand down!"

Johnny kept his finger taut against the trigger, felt it slowly coming back, applying more and more pressure. In a second, it would turn Flagg's head to pulp.

"Johnny." Sheila came up beside him, gazing up at him, her eyes wide now, fearful. She stopped just off his left knee and reached up to place a gloved hand against the shotgun's double bores. "Please," she said with quiet gentleness, keeping her eyes on his. "He's not worth it." She shoved the cannon down and to one side.

Yielding to her, Johnny eased the tension in his trigger finger.

He lowered the weapon and cut his gaze to Flagg still down on one knee, cowering like a dog caught stealing chickens. "See how fast you can make yourself scarce, Flagg, or I'm gonna blow your legs out from under you."

"Christ!" Flagg lowered his hands and rose unsteadily, still looking at the shotgun that Johnny held at half-mast.

Sheila turned to the town marshal. "You heard him, Jonah."

Backing away, his face flushed with anger and humiliation, Flagg glared at her. "You're as crazy as he is!"

He turned, slipped on some fresh horse fritters, regained his balance with a curse, then hurried away, glancing cautiously back over his shoulder. He turned down a side street, cast one more stricken look behind him, then disappeared around the far side of a harness shop.

Sheila looked up at Johnny, scrutinizing him all over again.

His cheeks warmed. What kind of man did she see before her now?

"Well," he said after a while, "I reckon if we're goin' . . ."

"Yes," Sheila said, nodding slowly. "I guess we'd better get going."

She turned away, mounted her filly, swung the horse into the street, glanced at him once more, then booted the filly west.

Johnny rode up past the pack mules and untied their reins from the hitchrack. He swung his cream around and tossed Bear the mules' lead lines.

"Here you go," he said. "You might as well start earning your pay."

"Thanks," Bear growled.

"Don't mention it."

CHAPTER 15

Johnny felt as though Flagg had tied his gut in a tight knot.

Guilt racked him anew. It hung heavy on his shoulders.

Now began the test, he thought, as he and Bear and Miss Bonner left Hallelujah Junction behind and below them as they started the long, three-day trek high into the mountains. Now he was on his own. He had no whiskey with which to help fight back the fork-tailed, green-toothed demons of his memories.

It was just him and them. They were bigger and better-armed, and he stood naked against them.

At first, as usual, he wanted to flee. His first impulse was to turn around and gallop back to town and dash into the first saloon he saw, buy a bottle, and grab the first girl who entered his field of vision . . .

Those first few miles into the mountains were long and hard. All of his muscles and sinews were drawn as taut as freshly stretched Glidden wire. The wails and screams and the blasts of the shotgun that had obliterated his son echoed loudly inside his skull.

But as he put more and more distance behind him, as his three-person party led by Bear and the packhorses, with Sheila riding second, and Johnny bringing up the rear, rose higher into the pines and spruces, where the air was winey with the smell of the mountains, the harsh colors of his memories softened. The screams and the shotgun blasts drifted farther and farther away, tempered by the piping of mountain birds and the ratcheting cries of hunting hawks and eagles, the sonorous soughing of the wind in the high branches.

The horses' hooves thudded softly. The saddles squawked. Occasionally, one of the mounts clipped a rock, sent it thudding off the trail.

Still, out of nowhere, Flagg's voice returned again to speak in Johnny's ear: "You see, rumor has it Shotgun Johnny was steppin' out on his wife . . . the lovely Lisa . . . an' he had a few drinks out with this other gal before he come home . . ."

After two hours on the trail and already deep into the mountains, they stopped for water at Rushing Creek. They watered the horses and the pack mules first then staked them out to graze in the shade of the tall pines and spruces.

Johnny filled his canteen then lay belly down against the grassy ground and hung his head out over the creek. He removed his hat and dunked his head in a cool, dark back eddy of the creek tumbling down its steep, shelving, rocky bed shaded by the forest pressing in close on both banks.

The water was refreshing, bracing. Johnny lifted his head then cupped water to his lips, drinking lavishly of the tooth-splinteringly cold, wet snowmelt that tumbled down from high glaciers feeding

Rainbow Lake before overflowing into several creeks of which Rushing was one.

When he had finished drinking, he turned to see Bear kneeling beside him, screwing the cap onto one of his two canteens. The older man regarded Johnny with concern.

"You all right?" he asked above the creek's soft roar.

Johnny nodded, swept his cropped wet hair back, and ran his fingers through it.

"You shoulda shot him, maybe," Bear said. "For lyin' like that . . ."

Johnny gave a mirthless chuckle. "Who said he was lyin'?"

Bear studied him skeptically. Johnny turned to see Sheila kneeling on the other side of him but farther away. She was regarding Johnny with much the same expression as Bear. When their eyes met, she turned her head slowly away then reached into the creek to cup the refreshing water to her face.

Ten minutes later, they were back on the trail, making their way gradually higher, riding up and over passes and following sloping canyons fed by creeks to yet another pass then down, down into the next watershed fragrant with the pine forest hovering close about them. Several times they passed small clusters of prospectors' cabins, the prospectors themselves toiling along creeks with picks and shovels and standing out in the sliding brown water, swirling gravel in pans and watching for gold dust glinting in the sunlight with the promise of wealth or, at the very least, enough grub and supplies to last them another week.

The men, most of whom were likely single and lonely, swiveled their heads to follow the three passing riders, their eyes instantly pinning on the young brunette riding between the burly lead rider trailing the packhorses and the tall, dark, younger man with the shotguns sheathed on his thighs and straddling the handsome cream. A couple of the toiling prospectors elbowed each other or jerked their chins to indicate the girl, and grinned and moved their lips with bawdy comments.

Johnny couldn't hear the comments from this distance, but he knew what they were saying.

Once while garnering such unwanted attention, Sheila glanced over her shoulder at Johnny and curled her upper lip in disdain. "Men."

"Yep," Johnny said. "They sure are."

She was holding up well otherwise, though. He couldn't help noticing that she sat the sorrel filly with aplomb—straight-backed and loose-hipped, swaying along with the animal, at ease with its movements. She knew how to command the mount, going easy on the spurs and reins, sometimes using only her knees to relay commands. The main trick about riding was knowing when to command and when to surrender. She was at least as well-trained as the horse obviously was, which meant this was neither one's first ride.

"Where'd you learn how to fork leather, Miss Bonner?" Johnny asked later that afternoon as they rode along the bank of another narrow gurgling creek, heading gradually up yet another valley between high, forested ridges.

"I was a member of a horse club back east," she said. She leaned forward to pat the filly's right wither. "Ezzy here was a birthday gift from my father, just before he came west. I had her shipped out here not long after I arrived in Hallelujah Junction . . . when it became apparent I was destined to stay here and try to make a go of the Bank & Trust."

"You've been riding her, I take it."

"Short rides, mostly. On Sunday afternoons." Sheila looked again at Johnny over her right shoulder and crooked a wry smile. "Nothing as long as this one, and certain parts of me are reminding me of that. Not to worry, though, Mister Greenway. This nipped an' tucked young lady will not slow you down in the least."

"So far, so good," he said. "But, then, we've just started."

"Like I said, not to worry, Mister Greenway."

"You might as well call me Johnny," he said. "Since we're sharin' the trail an' all."

Again, she looked back at him. This time her eyes were cast with a schoolmarm's chiding. "Now, Mister Greenway—I am your employer. You are my employee. And this is no Sunday ride but a business trip. I am Miss Bonner to you and you are Mister Greenway to me. Now and forevermore."

"All right," Johnny said with a wry chuckle. "Have it your way, Miss Bonner."

"Yes, I like the sound of that," she said, turning her head back forward.

Johnny smiled at the young woman with admiration. Nipped and tucked, she might be. But she had pluck, too. She wasn't afraid to let a man know how she stood.

"Looks like a good place to camp over yonder," Johnny said an hour later, when the sun had fallen behind the mountains and cool, purple shade was stealing out from the valley's western wall. Already, a chill grew.

Bear drew rein, stopping the two pack mules. Sheila checked the filly down behind him.

"Where?" Bear asked.

Johnny pointed toward a relatively level area in the trees off the trail's left side, opposite the creek but close enough to it for a handy water source.

Bear scrutinized the area then turned to Johnny. "Might be too good. Comprende?" He glanced at Sheila.

"Right," Johnny said.

"Come on," Bear said, booting his clay forward. "I know a place."

Sheila turned to Johnny, frowning. "What's wrong with that place?"

"Nothing. That's what's wrong with it."

"Please speak plainly, Mister Greenway," she said with a tolerant pitch to her voice, canting her head to one side.

"We'd likely be expected to camp there," Johnny told her. "Best to find a place a little less good, and not as close to the trail."

Sheila shook her head. "I don't understand. We don't have the gold yet."

"No," Johnny said. "But we have you."

Scowl lines knifed across her forehead, beneath the brim of her broad-brimmed hat. "I don't under . . ." Then she caught on. "You mean, you think . . ." She cast her gaze along their back trail. Turning back to him, she said, "Some of those men . . ."

"Might be lonely enough to have dangerous notions," Johnny said. "Especially after they saw such a beautiful woman passing along the trail."

She drew an angry breath and scowled at him, shaking her head with acrimony. "Men."

Johnny jerked his chin up the trail. "After you, Miss Bonner."

"Ma'am, you like rabbit?" Bear said later, after they'd pitched camp for the night.

The former mountain man held up the two big jacks he'd shot earlier that day with his old Spencer repeater, when they'd stopped to water their horses again and he'd stolen out away from Johnny and Sheila. He grinned, broadening his bearded mess of an aged, haggard, sun-seasoned, wind-burned face partly concealed by his thick, tangled beard.

He held the rabbits high, testaments to his hunting prowess and wilderness kills.

"I do like rabbit," Miss Bonner said. "But even if I didn't, after that ride I'm so hungry I'd eat them, anyway. Are you sure two is enough?"

"They're pretty big," Bear said. "I figured we'd make a stew. I got a couple taters in my grubsack."

"So do I," Sheila said, grabbing the rabbits out of the old man's hand. "And I will do the honors."

Bear frowned down at her. "You're gonna cook?"

"Indeed. We each have a job. Yours is guiding, Mister Greenway's is guarding the gold, and mine shall be cooking. Leave all of the cooking to me, gentlemen. You're in very good hands, if I may say so myself!"

Jacks in hand, she flounced off to where Johnny had piled wood he'd scavenged from the surrounding woods. Bear glanced at the younger man, who was down on his knees, coaxing a fire to life. They shared a shrug.

The horses and mules were tied to a picket line. They'd all been rubbed down carefully and watered. They now had feed sacks draped over their snouts, and were munching away contentedly on parched corn and oats. Sheila had tended her own filly, though Johnny had offered to perform the task for her since it had been a long day for her. She'd insisted that she needed no help and fully intended to carry her own weight, which, apparently, also meant she'd do all the cooking, as well.

Johnny had admired how she'd cared for her horse, rubbing it down with burlap and tending its hooves and frogs, removing trail debris, and brushing the burs out of its mane and tail. She accomplished the task like someone going down a checklist, not like someone who did it all the time or who'd taken to it naturally, but he couldn't fault her for that. She worked in a bank, after all. She wasn't a trail wolf like he and Bear.

He also wouldn't fault her for taking on the cooking chores. At least, he didn't fault her until she'd dished up plates of the steaming stew and passed one each, with a cup of black coffee, to Johnny and Bear, who were now lounging around the fire where they'd piled their tack.

"Ah, thank you, ma'am, thank you, ma'am," Bear sang, grinning down at the plate as he took it in his big, thick hands. "Mmmm. Sure smells good!"

"Sure does," Johnny agreed. But when he'd stuck the first forkful into his mouth and began chewing, he stopped chewing, and glanced at Bear. The big man glanced over at him. He'd also stopped chewing.

"Well, how is it?" Miss Bonner asked as she spooned some onto her own plate, glancing at each man with wide-eyed expectation.

Johnny chewed slowly, doing his best to manufacture a delighted expression. It wasn't easy.

She'd overcooked the rabbit and undercooked the potatoes, carrots, and the wild onions Johnny had found when he'd been out gathering more firewood and had passed along to her for the stewpot. The gravy—if you could call it gravy, for it was nearly as thin as soup—tasted scorched but otherwise relatively flavorless despite all the pepper she'd obviously added. In fact, the pepper was about the only thing he could taste, so that the broth tasted like a weak soup into which someone had spilled pepper.

Bear said, "Uhhh . . ."

"Hmmm," Johnny said. He picked up the baking-powder biscuit she'd set on his plate, hoping to find some measure of satisfaction in the roll. He dug his fingers into it. Or tried to, rather. It was about as yielding as a rock. Johnny dunked the biscuit into the so-called gravy—soaked it good, in fact—but it was still like taking a bite out of a ball of nearly set plaster of Paris.

"Well?" the young woman said, chewing her own food and raising her eyebrows speculatively. "Not bad, eh?" She swallowed then forked another bite into her mouth. "Yes, I think the rabbit tastes pretty good." She glanced at the men again. "Don't you, gentlemen?"

"That's what I was just gonna say," Johnny said quickly after swallowing a mouthful of the putrid stuff and trying desperately to hold off a laugh despite glimpsing in the periphery of his vision Bear eyeing him closely with a big, ironic grin on his own bearded mug. "The rabbit is . . . well . . . the rabbit's just plumb . . ."

"Tasty as hell," Bear finished for him, swabbing his biscuit in the gravy several times, trying to work some pliancy into the overcooked dough. "And the vegetables . . . well . . ."

He glanced over at Johnny, who took a deep ragged breath to stifle a laugh.

"Yeah, them vegetables," Johnny said. "I don't know what you did to them . . ."

Bear snorted then quickly shoved another forkful of the food into his mouth and turned away as he chewed, though Johnny could see the big man's shoulders jerking as he tried desperately to contain himself.

"Really?" Sheila asked hopefully, eyes as wide as those of a hopeful bride. "You do like it?"

"I don't know what you did to the vegetables," Johnny repeated, trying to impale another charred chunk of the meat out of the watery broth, "but they sure . . . they sure do add a fine flavor . . . wouldn't you say, old pard?"

Bear chewed the biscuit he'd just dipped in the gravy again, as though he were chewing the leather of an ancient boot, and sighed to cover yet another laugh. He swallowed the large lump like a snake devouring a gopher, then brushed his fist across his nose and cleared his throat. "Took the words right out of my mouth," Bear said. "They add a fine flavor, I tell you. Fine, indeed. Mighty fine!"

"You're not just saying that?" Sheila asked as she dipped her biscuit into her own gravy. "I mean, I really want you to be honest. Father always loved my cooking, though he insisted I stay out of the kitchen and let the housekeepers prepare and serve the meals."

"He did, did he?" Johnny asked, choking back a guffaw.

"Nah!" Bear said with feigned astonishment. "Your pa hardly ever let you in the kitchen, despite his lovin' your cookin' so much?" He glanced quickly at Johnny, who stared straight down at his plate, desperately trying to maintain his composure. "Well, I reckon he just knew you were cut out for better, more important things."

"I guess so," Sheila said with a shrug as she continued to eat. "Too bad, though. I've always enjoyed the kitchen and the satisfaction of throwing together a hearty meal, but Father just wouldn't hear of it!"

Both Johnny and Bear almost strangled on their food, suppressing and covering their laughter by eating as quickly as possible and trying not to look at each other. If they'd so much as glanced at each other at this point, they'd have broken down in wild laughter and likely gotten the rest of the stew tipped over their heads for their indiscretion.

CHAPTER 16

The next day around noon, Johnny, Bear, and their chief cook and bottle washer, Sheila Bonner, rode out of the timber at the bottom of a ridge and down into a narrow valley bisected down its middle by a slender stream.

A wooden bridge spanned the stream. On the other side of the stream, a long log cabin sat, smoke unfurling from its broad brick chimney to send a blue haze out over the stream and the jade beaver meadow enshrouding it. A broad wooden sign stretched across the cabin's second story, just up from the roof over its front porch.

The words RILEY DUKE'S SALOON had been hand-painted in bold red lettering across the sign, which was a good six feet high and twenty feet long. A dozen saddled horses were tied to the two hitch-racks fronting the place. All of the horses had rifles snugged down in saddle scabbards. At least that many men lounged around on the saloon's roofed porch in chairs, stools, or on the floor, some sitting with hips hiked on the rail.

They held bottles or stone mugs in their hands.

Several were smoking pipes or cigars. Tobacco smoke billowed out from beneath the porch roof.

As Johnny, Bear, Sheila, and the pack mules followed the trail on down the slope then clomped across the wooden bridge, over the stream of clear brown water sliding over its sandy bed between banks tufted with wolf willows and mountain sage, all heads on the porch turned toward them. Eyes smoldered in shaded faces, slowly blinking, as Riley Duke's clientele regarded the three riders.

"Well, this ain't good," Bear said in a high, thin voice, glancing over his shoulder at Johnny riding behind Sheila.

Sheila frowned at him. "What's wrong?"

When Bear didn't reply, Sheila turned to look at Johnny over her right shoulder. "What's wrong, Mister Greenway?"

"Just keep riding, ma'am."

Bear glanced over his shoulder at her. "This is a nasty ole place, and it just happens to be jam-full today. Just keep ridin', Miss Bonner. Keep your eyes straight ahead."

They followed the trail up the slope toward the roadhouse and then followed it as it swung left, skirting the edge of the saloon's hard-packed yard and continued toward the forested ridge rising in the northwest.

"Hello!" rose a man's voice from the roadhouse porch. "Hello, hello, hello, my good lady!" Johnny looked over to see a man sitting with one hip on the porch rail raising his bowler hat high above his bearded head. "Why don't you bid adieu to those raggedy-heels in your company, and join us fine gentlemen of culture and high breeding over here at

Mister Duke's stylish establishment, where you'll find not only fine spirits but learned conversation and rarefied male charm!"

A fusillade of raucous whoops and howls rose from the men around the first speaker, who'd spoken in a heavy British accent. Several men clapped and stomped their boots on the porch's wooden floor.

"Oh, boy," Bear said, as they rode on past the roadhouse, heading toward a ridge rising in the northwest.

Sheila glanced over her shoulder at Johnny and gave a reproving curl to her upper lip.

"I know," Johnny said with a sigh. "Men."

"Indeed." She blinked slowly then turned her head forward.

They and Bear followed the trail up to the crest of the next ridge, which was barren of trees and covered in only short, lime-green grass and a few widely scattered, mossy rocks.

"Let's hold up here," Johnny said, stopping Ghost and stepping down from the saddle.

"What are you going to do, Mister Greenway?" Sheila asked.

He dipped a hand into a saddlebag pouch and withdrew his field glasses. "Gonna have a look behind us."

Johnny dropped his reins and, hanging the binoculars, cased in red baize-lined leather, around his neck by their leather strap, he stepped off the trail and climbed a low hill. He stood atop the hill, which was the highest point on this high ridge, and looked out over several lower, pine-covered ridges to the southwest.

With his naked eye, Riley Duke's Saloon was about the size of his thumbnail from this distance.

When he raised the spyglass and adjusted the focus, the saloon grew larger and more detailed. He could make out enough details to see that the dozen or so horses that had been tied to the hitchracks earlier were no longer there.

"We got trouble?" Bear called from where he sat his claybank's saddle.

Johnny swept the country around the saloon with the glasses. He saw no sign of the horses.

"Could be," he told Bear.

"Ah, hell."

"Yeah." Johnny lowered the glasses and made his way back down the hill.

Sitting her dun filly, Sheila frowned curiously at each man in turn. "I don't . . . understand."

Johnny dropped his glasses into his saddlebags and turned to Bear. "Why don't you and Miss Bonner mosey on down the trail? I'll wait here and, if we're being shadowed, I'll show our shadowers the error of their ways."

"You sure?" Bear said.

Johnny nodded. "Be careful. They might have split up, hoping to work their way around us."

"All right." Bear glanced at Miss Bonner. "Come on, ma'am."

"Are you serious?" Sheila asked Johnny, her voice pitched with incredulity. "Do you really think those men at that saloon are after us? After *me*?" She opened her arms and gloved hands as though to display herself.

Johnny looked at her—about as pretty a woman as he'd ever seen, her chestnut hair, gathered into a mare's tail, snaking forward over her right shoulder. She was even prettier now than before, for the sun had lent an earthy tone to her formerly pale cheeks. Her white, sweat-damp blouse drew taut against her bosom as she breathed, revealing more than she intended it to.

Johnny glanced at Bear then returned his gaze to Miss Bonner. "Yep," he said with a fateful sigh and a wry pitch to his voice. "Yeah, I do."

"Come on, ma'am," Bear repeated.

When they were gone, Johnny led Ghost well off the trail and tied the horse to a pine branch. He slid his Winchester from his saddle boot, racked a round into the action, then depressed the hammer. He walked back down the trail and pulled up to within thirty feet of where the trace, curving up the ridge through widely scattered pines, opened out into the clearing capping the ridge.

A boulder roughly the size of a stagecoach stood along the trail's right side. Johnny stepped up behind the boulder, on the trail side, and dropped to a knee.

He waited, pricking his ears, listening.

Nothing but birds piping in the brush and the low, raspy whistle of the breeze.

Hoof thuds came to his ears softly at first. They quickly grew in volume. They were coming from the forest on the side of the mountain. The riders were galloping toward him. Impossible to tell how many for sure. The vigor with which the horses were galloping up the incline told Johnny that the riders weren't merely heading back to their mines or homestead claims.

They had more nefarious intentions in mind.

Johnny looked out from behind the boulder,

staring at where the trail curved up out of the pines. Sunlight bathed the pale, powdery trail. The dark-green forest appeared black in contrast to it.

The thudding grew louder, louder, as did the jangling of trace chains and the clanking of iron bits against teeth.

He saw several hatted heads bobbing just above the line of the slope as the first riders galloped into sight.

Johnny leaned his rifle against the boulder then stepped out onto the trail. He unsnapped the keeper thongs from over the Twins' hammers.

The first two riders, riding side by side, saw him and hauled sharply back on their running mounts' reins.

"Whoahhh!" one of them cried.

Two of the four flanking the first two riders ran their own mounts up into the rumps of the first two. The men cursed. There was a skittering, dusty bottleneck for several seconds, the horses whickering and whinnying and churning the dust with their chopping hooves as the riders got them under control while casting wary gazes toward the tall, dark-haired man standing on the trail before them, a red silk neckerchief drooping down his chest and two double-bore shotguns holstered on his thighs.

"For *chrissakes!*" bellowed one of the six men in the back. His own mount, a strawberry roan, had dropped to a knee and was now righting itself with an indignant whinny.

Finally, when they'd all gotten their horses settled, the riders stared at Johnny through the billowing dust.

The near rider on the right smiled beneath his dusty brown bowler hat. He was a tall, thin man with yellow hair, a spade beard and trailing mustache, and a long, tan duster. "Shotgun Johnny!" he yelled as though in unabashed delight at seeing an old friend he hadn't seen in years. His blue eyes twinkled.

He was the British gent who'd called from the saloon.

"Hi, Jim," Johnny said with an affable smile.

The man's name was Bryce Jimson, "Jim" for short. Jim was a notorious, small-time stage robber who wasn't above robbing prospectors and miners of their pokes. He'd been stalking the mountain trails from Colorado to California for years, plundering the defenseless. Johnny had arrested him one time for murder, but the case had died in court due to a lack of witnesses, and Jim had flounced free to continue his depredations, which included rape of female stage passengers.

"Long time no see, my good friend!" Jim said. He leaned forward against his saddle horn and shaped an expression of mock concern. "I heard you'd fallen on hard times, Johnny . . ."

"Shut up," Johnny said.

Jim frowned as though deeply offended. "Why, John . . . that's no way to talk to an old friend. Why, you and I traveled many miles together. Of course, I was cuffed an' shackled—now, wasn't I?"

He grinned over his shoulder at the other five men in his pack. "Judge Freeman freed me. Very aptly named, Judge Freeman—wouldn't you say, Johnny?"

"You're after the woman," Johnny said blandly.

"What?" Jim said, glancing at the others as though wondering if they understood what this madman was talking about.

"Turn your limey ass around, Jim," Johnny said. "Ride back to Riley Duke's Saloon and have another of Riley's dark ales. Good stuff. I remember it well. It's a helluva lot better than snuggling with the diamondbacks, which is what's gonna happen if you or your dull-witted friends here take one more step forward."

"You can't tell us what to do!" shouted the man sitting his horse directly behind Jim, leaning out from his saddle to see around the Brit. "It's a free country, an' you don't own the trail!"

"Besides," added one of the others, "you ain't a lawman no more. Last I heard, you was nothin' but—"

"I'm not gonna tell you again," Johnny said with quiet menace. He tucked his coat flaps back behind the Twins.

"You can't pull them cannons quicker'n we can pull our pistols, Mister," said a paunchy gent on a nervous sorrel. He wore a low-crowned black hat. A dark-gray mustache hung down over both sides of his mouth. He eyed the Twins and slowly slid his gloved right hand toward the grips of an ivory-gripped Bisley holstered on his right hip.

Jimson held up a placating hand, scowling down at Johnny. "Easy, fellas. Easy, now. He can pull them Twins of his, as he calls them, faster than any of us can pull our hoglegs." He grinned coldly. "I found that out the hard way."

"And damn near got a big, round tunnel bored through your brisket," Johnny pointed out.

"We'd best mosey," Jim told the others.

They all glared at the man with the shotguns, reluctant to yield the trail.

"Do as he says," Johnny said. "He's a wise man, Jim is. Might not look like it, but . . ." He gave a mocking half-smile.

Jim returned the smile and tapped two fingers to the narrow brim of his bowler. "Till we meet again, Shotgun Johnny."

"It's your funeral."

Jim began to rein his steeldust gelding around. The others followed suit, keeping their hard gazes on Johnny, who continued smiling up at them in mockery. Jim had just taken his eyes off of Johnny when he whipped his head back toward him, his right hand moving in a blur toward the Colt holstered on his right thigh.

Johnny knew Jim well enough to know that the move had been forthcoming.

He was ready for it. In fact, he was eager to scour the West of the low-down, scurvy, woman-savaging dog of Bryce Jimson. He whipped up the Twins as fast and as pretty as you please, leveled the right one on Jim, and tripped the left trigger. Jim had seen his mistake at the last quarter-second. He widened his eyes and mouth in terror and screamed, *"No!"*

Too late.

The word hadn't cleared his lips before the cannon thundered and the fist-sized bunch of double-ought buck plowed through his breastbone, shredding his heart and throwing him back off his horse and into the man directly behind him. The second man screamed, as he, too, was thrown off his horse to bludgeon the blood-splattered trail.

The others had had the same notion as Jim. All four reached for their own sidearms, cursing through gritted teeth, eyes round with fury.

Their eyes grew even wider when they saw the Twins slide toward them.

Johnny tripped the right-hand popper's right trigger at the same time that he tripped the same trigger on his left-hand ten-gauge. The men were so tightly grouped on the trail before Johnny that the twin blasts blew three of the trail wolves off their horses, howling.

Johnny took the third man with the left popper's second barrel just as the man's own Remington cleared leather. The man dropped the gun as he rolled ass over teakettle straight off the rump of his prancing buckskin to hit the trail with a thud and a hard grunt.

Johnny stepped off the trail as two horses thundered toward him, whinnying shrilly and buck-kicking, horrified by the ten-gauges' ear-numbing thunder. As the other horses ran back in the direction from which they'd come, Johnny holstered the Twins and picked up his Winchester. He turned back to the trail.

All six men were down. Three were dead. Two were dying. The fourth, the man who'd merely been thrown from his horse by Jim, just then sat up and, glaring through the horses' wafting dust at Johnny, raised the Colt in his right hand.

Johnny raised the rifle and thumbed the hammer back.

The man dropped the pistol and screamed, "I give up!"

"You're a bad dog." Johnny lined up the beads on the man's forehead over which his mussed, sweaty hair hung. Johnny tripped the Winchester's trigger, punching a quarter-sized hole through the middle of the man's forehead, just above the bridge of his nose. "Bad dogs die."

Then he ceased the howling of the other two, looked over his work with satisfaction, reloaded the Twins, and retrieved his horse. He held up his right hand. It shook only slightly.

Not bad, he thought. *Not bad at all.*

He galloped on up the trail toward Bear and Miss Bonner.

CHAPTER 17

Bear might have been old, but his hearing was still raptor-sharp. So were his eyes. It was other, unmentionable parts of his body that didn't work so well anymore. Thank God those didn't come into play here!

"Listen," he said, holding up his hand and checking down his beefy clay and the pack mules just off the clay's right hip.

Behind him, Miss Bonner stopped her dun. "What is it?"

"You don't hear it?"

"I don't . . ." She let her voice trail off when her own ears must have picked up the thuds of approaching riders. "Yes . . ." Her voice was thin with fear.

Bear threw out his arm and poked his gloved right finger toward the timber off the trail's right side. "That way! They came up through Coffin Gap to cut us off!"

"Oh, dear." The woman was behind him. "What're we going to do, Mister Musgrave?" She glanced behind. A few minutes ago, they'd heard the roars of Johnny's Twins with a punctuating belch from his

Winchester. At least, Bear thought it had been
Johnny's rifle. He hoped so.

The woman was likely hoping that Johnny would
get his behind up here to help this old man—Bear—
with the approaching cutthroats who no doubt intended great harm to Miss Bonner but only after
inflicting even greater and lasting harm to her old
benefactor.

Well, Bear might've been old, and all of his parts
might not have been in good working order, but he
had his eyes and his ears, and he had his good old
Remington revolver and his good old Spencer .56
repeating rifle, by God! He also had the bowie knife
he carried in a sheath hanging from around his
neck. He kept a razor's edge on the pigsticker—
sharp enough to shave a frog . . .

He turned to Miss Bonner, who was now staring
worriedly off toward where Johnny would come
from—if he came. If he was in any condition to
come.

"Miss Bonner."

She whipped her head to him.

"Come on," he said softly. "Follow me. Hurry!"

He reined Bronco off the trail's left side, tugging
the two mules along on their lead lines. The thuds
of the oncoming riders were growing louder. Miss
Bonner followed Bear and the mules into the forest
and around behind a large, fallen Douglas fir that
had been yanked up by its roots and now served as a
barricade of sorts. Bear stopped his horse and the
mules behind the great ball of roots that was nearly
the size of a small cabin, and stepped down from
his saddle.

"There!" a man shouted above the loudening din of the galloping mounts.

"Damn," Bear said to himself. He and the woman had been spotted.

Bear stepped up close to the root ball, edged a look around its right side. Yep, they'd been spotted, all right. The riders were just then galloping across the trail and into the woods, heading toward Bear and the woman.

"Step down, Miss Bonner," Bear said, trying to keep his anxiety out of his voice. He tied Bronco's reins and the mules' ropes to the tangle of roots protruding from the ball. "You stay here. Stay down." He slid his Spencer from the boot strapped to his saddle, and worked the trigger guard cocking mechanism, sliding a live cartridge into the breech. "No matter what happens, you stay here and wait for me or Johnny."

"Oh, God," she said.

Yeah, a prayer couldn't hurt, Bear thought. *'Specially if Johnny bought the farm back up the trail a piece.* The ex–mountain man did not voice this sentiment to the woman.

He stepped out from behind the ball of roots.

The riders were coming. There were six of them. They were coming like jackals with the smell of baby lambs in their nostrils. They were spread out side by side, galloping through the woods, weaving around the tall pines and spruces, making a beeline for Bear and the girl.

"Right there! It's the old man!" one of the riders shouted, jutting an arm and pointing a finger toward

Bear, who calmly raised his Spencer and blew the man out of his saddle.

"Whaohhh!" yelled the man riding six feet to the right of where the first man was rolling wildly upon the forest floor.

Bear wheezed out a soft curse as he cocked the Spencer, pumping another round into the action. He raised the rifle and lined up the sights on the hatted head of the man to the right of the first man he'd drilled. The second man was hauling back hard on his horse's reins. The horse had its legs locked up and was skidding forward, eyes round and white-ringed, ears laid back against its head.

The rider's eyes were wide, as well. And cast with horror.

He saw the big, bearded man aiming the Spencer at him. He opened his mouth to scream but no sound escaped his lips before he, too, was thrown off his skidding horse to roll wildly upon the ground, kicking up dead leaves and pine needles. Bear cocked the Spencer again, ejecting the spent cartridge, which went smoking over his right shoulder. Before he could get the new cartridge seated in the chamber, another of the marauders bore down on him, aiming a pistol straight out from his shoulder.

"Ah, hell," Bear wheezed out, knowing he was about to be taken to the dance.

Just then thunder pealed. The man hard-charging Bear triggered his pistol wide just before he flew sideways out of his saddle with a shrill scream. It was as though he'd been hit from the side with a giant, invisible hammer.

As he hit the ground and rolled, thunder pealed

again. Only it wasn't thunder. Johnny Greenway was charging in from the forest ahead and to Bear's right, maybe thirty feet away and crossing in front of Bear at a slant, his reins in his teeth, both shotguns aimed straight out in both his big, black-gloved hands.

Lightning ripped from both poppers at once, and the two riders that had been homing in on Bear from Bear's left also left their saddles in a hurry. One of the two horses stopped and reared, screaming. It whipped around, inadvertently kicked its now-fallen rider in the head with a loud smacking sound and galloped back in the direction from which it had come, buck-kicking its disdain at the violent turn of events.

The sixth rider had dismounted his horse a couple of seconds earlier and now ran for the cover of a broad spruce. Johnny neck-reined Ghost in the direction of the fleeing rider. Johnny and the cream bulled the man down. He fell screaming as Ghost's hooves ground the man's flesh and bones before continuing forward, leaving the man howling and writhing and rolling in the horse's wake.

Johnny turned back to the man who was now on his hands and knees, cursing shrilly. "You crazy son of Satan!"

Johnny rode slowly up to the man, who lifted his hands high above his head and wailed, *"No, please!"*

Johnny let Ghost take two more strides toward the man. The shotgun in Johnny's left hand thundered, lightning jetting from the right maw. The buckshot picked the man up off his knees and hurled him straight back and bounced him violently off a ponderosa pine. He flew forward and dropped belly down on the ground, leaving the pine behind him splattered with red blood and viscera.

Johnny stared at his latest victim, both of his smoking Twins hanging straight down at his sides. Sudden silence fell over the forest, save for the thuds of the still-fleeing horse. The thuds dwindled quickly, and then silence reigned until Miss Bonner looked up at Bear from where she knelt behind the root ball.

"What . . ." she said, haltingly, her voice thin with fear. "What is it?"

Bear glanced at her then looked off again toward where the tall, hawk-faced former Juan Beristain stared down at the last man he'd blown through the smoking iron doors. Johnny turned his gaze toward Bear.

Bear gave a dry chuckle. "That?" He drew a deep breath, glad to feel his racing heart finally slowing. "That was Shotgun Johnny. He's back!"

Johnny rode slowly around to each of the bodies, making sure all of the attackers were dead. As he did, he reloaded his shotguns and shoved them down into his holsters. He gigged the cream over to where Bear and the woman stood watching him, a vague disbelief creasing their foreheads.

"You two all right?"

Bear glanced at the woman. She stood staring up at Johnny, her cheeks a little pale beneath her new tan. She didn't say anything.

Bear said with irony, "Thanks for the help, but I was about to get 'em on the run."

"Well, I was in the area, so . . ." Johnny smiled. He turned to the woman. "You all right, Miss Bonner?"

Keeping her vaguely apprehensive, faintly approving eyes on him, she nodded. "I guess I really did hire the right man, after all."

"Don't count your chickens before they're hatched."

"No, I never do. Still, I can't think of another man who could take down so many men so efficiently. So . . ." She glanced around at the dead men whose bodies glistened with the blood leaking out of them. Already, some crows had found the bodies and were dipping their beaks into the wounds for fresh meat. The woman clapped a hand to her chest, gagging, then abruptly turned away. *"Oh, God!"*

She hurried off into the brush.

Bear turned to Johnny and shrugged. "She's right impressed. So am I." He canted his head to one side, scrutinizing his younger, slimmer friend. "How 'bout you?"

"Impressed?"

"Yeah. A year ago . . . hell, a *week* ago . . . I bet you never saw yourself back . . . well, doin' what you do so well."

"Killin' folks?"

Bear shrugged again. "Call it what you want."

"You know what, old friend?"

"What?"

"I don't feel a damn thing," Johnny said. "Nothin'."

It was true. He'd felt no hesitation, no fear when facing the killers. No exhilaration or rage, either. He didn't think his heart had even beat much faster than normal.

It used to be he'd feel some guilt about the men he'd killed, even if he had killed them in the legitimate course of his job. Now he didn't even feel that. He felt no differently than he would have felt had the men been bloodthirsty wolves.

This lack of feeling was odd. It made him feel like a husk. It might be unsettling if he thought about it too long, which he did not.

At least he wasn't drinking and continuing to make a fool of himself. For that at least, he did feel some gratefulness.

Bear continued gazing at him curiously. Finally, he nodded slowly, then glanced around at the dead. "Well, what're we gonna do with them?"

"Not a damn thing," Johnny said. "We leave them where they are." Such men didn't deserve a proper burial. Such men deserved to lie where they'd fallen, a feast for the blackbirds and crows who, once word had made its way around the vicinity that fresh carrion was available, would be usurped by bigger birds and, finally, by the wolves or the big wildcats.

"All right, then," Bear said with a sigh, brushing a hand across his bearded mouth and tugging his blue cap down on his forehead. He stepped back behind the ball of roots to grab his claybank's reins.

"We're just gonna leave them?" the woman asked later, when she and Bear had mounted their horses and were following Johnny back toward the trail. She glanced around again, still looking a little green around the gills.

"Crows gotta eat, too," Johnny said.

CHAPTER 18

Late the next day they climbed above the timber-
line and rode along the north side of a stony ridge
that rose like a gray dinosaur spine from the top of
the mountain.

Last winter's dirty snow, still sculpted into drifts,
slanted out from the side of the ridge. Fingers of
melting water trickled out away from the snow, glinting in the late-day sunshine, to run off down the
gravelly slope and into the broad, barren, funnel-like
canyon below, the chasm's steep walls strewn with
gray slide-rock.

The riders followed the gentle curve of the ridge
crest for a mile beyond the canyon and then down
into deep timber again and through the mouth of
yet another, shallower, narrower side canyon. A
hand-painted, badly faded sign appeared amongst
rocks along the narrow trail, announcing NO-NAME
TOWN.

"Well, I'll be hanged," Bear said from where he
rode ahead of Miss Bonner, trailing the mules by
their lead lines. "Last time I was up thisaway, there
weren't nothin' but that cabin over yonder."

He pointed out a low, shake-shingled shack off the trail's left side, at the edge of a beaver meadow. The cabin had no front door, and its mossy roof was partly caved in. "Healy Morgan built that shack back in sixty-four, an' I spent one summer with him there, trappin' these meadows and huntin' grizzlies up on them ridges yonder. That's all there was up here then."

"Well, there appears a good deal more up here now," remarked Miss Bonner as they rode on past the sign.

"Yeah, I can smell it," Bear griped as he lifted his nose to sniff the air.

Riding behind Sheila Bonner, Johnny could smell it, too—the stench of overfilled latrines and ripe trash and animal carcasses. There was also the smell of pine smoke from cook fires. Johnny thought he detected the faint, cloying aromas of women's perfume—that of the cheaper variety.

Sounds grew, as well, as the three entered the settlement oddly dubbed No-Name Town, which had been built in a slight clearing in the pines and rimmed in steep, gray ridges peppered with the black gaps of mine openings fronted by the drooping gray tongues of tailings. Men worked with picks and shovels along the ridges, some with carts pulled by donkeys and bristling with prospecting implements. There were the occasional explosions of reverberating dynamite blasts as the miners plunged deeper into the mountain, following veins.

The town itself pushing up around Johnny and his trail partners wasn't much more than hastily erected, dirty canvas tents with tin pipes angling up from their roofs and unfurling blue smoke into the air over the settlement. Dead deer and elk and even a bear hung here and there from pine boughs, and bearded men plundered the carcasses' innards with skinning knives, laying out meat chunks on crude wooden tables or on the tops of barrels—in one case, a man was laying out his own meaty harvest on planks laid over a handcart.

The tent shacks, hastily erected so they could be quickly razed before the first snows of winter blew across this high-country no-man's-land, bore signs announcing LEATHER GOODS, HORSE FEED, BLACKSMITH, JOHS LIVERY, ALE, GOOD FOOD, H.J. WALTHAM DOCTOR OF DENTISTRY, MADAM BERLIOZ'S PARLOR HOUSE (this, too, was merely a sagging dirty tent), BENJAMIN J. CARSON, M.D., and similar other establishments that were part and parcel of high-country boomtowns.

This one had apparently grown up around the Reverend's Temptation gold mine. The sign for the mine, a heavy piece of timber stretched across two tall pine poles, lay at the far end of the settlement and at the foot of a rocky slope upon which were strewn crude wooden buildings and a stamping mill, which vaulted its steady drumming roar above the din of the town.

"You been up here before, Miss Bonner?" Johnny called above the racket of two fighting dogs and two men shouting at the dogs that appeared to be contesting the ownership of a big thighbone—likely having belonged to a bear—in heavy German or Scandinavian brogues.

"No," Sheila said, raising her voice also as they continued riding along the muddy street between the dirty tent shacks. Smoke from chimney pipes swept over and around them. "My father was only up here a couple of times. He said it was a good place to stay away from, and now I see why."

She'd stopped her sorrel to gaze at one of the few permanent establishments in the town. It was a large log building with a broad, wraparound veranda. A balcony ran along its second floor. Men and women milled on both the first-floor veranda as well as on the balcony. The women were dressed in the frilly garb of parlor girls—those who were dressed at all, that was—and the men wore the dungarees, cloth caps, and heavy-soled, high-topped boots of miners.

Beards hung a good way down their chests. One beard dropped all the way to the big, brass buckle of one man's belt, and a porcelain pipe poked out of the man's mouth.

A big sign hung over the front veranda, its large, stylish red letters fairly shouting WELCOME TO YVETTE'S HOUSE! A smaller sign nailed to a post teased: FREE BEER WITH EVERY GIRL!

"What a deal!" Bear exclaimed. He, too, had stopped to admire the establishment.

"Hello, there, you big lug!" The greeting had come from a largely built woman standing on the veranda gazing down into the street in general and at Bear in particular. She had to have weighed well over two hundred pounds and worn at least ten pounds of paint and rouge. Her eyelashes alone must have weighed close to a pound apiece, though she didn't seem to mind fluttering them as she sized up the big man on the street below her.

She wore too little for her hefty size. Way, way too

little. What she did wear was all dark lace and taffeta from which her ample self sprouted like a giant, pale bud.

"Well, hello there, yourself!" Bear returned, grinning up at the gal. "Let me guess," he said, then pressed his thumb to his bearded chin in a mock gesture of exaggerated pensiveness. "You're Yvette!"

She cackled a laugh. "How'd you know, sweetie?" She looked askance at him. "Have you been here before? Pardon me if I forgot, but I get all kinds through my, uh . . . hallowed halls. Hah!"

Bear laughed. "No, no, Miss Yvette. It's been years since I was last up this high in the clouds."

"Beautiful, ain't it . . . ?"

While Bear continued flirting with the hefty doxy, Miss Bonner turned her horse nose to nose with Johnny's, and said, "I'm going to ride on up to the mine and meet with Mister Nolan. We have much to discuss, and it's getting late. I'd like to start back down the mountain as early as possible tomorrow morning, so . . ." She tossed her head to indicate Bear still laughing and palavering with Miss Yvette. "Keep your friend out of trouble, will you?"

"Don't worry—I'll throw a catch-rope over him if I have to."

She studied the big man briefly. Bear was waving and gesturing, laughing with the whore. Turning back to Johnny, Sheila said with only a little irony, "You might have to."

She paused and looked around, then turned her gaze once again to her gold guard. "I was told there was a boardinghouse here in No-Name Town. That must be it over there." She indicated what appeared to be another permanent structure in the settlement—a boxlike frame building sitting just up the street from Miss Yvette's place. "I will secure rooms for us there. I was told it's quite rugged, but the bedbugs aren't deadly and the food they serve in their so-called dining room is passable."

"Passable, eh?" Johnny scraped a thumb down his jaw, reflecting that it couldn't be any worse than what he'd padded out his belly with lately.

As though reading his mind, Sheila said with a twinkle in one eye, "I'm sure it's nothing compared to my cooking, but it won't kill us for a night." She gave a dubious half-smile. "Let's meet bright and early tomorrow morning in the dining room, then, shall we?"

Johnny nodded. "Good luck with Mister Nolan."

Sheila nodded and reined her filly away. "Thank you." As she rode down the muddy street toward the mine, several of the unwashed citizens of No-Name Town called out to her bawdily, some whistling.

Sheila continued riding, keeping her head forward, enduring the onslaught with her customary cool disdain, her back taut, silently defiant. Johnny felt he should have accompanied the woman to the mine, but she obviously thought she could take care of herself. Besides, the business she had to discuss with the mine superintendent, laying out her financial troubles, was a private matter.

Oh, well. The mine wasn't far. If she needed help, he'd be one scream away.

Johnny turned to Bear. The big man was looking at him. Yvette was no longer on the balcony.

"Where's your friend?" Johnny asked.

"Customer."

"Aw," Johnny said in mock pity. "You two were just startin' to get along."

"That's too much woman fer me, anyways." Bear jerked his head to indicate Sheila. "Where's she off to?"

"Business."

"Ah."

Johnny put Ghost up to a hitchrack fronting Yvette's place. "Come on," he said. "I'll buy you a drink or two."

"Hold on," Bear said, scowling at the other man. "You ain't goin' in there. Hell, they serve . . . well, you know what they serve in there."

Johnny swung down from his horse's back and looked up at the sign running across the veranda roof. "Well, since it's obviously a whorehouse, I'm guessing they don't serve sermons, tea, and crumpets. Probably whiskey an' women."

"You got that right. An' while I don't believe you've sworn off wimmen, you have sworn off—"

"Yeah, but you haven't."

"Haven't what?"

"Sworn off whiskey. Maybe you've sworn off women, though not because you wanted to." Johnny gave a wry chuckle.

"Shut up about that, you young devil. And quit tryin' to muddy the water. You can't go in a place like that, Johnny. You just can't do it!"

Johnny tied Ghost to the hitch rail. "Watch me, old-timer."

"Johnny, gallblastit!" Bear exclaimed, nudging Bronco up to the hitch rail beside the cream. As

Johnny walked up the porch steps, Bear swung down from his saddle, quickly tied his mount to the hitch rail, then hurried up the porch steps behind Johnny.

Johnny nodded to several men and "ladies" regarding him and the older man skeptically, their eyes touching on the Twins strapped to the younger man's thighs. The holstered ten-gauges were always objects of curiosity. In the past, they and his deputy U.S. marshal's badge, of course, had marked him as the lawman he'd been. When he hadn't worn the badge but only the Twins, for the moon-and-star had often made him an easy shooting target, most folks had mistaken him for a bounty hunter, as they likely would now.

That was all right with Johnny. That meant they'd probably give him a wide berth. He liked when folks gave him a wide berth. He felt none too friendly these days.

He pushed through the batwings, Bear at his heels rasping out, "Johnny, dammit! Listen to me, will ya? You can't—"

"Come on, old-timer, I'll buy ya a couple shots of who-hit-John."

The plain pine bar, flanked by leaded looking glass and shelves bearing up under the weight of many unlabeled bottles, stretched across the back of the room. Most of the customers were apparently either upstairs or on the veranda, for the main saloon was nearly deserted. From the ceiling could be heard the sounds of several beds getting good workouts. Women moaned and men grunted. Several miners were deeply involved in a game of five-card stud on the room's right side while a man and a blond young woman sat on a red-velvet sofa shoved up against the wall to the left.

The girl wore only pantaloons and a corset. She had feathers in her hair, and she was barefoot. The paint on her cheeks and lips was badly smudged, so that she looked like a fresh watercolor painting left out in the rain.

She was obviously distraught about something, for she dabbed at her eyes with a lace-edged handkerchief and muttered to the jake sitting beside her. The jake, a middle-aged man with a salt-and-pepper beard and long, tangled hair of the same color, was trying to listen to the girl's prattling, but he was having a devil of a time staying awake. His unfocused eyes kept closing, and his chin kept dipping to his chest just before he caught himself and jerked his head back straight on his shoulders. This happened over and over again as Johnny watched. The sleepy gent held a half-full bottle of busthead close beside him, between him and the sobbing girl.

"Cat died," said the barman as Johnny approached the bar, Bear in tow, scowling at him reprovingly.

"What's that?" Johnny asked the tall, pale man with short, black hair shiny with pomade. He had a pencil-thin mustache and deep pockmarks on his cheeks and forehead.

"Her cat died. She's been a wreck all day."

"Oh, that's too bad," Bear said, switching his attention to the girl.

"It is too bad," said the barman. "She's Yvette's best moneymaker, but she ain't done a lick o' work all day. Just clouds up and rains. Chews the ear off anyone who'll listen. I reckon it's poor Knute's turn now. Yvette's got a tender heart. I'd have thrown Josie out on the street by now, but not Yvette. Anyway, can I set you fellas up with a coupla whiskeys? Or do you wanna start out with beer? I brew my own out back. An old recipe long in my German family. Grow the hops myself. A nickel a bucket. Can't go wrong with the ale, no sir!"

"Whiskey for my friend," Johnny said. "And coffee for me."

The barman scowled at him. "Coffee?"

"As strong as you got."

The barman studied him closely, as though he thought he were joking. Then he hocked phlegm from his throat, spat it into a sandbox behind the bar, and said. "Well, I think I still got some on the stove in the backroom. It's been on the warmin' rack since mornin,'" he warned.

"As long as the six-shooter's floating on top."

"Well, it is, at that—it purely is!" The man chuckled as he set a shot glass on the bar and splashed whiskey into it from an unlabeled bottle. "Leave the bottle," Johnny told him. "My friend's thirsty."

The barman shrugged then disappeared through a curtained doorway. Bear looked from Johnny to the whiskey, from the whiskey to Johnny, licking his lips and rubbing his hands nervously on his smoke-stained buckskin trousers. He was trying to say something but was having a devil of a time getting the words out.

"Good Lord, Bear," Johnny said. "Did you swaller your tongue? Should I send for a sawbones . . . er, a tongue-puller?" He slapped the bar, chuckling.

"Stop your teasin', you nasty pup. You expect me to drink that stuff in front of you?"

Just then the barman came through the curtained doorway holding a thick stone mug filled to the brim with steaming black coffee. "Here you go," he said, setting the stout mug on the bar. "On the house. I gave you the bottom of the pot so I ain't gonna vouch for as how it won't bore a hole clear down to your boots. Might even burn through your boots and into my floor!"

"That's how I like it."

Johnny paid the man for the whiskey then jerked his head. "Come on, old-timer. Let's take a load off. We got the rest of the day and night to burn in this perdition. Might as well do it sittin' down."

Bear grimaced as Johnny made his way over to a near table and kicked out a chair. Bear looked at the bottle, his expression like that of a man led by shotgun to a church altar to marry the plainest girl in town.

Finally, apparently choosing the bride over a load of buckshot, the big man grabbed the bottle and his glass. He moved over to the table, kicked out a chair opposite Johnny, and set the bottle on the table. Holding the small glass between his sausage-sized index finger and even thicker thumb, he took a slow sip of the whiskey, closing his eyes as he did so, savoring the flavor. Swallowing, he eased his heavy bulk into the chair.

He set the shot glass gingerly on the table, as though it were fine china.

He looked up guiltily at Johnny, narrowing one eye. "That don't devil ya?"

Johnny blew on his coffee, sipped, and swallowed. "Sure."

"Why, then . . . ?"

"I can't go the whole rest of my life avoiding saloons or men who drink. Sure, I'm gonna want a drink from time to time. Hell, I want one now. But I don't deserve that stuff. I realize it now. There's no way I'll ever allow myself another swig of liquor again."

"What do you mean you don't deserve it?"

"I drank to soften the blows of guilt. I didn't deserve that. The drinkin' only added to the guilt. I don't think I fully realized that until I stared down into Lenore's dead face. In Lenore, I saw my wife. I saw Lisa. It about killed me, an' right away I wanted a drink. Right away, I told myself *no.* I don't deserve to have those blows softened. No more."

Johnny stared gravely across the table at his old friend. "From now on, I face my demons, drink my coffee, and try to live as good a life as I can for the time I have left. I owe that much to my dead wife and my dead boy. That, at least, I *can* do."

Bear studied him for a time, as though plumbing the depths of his sorrow. As though having peered into those murky depths where red devils wallowed, snapping their toothy jaws and flicking their forked tails, the burly man winced and sat back in his chair. He took a sip of the whiskey, wagged his head. "I didn't know, Johnny. You never told me about . . ."

"Yeah, well, I didn't want to talk about it. I reckon the rumors followed me from Carson City, though. That's how Flagg knew. I could tell by the eyes of most of the other folks in Hallelujah Junction that they knew, too."

"About the . . . the . . . other . . . gal."

"Yeah."

Bear nodded grimly, staring into his whiskey. He looked up at Johnny, and beneath his blue knit cap his face became a deeply etched mask of misery as he said, "Johnny, you can't let guilt eat you up over that. You're a man like all the rest of us, an' all the rest of us have done some bad things we feel real bad about."

"Yeah, well, I feel real bad about it."

"Hell, Johnny," Bear added with a mirthless chuckle. "You're *Basque*. French and Spanish. That's a powerful mix of blood. You know what ever'body says about the Basques. Why, they—"

"Smell like sheep dip," another voice finished for the older man. "Hell, I can smell it from here!"

Johnny hadn't realized until now that two more men had entered the saloon and were standing nearby.

CHAPTER 19

The two newcomers stood at the bar, each with a filled shot glass before him. Both were dressed in the tony garb of the better card sharps. Both wore claw-hammer coats, flowered waistcoats, and pinstriped trousers. They had long, brushed hair and thick mustaches and side whiskers.

One was tall and blond. The other was of medium height, dark, and stocky. The blond was the one who'd made the sheep-dip comment, which was not a new insult to Johnny's ears. Having been raised in a sheepherding family, he'd heard the insult many times, usually when his family had stopped in towns for supplies.

He knew that particular insult as well as many more. The cattlemen had been very inventive in finding new and different ways of insulting the sheepherders, and of killing them, too.

In this neck of the woods—northern California and southwestern Nevada—most folks recognized the men and women of Basque blood. Such people were often, like Johnny, ruddy-skinned with high broad cheekbones, brooding eyes beneath sharply

ridged brows, wide mouths, and aquiline noses. Most
Basques whom the former Juan Beristain had known
were short and stocky, with large hands and feet, suit-
able to hard labor and much walking.

The only difference in Johnny was that he was tall,
with long legs and broad shoulders. Otherwise, he
had Basque written all over him.

The blond, Louis Baumgartner, had recognized
him. Johnny had known Baumgartner for some time,
for the man was an infamous drunk and lout who
haunted the trails between boomtowns the way bur-
infested curs followed gut wagons. He plundered
small gold fortunes via poker.

The darker man was Charles Bishop, milder than
Baumgartner but only by a little. He was a gambler
with small eyes and a quietly seedy manner.

"I'm sorry, Louis," Bear said, "but we wasn't talkin'
to you." Bear knew the men, as well. Most around the
area did.

Baumgartner manufactured a mock expression of
surprise. "Oh, I'm sorry. I didn't see you two fellas
there. Like I was just sayin' to my friend Charlie here,
I smelled sheep dip." He glowered at Johnny. "Now I
see why."

Johnny stared back at the man but he didn't say
anything. Annoyance touched him, but nothing
stronger than that. He knew the man was just bored
as he waited for the more moneyed prospectors to
roll in from their diggings clutching pokes of gold
dust in need of lightening. Continuing to hold the
gambler's insulting gaze, Johnny quirked his mouth
corners in a faint grin then reached inside his coat
for his leather makings sack.

Baumgartner turned toward his friend Charlie

Bishop, who grinned back at him in boyish delight at the ribbing. Baumgartner snorted dryly, shook his head with disdain, then turned around to face his drink on the bar.

Bear turned to Johnny and rolled his eyes. Johnny shrugged as he dribbled Kansas City tobacco onto his El Oso wheat paper. "Now as I was sayin'," Bear said. "You know that Basques are known for their hot-blooded ways. Passions run strong in you folks. You can't blame yourself, Johnny."

"Just the blood, eh?" Johnny said as he licked the quirley closed and scratched a match to life on a table leg.

"Right enough."

"Oh, well . . ." Johnny touched the flame to the cigarette. "I don't want to talk about it."

"How come you're not drinkin', Johnny?" This from Baumgartner again.

Johnny looked up to see the man standing with his back to him, leaning forward against the bar. The man's eyes met Johnny's in the backbar mirror.

"I mean," the blond man continued, "you look good. Looks like you crawled up out of the mud and dung . . . all the trash I heard you was sleepin' in . . . and *with* . . ." He curled his lip, mockingly. "I mean, if you don't have money, I'll buy you a drink, Johnny."

Johnny stared at the man in the mirror. Anger had begun to flare in him when the man had emphasized the word "with." Johnny knew what . . . or who . . . he'd meant. He'd meant Lenore.

Bear glanced at Johnny uneasily. "Don't mind him," he said quietly. Turning to Baumgartner, he said, "Louis, do you mind? We're havin' us a private conversation over here. Johnny thanks you for the offer, but he don't drink no more. The coffee's fine. Now stop spoilin' for a fight."

"Easy, old man," Baumgartner said to the reflection of Bear's face in the mirror. "Don't get your bloomers in a twist."

Baumgartner grinned then lowered his head, jerking his shoulders in laughter.

Bishop lowered his head, as well, also laughing, making wheezing and rasping sounds as he did.

"You boys is real funny," Bear said. "Real funny."

Baumgartner threw back the last of his drink then turned to Bishop. "Come on, Charlie. You can buy me supper. Gonna be a long night."

When Bishop had thrown his own drink back, the men donned their bowler hats. Baumgartner turned away from the bar and pinched his hat brim to Johnny and Bear, and said, "Stench is a little thick in here, anyway." He winked then started walking past Johnny.

Johnny hadn't intended to do what he did next. It was pure impulse to stick out his right foot and trip Baumgartner. It couldn't have worked more beautifully had he planned the move well ahead of time. The blond gambler got his right half-boot caught under Johnny's ankle and his forward momentum carried him forward and down.

He plunged to the floor with a loud slap of his hands and a *boom!*

"Ah, no . . . no," Bear mourned.

Baumgartner cursed shrilly as he rose to his hands and knees and shook his head to clear the cobwebs. He started to climb to his feet, but then Johnny rose from his chair, grabbed the collar of the man's shirt with one hand, and whipped Baumgartner back behind him. Limbs pinwheeling, the gambler flew through the air, gracelessly pirouetting on the toes of his boots, to fall hard to the floor again and to slide up against the bar with another *boom*!

"Holy . . ." Bishop stood looking at Johnny and his blond partner in shock and dismay, lower jaw hanging.

Johnny reached down, pulled the blond off the floor once more, and held him before him. Baumgartner blinked his eyes in exasperation, then winced as Johnny pulled his own right fist back behind his shoulder, cocking it for a decisive roundhouse.

Before Johnny could deliver the crushing blow, someone wrapped a hand around his right bicep, which hovered level with his right ear. The hand squeezed none too gently.

"Oh-oh," Bear said.

Johnny looked down and to his right. He followed the small, female hand dug into his thick bicep, to the attractive brown eyes of Sheila Bonner staring up at him. She arched an ironic brow and said, "If you'll pardon the interruption, Mister Greenway, there's a matter we need to discuss."

She released his muscle, lowered her hand.

A man stood beside the young woman. He was middle-aged, slender, gray-haired beneath a frayed brown bowler, and all business. He wore a cheap suitcoat over a white shirt and vest, all very rumpled, as though he slept in his clothes. He was smoking a brown cheroot. Johnny released Baumgartner, who fell back against the bar with a curse, angrily straightening his collar. His gaze lingered with typical male interest on the pretty young woman who had likely just spared him a broken nose.

Johnny turned to the young woman and the man. He frowned curiously.

"This is Mister Nolan," said Miss Bonner, canting her head toward the man standing beside her. "He has something he'd like to show us."

"What is it?"

Nolan jerked his head toward the saloon doors. "Come on."

While he started toward the batwings, Johnny looked at Bear, who shrugged. Miss Bonner stood before Johnny, looking up at him with that faintly ironic expression again. She glanced from the two gamblers to Johnny to Bear, and said, "You are on my time now, Mister Greenway. I guess I should have admonished you to behave yourself, but I guess I thought it perfunctory."

Bear scowled at Johnny then turned his questioning gaze to the young woman. "Per-*what*?"

The woman sighed. "Come with me and Mister Nolan, please."

She turned and headed for the batwings, near which Nolan waited, puffing his short cheroot.

Johnny grabbed his hat off the table. Bear grabbed his bottle off the table, and stuffed it into a pocket of his coat. He threw back the rest of the whiskey in his glass, and then he followed Johnny toward the batwings.

"Watch your back, Shotgun Johnny!" bellowed Baumgartner behind them.

"Oh, I will," Johnny muttered, then followed the woman and the mine superintendent through the doors.

"Right this way," said Nolan as he tossed the stub of his cheroot into the street then, exhaling the smoke from his last drag, moved down the porch steps before swing to the right.

"Where we goin'?" Johnny asked Miss Bonner, walking ahead of him, following Nolan.

Nolan glanced at him over his shoulder. "You'll see."

Johnny glanced at Bear behind him. Again, the big man shrugged.

Johnny and Bear followed Nolan and Sheila around behind Miss Yvette's place. They strode down one wide alley and then down a narrower, intersecting alley. They walked out into an area flanking the town proper and stippled with firs and spruce trees. They weaved around tent shacks and cook fires and makeshift stables in which stock milled. Chickens and several loose goats scattered at their feet.

They walked around a fir tree where yet another man was butchering yet another hanging, gutted deer, and pulled up in front of a square shack comprised of vertical pine planks and sheathed in evergreen shrubs. Pine branches had been thrown atop the roof as though to keep sunlight from streaming through the cracks between the planks.

Nolan turned to Miss Bonner. "This is the communal icehouse." He wore a grave expression on his gray-mustached face. "Maybe you'd better wait out here, Miss Bonner."

She pondered the suggestion, chewed her lip, then shook her head. "I want to see."

"See what?" Bear asked in building exasperation.

"Hold on." Nolan removed the latching bar and swung open one of the two doors.

He stepped into the cool shadows. Johnny could

see the piled ice blocks sprinkled with bark and sawdust. Blanket-wrapped bundles slumped atop the ice, sagging down the sides of the blocks. There was a cloying sweetness in the air.

"Let's see," Nolan said, pausing, looking around. "I think this is the one."

He walked over to one of the bundles, drew a folding knife from his pocket, opened the blade, and cut the ropes lashing the blankets closed. He removed the rope and jerked the blankets open to reveal a man's face glaring up at him. A deathly pale, blue-tinged face. The wide-open eyes were glassy, but, even in death still touched with a lingering horror.

Standing to Johnny's left, Sheila stifled a gasp.

Johnny walked to the dead man staring up at him. "Well, well . . . if it ain't Deputy U.S. Marshal Lyle Wallace."

"Hmmm," Bear said. "And the others?"

"The men he goaded into joining his posse," Nolan said, closing the blankets over Wallace's face. "Five of 'em. At least, I assume they were a posse Wallace led after the gold thieves."

"And found them," Miss Bonner said.

"Or the gold robbers found Wallace." Johnny turned to Nolan. "Where'd you find them?"

"I didn't. Some prospectors from Murphy's Hollow did. Found 'em hanging like ripe fruit from several trees along the South Fork of Washo Creek. Flagg's men had been camped there, horses tied to a picket line."

"So the gold robbers did find them," Miss Bonner said.

"Looks like," Nolan said. "The prospectors bundled

them up in their own soogans, tied 'em over their own horses, and hauled 'em to town."

"When?" Bear asked.

"Day before yesterday. But they were dead at least three days before the prospectors found 'em. Already turning stiff and starting to stink."

Miss Bonner gagged then covered her mouth with her hand.

"Sorry," Nolan said, sheepish.

"No." Sheila shook her head defiantly. "I wanted to see for myself." She glanced at Johnny. "I wanted to know what we might be running into."

"Right helpful," Bear said, staring down at the blanket-wrapped Marshal Wallace, his voice pitched with wistfulness. "Right helpful . . ."

"Maybe we'd better hold off on that gold run," Nolan suggested, keeping his eyes on Sheila. "You'll be robbed for sure. Whoever's after the gold is still out there. And they obviously got you outgunned." He paused. "You're gonna need more men. Hell, you're gonna need a small army, Miss Bonner. Pardon my French."

"Even if I could afford a small army, which I can't, I have no idea how large a small army would be large enough. I have no idea how many men are robbing the gold. No one who's seen them has lived to tell about it." Miss Bonner's voice grew brittle with her understandable frustration. "And I can't wait. I have to get that gold to the mint so I can pay your men and keep the mine as well as the bank open. My main source of reliable revenue at the moment is the Reverend's Temptation. I just need to get the gold down to the consarned bank in one piece!"

She gave a deep sigh of consternation as she crossed her arms on her breasts, kicked a stone against the wall, and swung around to stare out the icehouse's open door.

Johnny placed a hand on her shoulder. "We'll get it down safely."

Sheila looked up at him. Her mouth corners lifted a wan smile, and she nodded. "I know you'll do everything you can." She glanced at Bear. "Both of you."

She'd barely gotten the last word out before her eyes widened in shock, and she gave a shrill cry. She threw herself against Johnny, wrapping her arms around him as a guttural growling and thumping sound rose to Johnny's right.

"Tarnation!" Bear exclaimed, leaping forward as some furry gray creature dashed out from the bowels of the icehouse and bolted through the door, snarling.

"Damn!" Nolan exclaimed. He'd also jumped. "Coyote!" He gave a nervous laugh. "Just a coyote. Must've dug under one of the walls, the nasty devil!"

Johnny had closed his hand around the neck of the Twin on his left hip, but now he removed it. Sheila shuddered as she pressed her right cheek against his chest. Seeking protection, she'd squeezed him hard, wrapping her arms around his waist. Now she loosened her grip.

She looked up at him, her pretty cheeks turning red with chagrin.

Johnny stared down at her. His ears warmed as his gaze held hers. She felt fine and warm and supple against him. That feeling must have been reflected in his eyes. She held his gaze for another second then looked abruptly away.

Her cheeks turned an even deeper red as she dropped her arms and stepped back quickly, glancing around in embarrassment.

"Well, that . . . was certainly . . . startling . . ." She gave a nervous chuckle, fiddling with her hair.

Nolan and Bear regarded her wistfully. As they switched their gazes to Johnny, his ears turned even warmer, and he said, "Yeah . . . had me goin'. Just a coyote, though. Nothin' to worry about."

Bear favored him with a wry grin. "Nah, nah. Nothin' to worry about." He'd said the words slowly, ironically, arching his brows insinuatingly.

Johnny scowled at him, changed the subject. Glancing at the dead men slumped over the ice, he said, "Well, now that we know what we're up against, I reckon we got some plannin' to do."

"Yes, planning," Sheila said, her cheeks slow to lose their blush. "Why don't we do so over supper?" She swung around and walked outside.

Johnny watched her go. He felt eyes on him. He turned to see both Bear and Nolan regarding him with smirks on their lips.

"What the hell you two lookin' at?" Johnny said, peeved. "You heard the woman. Supper time!"

He left the icehouse.

She had felt mighty good, though.

Chapter 20

"Mighty fine grub," Bear said a half hour later as he cut a chunk of meat off the big elk steak on his plate, in the dining room of Big Lars's Boarding House at the north edge of No-Name Town. He was about to fork the meat into his mouth but stopped and glanced guiltily at Sheila sitting across the table from him. "I mean . . . not nearly as good as your cookin', though, ma'am. I didn't mean to give offense."

Johnny turned an amused chuckle into a cough, and kicked his friend under the table.

Sheila smiled over her steaming stone coffee mug at the burly old-timer. "Why, thank you, Bear. How nice of you. I have to confess, though . . . Big Lars's digs here might be humble, indeed, but his cooking is going down right well."

She switched her smile from Bear to Johnny. Johnny returned the smile with a warm one of his own, feeling his innards twisting behind his cartridge belt. He couldn't get the memory of her body pressed against his out of his mind, and now he found himself basking in the luster and comfort of her rarefied smile. He liked how her almond-shaped brown eyes crinkled slightly when she formed the expression, how her full lips drew up at the corners, making her cheeks dimple.

She looked down quickly, another flush rising in her face. It was then that Johnny realized that their gazes had held just a second or two too long. He looked away quickly, too, and resumed cutting his meat and forking chunks into his mouth, along with the gravy-drenched fried potatoes and bits of applesauce.

Again, his innards twisted. His heart was beating faster than normal. Damned perplexing.

What in the hell was happening here?

This woman was not only way too good for him, she was his employer. What's more, these odd sensations that came to him from time to time . . . that had been coming to him along the trail up here, as well, if he were honest with himself . . . racked him with guilt. They brought back memories of the night Lisa and David had been killed. Memories of what he'd been doing before he'd gone home and that door had been kicked open and all hell had broken loose, and the devil's own hounds had run wild through his life, ripping and tearing, destroying everything— all that he'd loved.

Get yourself straightened out, you damn fool, he silently told himself, chewing, trying very hard to keep his eyes off the beautiful woman across the table from him. *She's off limits for many reasons. Even if she wasn't off limits because she's not only your employer but way better educated than you—and just plain better than you all around!—you couldn't have her.*

You don't deserve to be happy again. Not with Lisa and David lying cold in their graves because of you.

He sucked down nearly half of his scalding coffee to drive such sharp-edged musings from his mind, and consciously turned his attention to the problem all three of them were facing.

He cleared his throat. "Tell me somethin', Miss Bonner."

She glanced up at him from beneath chestnut brows.

"Are you sure Mister Nolan is trustworthy?"

After the visit to the icehouse, Nolan had gone back to the mine. It was just Johnny, Sheila, and Bear dining together in Big Lars's humble dining room, on the first floor of his rustic boardinghouse. A couple of men who looked like salesmen sat a table on the other side of the small, low-ceilinged room lit by two bracket lamps and a candle lamp, conversing in desultory tones. They were the only other diners. Big Lars and his dour daughter, Louise, could be heard banging pots around in the kitchen off the dining room.

"I believe so," Sheila said, frowning across the table at Johnny. She swallowed a bite of food, then shook her hair out of her eyes as she stared at him curiously. "My father seemed to think he was trustworthy, anyway. Why do you ask, Mister Greenway?"

Bear answered for Johnny, cutting his dark gaze between Johnny and the young woman. "Somebody from the mine must be passing word to the robbers when the gold is being hauled out of the mountains."

Johnny looked at him, one brow arched. "You figure it, too?"

"I'm smarter than I look."

"Why do you think that?" Sheila asked them both.

"The thieves have been up here a long time," Johnny said. "They'd have to be very patient men to keep a close eye on the trail every day just in case a shipment of gold was heading down to Hallelujah Junction."

"Owlhoots ain't the most patient men in the world," Bear added with a crooked grin. "That's one reason they're owlhoots."

Johnny ate his last bit of steak and dropped his fork on his plate. "I think they're holed up in the mountains somewhere. Maybe a cabin, maybe an abandoned ranch. Someone's either sending word down from the mine when the gold is being shipped, or . . ."

"Someone's sending word up from the bank," Sheila finished the sentence for him, frowning down at the table, thinking it over. She wrinkled the skin above the bridge of her nose, shook her head. "Word has to be coming from the mine. The only other person at the bank who know when the gold is being shipped is George Poindexter."

"You trust Poindexter?" Johnny asked.

"Absolutely." Sheila nodded. "He's been a good, loyal friend and business associate of my father." She thought about it some more, shook her head again. "No. It can't be George. However . . ."

She let her voice trail off as another concern distracted her.

"Yes?" Johnny said.

"There is usually one other person in addition to me, George, and Mister Nolan who knows when the gold is being hauled down from the mine. That would be the messenger Nolan sends down to Hallelujah Junction informing me that the mine has enough ingots for another run. That's how I know when to send a man up for it. The messenger usually delivers a short note to me, but he wouldn't have to open it to know what it says. Wouldn't it be obvious that the gold will soon be shipped? The messenger might be the one relaying the information to the robbers either on the way down or on his way back up."

The three thought in silence.

Johnny sighed and shrugged. "Well, there's nothing we can do about that situation now. Now we have to assume that the robbers have learned we're hauling the gold down the mountains tomorrow."

"I should have thought of this," Sheila said. "We could have planned differently."

"Is there only the one route out of the mountains from here?" Johnny asked her.

"As far as I know."

"You mean the same way we came up?" Bear asked.

"Yes," Sheila said.

"No, no." Bear shook his head. He shoved his plate away. The platter was empty save for the large bone and a few smears of applesauce. He held his cup out for Big Lars's unsmiling daughter to refill it. The thickset girl had just then approached the table with the big speckled pot in her hands, her round spectacles sagging on her doughy nose.

Back in the kitchen as he worked, Big Lars was singing a song in Norwegian. He sang loudly and with great feeling. It was hard to believe he'd fathered such a colorless child as his daughter, who returned to the kitchen after refilling Sheila's and Johnny's cups and then those of the two drummers, as well.

Bear spooned sugar into his coffee, blew on the hot liquid, sipped, then set the mug down on the table.

He leaned forward, crossing his thick arms on the table before him. "There's Sacramento Ridge and the Devil's Horns Pass."

"The Devil's Horns?" Johnny said, incredulous. "This time of year? It's probably damn near winter up there."

"Might be hairy. And it would add a good two more days to the journey. Maybe three." Bear looked at the young woman, who stared back at him with keen interest. "But I could get you through that way if my old ticker don't give out on me. The Devil's Horns is almost fourteen thousand feet high. Air's thin up there. I used to go up there with a pick an' shovel when I was a young man. I told myself I was lookin' for gold, but truth was I just plain liked it up there. All rocks and hawks. No other men. Might be different now."

Bear looked around, scowling, as though his field of vision were encompassing this cesspool of a town up here where he remembered it being so pristine not all that long ago. "But I doubt it. Leastways, them robbers wouldn't expect us to go that way if they even know about it. I'm bettin' they don't even know about it. The only folks who know about the Devil's Horns is the feeble old mountain men like myself who used to trap or hunt gold up thataway when we were young and didn't know better."

"Long, hard ride up to the Devil's Horns," Johnny said.

"And there's a chance the weather won't let us get over it," Bear warned. "It's a narrow trail between very steep ridges after a steep climb through a boulder field. If there's ice up there already, which there could be, we won't make it. We'll have to come back down and go the usual way. Awful hard on horses."

Johnny sipped his coffee then turned to Bear. "Let's say we make it over the Devil's Horns. How do we get back down to Hallelujah Junction from there?"

"Around Crater Lake and back east along Three-Grizzly Creek."

"Damn," Johnny said, brushing his fist across his nose and regarding his friend with renewed appreciation for his past adventures. "I've never even seen that country from a distance, though my first pa, Joseba, told me about it."

"I used to come down the mountains that way when I had a cabin at Star Lake. I wanted to go the long way because I was livin' with a nasty ole Paiute squaw at the time, an' I was in no hurry to get home!" Bear slapped the table and laughed.

Johnny and Sheila laughed, as well. Sheila had a beautiful laugh, her eyes glistening. Johnny liked the way she laughed as much as the way she smiled, and he liked the way her eyes danced with humor. It was too bad she didn't have reason to smile and laugh more often.

She caught him gazing at her fawningly again, and she flushed as she flicked her eyes away, leaning toward Bear. "Let's do it," Sheila said. "Let's go that way, Mister Musgrave."

"You ready for a long, hard ride, Miss?"

"I am. I have to get that gold out of these mountains or I'm ruined. Mister Nolan said he thought he could convince his men to wait another few weeks to get paid, but no longer. They're grumbling at the Reverend's Temptation, and I don't blame them. They work hard; they deserve to be paid promptly. The only reason they're staying on is because they have few other options this late in the year, and they need a stake for the winter." Sheila narrowed a probing eye at Bear. "What about you? Remember what you said about the air being thin? I don't want you to endanger yourself."

"Ah, heck." Bear flushed under the beautiful young woman's ministrations. He lightly punched his thick, brown fist against his chest. "I got the ticker of a grizzly bear. That's why they call me Bear, don't ya know? Besides, the Devil's Horns wouldn't be such a bad place to give up the ghost. A feller could do worse than spend eternity up there." He smiled dreamily, remembering that sacrosanct place high among the rocks and clouds.

Johnny and Sheila silently conferred.

She nodded.

Johnny nodded, then, too. "All right," he said. "It's settled. The Devil's Horns it is."

CHAPTER 21

They started out early the next morning, first picking up the eight gold ingots from the mine and then heading along the outskirts of Hallelujah Junction while most of the residents except some night-hunting dogs still slumbered. One of the dogs, heading back to town after spending the wee hours hunting or sowing his wild oats in the countryside, kicked up a short but noisy ruckus.

Drawing attention to themselves as they stole out of town was the last thing the three travelers had wanted—it was the very thing they'd pulled out early to avoid, in fact—but it couldn't be helped. The dog probably wasn't used to seeing anyone up this early, around four A.M., and was more startled than angry. The indignant mongrel soon lowered his hackles and slinked off toward town and likely a bone-littered bed in the back of some barn or under a boardwalk.

On the way up into the mountains, Bear took the lead. He led one mule while Johnny led the other one at his position behind Sheila. Each mule carried four twenty-five pound ingots worth roughly fifty thousand dollars.

Since it was still good and dark when they pulled out, they rode slowly, cautiously, skirting the edge of a beaver meadow then crossing a wooden bridge spanning a creek and heading into the timber to the northwest of Hallelujah Junction. It was especially dark in the timber, but the sky lightened quickly. The lemon ball of the sun soon followed, sending steam snaking up from the light frost in the lower areas of the forest floor, and from the dew-soaked brush.

Once beyond this first stretch of forest, they climbed a low ridge and dropped down the other side. Bear picked up an ancient trace in the next valley and, with the light now angling brightly through the pines, they increased their pace, following the meandering trail along the left bank of an unnamed creek. Following one creek and one canyon after another, they made their gradual way into the high ridges surrounding Hallelujah Junction until, at midday, they rode out onto the top of a bald, windy knob and stared back in the direction from which they'd come.

All they could see of the town from this distance was a very small patch of cream and tan beneath a gauzy layer of woodsmoke two ridges to the southeast, between high, hazy, blue-green ridges.

Bear turned his head and pointed ahead of them. "That there is Sacramento Ridge."

Johnny and Sheila shaded their eyes with their hands as they stared at the long hulk of a camelback ridge, its sides spotted with old snow, humping up before them. The top was barren while the ridge's slopes were green with pines and golden with changing aspens.

Dead timber slash lay strewn along the sides of the

mountain like strewn matchsticks. There was a good
bit of gray shale, as well. From this vantage, it looked
like a wild and rugged country up there, with no way
up nor through it.

Bear knew a way, however. If anyone would know,
Bear would.

"And that," the old-timer said, lifting his arm and
pointing several inches higher with his finger, "is the
Devil's Horns Pass." He cackled a delighted laugh and
turned his gap-toothed grin on Johnny and Sheila.
"Ain't it divine?"

The Devil's Horns Pass towered over Sacramento
Ridge, from its north side. It was a bald, craggy mass
of rock with no green on it whatever. Only pale
orange rock. Two pillar-like, vaguely horn-shaped
formations, showing yellow now in the midday light,
were separated by a level area about as wide as
Johnny's thumb from this distance. The near side of
that ridge was a devil's playground of strewn boulders, some appearing as large as cabins and bigger—
the size of large ranch houses. The rocks lay in all
positions, leaning against and lying on top of each
other, each supporting another, many appearing to be
precariously positioned on the steep incline so that
a light breeze might send them tumbling into the
others until there was one big, earth-shattering land-
slide.

The sky was cobalt blue and clear. However, several creamy masses of clouds appeared to be piling
up over the two flamed-shaped formations comprising the Devil's Horns Pass. Bear must have been
sizing them up, as well, for he shook his head and
said, "Weather's already moving in over the pass.
The Devil's Horns makes its own weather, and it's

gonna have somethin' in store for us soon . . . the farther we climb."

"How bad does it get?" Sheila asked.

"Cold rain with drops the size of silver dollars. Sideways wind. Hail. Sometimes even snow this time o' year. That's not the worst. The worst is when it gets cold at night up there, and the rain and hail freezes on the rock. If that happens, we're gonna have a helluva time negotiating the back side of the pass." Bear shook his head. "I don't know. This may not have been such a good idea, after all."

Johnny turned to Bear. "Your call, old-timer. You know the country. If we're gonna turn around, we'd best do it now."

Bear flared a nostril at him. "Bear don't turn tail." He neck-reined Bronco around and booted him north, pulling the mule along behind him. "Even when he should," Johnny heard the older man add darkly.

Johnny and Sheila exchanged fateful looks.

They reined their own mounts around and followed Bear down off the knob. They had trouble getting the horses and the mules down the slope and into the next valley beyond. Slash impeded their way at every turn so that they had to follow a careful, switchbacking route, sometimes dismounting and leading their horses and the mules around the piled rubble of fallen, ancient trees littering the slope, like the bones of a thousand dead giant warriors felled on the field of battle.

Where the slash thinned, slide-rock stepped in to offer its own danger. The riders dismounted and led the horses and mules over these long stretches of talus, the men and the woman and the four-legged mounts slipping and sliding on the sharp-edged rock heaving up out of the mountainside where the shallow soil had been eroded away by wind and gravity.

When they'd mounted again after negotiating their second large patch of slide-rock and were still making their way down the ridge, Johnny turned to Sheila. Her face was pale, and her eyes were cast with wariness.

"You all right?" he asked her.

She glanced at him quickly, drew a sharp breath, shook her head. "I'm afraid." She looked at the vast country around them, the steep slope they were on. "Bear described it well, but . . . still, it's a shock. This country. It's so . . . big. I feel so *small*!"

Johnny glanced at the world around them—a rugged canvas of violent natural beauty over which they crawled like bugs on the moon of some unpopulated planet at the farthest reaches of space and time. Seeing it the way the young woman saw it, through eyes that had likely never looked upon such a remote and formidable wilderness before, Johnny felt the muscles draw taut between his shoulder blades.

"On the bright side," he said, hipping around in his saddle to see behind them, "I don't think we have to worry about being followed."

"No," Sheila said, her voice vaguely amused but still brittle and quivering slightly as her horse dropped jarringly down the steep incline. "No . . . I would think not."

When they reached the bottom of the valley, they paused to water themselves and the mounts at a wild, high-country stream winding through thick tamaracks and balsams. Johnny built a fire from dead pine branches and brewed coffee over an iron spider. Sheila sat down and leaned against her saddle, throwing her hair back.

The sunlight danced in it, shimmering. It glistened in her eyes, too. Judging by the expression on her face, her mood had improved.

She drew a deep breath, filling her lungs, her bosom expanding behind her white blouse. "Ohhhhh," she said, releasing her breath. "The air smells like wine fermented from pure pine and sunshine! I've never smelled air so fresh, tasted water so pure and cold." She looked at the stream chugging over rocks to her left and sending a fine, refreshing spray into the air around them. She turned her dreamy eyes on Johnny. "Paradise."

Johnny poured up three cups of black coffee. "It is that." He glanced around. "I grew up in this country. At least, the first several years. My first memories are of country just like this, only me an' my old man and older brother and a herd of sheep grazing in the trees around us. We'd pitch a tent, spend a day here, a day there, nights cold and clear and the stars hanging like Christmas glitter . . . always on the move . . . always through country like this right here."

He passed a cup to Sheila and Bear, who immediately blew on the black java and sipped. There was nothing like a cup of hot coffee after a half a day's hard ride in the high country. It made the cool, fresh air even more intoxicating and invigorating than it was in its pure rawness. Especially with a little gray ash floating on the inky black surface, with the steam rising and adding its own perfume to the cold stone, pure river, and forest smells of the country.

"Me, you know what I see out here?" Bear asked

when he'd slurped down a good third of the hot brew and stared through the steam rising from the cup out along the river to the east: "I see a Northern Ute village spread out along the bank there. The chief of the village was a friend of mine. In fact, I married one of his daughters." He smiled. "This chief, Who Runs Like the Water, had an old flintlock rifle he once traded Hugh Glass some pemmican and a couple horses for."

"Pshaw!" Johnny said. He glanced at Sheila. "You can believe only half of what he says and you'd best be mighty skeptical of the other half, to boot!"

"No, no—it's true! Ahh, how I remember layin' out here of a spring afternoon and watchin' the maidens take a break and go for a swim. There was one partic'lar long-haired, chocolate-eyed lass that caught my eye. The one I married the next year. Leaping Fawn was her name. Oh, she was a looker, that one. Cost me eight horses, five blankets, a bowie knife, and a whole passel of trade beads!"

He looked askance and with off-color irony at Johnny and Sheila. "An' she was worth every blanket, bead, blade, an' hide. Hah!"

He slapped his thigh, had a good laugh.

The dreamy expression returned to his bearded face as he looked at the river and said, "I can still see her the first time I seen her . . . with four or five others. She stuck out, I tell you. The purtiest maiden of the flock. I can see her right now, skinnin' out of them deerskins, tossin' 'em over a branch, throwin' her long, black hair back, an' diving into the cold, black pool yonder. Fine and long, tall an' proud, filled out in all the right places, with copper skin and . . . well, you know . . ."

He chuckled with sheepish lust, brushed a hand through his beard, and shook his head. "Oh, how she could swim!"

Johnny found himself held rapt by the story and staring at Sheila. He didn't realize that she was gazing back at him with probably much the same expression as his own until they'd held each other's gaze for a good five or ten seconds. Suddenly realizing, he lowered his eyes quickly, raised his coffee, and muttered through the steam, "Yeah, well . . . you can only believe about half of what the old mossy-horn says . . ."

He glanced up again to see Sheila's eyes still on him. She smiled at him obliquely. Hard to tell what she was thinking, but whatever it was, her eyes tugged at him.

A bugling cry vaulted over the valley. It sounded like the roar of a hoarse, angry lion.

Sheila gasped.

Johnny looked at Bear. "Is that what I think it is?"

Again, the cry sounded, shriller and more brittle this time.

Bear looked toward the ridge down which they'd come. "Sure sounds like a bear to me."

"A bear?" the woman asked, placing a hand to her chest as though to calm her heart.

The bruin again gave its shrill cry. It was longer this time, more quavering, angrier. It was followed by the rifle-like report of a snapping branch.

Johnny ran over to where he'd piled his gear near the horses and mules, which they'd unsaddled to give the beasts a better rest. He pulled his binoculars out of his saddlebags, removed the glasses from their case, then strode out away from the fire. He raised the glasses and adjusted the focus.

"I see him," Johnny said. "And he's comin' this way."

"Ah, hell," Bear said. "And here I was gettin' so relaxed I was starting to think this might be a good place to camp for the night."

"Best think again, old-timer." Johnny watched the bruin make its way down the ridge at an angle, weaving around slash, its chocolate coat dancing over its muscular frame as it made the fast descent. Occasionally the big grizzly, roughly the size of a Concord coach, stopped to lift its broad, thick snout, sniff the air, and bellow its threatening wail, which echoed menacingly off both ridges, swirling over the valley. "He apparently has this here valley staked out as his very own, and he's all-in for discouraging interlopers."

"Discouraging, eh?" Bear said, removing the coffeepot from the fire and quickly kicking dirt on the flames. "More like tearing flesh from bone, I'd say!"

"Oh . . . no . . ." Sheila said.

Bear looked at her. "Sorry. I didn't mean to frighten you unduly, Miss, but that's about the size of it, I'm afraid."

"Then I guess I am not unduly frightened, am I?" Sheila gained her feet stiffly, her face bone-white beneath her tan.

"He's got us scented," Johnny said. "He's downwind."

He lowered the glasses then hurried back over to his gear, returning the glasses to his saddlebags. He lifted his blanket and saddle, tossed them over Ghost. While Bear quickly geared up his own horse and mule, Johnny outfitted his mule then helped Sheila finish bridling and saddling her sorrel. She was having trouble with the buckles and straps, for her hands were shaking.

"I'm sorry," she said.

"Don't apologize." Johnny could more clearly hear the crunching and snapping and thrashing as the bear bore down on them, within a couple of hundred yards of the valley floor and fairly hurling itself down the ridge. "Nothing like the cry of a rogue bruin to tie my insides in knots."

He grabbed Sheila and fairly threw her up into her saddle. She gave a clipped cry of shock, glancing down at him incredulously, color touching the nubs of her cheeks.

He winked up at her. "We'll be all right. We just need to ride like hell, that's all. Uh . . ."

"Pardon your French," Sheila said. "Of course."

"Yeah," Johnny said. "Somethin' like that."

CHAPTER 22

Johnny was on Ghost now, tugging on the lead line of his mule.

He turned to Bear. "Lead off, partner." He glanced back to see the griz hurling itself toward them across the valley floor, shaking his head as though he couldn't believe anyone would have the gall to intrude on his territory.

Whipping his head back to Bear, Johnny said, "Best make haste!"

As if to validate his opinion, the bruin roared again. This time the wail was so loud, the bear drawing nearer and nearer, that it almost made Johnny's eardrums rattle.

"You can say that again!" Bear nudged Bronco into an instant gallop, heading downstream through stirrup-high grass. "Time to haul our freight, ladies and gents!"

Johnny slapped the filly's rump with his open hand, and the horse lunged off after Bear and Bronco, Johnny bringing up the rear, holding the mule's reins taut in his left hand. He and Sheila followed Bear across the stream via a shallow, gravelly ford, the horse's hooves' splashing up the water into sunlit rainbows.

Halfway across the stream, Johnny turned to see the bear still charging toward them, making less noise now since it was out of the slash and too intent on the chase to bother with further bellows. A cold stone dropped in Johnny's belly. The bear was within a hundred yards now and chewing up the ground with each lunging leap. Its long fur buffeted wildly across its hump and broad chest, rippling down its thick legs, flashing in the sunshine.

"Oh, boy," Johnny said under his breath as Ghost lunged up the stream's opposite bank. "Oh, boy . . . oh, boy . . ."

Bruins could run faster than a horse. He'd never actually seen it up close, but he'd heard spine-tingling tales of such doings, and he had a feeling he was about to see it for himself in a matter of minutes, possibly seconds . . .

"This way, folks!" Bear said, glancing back as he put Bronco up the steep slope through thick timber.

Sheila and her filly bounded after him. Johnny turned Ghost onto the old Indian path, as well, and leaned forward in the saddle as the cream dug its front hooves into the thick forest duff, climbing heavily, springing off its rear legs. Hunkered low, Johnny dared another look over his left shoulder.

His gut dropped. He felt as though Ghost had just run off a high cliff and was plunging through thin air.

The bear was lunging up the slope behind him, so close now that Johnny could smell the wild, gamy, sour smell of the savage beast, see the long, curved, white fangs as the bear glared at him through its flat, black eyes. It rushed toward him so fast, barreling up the slope, that its fur was brushed straight back against its thick, muscular frame.

Knowing that the bear would throw itself on him and Ghost in less than a minute if he didn't do something fast, Johnny dropped the mule's lead rope. The mule continued lunging up the slope, braying wildly. Johnny jerked Ghost hard left, curveting him on the trail. He flipped the reins into his teeth, released the keeper thongs from over the Twins' hammers, and jerked both sawed-off ten-gauges from their sheaths.

He clicked all four hammers back with a single brush of each thumb, aimed straight out, then slanted all four barrels down at an angle before him.

The Twins roared, orange flames roiling from a single barrel of each popper. Both wads of buckshot struck the trail, blowing fist-sized clumps of dirt and ground pine needles and moldering leaves out of the ground.

The concussive din of the rocketing blasts slowed the bruin.

Johnny triggered the second barrel of each popper, adding two more small craters to the trail before him, ten feet in front of him and ten feet in front of the bear.

The smashing blasts rolled out over the valley, chasing each other, swirling as they died.

The bear stopped suddenly, plowing up ground as it reared back on its haunches.

It came to a full stop over the four craters in the trail, looking up at Johnny through those button-black doll's eyes, glassy with malign intent. It tipped its head with a doglike curiosity, working its large black nostrils, sniffing, likely detecting the peculiar, malevolent smell of cordite.

Slowly, his heart beating a tom-tom rhythm in his chest, Johnny shoved the Twins back into their holsters. Just as slowly, not wanting to make any sudden moves and encourage the cowed bruin before him to resume its rampage, Johnny slid his hand to the Winchester jutting from the scabbard on the right side of his saddle.

He hoped he wouldn't have to use the rifle. It wasn't of a large enough caliber to do much except infuriate the bruin further. To do any real damage, he'd have to punch a .44 pill through an eye. Even from this distance, he didn't think such an inadequate round would penetrate the heavy fur and thick hide. To hit an eye, he'd have to be awfully steady, and he didn't think he could be that steady, especially not with Ghost prancing around beneath him.

The cream was well-trained and brave. But no horse could sit still with a seven-hundred-pound bruin bearing down on him. In fact, Johnny marveled that Ghost hadn't yet thrown him and fled.

Chewing his bottom lip, Johnny pulled the Winchester free of the leather and very quietly began to work the cocking lever, pumping a live cartridge into the action. He'd gotten the lever pulled straight down when he froze.

The bear pushed back up onto all fours. Regarding Johnny through those menacing, inky black eyes, the bear opened its jaws wide and loosed another ear-ringing wail. It shook its enormous head, pawed the ground once with a paw the size of two dinner plates and claws like bowie knives, then swung around and moseyed back down the ridge, swinging its stout hips and glancing behind it to give another wail of deep chagrin and frustration.

Johnny watched the retreating beast in hang-jawed shock. He was still holding the half-cocked rifle straight up and down in his hands. His racing heartbeat slowed very gradually.

"Well . . . I'll . . . be . . . damned," Bear said softly up the trail behind him.

Johnny kept his eyes on the bear that bottomed out in the valley now and angled back toward the stream, drifting ever so gradually from sight.

"Hah!" Bear laughed. "He either realized how notional them Twins is or he really didn't like how you look, Johnny. Hah!"

Johnny went ahead and finished racking the fresh cartridge into the Winchester's chamber, just in case. He off-cocked the hammer, returned the rifle to its leather, then looked up the trail behind him. Bear and Sheila sat their own mounts sideways to the trail, staring back at Johnny. They were fifty and thirty yards away, respectively. Both their horses were whickering and shivering, shifting their weight from one hoof to the other.

Bear's mule was staring down the trail past Johnny, braying up a storm. Johnny's mule stood several yards up the trail beyond it. Apparently having decided the danger had passed, the pack beast was idly grazing.

Bear was grinning and shaking his head in disbelief. He narrowed an eye at Johnny. "I thought for sure you was gonna be the guest of honor at that beast's table tonight." He glanced at Miss Bonner. "What about you, Miss—didn't you think so, too?"

Sheila didn't say anything. She just stared down the trail past Johnny as though still not quite convinced that the grizzly was gone. Or maybe she was expecting it to have a change of heart and return on a wild tear up the slope . . .

Johnny was, too.

"Come on, Ghost," he said, tugging at the cream's reins. "Let's us mosey, I think."

The horse gave him an owly, white-ringed-eye look as though to say, "Took the words right out of my mouth, pard," and started up the trail. Johnny could feel the poor beast's heart still racing under the saddle, as though it were hard-charging through deep woods.

But, then, Johnny's hadn't slowed much, either.

"What do you say, you two?" Bear called as he rode on ahead, chuckling. "We havin' fun yet?"

They gained the top of the ridge an hour later.

After a brief rest, they headed northwest along a broad, barren plateau carpeted in widely scattered patches of low-growing shrubs, bright orange and deep purple wild flowers, fine gravel, and rock. There was a lot of rock. Some of the larger escarpments still had dirty snow on their lee sides. The colorful flowers stood out in this otherwise barren landscape like fresh bouquets happened upon unexpectedly in an abandoned desert cemetery.

The only animals Johnny saw at this altitude of eleven or twelve thousand feet, were the little, dark, gopher-like pikas, which peeped amongst the rocks.

After an hour of travel along the plateau he saw several bighorn sheep grazing along a camelback escarpment to the west. A few small hawks darted here and there, giving their ratcheting cries.

It was a sun-battered, wind-scoured country of utter desolation. The only sounds were the chirps of the pikas, the occasional cries of hunting raptors, and the ceaseless, low whoosh of the wind. The wildflowers added occasional color of astonishing brightness and beauty.

Despite the hammering sunshine, the air was cool. Johnny could tell that the temperature was dropping fast ahead of a mass of forbidding-looking clouds moving in over the Devil's Horns jutting straight ahead of them now. The formations looked lens clear in this high-altitude light, and close enough to reach out and grab.

Johnny knew the high country well enough to know that the nearness was an illusion. That was even more apparent when he saw the broad canyon dropping abruptly ahead. As they approached the chasm, he saw the boulders lining the bottom and the opposite side of the ridge—all sizes and shapes of rock that had likely spilled down from the ridge, forming the Devil's Horns above and beyond it maybe millions of years ago.

"Incredible." Sheila said when they paused to stare down at the canyon and at the Devil's Horns jutting on the other side of it. She turned to Bear. "Do we continue across the canyon to the Horns? I mean, is that where you plan on camping tonight?"

The bearded old-timer shook his head. "We'll never make it. One, these mounts is weary. Two, this old mossyhorn is weary." He gave an ironic grunt then narrowed an eye at the cloud mass moving over the Devil's Horns. As he did, the clouds blotted out the sun. It was as though a pale curtain had been thrown over a lamp, turning what had been a bright high-country afternoon into an eerie, shadowy dusk.

Thunder rumbled. Johnny felt the reverberations in his bones.

In the dark clouds that now caught and tore on the two Devil's Horns, witches' fingers of lightning glittered. The wind gusted, blowing curtains of raw cold air pregnant with the fresh dampness of an imminent rain.

"Three," Bear continued, "that there's one helluva storm movin' in. We'd best hurry into the canyon and hole up amongst them rocks." He turned to Sheila. "I'm afraid, Miss Bonner, that you're about to witness just what kind of wicked weather this high country can throw at us. I hope you ain't cursin' me for takin' you this way."

"Of course not," Sheila said, sitting up straight and brave in her saddle. The wind blew her hair back behind her head. "This nipped and tucked young city-bred lady can weather a little storm, Mister Musgrave!"

"All right," Bear said, glancing darkly at Johnny then booting Bronco on down the meandering big-horn sheep trail they'd been following. "You just remember that come midnight . . ."

CHAPTER 23

If Sheila didn't remember Bear's warning, Johnny did.

Johnny had a feeling Sheila remembered, too, but she was too determinedly brave and polite to mention it. They were all awake at midnight, hunkered down under a hastily erected canvas lean-to in the relative shelter between two large, slab-sided boulders. They'd picketed the horses and mules nearby, and they could hear the mounts whickering and braying as the storm lashed at them all.

It had started with hammering rain. Soon, waves of hail curtained down from the Devil's Horns that were quickly lost above the clouds. The ice chunks hammered them relentlessly for nearly a half hour. Thunder cracked like Napoleon cannons. Lightning danced around them—above and to both sides, striking the higher escarpments and filling the air with the burnt-pepper smell of brimstone.

When the hail had stopped, the rain returned but with less vigor than before. When they'd first reached the canyon, they'd managed to tend the mounts, erect the lean-to, and arrange their camping gear just before the storm had hit. After that, there hadn't been time to do much since except hunker down and hope they weren't drowned by the rain pooling between the boulders, or blasted by the lightning barrage.

Despite the lean-to and the rainslickers they'd donned just after they'd started into the canyon, they each were soaked to the proverbial gills. Soaked and cold, for the wet wind had a wintry bite. They sat beneath the lean-to, their backs to the rock, legs drawn up, watching in silent amazement the torrential hell Mother Nature could kick up when she really put her heart and mind into it. It was like a massive assault by an army of zealots—mind-numbing in its relentlessness.

The storm gathered its lightning and thunder and its lashing rain and pulled away around two a.m. A lesser rain, intermittently a mere mist, remained over the canyon. Johnny, Bear, and Sheila all lay against their saddles and tried to sleep. Johnny could not, however. He was too soaked and cold and shivering for slumber. He knew that Bear and Sheila didn't sleep, either, because he saw them moving around him, shifting positions in a desperate attempt to find some small degree of comfort.

At one point, he saw Sheila shivering beside him. She lay on her side, knees drawn toward her chest. He slid over to her, wrapped his arm around her, and said into her ear, "I'm gonna hold you. I don't mean nothin' by it except to share body warmth. You all right with that?"

She glanced up at him in the rainy darkness. Her lips were trembling. She nodded.

He lay spooned against her from behind. Gradually,

he thought he could feel her shivering dwindle. He wasn't sure, but he thought she slept. He hadn't realized that he'd slept, too, until he felt the warmth of sunlight on his right cheek.

He lifted his arm from around her waist, and she jerked with a start.

"Easy," he said. "Just mornin's all."

She looked at him. She nodded and sat up.

"Well," he said, also sitting up and looking around at the sun-limned, dripping rocks around him. "That was about as much fun as I've had in one night in a long, long time. Spent a few nights with Joseba in such situations, high up like this, and I really hoped to never repeat them."

"I can see why." Sheila doffed her hat and ran her fingers through her wet hair then tilted her head to squint up at the sky. "The sun's on the rise, though. And I don't see a single cloud in sight."

Johnny rammed his right foot against Bear's backside, over where the old man snored on his side, head resting on his wet saddle. "Hey, old-timer. Rise an' shine. We're burnin' all this beautiful sunshine!"

Bear choked off a snore and lifted his head abruptly, looking around wildly, blinking his eyes. "What is it? What is it? *Arappy-hoe?*" He reached blindly for his rifle without finding it.

Johnny chuckled and turned to Sheila. "I'll be damned if he wasn't out like a blown lamp." He turned to Bear still looking around as though expecting a raging savage to stick him with a bowie knife. "Pull your horns in, old man. It ain't Arappy-hoe though only a few hours ago I was wishin' it was Arappy-hoe come to put me out of my misery."

He glanced at Sheila, who looked like a cold,

water-logged muskrat, albeit a beautiful one. Despite their discomfort, they both laughed.

Their good humor was short-lived.

When they got up and started moving around in their wet clothes, they realized they were unable to build a fire because there would have been no dry wood if there'd been any wood at all, even a stick, within several square miles. There were no trees up here, only rock. They each had a few bites of jerky and sips of water and then, in weary, soggy silence, saddled their horses and mules and began the rugged trek up the ridge through the boulders.

Rugged it was, too. The slope wasn't all that steep, but the boulders made almost unnegotiable obstacles in some places, forming box canyons and causing the three travelers to have to turn around several times and try yet another way only to find that that way, too, ended at a rock wall or in a passage too narrow to penetrate.

Mostly, they had to lead the horses and the mules through the narrow corridors of slanted rock, often having to climb up great mounds of strewn stone or embankments of eroded dirt and gravel in which wiry brush and the bright holiday bouquets of wildflowers grew. They didn't reach the bald crest between the two Devil's Horns until noon. When they did, their efforts were rewarded by a spectacular view of a broad, deep canyon beyond which lay a devil's maze of misty blue ridges foreshortening into seeming eternity.

The three paused to loosen the horses' and mules' saddle and pack cinches, respectively, and to give the mounts well-earned water. Bear and Sheila dropped to their knees and then to their butts, sitting up close to the lip of the canyon from which they stared out on the vast expanse of open air. The wind blew against them, blowing Sheila's hair back from her sun- and wind-burned cheeks, drying the sweat that had bathed all three of them once their clothes had dried quickly during the climb through the high, dry air.

Johnny gave Ghost a couple of handfuls of oats then walked over to stand at the canyon's edge, staring out into nothingness. The small sliver of what appeared a lone hawk or an eagle hovered far below him on a warm updraft. Gradually, the bird rose without moving its wings. Johnny saw the black body and the white head. The eagle floated up to maybe twenty feet below where Johnny stood on the ridge.

The wind rippled the feathers on the raptor's mottled blue-black body and at the edges of its wings, the short white feathers on its rounded skull. He'd never seen an eagle up this close before. It appeared nearly as large as a small horse—a horse with feathers and wings and a white head and hooked yellow beak.

The wind made a swishing sound as it played over and around the awesome creature.

The winged beast turned its head so that the man could see one savage copper eye and the hooked beak. The eye glinted in the sunlight. The beak opened. The bird gave a cry, as though in disgust to find intruders here in its high-country sanctuary, then banked away and swooped up and over Johnny and out over the canyon, its yellow talons with their sharp, black nails tucked up taut beneath it.

Johnny drew a deep breath of the fresh, cool air, and turned away from the ridge.

Bear didn't look well. The thin air was grieving him. He was breathing hard, wheezing. He looked pale and exhausted, his eyes red-rimmed. He sat there at the lip of the canyon without saying anything, heavy in his fatigue. Johnny was half the old man's age, and even he was tired. No wonder Bear looked beat. They'd had a long, wet night with brief, uneasy sleep followed by a savage climb in thin air.

After they'd eaten some jerky and drank more water, Bear heaved himself to his feet. Johnny wanted to linger here, give Bear more time to recover, but the mossyhorn would have none of it.

"We don't wanna be up here much longer," the old mountain man declared, staring warily off to the north. "Another storm'll roll in and we'll be fried to black crisps by lightnin', nothin' left but ashes washed away by the rain."

That and the memory of yesterday's storm was all the warning Johnny and Sheila needed. In a minute, they were on their feet and tightening their horses' latigo straps.

Johnny and Bear tied their mules to their horses' tails, so they could traverse the bridge in tight single-file. Leading Bronco by the clay's leathers, Bear led the way out over the narrow shelf of ground that jutted out from the backside of the left Devil's Horn. It was the only way across the canyon from here.

It wasn't much of a way at all—only a six-foot-wide natural bridge of slick, cracked, and eroded granite and limestone abutted on both sides by breath-taking and heart-twisting plunges of open, seemingly bottomless canyon. The grade on each side of the bridge had a bit of an angle to it, but not much. It was almost sheer, chipped, cracked, and crenellated rock. One slip of a foot would send a person, horse, or mule plummeting three hundred feet down that rock wall to the canyon's rocky bottom, for there was nothing on the wall to break their fall.

The distance from the left Horn to the other side was only about seventy yards, but the narrow width of the trail made it look longer.

Johnny saw Sheila staring at it, holding her filly's reins in her right hand.

"You all right?" he asked her.

She glanced over her shoulder at him. "Looks pretty narrow."

"It is. But you can make it. Just take it slow and keep an even hand on the filly's reins. She'll be all right. She made it this far. You both have."

Sheila regarded the bridge that Bear and Bronco and the mule appeared to be crossing with ease, the horse and mule switching their tails and flicking their ears but keeping to a straight line behind the man leading them.

"Did I mention I'm afraid of heights?" Sheila asked Johnny with a tremor in her voice that was half laugh and half groan.

"You're gonna be all right," Johnny said. "If you want, I'll tie the filly to my horse and lead both."

"No, no. I can do it. I'll pull my own weight." Sheila stepped out onto the narrow strip of rock dividing the canyon before them. "Come on, girl," she said, tugging on the filly's reins.

She led the horse onto the bridge. Johnny watched her closely. She walked slowly, stiffly, taking one step at a time, keeping her head forward, appearing not to look to either side at the stomach-churning sweep of canyon to both sides of her.

Johnny waited, watching, hoping neither she nor the horse lost her nerve.

Twenty feet out from Johnny's side of the chasm, the filly kicked a rock, sent it bouncing off down the steep ridge to their right, the thuds dwindling quickly. Sheila gasped, stopped. The filly stopped, as well, and, apparently sensing its leader's nervousness, shook its head and edgily shifted its weight.

It whickered.

"Keep going," Johnny called. "Nice an' slow. It was just a rock. Nothin' to worry about."

The woman continued leading the filly. They seemed fine now, moving slowly but smoothly.

Johnny glanced at Ghost. "No time to get notional now, boy." He glanced at the mule. The mule didn't worry him. Mules were notoriously sure-footed. While they sometimes did only what they wanted to do, the latter traits were exaggerated. Treated well, mules were often more dependable and level-headed than horses. The mule would be fine.

Johnny began leading both mounts out onto the bridge. Ghost stepped into line behind him, pulling back on the reins a little at first, when the horse saw the sweep of open air to both sides. Johnny kept a firm pressure on the reins, which he held up close to the bit. The horse relinquished control to its leader and stepped fluidly forward. It walked straight ahead along the bridge, only a couple of feet behind Johnny.

Johnny glanced off to both sides. So much emptiness pressing close to him made him briefly dizzy until he returned his eyes to the trail. That's where he kept them, focusing on the chipped and fractured granite path. Behind him, Ghost and the mule clomped along steadily, Ghost whickering softly, plainly nervous but following his leader without hesitation.

A cool wind gusted from the canyon off the trail's right side. It blew Sheila's filly's mane and tail sideways, to the left. It blew Sheila's hair that way, as well. It was a stiff wind, and Johnny had to lean into it a bit to keep his balance. Ahead of him, the filly stopped, shifting its weight dangerously. It lifted its head and gave a shrill whinny. The horse bobbed its head and stomped a rear hoof as though in protest of the precarious circumstance in which it had found itself— walking a tightrope between plummeting ridge walls.

Johnny drew a breath, held it. His blood quickened.

Sheila turned to the horse, spoke to it quietly. Johnny could hear the edge of fear in her voice. She pulled gently but firmly on the reins up close to the bit. The horse wasn't having it. The filly held its ground.

Johnny stopped. Inwardly, he cursed.

If the young horse reared just once and tried to turn, Sheila would lose it and might even get swept off the trail herself. He wanted to yell out to the woman, warn her to step back away from the horse, but that might only make it even more skittish and cause a sudden fatal move. The filly might even make the turn and gallop back in Johnny's direction, bulling him, Ghost, and the pack mule off the ledge.

His heart raced. Cold sweat trickled along his spine.

He stared over the horse and Sheila standing in front of it, talking to it gently, soothingly. Johnny admired her coolness. He doubted that he'd be nearly as cool in that situation, with the dark mouth of God yawning beneath him. Sheila spoke with her mouth up close to the filly's snout, smiling, patting one cheek, caressing with her fingers.

She glanced at Johnny from over the horse's left wither, and he could see the worry in her eyes, but there was a determination, an optimism there, too. With that brief look, she was reassuring him that she could handle it.

And she did, too.

A moment later, she stepped back and tugged gently but firmly again on the filly's reins. The filly followed, holding its head and tail down, compliant.

When Sheila and the filly and Johnny and his own horse and mule joined Bear on the other side of the natural bridge, Sheila dropped to her knees in relief.

"If I was a drinking man," Johnny said, smiling at her. "I'd buy you a drink or two or three."

"Here," Bear said. "Let me do it!"

The burly old-timer had pulled his bottle out of his saddlebags and had apparently taken a few pulls. Glassy-eyed, he extended the bottle to Sheila, where she knelt in front of the filly, regaining her wits.

She glanced sheepishly at Johnny.

He smiled again as he poured water into his hat for Ghost and the mule. "Go ahead," he said, chuckling with his own relief at having that major obstacle behind them. "You deserve it."

She smiled and accepted the bottle from Bear.

Hell of a woman, Johnny thought. If he ever settled down again, he'd like it to be with a woman like that. Only, he didn't deserve such happiness, so there was no point in thinking about it.

CHAPTER 24

They made camp a couple of hours later as the sun angled behind the toothy western ridges.

Bear chose the place well. They were a good thousand feet below the Devil's Horns Pass now, and back in thick timber and high green grass. It was wild country but not as savagely wild as above. It was also deserted. No one else was here, and it didn't look like anyone else had been here for a long time. Johnny scouted the place carefully. There were no fresh man or horse tracks, no campfire leavings. Only plenty of animal sign though no grizzly sign, he was relieved to observe.

Bivouacking, they first stretched a picket line for the horses and mules then built a cookfire at the edge of a fir forest already darkening and cooling now as the light waned. A lake sat at the bottom of the bowl-like, jade-green valley they were in, surrounded by gentle slopes thickly clad in the dark greens of spruces and firs and the sporadic yellows of the autumn-leaved, white-trunked aspens.

At this time of the day, light leaving the clearing, the water appeared a roughly heart-shaped pool of black ink.

When Johnny had first ridden into the clearing, three moose had spooked from the lake's far shore. The heavy, lumbering beasts with their paddle-like horns scurried off into the forest, making snapping and crackling sounds as they'd climbed the ridge. A lone coyote began yammering mournfully from a stony promontory behind the camp, where the low fire, built of readily available and well-seasoned deadfall, offered a long-yearned-for warmth at last.

Still, after the long, hard, perilous ride, the lake beckoned, cool and inviting.

"If you'll excuse me, gentlemen," Sheila said, when they'd settled in around the snapping flames, pleasantly exhausted but rimed with dried sweat and trail grime. She grabbed a towel and a carpetbag from amongst her piled gear. "This lady needs a bath."

She started off down the slope through the high grass toward the lake.

"Yeah, well, this fella needs a nap." Bear lay back against his saddle, rested his arm across his forehead, and was instantly sawing logs.

Sheila stopped near a fir tree and glanced back at where Johnny knelt by the fire. She didn't say anything for a moment, but gazed at him thoughtfully. Then, timidly, she said, "You can join me if you want." She shrugged and added quickly, "I mean, it's a big lake"

She turned and continued down the gentle slope toward the water.

Johnny's blood quickened as he watched her slender shape recede down the slope in the failing light.

He wasn't sure what to make of the offer. He decided not to think about it. There was no point in torturing himself. He couldn't have her for a whole list of reasons he'd already gone over. She knew that, too. She was toying with him. She meant no harm by it, only a pleasant distraction from all that they'd been through. A harmless, half-hearted flirtation.

A few years ago, he'd have jumped at the offer. But, then, a few years ago he'd have jumped on a lot of things . . .

No, he'd stay right here and start supper before she could. He didn't want to leave the cooking to her again. She meant well enough, but her place was in the bank.

He gave an amused snort at the thought and then started working on the small mule deer doe he'd shot an hour earlier, as they'd started into the timber. He'd field-dressed the deer, tied it up, and slung it over the mule's back. Now it lay near the fire, ready for butchering.

He picked up his bowie knife and started carving out a few tender steaks.

He stopped, rested an elbow on a knee, and brushed his fist across his nose. He couldn't get the intoxicating image of the young woman in the lake out of his head. Finally, after cutting out three nice-sized, inch-thick, blood-red steaks, he lay them in a pan, covered the pan with a swatch of leather, and cleaned his knife. He returned the knife to its sheath and turned to stare off between two firs toward the lake, which was even darker now with the sun nearly gone.

She shouldn't be alone out there, he told himself. *Might be someone on the lurk. Hell, this is grizzly country . . .*

He glanced over to where Bear was sawing away, his fat belly rising and falling slowly, luxuriant, the beard and mustache around his mouth blowing upward with each heavy, raking exhalation. Johnny chuckled at himself. What a ribbing the old man would give him if he knew how easily Johnny had been convinced to join Sheila at the lake.

Still, Johnny rose from his knees, swept his dark hair back over his head, and donned his hat. He grabbed an old blanket/towel from his saddlebags, slung it over his shoulder. He walked down the slope, angling between the firs. He could hear Sheila splashing in the lake but he couldn't see her. A high, rocky bank, peppered with a few stunted ponderosa pines, rimmed the lake, partly concealing it.

He stepped up onto a granite ledge. Her clothes were piled on a low rock—riding dress as well as underwear and boots. His heart gave a shudder. He looked out over the lake rolling away below him, dark and cool and ruffled by ripples. The water was silvery out where Sheila swam, thrashing like a young otter. The wavelets rolled away from her body, which was a creamy smudge beneath the surface.

She had her back to him at that moment, but she must have heard him or sensed his presence. She swept her wet hair back and turned to him, treading water. She stared across the water at him but did not say anything.

"Thought I'd better come down here," he called softly across the water. He was almost startled by how well his voice carried and echoed back to him off the surrounding, fast-darkening forest sloping up toward stony ridge crests. He patted the shotguns on his legs. "Ain't safe alone."

"I see you brought a towel," she said with a vague impishness in her voice.

Johnny didn't respond to that.

She gave a playful splash. He saw the white line of her teeth as she smiled devilishly. She leaned back in the water, kicked, and swam away from him, calling over her shoulder, "The water's wonderful!"

Johnny drew a deep breath.

Don't do it. Just sit up here and keep watch like you intended.

But, then, that wasn't really what he'd intended. *You brought the towel. Besides, now that you've come this far, you're not just gonna sit up here and "keep watch."*

He glanced again at the young woman's clothes piled on the rock. Again, his blood warmed.

Heart thudding, he swept his hat from his head in defeat. He tossed down his rifle. He removed the Twins from around his waist, and leaned the holstered shotguns against the base of a pine jutting from a crack in the stony granite slab. Facing the woman swimming around in the lake maybe thirty yards out from the slab, pretending to ignore him, he undressed quickly. Occasionally, he caught her glancing at him sidelong, out of the corner of one eye.

Still, she splashed and swam as though she were only enjoying the water.

He peeled off his long handles and socks, tossed them down, and stood up at the edge of the slab, leaning out over the water. She turned her head slightly toward him, stopped, started to turn away, then turned fully around to face him.

Their eyes met and held.

Her eyes flicked down his long, broad-shouldered body, and they widened. She shook her head slowly. "No," she said. "You stay there."

Johnny grinned then swung his arms up over his head and sprang off the slab, lowering his head and turning his body into a downward-arcing missile. He cleaved the water smoothly and was instantly enveloped by the sharp chill. His fingers grazed the sandy bottom and then he lifted his head and shoulders and swam up through the dark, black water, his head breaking the surface only about twenty feet away from her.

She narrowed a warning eye at him. "Stay away."

Grinning, Johnny moved slowly toward her. She watched him, her wariness growing. "Mister Greenway," she said. "Stay . . . away . . ."

Johnny swam toward her. She backed away from him.

"Mister Greenway, I am your employer. You are my *employee.*"

Johnny swam toward her slowly, within ten feet and closing, his grin in place.

"I'll scream for Bear," she said, backing away slowly, waving her hands in the water, keeping her admonishing eyes on Johnny.

"Bear's in hibernation."

"I'm warning you, Mister Greenway. I have a pistol." She glanced toward the rock on which she'd left her clothes in a neat pile.

Johnny slowed as he closed in on her, keeping his lusty gaze on her. "You'll never make it."

She kicked at him with one of her legs. He grabbed her foot.

She gasped.

Holding her foot in his left hand, he raised it up out of the water and lowered his head to it. He pressed his lips to the top of it, the wet, cool skin silky smooth against his mouth, and released it.

Her lips parted as she drew a deep breath. She hesitated, frowning, drew another heavy breath. "Don't do that again."

"Are you sure you don't want me to?"

"No." She frowned, flushing. "I mean—no, don't do it again."

He swam to within a few inches of her. He stopped when his lips were six inches from hers, when he could feel her warm breath on his own lips. She stared at him, her shoulders rising and falling sharply, heavily, as she breathed. She was no longer swimming backward but holding still, treading water.

Johnny let the grin fade from his lips. He stared into her eyes. She stared back at him.

A raging male hunger was a wild animal inside him. He drew back on its chain.

For several seconds they held there in the lake, treading water, staring into each other's eyes.

"Tell me no, Miss Bonner," Johnny said, his voice pitched with vague pleading. He hardened his voice, adding a tone of urgent warning. "Tell me no . . . Miss Bonner."

She opened her mouth, drew a long, deep breath.

She leaped toward him, wrapped her arms around his neck, and pressed her lips to his, kissing him hungrily. She clung to him desperately as they mashed each other's mouths together. Johnny wrapped his arms around her shoulders and waist, drawing her close against him, his need fairly exploding inside him.

He tipped her head slightly back and to one side,

kissing her with a hot, ungovernable passion. They barely stayed afloat, kicking their legs in unison. Her lips were warm and soft. They tasted like cherries.

With an iron will, he reached an arm up behind him and peeled one of her hands away from his neck.

She groaned, resisted his effort, dug her fingers deeper into his neck.

Again, Johnny pried her hand away. Then the other one. He pushed her arms down until she had to start treading water again on her own.

She frowned at him, desperation glinting in her eyes.

He started backing away from her.

"Johnny," she said softly, sadly. "You don't have to give up everything."

He continued backing away from her. Aside from burying his family, it was the hardest thing he'd ever done.

He smiled. "I came down here to keep watch—remember?"

She gazed at him curiously, crestfallen. He swung around and swam back to the granite slab.

He climbed onto the slab, toweled off, and dressed. He sat down against the base of the pine, stretched his legs out before him, crossing his ankles, and built a smoke.

She swam for a while longer then swam over to the granite slab. "I'm coming up," she said from the water at the base of the high slab, where he couldn't see her. "Close your eyes."

"They're closed."

He closed his eyes and heard her labored breath as she climbed the slab. He heard the wet sounds of her movement, the water streaming off her body onto the granite. He kept his eyes closed, smoking the quirley, as she padded past him, toweled off, and dressed.

"All right," she said. "You can open them, Mister Greenway."

He opened his eyes and smiled knowingly up at her. So they were back to the formalities again. That was all right with him. He preferred it to the other.

She had her back to him but she turned her head to gaze at him over her left shoulder. As she did, she took up the wet tail of her hair in both hands in front of her, and squeezed the water out of it. She seemed to be trying to read him, studying him closely. He gazed blandly back at her, smoking.

She sat on a rock and pulled her socks onto her feet, then her boots. Rising, she slung her now-wet towel over her shoulder and gazed down at him. "I don't know about you, but I could eat a horse."

"A whole horse?" Johnny asked with feigned incredulity.

"A whole horse."

"Pshaw!"

"Come on—I'll cook that beautiful doe you shot," she said, walking across the slab, heading back in the direction of their camp.

Ah, hell, Johnny thought. He should have stayed in camp and cooked the meat, saving him and Bear from another charred meal.

"I'll cook tonight," he said, stubbing out his cigarette then climbing to his feet.

"Nonsense."

"No, really," Johnny pleaded, walking up behind

her now as they left the slab and walked through the grass toward the camp at the edge of the forest a hundred yards beyond.

She was several feet ahead of him. She swung around, smiling at him again, this time playfully. "I'll race you," she said. "First one to camp gets to cook!"

Laughing, she swung around and ran through the grass, holding her skirts above her ankles, her wet hair swaying across her slender back.

Johnny caught up to her, grabbed her arm, and pulled her back behind him.

"Oh, no you don't!" She ran up and tripped him.

Laughing, Johnny fell. He lashed out with his arm, grabbed her ankle, tripping her.

She fell with a grunt, rolling, laughing. He gained his feet, running up the slope toward the fire glowing orange now as full darkness descended.

"That's cheating!" she cried.

Johnny slowed and let her catch up to him. Still playing like children on a playground, they tripped into the camp side by side, grabbing at each other's arms, breathless and laughing.

"Oh, no!" Sheila cried, stopping suddenly at the edge of the firelight.

"Hungry, kids?" Grinning, Bear held up the sizzling platter of freshly cooked venison.

After the meal, Johnny took the first night watch.

They were likely alone out here, this far from civilization and known trails, but one hundred thousand dollars in gold was tucked down in the canvas panniers stacked where they could keep a close watch over them. They weren't taking any chances.

Bear spelled him at two.

Each eyelid weighing as much as a blacksmith's anvil, Johnny rolled up in his soogan on the other side of the now-dead fire from where Sheila slept soundly in her own blankets.

The first blush of dawn pearled the eastern sky when he woke to a woman's terrified screams.

"Sheila!"

Johnny leaped to his feet, quickly stomped into his boots, grabbed the Twins, and ran off into the trees.

Chapter 25

"Sheila!"

A Twin in each hand, Johnny ran hard, leaping deadfalls dimly outlined by the thin brush of creamy dawn light through the dark pillars of the trees to his left.

He leaped another deadfall, stopped, and shouted again, *"Sheila!"*

Again, came the agonized cry. From off to his right.

He swung that way and resumed running. It was too dark to see all the obstacles before him. Low branches and shrubs clawed at him; blowdowns and deadfall crackled beneath his boots, sometimes tripping him and almost sending him to the ground.

He ran around a low pile of rock and brush and stopped, listening.

She screamed again . . . again . . . again, as though someone were beating her savagely.

"Johnny!" she cried.

Johnny looked around wildly. He couldn't pinpoint the origin of the screams. She seemed to be moving around, maybe being dragged away from the camp. She must have gotten up to tend nature and someone had grabbed her . . .

"*Johnny!*" Sheila screamed again.

Staring through the trees, he thought the plea had come from ahead and on his left. He bolted forward, running, leaping more blowdowns. He crossed a clearing and came to the deep cut of what was probably an old mine running along the forested slope on his right.

"Johnny!"

That time the scream came from the direction of the lake.

Johnny turned that way and, breathless and sweating now, he ran along a tailing pile abutting the gash of the mine in the ground to his right. Again, the scream rose. Much closer this time.

She was close. Very close.

A figure stepped out from behind a tree on the mine's opposite side and ahead of Johnny about thirty yards. Johnny stopped and raised the Twins, his thumb caressing the hammers.

He studied the figure. It was a woman, but not Sheila. This woman was tall and broad-hipped, bullet-shaped, vaguely Indian-looking. Long, grizzled, black and gray hair hung down to her shoulders. She wore a buckskin jacket decorated with Indian beads, and a long, black wool skirt over black leather boots.

She wore two pistols and a sheathed bowie knife on her broad hips. In her right hand she held a Winchester rifle. Though the swells of her body identified her as female, she appeared as much man as woman.

Her Indian-dark face was shaded by her black derby hat, though Johnny detected a feral cast to her eyes. Johnny saw the off-white line of the woman's teeth when she opened her mouth, laughing, and tipped her head back. The laughter died on her lips. Her face scrunched up, and she launched an ear-assaulting scream at the forest canopy above her.

It was the same scream Johnny had heard before. The same scream that had awakened him so abruptly. Befuddlement washed over him, carving deep lines of chagrin across his forehead.

The woman dropped her chin and stared at Johnny from across the narrow gash of the mine. *"Johnny!"* she cried, pitching her voice with feigned agony. "Oh, Johnny—please help me! Please, help me, Johnny! Oh, Johnny—they have me, Johnny! They have me an' the gold, Johnny!"

The woman's dark eyes danced with mockery. She threw her head back, laughing, pointing a mocking finger at him.

A hot wave of terror rolled through Johnny.

He'd been hornswoggled into leaving the camp.

The thought had no sooner rushed through his brain than a man said with quiet menace behind him, "Hello, Johnny. I been wantin' to make your acquaintance for a long time."

Johnny whipped around. Two men stood behind him, side by side and ten feet away. They'd stepped out from behind two fir trees, which they'd hidden behind as Johnny had passed, distracted by the phony pleas for help.

The man on the left was tall and black-bearded, wearing a battered tan hat, and cartridge bandoliers crisscrossed on his chest over a brown leather brush jacket. The man on the right had a broad, devil's grinning face with high, tapering cheeks obscured beneath a thick, sandy beard, and wicked slits for eyes.

Coarse, sandy blond hair poked out from beneath the battered Stetson stuffed down on his head.

Johnny recognized him, but he didn't have time to attach a name to the face before the man's grin broadened, showing a chipped eyetooth. Both men jerked rifles to their shoulders.

Johnny tripped a trigger of the Twin in his right hand. The shotgun thundered, and the black-bearded man was punched off his feet and backward as though engulfed by a great wind.

A quarter second later, the shorter, slit-eyed man triggered his Colt's revolving rifle, and Johnny felt a hard pinch in his left side. He grunted as he twisted around and fell backward, hitting the ground on his back. Still holding the ten-gauge in his right hand, he tried to raise it but stopped when he saw the sandy-haired gent striding toward him, cocking the Colt rifle and again aiming from his shoulder, drawing a bead on Johnny's head.

Johnny didn't have time to squeeze off another shot.

Instinctively, he rolled to his left and over the lip of the mine. He fell through a fringe of brush and then down through open air for a second or two before striking the steep side of the mine's open shaft and rolling over rocks, gravel, brush, and roots. He struck on the bottom of the mine with another, louder grunt, and the wind was punched from his lungs, pain biting him all over his body, like a pack of hungry wolves tearing at him.

Consciousness blinked out on him, and everything went black. Misery continued to rack him, his head throbbing. He could vaguely hear the crackle of a rifle and the shrill spangs of bullets ricocheting around him.

When he opened his eyes, bright sunlight stabbed at his eyeballs, impaling each with the pain of poison arrows. He groaned and closed his eyes again, resting his head back against the ground. For nearly a minute, all was foggy. He knew something bad had happened, but he wasn't quite sure what. He wasn't even sure where he was or what he was doing there.

Quickly, as he lay sucking air in and out of his lungs and parrying the blows of what felt like a large hammer against his brain plate, he remembered it all from the beginning—from waking up to the screams to the face of the man who'd called him by name and grinned at him through a thick, sandy beard on his devil's face a second before he'd fired that rifle into Johnny's side.

Harry Seville.

Johnny saw him clearly now as he lay with his eyes closed, enduring the starbursts of light exploding just behind his squeezed-shut lids and a tearing pain raked him on his left side, a few inches above his cartridge belt, where he'd taken the bullet. He saw the little slanted slits of green eyes, the tangled beard, the sandy blond hair poking out from beneath the battered Stetson.

Harry Seville.

Seville's brother, Sonny, had been one of the men who'd busted into Johnny's house. He'd been the man with the shotgun who'd blown young David into eternity before he and several others had stormed Johnny and taken turns beating him while they'd savaged Lisa in the kitchen, then cut her throat.

Sonny Seville. Dead now.

Blown into eternity near Elko by Johnny's Twins, though Sonny would be far removed from the eternity in which David now dwelled. If anything made any sense at all, Sonny Seville was swimming the eternally burning butane rivers beyond the devil's smoking gates, screaming his lungs out with the other burning sinners who'd killed children and raped women on this side of the sod.

Harry Seville had been in prison when Shotgun Johnny had killed his brother and the other murdering dogs in his party. Seville was out now, obviously. And he was one of those robbing the gold. One of the leaders, no doubt.

It figured. The gold robbers were a slippery, savage bunch, and there were few robbers or killers more slippery or more savage than Harry Seville, who'd been known to ride with a big Sioux half-breed every bit as savage as Seville—Louis Raised-By-Wolves, who, it was said, had come by his name honestly. Raised-By-Wolves had a mannish half-sister who went by the name Babe.

Just Babe.

Johnny had never seen her, only heard that she and Louis rode together, along with Harry Seville, and that she was sometimes Seville's woman, sometimes not. He'd also heard that she was as deadly, possibly deadlier, than both Seville and Raised-By-Wolves put together.

That was saying something.

Seville had been raised in this country. Someone must have gotten word to him that Johnny was guarding the bullion now, and being guided by Bear Musgrave. Seville likely knew Bear, likely knew that Bear knew these mountains well enough to be cagey enough to choose a different route down than the usual one, to avoid the robbers.

Johnny's battered, burning brain turned to Bear and Sheila.

Oh, God. His heart shuddered. He had to get back to camp.

He knew the gold would be gone. But what about the burly old-timer and the young woman? What condition would he find them in? Part of him—a large part of him—didn't want to know.

But he had to find out.

He choked back the throbbing in his skull and sat up.

"Oh!" He grabbed his head in both hands. The tumble down the steep ridge had knocked him unconscious and pushed up a couple of tender goose eggs. He wondered how long he'd been out. Judging by the light, maybe a couple of hours. The sun was well above the horizon.

He lowered his left hand to his side, swept it across a patch of blood staining his long-handle top. He poked his finger through the long, bloody tear in the wash-worn cotton fabric. He knew a moment's relief when he realized the bullet had merely nipped his side, carving a quarter-inch trough. It burned like hell, but it wouldn't kill him. He'd tend it later. At the moment, he had bigger fish to fry . . .

He holstered the ten-gauge he'd dropped during his tumble down the ridge, and heaved himself to his feet, grinding his molars against the pain but relieved to establish that, while he'd suffered several bad bruises and a graze, no bones seemed broken. When he'd rolled off the ridge, he'd fallen onto the sloping mine floor and rolled back toward the wall, partially protected by a bulging belly of overhanging rock. That was likely what had kept him from being pinked by one of the bullets he remembered hearing Harry Seville firing from up top.

He saw that one bullet had nipped the outside of his right boot, making a slight tear in the leather. The others must have ricocheted off the chipped rock and gravel around him, somehow missing him. Seville must have decided Johnny was dead. That's why he hadn't bothered to come down here to make certain-sure.

There was probably another reason Seville hadn't come down here, Johnny saw now as he lifted his gaze to the ridge down which he'd plunged. The wall was a good fifty feet high, and nearly sheer in places. Seville hadn't come down here because he'd seen that it would have been a difficult descent. Deciding that Johnny was dead had been the convenient decision. It had been a safe bet, too, that at least one of the several bullets Seville had fired into the mine would have hit its mark. The open shaft was only about twenty feet wide, making the mine a nasty arena for ricocheting bullets.

Johnny had been damned lucky none had hit him.

Now if he could just find a way out of the knifelike slash in the ground . . .

He looked around, frustration rising to mingle with his dread over the fates of Bear and Sheila. He strode up and down the pit, but there appeared no easy way out of the mine. His desperation growing, he quickly chose a route up the steep ridge, and began climbing.

A half hour later, he thrust the bloody point of his scraped chin up over the lip of the mine. He thrust his hands, also raw and bloody from climbing by his fingertips—and from sliding down the long rough wall when he'd made missteps—over the lip.

With a weary grunt, he hoisted himself up onto level ground carpeted in pine cones, needles, and dead leaves, and rolled away from the gash. He lay belly-up, breathing hard, cursing, groaning at the sundry raw aches and pains grieving nearly every inch of his body. Suppressing them, he heaved himself to his feet and looked around. He quickly gained his bearings and hurried off in the direction he decided the camp was.

He ran like a drunkard, crouched low, breathing hoarsely, tripping over deadfalls and other obstacles, falling, picking himself up, staggering forward, groaning. Dread was a heavy stone in the pit of his stomach.

"Bear?" he called as he ran, too exhausted to raise his voice much above a choked cry. "Sheila . . . ?"

It took him what seemed a long time to locate the camp. Twice, he realized he was heading in the wrong course, and, taking his bearings on the lake he glimpsed through the trees to the southeast, he adjusted his route and continued slogging, weaving around trees and shrubs and scattered rocks, tripping over fallen branches and uprooted trees.

He dropped again to his knees, having slipped on a patch of soggy leaves and pine needles, and started heaving himself back to his feet. He froze and, still on his knees, stared straight ahead.

His mouth went dry. A spider of horror climbed his spine.

A large object was suspended in the air over the camp, near the cold gray ashes of last night's

campfire and the strewn tack. The figure was long
and broad and silhouetted against the sunlight angling into the camp from the east.

"Ah, no . . ." Johnny's heart raced. "No . . . no . . .
no . . ."

He heaved himself to his feet, moved slowly forward. His heart swelled, twisting, as he moved into
the camp to stand near where Bear's worn, mule-
eared boots hung five feet above the ground.

"Dirty dogs," Johnny raked out as he stared up at
his dead friend. "Ah, you lousy, dirty dogs . . ."

Johnny sobbed, tears making a blurry window of
his vision.

Bear hung as limply as a side of beef, the heavy
knot of the noose snugged up against the back of his
neck, pushing his head forward and down. His tongue
poked out a corner of his mouth. His lids sagged
over his eyes, which stared down, opaque with death,
at Johnny. A cool morning breeze stirred, moving his
big body slightly to one side and then the other, the
rope creaking faintly.

They'd hanged him. But first they'd plunged his
own bowie knife into his belly.

"Dirty dogs," Johnny said again, a vast swell of
emotion mixing with the agony in his head. He
sobbed. Tears dribbled down his cheeks. "Dirty
damn . . . dirty damn dogs . . . !"

Sheila . . .

Gritting his teeth, Johnny stepped back, drew his
arm across his face, swabbing up the tears.

He looked around for the young woman, expecting to find that she'd been similarly treated. He
didn't see her. His and Bear's tack and bedrolls still

lay strewn around the cold fire ring, but the horses and mules were gone.

Only Johnny and Bear remained, Bear silent in death, turning slowly back and forth in the breeze.

But what of Sheila?

Johnny called for her. No answer. He scoured the area around the camp. No sign.

Her gear was gone. They must have taken her.

Again, Johnny raised his eyes to his dead friend. He tightened his jaws as he imagined the laughter of Bear's killers, mocking Bear as they'd killed him, mocking Johnny, doing God-only-knew-what to Sheila.

Slow hoof thuds rose behind him.

Johnny spun, clawing the Twins from their holsters. In his weariness and agony, he stumbled backward against Bear's legs, and nearly fell. He stared out ahead of him.

He lowered the shotguns.

Ghost walked toward him through the forest, ears twitching, switching his tail as though in relief at finding his rider alive. Johnny was even more relieved to see the horse than Ghost was to see him. Without a mount, he'd have had a snowball's chance in hell of running down Seville and Raised-By-Wolves.

Bear's horse, Bronco, came plodding up behind Ghost, sniffing the air and whickering darkly as though in sad acknowledgment of his rider's grisly fate.

Johnny turned to gaze up again at his old friend, his upper lip quivering with grief, fury, and determination. "I'll get 'em. Don't you worry, old friend. I'll get 'em. Seville's gonna regret not climbing down into that mine to make sure I was wolf bait!"

CHAPTER 26

Sheila rode slumped in her saddle, her hands tied before her.

She winced against the rope drawn taut around her wrists and then around the horn. After a day and a half of riding, the ropes had sawed through several layers of skin, causing them to bleed. She grimaced against the burn.

She looked at the broad back of the thickset woman riding ahead of her, leading the filly by the horse's bridle ribbons. "I need you to loosen these ropes."

Behind her, a couple of the men in the pack snickered.

Sheila looked at the woman riding ahead of her on a strawberry roan. The woman, who was called Babe, was ignoring her. "Say, there," Sheila said, raising her voice, "I need you to loosen these ropes."

Babe glanced casually over her shoulder. She looked vaguely Mexican, but Sheila understood from bits and pieces of the killers' conversation that she was part Indian and the sister of one of the two men riding out front of her and the others—a big Indian with a granite-like face and flat, savage eyes. Babe had a mannish manner to go with the men's clothes she wore—aside from her black wool skirt—including two pistols and a knife jutting from a sheath on her wide, black belt that strained around her thick middle.

"Say what?" the woman said, testily.

"I need you to loosen these ropes," Sheila told her, unable to keep the impatience from her own voice. "I'm bleeding again."

"We'll stop here," said the pack's leader, an uncouth brigand named Seville.

Babe drew her roan to a halt, stopping Sheila's filly, as well. They'd drawn up near a stream murmuring and flashing through a forest off the trail's left side. The woman kept her eyes on Sheila. Babe's eyes were as flat and savage as her brother's, whom everyone called either Louis or "Wolves," short for his full surname, which was, not unpredictably, Raised-By-Wolves. He certainly seemed like a man whom Sheila could see having been raised by a pack of savage wolves yet no more savage than the human wolves he now found himself co-leader of . . .

Early in the morning of the previous day, they'd killed Bear and Johnny. Sheila didn't know how they'd killed Johnny. She knew only that they'd tricked him into running off in the shadowy dawn, believing he'd been answering Sheila's own pleas for help. It had still been dark enough, and Johnny had been distracted enough that he hadn't noticed that Sheila had been lying not seven feet away from him, sound asleep in her bedroll, until Babe's phony cries had awakened Sheila, too.

She'd called out to Johnny but, hoarse from sleep,

she hadn't raised her voice loudly enough for him to hear her. And then he was gone.

And then Bear, descended upon by the cutthroats, had bellowed from where he'd apparently been keeping watch in the woods. There'd been the horrible sounds of a fight, and then, while several men converged on Sheila, holding her down, Bear had been dragged into camp, beaten and bloody.

One of the savages had stabbed the poor man with his own bowie knife. He'd still been dying when they'd hanged him in front of Sheila, forcing her to watch the poor, groaning, sobbing man die the most horrific death she could imagine, with his own knife in his guts.

Rage and sorrow mixed in Sheila as she remembered the grisly, horrific scene.

These men and this woman, Babe, weren't even people. But they weren't animals, either. No animal—not even the grizzly that had charged her, Johnny, and Bear yesterday—would have acted so savage. They were lower than the lowest person and the lowest animal on earth. They were going to kill her. She'd already decided that. That had alleviated her fear somewhat—the fear of the unknown, at least. She'd had ample time over these past thirty-some odd hours to have come to terms with the notion, to be resigned to death.

Now what she mostly felt was helpless frustration and rage.

"What are you caterwauling about, my queen?" Babe asked Sheila with a sneer.

"I said I need you to loosen these ropes," Sheila said bitterly. "They're cutting into my wrists."

Several of the men around Sheila snickered again

as Babe rode back to Sheila and pulled her big knife from its sheath. Babe stared coldly at Sheila then reached over and sawed carelessly through the ropes binding her wrists to the horn.

The knife nipped the bottommost wrist. "Ouch!" Sheila groused as she pulled her wrists free of the horn.

"Feel better, my queen?" Babe asked, her voice shrill.

"No, it doesn't!"

"How 'bout this, then?"

Babe smacked Sheila's cheek with the back of the fist holding the bowie knife. Sheila screamed as the blow threw her from her saddle. She struck the ground beside the filly, the wind punched out of her lungs. She lay writhing, trying to suck a breath, her cheek burning where Babe had struck her, her vision blurred from her hard meeting with the ground.

She rolled onto her side, clutching her belly and gasping. Babe dropped to a knee beside her.

The thickset woman grabbed Sheila's chin in her right hand and jerked her head up. She curled her thick upper lip and narrowed her eyes. "From now on, my queen, you don't tell anyone around here to do anything, understand? Here, you're *nobody*—got it?"

The sandy-bearded, devil-eyed, savage leader of the pack, Seville, chuckled incredulously as he stepped up beside the woman and placed a hand on Babe's shoulder. "Easy, there, Babe. Don't damage the goods."

"Yeah, Babe—go easy," admonished Babe's big

Indian brother, gazing goatishly down at Sheila.
"Don't hurt her. She's . . . hell . . ." He prodded
Sheila's behind with his boot toe, seedily, caressingly,
as though judging the quality of farm stock. "She's
real . . . soft." He grinned, showing rotten teeth.
"Real *nice!*"

"Soft an' nice, eh?" Babe smiled coldly at the two
men. "Soft an' nice an' *off-limits*—you understand?"

"Oh, fer chrissakes!" intoned Seville with exasperation.

The other men had gathered around, and they,
too, were voicing their poor opinions of Babe's re-
monstration.

"What the hell we take her for if we can't have fun
with her?" asked one of the lesser lights in the wolf
pack. To a man, they had the look of hungry wolves.
Even more so now as they stared down at their
hostage, who was just starting to draw air into her
lungs again though her head still ached.

"I done told you fellas a dozen times, already,"
Babe said in exasperation. "We brought her for *insurance.* It's a long way to Mexico, amigos, and the
telegraph wires run all the way to Juárez these days.
When that gold and this pretty white girl doesn't
make it to Hallelujah Junction, word will go out over
the telegraph that a gang of gold thieves is heading
for Mexico. Where else would we head with all that
gold? When word of how much gold we're packin',
and the purty little white gal we've taken, reaches all
corners of the west, every bounty hunter and lawman
on the frontier will be looking for us."

Babe gritted her teeth. "*Can you finally get that
through your thick skulls?*"

Babe reached down and jerked Sheila's head up by her chin again. "This here pretty little white girl is our insurance they won't shoot first and ask questions later!"

"Sure, sure," Seville said, chuckling and holding his gloved hands up in supplication. "I savvy what you're sayin', Babe, but . . . just because she's insurance don't mean me an' the boys can't have a little fun with her!" He laughed and slid his devil's eyes to Sheila.

"It sure as hell does!" Babe bellowed, leaning forward, both fists on her broad hips. She had a low, mannish voice, and it sounded even lower and more mannish when she raised it. "If all you peckerwoods have a go at her—*every man-jack one of you*—she'll end up dead one way or the other. You fellas know how rough you all are. This girl's made of china." She looked down at Sheila, ran a tender finger along the bruise already coloring up on Sheila's left cheek. "Why, look how she bruises so easily . . . poor child."

"Bruises easily?" Seville laughed in exasperation. "Hell, you sucker-punched her off her horse, Babe!"

"Just to teach her a lesson!" Babe turned to Sheila again. "You've done learned it, too—haven't you, my queen?"

Sheila glared up at her.

Raising her voice, Babe said, "Haven't you . . . *my queen?*" She drew her foot back as though preparing a swift, sound kick to Sheila's stomach.

Sheila looked away and gave a grudging nod.

"See there?" Babe said, proudly, rising up on the toes of her boots. "Tame as a kitty-cat. I'll have her eatin' outta my hand soon."

"She can eat outta my hand any ole day o' the week," said one of the other men in the pack standing around Sheila, lustily ogling their captive.

"You gotta keep your men away, Harry," Babe said, eyeing the wolfish men warily. "They'll kill her, an' you know it. They'll kill her without even tryin'. We need her for insurance."

Seville looked down at Sheila. He tugged on his beard, thoughtful, then turned to Louis Raised-By-Wolves standing beside him. The big Indian had his thumbs hooked behind his cartridge belt as he stared stonily down at the white woman. He looked at Seville, the savagery so apparent in the big Indian's eyes that even Seville recognized it, and he chuckled his acknowledgment that Babe was right.

"All right, Babe," Seville said with a long sigh and a wry chuckle, still pinching his sandy, dusty beard and staring with his devil's eyes at Sheila. "I reckon you're right."

He reached down and grabbed up a lock of Sheila's long hair, rubbed it between the thumb and index finger of his gloved right hand. He dropped the hair and turned his own hard, menacing eyes on Babe. "For now, we'll do it your way. You just make sure she ain't no trouble, or we'll have our fun with her an' cut her throat. And you remember one more thing, Babe." He curled a nostril at her. "You remember that what's good for the gander is good for the goose."

Several of the other men, including Babe's half-brother, snickered.

Babe flushed and glared at Seville, but she didn't say anything. Seville was obviously the pack leader, with the big Indian, Raised-By-Wolves, second in command but with Babe a close third. Seville rode herd on the pack, as the saying went, but he reluctantly allowed that Babe was a voice of reason. Still, he'd let her push him only so far.

Babe might be a savage in her own right, but Sheila likely owed her life to her, and for that she was nominally grateful. Without Babe, she'd likely be dragged off into the brush and horrifically savaged.

Somehow, she had to stay on Babe's good side.

Until she could find a way out of the predicament she was in.

As the men dispersed around her, she glanced back along the trail, in the direction in which Johnny and Bear lay or hung dead from a tree. A hollow, cold, hopeless feeling washed over her, and she choked back a sob.

Babe dropped a canteen in the dirt beside her. "Have you some water, Queen. Maybe pour a little over them wrists."

Sheila lifted the canteen, unscrewed the cap. A wooden smile passed across her lips as she choked back her rage and said, "Thank . . . thank you, Babe."

Babe chuckled. "Now, that's what I like to hear . . . in the tone I like to hear it in." The thick woman reached down and slid a lock of Sheila's disheveled hair behind her ear. "I think you an' me are gonna be friends, Queenie. Huh? What do you think?"

Sheila gave a wooden smile then sipped from the canteen, her skin crawling.

When she lowered the canteen, Babe took it from her. "Tell you what—looks like the fellas are gonna take 'em a break, have a little coffee."

Sheila followed Babe's gaze toward where the men

were leading their horses into a broad horseshoe bend of the creek. A thin, roiling cloud of tan dust rose behind them, obscuring them. Some were already gathering wood for a fire. "Let's walk on down to the stream and bathe them pretty wrists of yours." She clucked and shook her head. "Some mighty tender skin you got there, Queenie. Spend too much time inside, is your problem."

Babe swung around and led her strawberry roan and Sheila's filly into the forest. "Come on. Don't try runnin', now, or I'll shoot ya down like a dog." She chuckled.

Sheila watched the woman walk away from her. Her heart quickened with the possibility of escape. It would be foolish to make the attempt now, however. Like Babe had promised, she'd only be shot down. She had to bide her time, be patient. When the first opportunity showed itself, she'd exploit it for all she was worth.

She followed Babe and the horses into the forest. The trees sloped downward toward the stream that ran along the base of a steep, red stone ridge roughly fifty yards away. The stream rippled over shallow rocks, its cobalt surface flashing golden in the sunshine.

A lone hawk soared high over the top of the red ridge.

Babe appeared to be angling off to the left of where the men were unsaddling their horses and throwing down their gear in anticipation of a long break, probably coffee and a nap. Two of the men were stripping the pack saddles from the two mules, as well—the mules that were hauling Sheila's one hundred thousand dollars in gold bars.

More gold, gone.

Those ingots represented Sheila's last chance for survival out here in the West. There was no point in thinking about that now, however. Now, she had to forget about the gold and concentrate instead on her own personal survival. If she didn't find a way to escape her captors, there was no doubt in her mind that she would soon be dead.

After being thrown to the proverbial wolves, that was.

Sheila paused, frowning as she gazed over at where the men were throwing down in the shade upstream, and then at where Babe was leading Sheila down toward a rocky outcropping to the left, downstream and down a slight grade from the men. A good hundred yards away from them, in fact. The stream tumbled down a low falls over there.

Again, Sheila's heart quickened. Maybe her opportunity to make a run for it had shown itself even sooner than she'd expected.

CHAPTER 27

Sheila continued walking toward where Babe had stopped the horses on the grassy shore of the stream near the falls.

She glanced toward the men. They were at least a hundred yards away, up the grade to her right, almost out of sight. Likely by some queer design, Babe had led Sheila away from them. They were alone over here.

A low waterfall rumbled straight out ahead of where Babe was now loosening the latigo straps of her roan. The falls would cover any sound Sheila might make. She stopped and looked at Babe, who was crouched forward, loosening the latigo. Sheila's pulse throbbed in her temples. It pounded harder when she scoured the ground for a rock and found one.

She was about to reach for it when Babe turned to her and said, "What the hell you doin', Queen?"

Sheila jerked her chin up. She raised her bloody wrists, feigning a wince. "They hurt."

Babe jerked her chin toward the water. "Well, go over to the stream and dip them in. That's why we came down here. You sure are pretty, but I guess it's right what they say about pretty wimmen." She gave a caustic laugh.

"Right, right." Sheila walked past Babe, heading for the stream. "That's what I'll do—I'll bathe them."

"There you go!" Babe said with another mocking laugh.

Sheila walked to the edge of the stream. She looked upstream toward where the men were lounging around a small fire. She glanced behind her at Babe, who was just then loosening the filly's saddle cinch. The woman wasn't looking at her. She must have had full confidence that Sheila was no threat to her. As benign as a child.

Good.

Sheila dropped to her knees and dipped her wrists in the water. The cold fluid stung the burns, but she barely noticed. She had her mind on escape.

"How you doin', Queen?" Babe said when she'd tied both horses to a spindly aspen.

"You were right, Babe. The water feels so good."

"See, I told ya!" Babe chuckled.

Sheila glanced over her shoulder at the woman. "Do you think . . . um . . . you wouldn't happen to have a little salve, would you?"

"Salve?"

"Yes, I'd like to rub some salve into the burns."

"I reckon I have a tin of stuff I use on saddle galls. Hiram Harveys' Somethin'-Or-Other."

"That would do."

Babe walked over to her horse and dipped a hand into a saddlebag pouch. She walked over to where Sheila knelt by the stream. Babe held a small, square tin in one hand. She removed the lid with her other hand, and said, "Try some of this here."

"Would you rub it in for me, Babe?"

Babe flushed a little, averted her gaze, suddenly bashful. "Why, uh . . . sure."

Sheila stood, holding her hands together, palms down, fingers curled inward. When Babe dipped a finger into the dark-green salve, Sheila lifted her right fist above her head. She smashed the rock she held clenched in her hand down against Babe's left temple.

There was a dull, smacking thud as the rock connected with Babe's skull.

Babe dropped the tin.

"Oh," she said, stumbling backward, shock making her eyes dance. "Oh . . ."

She clamped her pudgy hands to her temple, scrunching up her face in pain.

Sheila's heart was racing. She'd never assaulted another human being before. Doing so now made her sick, made her knees turn to mud, threatening to buckle. She stared at Babe. She had to hit her again. She had to knock her out, or Babe would alert the others.

She lifted her hand, squeezing the rock, hesitating.

Babe lowered her hands and cast Sheila a look of unbridled fury. Sheila lunged forward with a low, inadvertent scream, and smashed the rock against Babe's head again. The woman continued stumbling toward her, compressing her lips into a thin white line.

Sheila stepped back, sobbing with anxiety and revulsion for her own actions, and smashed the rock once more against Babe's temple, further opening the same gash she'd opened with the first blow and that now bubbled dark red blood.

Babe stopped. She wobbled on her broad hips,

her eyes appearing to lose focus. She dropped to her knees in the green grass at the edge of the stream, her arms hanging slack at her sides.

Sheila shifted her feet, looked from Babe toward the men lounging in the grass by their fire, sipping coffee, the smoke from the fire partly obscuring them. She could only see a few of them above the rise of ground between her and their camp. That was good; it meant they didn't have a clear view of what was happening down here, either.

Sheila looked at Babe again. The woman's eyes seemed to have regained their focus. Grunting and wheezing, Babe bunched her lips and, reaching for Sheila, started to heave herself to her feet.

"No!" Sheila lunged toward her again and slammed the rock even harder than before against her head with a wet smacking thud as the rock found the bloody gash again.

Babe's head jerked far back and to one side, toward the stream. All the blood appeared to rush out of her face and ooze up out of the wound.

Her heavy body followed her head, and she collapsed on her side, quivering, eyes rolling back in their sockets, odd sounds issuing from deep in her lumpy chest.

Sheila dropped the bloody rock. She looked from Babe to the men's camp. No one appeared to have spied Sheila's assault on Babe.

Quickly, breathless, emotion causing her body to tremble, Sheila hurried over to the filly that stood watching her warily but bobbing its head as though in approval of her actions. Babe's horse was idly cropping grass, oblivious.

"Okay," Sheila heard herself say, addled by panic,

trying to think through her anxiety to what she needed to do next to escape.

She grabbed the filly's reins and hurried to the horse's left side. She stepped onto a rock, grabbed the saddle horn, and started to poke her left boot into the stirrup. But then the saddle slid toward her, and she remembered that Babe had loosened the latigo.

Quickly, she tightened the straps, crying, "Please, girl, just this once don't fill up your lungs . . . !"

The filly must have understood and, even more surprisingly, obeyed. The horse did not fill its lungs. With a jerk, Sheila pulled the latigo taut and secured the strap through the cinch. She stepped up onto the rock again, grabbed the horn, poked her left boot through the stirrup, and swung into the saddle.

Her heart pounded as she cast another enervated look back toward where the men were gathered around the fire. She was higher now, being atop the filly, so she could see them more clearly. They would see her now if they turned toward her, which at least one of them was bound to do in a second or so . . .

She was so terrified that she couldn't look at them again, as though her doing so would cause them to notice her in return. She reined the filly out away from the stream and booted it north, opposite of where the men were lounging around the fire. It was open ground this way until the trees started roughly a hundred yards away. She didn't have a choice of which route to take. There was really only one.

"Let's go, girl," Sheila said under her breath, her frayed nerves leaping around just beneath her skin.

She crouched low and forward in the saddle, trying to make herself as small as possible. She wanted to boot the filly into a gallop, but she was afraid the men would hear the thuds of the horse's hooves, so she kept it to a trot. Her heart was dancing around inside her chest, skipping beats, and a high-pitched ringing assaulted her ears. She was sweating, her breathing shallow.

The trees at the far end of the clearing grew larger before her.

Larger and larger . . . beckoning.

Soon, in less than a minute she'd be in them, out of sight.

She couldn't resist a glance over her right shoulder. She gasped sharply. Several men had risen from where they'd been sitting and were now walking toward her, spreading out, apparently wondering what was happening. Others were just then gaining their feet, as well, and walking away from the fire toward Sheila.

"Oh, no!" Sheila jerked her head forward and rammed the heels of her boots into the filly's loins. "Go, girl! Go! *Goooo!*"

"Hey!" a man shouted angrily behind her.

More shouts rose but then Sheila was in the trees and the horse's loud hoof thuds drowned out all other sounds.

"Go, girl!" she cried, glancing behind her, seeing the men now running for their horses. She turned her head forward again and laid against her saddle horn. "*Goooo!*"

The filly stretched out her long legs, running hard, turning around trees, which fortunately were fairly widely spread apart. The horse leaped deadfalls and blowdowns and bulled through thin clumps of brush. Sheila reached the end of the woods and climbed an open slope beyond it. When she'd gained the crest of the hill, she heard whooping and hollering and the drumming of hooves behind her.

"Oh, God . . ." Judging by the sounds, the human wolves weren't far behind. They'd have no mercy on her now. Not after what she'd done to Babe. If they caught her . . .

She gave her head a single shake, trying to dislodge the horrifying thought.

It would not give ground, however. It followed her down that ridge and up the next one, and into another forest, climbing . . . forever climbing—toward where or what, she had no idea. She was just running, trying to escape her savage captors and certain, slow, painful death.

Hoof thuds rose sharply behind her, louder than before.

Sheila turned a wide-eyed look over her shoulder and gave another sharp gasp when she saw two riders entering the forest fifty yards behind her and closing fast. More riders flanked them, also coming hard.

"No," Sheila sobbed. *"Nooo!"*

She turned her head forward. A low branch swept toward her. She saw it too late. It slammed into her chest and rolled her backward off the filly. The horse continued lunging up the steep, shaded incline while Sheila hit the ground and rolled wildly down the slope.

When she came to a stop against a deadfall, she looked up to see one rider approaching, whooping and yowling like a wolf on the blood scent. The man drew rein a few feet away from her and leaped out of his saddle.

"Whoo-whoooo!" he howled, grinning down at her from beneath the brim of his weathered Stetson. Two pistols bristled on his hips. He glanced back at five or six more men approaching at a dead run behind him. "Gonna have us a good ole time now, boys!"

He moved toward Sheila, who was too dazed from the tumble to do anything more than stare at him in horror, shaking her head, muttering, "No . . . no . . ."

The man laughed again and strode toward her.

He stopped suddenly when the squawk of leather and loud hoof thuds rose abruptly on the upslope somewhere behind Sheila. A horse gave a fierce snort. Sheila turned her head to see a horse and rider bounding down the slope, the black-clad man with the pale horse's ribbons in his teeth, two short, double-barreled shotguns in his hands.

Sheila's assailant gave a yelp of surprise then reached for the pistols on his hips. He didn't get his hands closed around either handle before—*Johnny*—extended his left-hand shotgun at the man. Orange flames and gray smoke lapped from the large barrel as thunder pealed so loudly that Sheila was thrown backward by the concussive blast.

She looked away as her attacker's face and upper chest turned red as he was thrown backward down the hill, rolling wildly, already silent in death.

Ghost hadn't broken stride as horse and rider continued down the steep hill past Sheila, heading toward the small horde of riders that had pursued Sheila. Several of the gold-robbing gun wolves, surprised by the unexpected appearance of her savior, jerked back sharply on their reins, while others reached for guns.

Johnny extended both shotguns. The big weapons

thundered again loudly, sending several men flying off their horses, screaming. Ghost took two more long, lunging strides down the hill as two or three riders hurled themselves from their saddles and dove for cover.

Johnny blew two more riders off their own horses with his last barrel.

One man remained on his galloping mount, cocking a rifle as he rode toward Johnny.

Greenway flipped both shotguns in his hands, catching them by their barrels. He swung the right one club-like against the head of the man just then aiming the rifle at him. The man triggered his rifle wide and yowled as he went caroming over the arched tail of his exasperated horse.

He hit the ground and rolled.

At the edge of the woods below Sheila, who gazed at the commotion in hang-jawed shock, Johnny reined Ghost around sharply, wheeling. Horse and rider lunged back up the slope, Johnny crouching low as several of the men who'd gone to ground now fired at him from cover, cursing loudly in frustration as their bullets hammered tree trunks and snapped low-hanging branches, missing their target by inches and feet as Johnny sped past them.

He reined Ghost toward where Sheila knelt on the slope. He stopped the horse beside her and extended his hand to her.

"Hop on!" he bellowed.

Sheila heaved herself to her feet, threw her hand at him. He grabbed it, swung her smoothly onto Ghost's back behind him, then ground his boot heels into the gelding's loins. Ghost gave a determined whinny as the big mount lunged off its rear hooves and heaved itself up the steep slope, the shooters' bullets whistling and buzzing through the air around them, plunking into trees and thudding into the ground to each side.

They'd ridden maybe fifty yards, the shooters well behind them now and no longer firing, when Johnny angled Ghost over toward where the filly stood, reins dangling, staring incredulously toward the two people on the pale horse moving toward it.

"Get back on your mount," Johnny ordered, glancing quickly, anxiously down the slope behind them. "I'll keep the reins so we don't get separated!"

He threw a hand back to help Sheila to the ground. She ran over to the nervous filly, which sidestepped away from her, whickering, twitching its ears. Sheila took the reins, swung up onto the saddle, then nudged the horse toward Johnny, flinging her reins to him.

"Hold on tight!" he yelled.

Johnny clutched the reins tightly in his right hand and ground his heels into Ghost's loins once more. Again, the big horse lunged up the steep incline. Sheila crouched low over the filly's mane as the young horse whinnied her disdain for the loud and dangerous turn of events, and lunged off after the big pale gelding.

Horses thundered behind them.

Sheila glanced over her shoulder and, touched with dread once more, said into Johnny's right ear, "We've got company!"

CHAPTER 28

Johnny looked over his right shoulder.

Sheila was right. Some of the gang were tailing them from about forty or fifty yards back, weaving through the trees, yelling amongst themselves, a couple sporadically triggering pistols.

Ghost lunged up onto a bench. Johnny drew back on the horse's reins, stopping, looking around then booting the pale horse down the bench's opposite side, pulling Sheila's filly along behind him. When they were roughly twenty feet down the side of the bench, Johnny checked Ghost down again, swung his right leg over his saddle horn, and dropped to the ground.

"Come on," he said, thrusting a hand up to Sheila. He helped her dismount, then gave her the filly's reins. She looked up at him searchingly, curiously, obviously wondering how he was still alive.

Explanations would have to come later.

"Mount your filly and ride up that next ridge there." Johnny pointed to another bench above a short stretch of forest and running along the base of a bald crag. "Follow it to the northeast, through that gap yonder. You'll come to a canyon on the other side. Wait for me there."

"What're you going to do?"

Johnny had already broken open his right-hand Twin and reloaded it. Now he broke open the left-hand one and pinched out the spent wads. "I'm gonna cull the herd a little more."

Sheila gave him a worried look, her cheeks flushed with fear, but she hesitated for only a second before she swung up onto the filly's back and galloped off down the bench. In seconds, she gained the bottom of the bench and started up the next ridge through thick forest.

Leaving Ghost ground-reined, Johnny hurried back up the slope. Several feet from the crest, he dropped to a knee, hunkered low, and waited.

The thuds of the jackals' hooves grew louder and louder as did the snapping of branches and the crunch of pine needles. When Johnny judged they were close, he scurried to the top of the bench and straightened to his full height, thumbing back the Twins' hammers, extending the savage poppers straight out in both hands.

The riders materialized from the foliage, two groups riding roughly twenty feet apart and emerging from the forest in two ragged clumps. Johnny flashed briefly on his old friend Bear Musgrave hanging from the tree in their former camp, Bear's own bowie knife sticking out of his guts, and he gave a cold smile as he aimed at the two riders riding close together on his left, very pleased to see that one was a big Indian—most likely Harry Seville's bosom buddy, Louis Raised-By-Wolves.

"Whoah!" Wolves grunted, widening his flat, black

eyes and jerking back on his reins when he saw the tall, black-clad man standing atop the bench with the sawed-off shotguns extended from his shoulders.

Johnny tripped the left trigger of the left blaster.

The quickly spreading double-ought buckshot sprayed both Raised-By-Wolves and the man on his right, tearing into their faces and necks and upper chests, ripping through shirt collars and neckerchiefs and throwing both men off their saddles with bellowing wails. Their horses pitched, wheeled, and whinnied shrilly.

"That was for Bear!" Johnny bellowed.

He aimed quickly at the clump of men on his right and tripped the right trigger of his right-hand Twin.

"That one's for Bear, too!" Johnny shouted on the heels of the ten-gauge's resounding blast as two more men went flying ass-over-teakettle from their saddles.

Johnny leveled the left-hand Twin again and tripped the second trigger, blowing another man galloping toward him nearly in two before the man's bloody carcass hit the slope and rolled back down into the forest. As the man's screaming horse galloped buck-kicking past Johnny before wheeling and heading eastward along the crest of the bench, Johnny aimed his right-hand shotgun at one of the men he'd blown out of his saddle.

The man, bloody from a hundred pellets chewing into him, was trying to get two pistols raised while he screamed.

Johnny calmly cleaved the son of a buck's head from his shoulders with the right-hand Twin's second barrel. As the head rolled back down the slope and into the forest, where the other riders had fled when they'd seen what they were up against, Johnny wheeled. He ran down the side of the bench, sheathed the Twins, leaped onto Ghost's back, and rammed her heels into the gelding's loins.

The horse plunged down the bench and then up the steep slope through thick forest. It was a hard run, and Ghost was blowing hard, white froth basting his snout and neck, when he gained the bench at the base of the bald crag. Johnny booted the weary horse east along the bench, across a broad meadow and then down into the canyon beyond it.

Sheila waited by a creek wending its way through the bottom of the rocky, willow-choked canyon. She stood by her filly, straight and tense, her shoulders slackening when she saw him galloping toward her. Her chest rose as she drew a deep breath of relief.

Johnny stopped Ghost and swung down from the saddle.

Sheila ran to him, placed her hands on his chest, and stared up at him as though she were staring at a ghost. Her eyes seemed to be searching his, darting from one of his eyes to the other.

"I don't . . . I don't understand," she said, shaking her head. "I thought you were . . ."

Johnny took one of her hands in his, lightly squeezed it. "I got damn lucky. I got hornswoggled, my partner dead, you almost killed. You hired a damn fool."

Again, Sheila shook her head. "It wasn't your fault. There's so many of them. Besides . . . you saved my life, Johnny." She slid her hands down his chest then frowned at his lower left side. She brushed her fingers across the bloodstain on his black frock coat, over the lump of the neckerchief he'd placed over the bullet burn, under his shirt. "You're injured."

Again he took her hand in his. "Just a burn. Like I said, I got damned lucky."

"It needs tending."

"Later." Johnny looked back in the direction from which he'd come. "I think I've delayed Seville's bunch. They'll be licking their wounds for a while, and they won't be able to track us across that rocky bench. They been burned, though. They'll be scouring the whole area soon. We'd best get to cover."

Sheila looked around. "What cover?" The canyon floor was flat and nearly barren. It appeared to be the bed of a long-dry lake.

"Mount up," Johnny said. "I know a place. They won't find us. Leastways, not for a while."

He helped Sheila onto her horse and then swung up onto Ghost's back. He rode out, leading Sheila and the filly to the southeast, across the dry lake bed, wending their way around boulders and clumps of willows.

"How'd you ever find me?" Sheila asked.

"Been tracking you."

Johnny had cut Bear down from the fir tree and given him a hasty burial, planning on returning to the spot later to erect a permanent marker. Bear deserved that much. Once Johnny had gathered his gear and saddled Ghost, he'd set out following the tracks of Seville's bunch. That many men—over twenty—hadn't been hard to track. Getting close had been another problem, for Johnny knew they were a veteran, savvy bunch of robbers and killers.

Sheila had taken care of that problem, however.

"How'd you ever get away from them?" Johnny asked her.

Riding beside him now as they walked their tired horses up the low ridge on the lake bed's southeast edge, Sheila shuddered. "I . . . don't think I want to go into it."

Johnny glanced at her. "That bad?"

Sheila looked over at him, her eyes stricken. "I think I killed someone. A woman."

"Babe?"

"If I didn't kill her, I severely injured her. If she's alive, she won't forget me—that's for sure."

Johnny looked at her with renewed appreciation for her toughness, which a few days ago he hadn't realized she'd had. "Neither will her half-brother."

"Raised-By-Wolves?"

Johnny nodded. "The worst of the worst. Both him and Seville are."

"You know their reputations, I take it."

"Oh, yeah." Johnny felt the burn of rage again as he remembered Sonny Seville bursting through the door of his house in Carson City. "Him and ole Louis an' Babe carved a wide swath across this California-Nevada country. Sometimes just the three of them, sometimes with a gang of men just as low-down and no-good as they are. I didn't realize Seville was out of prison until he came up behind me." Johnny drew a deep, self-recriminating breath, and shook his head again quickly.

"Like I said, a lot of them. Nolan was right. I needed an army."

"You didn't know how many there were."

"Now I do. Now I know it's useless to think I'll ever get that gold back."

"Not necessarily."

Sheila raised a curious brow at him then turned her gaze ahead in surprise, and said, "Where are we?"

They were angling down through another fir forest. At the bottom of the ridge sat a brush-roofed log cabin, its back to the ridge down which Johnny and Sheila were riding. Firewood was stacked against the cabin's back wall.

Behind the shack lay a privy. To one side, there was a pole corral and a small log stable. Beyond the cabin sprawled a lush beaver meadow on the far side of which a fast-moving river flowed, the white water flashing in the late afternoon's deep gold light. Several elk were foraging along the stream's far side, their cinnamon coats glistening, the horns of a couple of big bucks appearing as large as small trees.

"One of Bear's old cabins," Johnny said, his voice catching a little on emotion. "Him and another older trapper built it. That was the fella that started Bear out in the mountains, after he came out here from Illinois to live the wild life he was destined for, sure enough."

"Bear built this cabin?" Sheila said as they bottomed out in the meadow and rode toward the cabin's rear, the privy coming up on their left.

"He helped. When the old-timer who mentored him died, Bear married a Paiute woman, Two Crows. That's when my pa introduced me to Bear. I was only six, maybe seven years old. We ran sheep through this meadow, and Pa and Bear were friends. We stayed here several times with ole Bear and his wife—a nice woman. Pretty, as I remember. And quiet. She had a white streak running through her long black hair. She had a muskrat for a pet, and she give me pretty baubles made from rocks and the teeth and claws of the animals Bear trapped."

As they rode wide around the side of the cabin, Johnny cupped a hand around his mouth and called. "Hello this place! Anyone home?"

There was no response.

Johnny stopped Ghost in front of the cabin and sat staring at it.

The front, halved-log door was closed. A badly rusted tin washtub hung from a nail beside it. There was a low boardwalk running along part of the front wall, decorated with many deer and elk horns. The boardwalk looked rickety, in poor repair, its slender pole rail worn to near nothing where reins had been tied to it.

While the ground out front of the cabin was worn bare by the hooves of many horses and mules, brush and grass grew high along the cabin's stone foundation and along the front of the boardwalk fronting it. A couple of shaggy shrubs were as high as the two front windows.

Planks had been placed over the top of the field-stone chimney running up the wall on the cabin's right side, to keep debris, birds, and other creatures out.

"Nobody here?" Sheila asked.

Johnny shook his head. "Abandoned at the moment. I've been through when folks were living here. Prospectors, mostly. The last one was a man named Maurice Sullivan. Odd little man, prospector. Didn't say much. I thought he might still be here."

Johnny swung down from Ghost's back. "It's all ours, I reckon. For a night, anyway."

He glanced up at Sheila. She glanced back at him. A pink flush touched her cheeks. She looked away, and then Johnny did as well, his ears warming a little.

CHAPTER 29

"What you said about the gold," Sheila said a few minutes later, when they'd corralled their horses and were rubbing them down with burlap. "When I said I'd never see it again—you said 'not necessarily.'"

"Yeah." Johnny gave Ghost's left wither a good scrubbing while the horse nibbled oats from a nose bag.

"What did you mean by that?"

Johnny shook out the burlap then ran it across the horse's sleek coat once more, working now on the stout left shoulder. He wasn't sure how to answer the question. While he considered a response, she said, "Johnny, you're not thinking about going after those killers . . ."

Johnny drew a breath, shrugged a shoulder. "I'm going to get you safely back down to Hallelujah Junction. We're only two days away."

Sheila arched a brow at him over the filly's back. "And then . . . ?"

Johnny didn't respond. He kept working, grunting as he scrubbed at Ghost's cream coat, dislodging dried sweat, dust, and burs, noting cuts and abrasions that would need tending later. He winced as the brisk movements kicked up pain in his side. His head still ached dully from his tumble into the open mine shaft, but the bullet burn in his side galled him relentlessly, especially after the violent riding he'd done when confronting the gang earlier.

He was lost in thought about Bear so he hadn't heard Sheila approach him until he saw her boots on the ground near where he now knelt, going over Ghost's left rear leg. He straightened. She stared at him with concern, holding her own pieces of burlap in her hands, down low at her sides.

"Don't," she said quietly, slowly shaking her head. "Don't go after them, Johnny." She'd put a little more steel into her voice that time.

"It's got nothing to do with you or the gold. If I can get it back, I will. But . . ."

Sheila stepped toward him, placed a hand against his cheek. "Bear's murder is my fault, not yours. In my stubbornness and stupidity, I sent you two up into those mountains to do an impossible job. Nolan was right." Her voice turned shrill, brittle, and her upper lip quivered with emotion. "That job required an army, but I couldn't afford an army, so I threw you two and even myself to those wolves."

She paused, staring at Johnny with her grave brown eyes, shaking her head. "The fault is mine."

"The only ones at fault are Harry Seville and Louis Raised-By-Wolves." Johnny gritted his teeth, and his voice quavered with sadness and rage. "They butchered Bear, and they're gonna pay. Seville is gonna die the way Bear died. *Hard.*"

"John—"

"That's all there is to it." Johnny shook out his

burlap again, then resumed his work. "I don't want to talk about it anymore."

Harry Seville rode up through the trees, fuming. He didn't say anything, but rage was a fire-breathing dragon in his chest.

More men lay dead around him, twisted this way and that, blood oozing from what the gang leader recognized as shotgun wounds. Several wounded men were cursing and groaning, writhing on the ground, the uninjured men in Seville's pack standing around them, talking amongst themselves, some down on their knees, rendering aid to the fallen. Seville turned his horse to the left and a group of five men turned toward him, parting a little so that Harry could see that his partner, Louis Raised-By-Wolves, was one of the fallen.

Wolves sat back against a rock, drinking whiskey from a bottle as though the substance would soon no longer be distilled.

"Ah, hell," Seville said, and cursed. "You, too, Wolves?" That was his nickname for the big Indian, who held a wadded-up bandanna over his right eye. He had several buckshot wounds in his cheek, and the top of his shoulder looked like freshly ground beef. Seville thought he could see part of the bone through the torn, bloody flesh.

One of the other men, "San Francisco" Tommy Blackmoore, was dabbing at Wolf's shoulder, trying to mop up some of the blood. San Fran shook his head, sucking sharp breaths through his teeth.

He turned his mustached face to Seville and

said, "Don't look good, Harry. He lost his left eye. Shredded!"

"Shut up!" Wolves yelled after he'd pulled the nearly empty whiskey bottle back down. "Stop sayin' my eye's shredded, San Fran! I don't wanna hear that! It ain't that bad! Hell, it don't feel that bad!" The big half-breed turned his good eye to Seville, and said, "It'll heal! I'll be just fine, partner!" He took another deep pull from the bottle, draining it.

"Oh, Louis!" This from Wolves's half-sister, Babe, riding behind Harry on his buckskin stallion. "What happened, Louis?" She'd wrapped a white cloth torn from her petticoat around the top of her head. Dark-red blood had soaked through the cloth over her left temple.

"Crazy son of Satan came out of nowhere," said one of the men standing around Wolves. Wallace Demry, an outlaw from west Texas, was smoking a cigarette, his angry dark eyes on Seville. "Just like some ghost of the forest—there he was, a shotgun in each hand. Can you imagine? A shotgun in each hand—blasting away!"

"A shotgun in each hand?" Seville asked, incredulous, his heart quickening.

"Oh, Louis!" Babe said. "Help me, down, Harry. Help me, down!"

Seville dismounted and then helped Babe down from his horse. She stared straight ahead, her eyes not focusing. She held her hands out, waving at the air.

Wolves looked at his half-sister, frowning. "What the hell happened to you, sis?" he asked, pressing the bandanna firmly against his right eye.

"Where are you, Louis?" Babe asked, waving her hands out before her again. "Harry, take me to my brother."

Seville winced as he looked over at Wolves. "Blind," Seville said. "That catamount woman smashed her head with a rock. Musta done somethin' to her eyes. She can't see, Wolves. I'm sorry."

Seville had stayed back when the rest of the men had gone after the fleeing woman. Hell, it didn't take twenty-three men to run down one woman. But he hadn't been expecting her to get help from a man wielding two shotguns.

Two shotguns? But he'd killed "Shotgun Johnny" Greenway!

Leastways, he thought he had . . .

There'd been a lingering doubt in his mind. And now that doubt doubled. Tripled . . .

When he'd heard the shooting, Harry had saddled his own horse, but he'd been waylaid by Babe staggering around, screaming and waving her hands out in front of her, much the way she did now with one hand as Seville led her by her other hand over to where Wolves sat back against the rock.

"What happened, sis?" Wolves said, worriedly, as the men standing around him stepped back to make way for Seville and Babe. "She hurt you bad?"

"Bashed me with a rock." Babe dropped to her knees beside her brother, winced as she touched two fingers to her head, over the bloody wound on her temple. "I was only tryin' to be kind. I was tryin' to help her with her wrists—you know, where the ropes cut her? I was going to give her some salve . . ."

"And she beat you with a rock," Wolves said,

wrinkling his lips and narrowing his one eye in fury. "It's all because o' her—my eye, *both* your eyes!" He looked sharply at Seville. "I thought you said you shot him, Harry!"

Babe turned to look up at Seville. At least, she tried to look up at him. Her gaze, if you could call it that, was somewhere to his left and behind him. "It'll come back, Harry!" Babe assured him. "My eyes'll be just fine. They just need some time to heal's all. I won't be no trouble at all, Harry. You'll see."

Wolves looked anxiously up at Seville. "She'll be okay, Harry. I'll tend her till she's well. She can ride with me. I thought you said you shot the shotgun feller . . ."

"You all shot up, only one eye?" Seville said, skeptically. "Her with no eyes at all . . . ?"

The outlaw leader shook his head and turned to walk away.

"She'll be fine, partner!" Wolves called to Seville's back. "I'll tend her till she's well. Hell, I got another eye, Harry. That one's just fine."

"We'll be just fine, Harry!" Babe called shrilly, desperately.

The others stood around, regarding Seville gravely, expectantly.

Harry stopped to stare down at one of the other wounded riders. He was Fred Tatum from Tennessee, former Reb. Seville had met him in prison. In fact, they'd broken out together—they and the man who was just now kneeling beside poor Tatum, using a tweezers to try and pluck pellets from the bloody wounds peppering Tatum's chest and right arm. His name was Bill Donaldson—a big, thick, bullet-headed man from Oklahoma.

"How's he doin'?" Seville asked Donaldson. Tatum appeared only part-conscious. He turned his head from side to side, his face a mask of pain, half-open eyes glassy with agony.

Donaldson looked up at him grimly, shook his head.

Seville turned away and walked over to where the other two men lay writhing from their wounds. One, Sandy Cornish, had been hit in the leg bad, and he, too, was drinking whiskey from a bottle. Todd Elsbernd, from Nebraska, had been gut-shot. Seville had no idea why Todd was still alive.

Not for long.

The two men hunkered down beside Todd looked warily up at Seville. When they saw the heavy Colt in his hand, they rose and stepped back. Todd's eyes were closed. The short, bald man was shaking, his narrow chest rising and falling heavily.

Seville clicked back the Colt's hammer, aimed, and fired.

All the men in the bunch jumped though they'd been watching him closely, knowing what he was going to do.

Seville turned to Sandy Cornish. The men gathered around Cornish fell back.

Cornish was wiry and bearded, and he was holding the whiskey bottle up close to his face. He was sweating, his face pain-wracked.

"Ah, bloody hell, Harry," Cornish said in his heavy Irish brogue, setting the whiskey bottle down beside him. He gazed in terror at Seville's Colt, which Harry again cocked as he walked over to the

Irishman. The terror in Cornish's eyes was tempered by fateful resignation.

He knew the rules. No one slowed down the group. Besides, Cornish knew he wasn't going to make it. He was proverbially and literally on his last leg. Still, he sucked back a hoarse sob. Even the toughest, nastiest men on the frontier—and Cornish was certainly one of these—were afraid of death.

He turned the terror in his eyes to bald defiance as he stared at Seville and said, "You go to hell, Harry!"

Seville's bullet drilled a quarter-sized hole through the dead center of Cornish's freckled forehead.

Several men hurried out of Harry's path as the outlaw leader turned from where Cornish lay flopping his arms in death, and walked back over to Fred Tatum. Bill Donaldson looked at Seville and bunched his lips. He heaved himself to his feet and stepped away.

"We rode a lot of miles together—Tate an' me," he said. "We wouldn't have got outta the pen without him, Harry. You remember that."

Seville stood over Tatum, who opened his eyes, as though he suddenly understood what was coming. He lifted his head. Sweat streaked his face, and the waning sunlight shone like liquid gold in his eyes.

He regarded Seville and then he looked at the others all standing around resembling mourners at a funeral. He turned back to Seville and said, "No . . . now, *wait*! I don't wanna—!"

Seville's Colt thundered.

One of the men around him gave a hushed curse.

Seville lowered the Colt. Holding it down low against his right leg, thumb on the hammer, index finger resting against the trigger, he walked back over to his partner, Raised-By-Wolves and Wolves's sister Babe kneeling beside him, her sightless eyes fixed somewhere to Seville's left, her mouth forming a perfect "O" of apprehension. A tear dribbled down from one of her sightless eyes.

"Easy, now, Harry," Wolves said, holding up his left hand, palm out. "We . . . me an' sis . . . we'll be all right. We won't hold you up none. Not a bit."

Babe shook her head slowly, slowly moved her mouth as she shook her head and said, "Not a bit, Harry."

Seville looked at the shredded shoulder of his big Indian partner. "For you, Wolves, that ain't much worse than cuttin' yourself shavin'. Hell, after a good, warm winter down in Mexico, you'll be right as rain, good as new!" He chuckled but his slitted eyes turned dark when he turned to Babe. "But her, now . . . on the other hand."

"I'm good, Harry," Babe said, raising her voice. "I mean . . . give me a day or two, an' I'll be seein' again. As sharp as a hawk!" She turned her opaque gaze in the general direction of Wolves and said, "Please don't let him shoot me, brother. You an' me been through thick an' thin together. Why, I stuck with you when your no-good squaw ma left you with my no-good squaw-dog pa. You know that, little brother! I looked out for you when the other boys kicked your Injun ass. You remember that—I know you do!"

Tears dribbled down her unattractive face.

Wolves turned to Seville. The Indian still held the wadded bandanna against his ruined eye. Tears were flowing down from his good eye. His gaze was dark, stricken.

Seville sighed, flipped the Colt in his hand, and extended it butt-forward to his friend.

"Ah, hell, Harry," Wolves said, his deep voice pinched with misery.

Seville dipped his chin in a single nod then canted his head toward Babe regarding them both, her plump cheeks ashen. "What's goin' on?" she asked. "What's goin' on, Harry? You ain't gonna let him kill me, now—are you, little brother?"

Wolves glanced at the big pistol in Seville's hand.

The other men gazed at all three of them—Seville, Wolves, and Babe—in hushed fascination. A couple were smoking, some were passing a flask, but no one said anything. There was only the sound of the wind in the pine crowns and the ground-reined horses standing around snorting and cropping grass, switching their tails or swiping with their back feet at flies.

The sun was sinking behind the western mountains, shadows growing long, a knife-edged chill falling over the high country.

"What's goin' on?" Babe pleaded. "What the hell's goin' on, dammit?" She was sobbing now.

Wolves glanced into Seville's eyes, then drew his mouth corners down as he wrapped his big, bony, copper-colored hand around the ivory handle of his partner's Colt.

"What's goin' on?" Babe said, her voice thin now, her lower jaw hanging.

"Ah, hell," Wolves said, raising the pistol.

"What is it, little brother?" Babe asked.

"I'm sorry, sis," Wolves sobbed, sucking an anguished breath as he clicked the Colt's hammer back. "I'm so sorry!"

He pressed the barrel to Babe's forehead and squeezed the trigger.

When Babe flopped back on the ground, dead, Raised-By-Wolves turned his agonized good eye to Seville and said through his hoarse sobs and his tears, *"I thought you said Shotgun Johnny was dead, Harry!"*

CHAPTER 30

Sheila moved out onto the porch with a steaming bowl of water in her hands. She drew the door closed with her foot, wanting to keep inside the heat from the fire she'd built in the hearth. They'd need that heat later, as already now in the early evening the air was growing cold.

A breeze was building as clouds moved in, likely bringing a storm. Even as the thought passed through her mind, thunder rumbled.

Johnny was walking up to the cabin, his rifle on his shoulder. His red neckerchief blew back over his shoulder in the growing wind.

"I scouted the whole area," he said as more thunder rumbled in the mass of dark-purple clouds catching on the craggy peeks jutting on the other side of the river beyond the cabin. "We're alone here."

"If Seville knows about this cabin, he'll know we probably came here," Sheila said, resting the bowl of water on the boardwalk's rail. "He might come after dark."

Johnny stopped and thumbed his hat brim off his forehead. "He doesn't know about it."

"How do you know?"

"He'd be here by now." Johnny glanced at the clouds behind him. "That storm will keep him from trying to track us tonight. It's gonna be a gully-washer for sure. Looks like it even has hail in it. Most storms do up here." He glanced at the steaming bowl. "What's that for?"

"Your side."

Johnny grimaced. "Now, I told you it was nothin' but a—"

"Scratch, I know. But I can see that it's more than that." Sheila canted her head to one side in beseeching. "Please let me clean it for you. I hate to think of you going around with a dirty wound. It could get infected."

Johnny sighed. "If it'll make you feel better."

"It will." Sheila lifted the bowl off the rail and turned to the door. "Let's go in. It's chilly out here."

Johnny reached around in front of her and opened the door for her. She glanced up at his tall, hawk-faced figure towering over her, then looked away quickly, feeling a warm sensation in her belly that she chose to ignore, hard as it was. She'd been having that feeling more and more lately.

As she stepped into the small, crudely and sparsely appointed cabin, with the fire snapping in the hearth to her right, she remembered the image of that tall, dark rider bounding toward her on his cream horse only a couple of hours earlier. She remembered that his eyes had the look of a raptor's eyes, a falcon's eyes, to go with his hawk-like nose, as he'd extended both his shotguns straight out from his shoulders, thumbing the hammers back.

On a Sunday morning horseback ride in the country around Hallelujah Junction, she'd seen a gold eagle up close. The bird had been perched on a boulder looming over the trail, and it had that same gold glint in its eyes just before it had lighted from the rock and swooped down out of sight on the rock's far side. A second later, the sudden, sharp squeal of a rabbit had cleaved the air and made Sheila's heart shudder.

She felt herself oddly attracted to and repelled by the darkly handsome man known as Shotgun Johnny. The man was none the less compelling for being such an odd match for her. She'd been raised in a society so much softer and more civilized—"nipped and tucked"—than the one that the former Juan Beristain had obviously been fostered by.

Her attraction not only puzzled but frightened her a little, as did the man himself.

"Why don't you sit on the bed over there and take your shirt off?" Sheila turned away from the big man, knowing that her cheeks must be coloring.

"You sure are bossy!"

"Well, I'm a woman, aren't I?" she said, giving a wry smile.

Sheila sat down on the room's only bed. Covered by a bearskin, it stretched along the front wall, near the hearth. She pulled one of the two hide-bottom kitchen chairs over to it. As she did, Johnny doffed his hat and his neckerchief, setting both on the table.

He sniffed the air and looked over to where a coffeepot steamed on a hook hanging over the fire. "Smells good. Coffee, I take it?"

"I'll reward you with a cup once I've gotten that wound cleaned."

"It's a burn, not a wound."

"I'll be the judge of that."

When Johnny had pulled off his shirt and thrown it over the back of the chair on which Sheila had placed the water bowl, he unbuttoned his long-handle top. As he did, he stared out the window left of the door. They'd swum naked together. Still, he was self-conscious about exposing his torso to her.

"Please, don't be embarrassed," Sheila said, her voice quiet, intimate. "I've seen more than your bare chest, Johnny."

Peeling the underwear top down his arms, Johnny narrowed a curious eye at her. "What happened to 'Mister Greenway'?"

She couldn't help giving a crooked smile. "I drowned him in that lake we swam naked in together." She'd be darned if she couldn't help teasing him, enjoying herself very much, indeed. "Such formality on the heels of that sort of thing would seem a little silly—don't you think?"

He walked over to her, bare-chested, and stood staring down at her. She looked up at him, unable to keep her eyes from roaming across his broad, hard chest and flat belly. He had only a little dark hair between the pronounced lumps of his pectorals, and down his thick, corded arms. His hands were large, thick, and brown, the nails standing out pale against them. "You saw more of me than I did of you," he said accusingly.

She'd be damned if he wasn't the most handsome man she'd ever known. In stark contrast to the sniveling, lascivious drunk she'd first met in the Silver Slipper Saloon, he was a darkly handsome and dangerous man she yearned to have wrap his large arms around her and draw her to him brusquely, to close his mouth over hers the way he'd done that night in the lake.

She'd never wanted anything so much as she'd wanted him that night. When he'd pulled away from her, she'd almost screamed. No man had ever had that effect on her before. Like the man himself, it scared her even while it mesmerized her. He held her captive in his dark aura.

Sheila drew a calming breath, composing herself. "I think I know you well enough, and you, me, that we can use each other's first names. At least when we're out of hailing distance of town." She looked pointedly up at him, hooking half of her mouth in a wry smile. "Don't you?"

He didn't say anything. He continued staring almost coldly down at her with those dark, raptorial eyes with their savage, golden glint.

She patted the bed beside her. "Sit."

"A lady would keep her distance."

She gave an impatient chuff and glanced at the wound in his side and over which he'd carelessly stuffed a folded bandanna, which was glued by dried blood to his skin. "How would I clean that for you from a distance?"

Johnny smiled sidelong, as though he knew a secret about her. He sat down on the cot beside her, on her right, a few inches away from her. She placed a hand on his chest. "Lean back against the wall."

He reclined across the bed, propping his head

and shoulders against the wall. On purpose or inadvertently—she wasn't sure which—he slid his leg against hers. She could feel the warmth of his flesh through his pant leg. Trying to ignore it, Sheila carefully peeled the folded bandanna away from the wound. "It's stuck pretty good," she said, warningly, as she continued very slowly and gradually pulling the bandanna up from the dried blood. "Hurt?"

Johnny shook his head slightly, staring straight ahead, his eyes reflecting the fire's dancing orange flames.

It was raining now, the drops streaking the window behind him. Thunder rolled distantly over the valley, rumbling, sounding like the coupling of distant train cars. Lightning lit up the windows once every few seconds. The wind blew under the door, causing the two burning candle lamps to flicker wildly, casting shadows around the cabin.

When Sheila had pried the blood-soaked bandanna from the wound, she set it on the chair by the bowl and inspected the bullet's damage. She looked up at him, pulling her mouth corners down, chidingly. "That's more than just a burn."

He lifted a shoulder, dismissively.

She wrung out the cloth in the bowl and dabbed at the blood crusting the furrow running along his side. She worked for a time, dabbing gently at the blood, wringing the cloth out in the bowl. Rain pattered on the cabin's roof and on the windows, but it was relatively safe and secure in here. It was pleasantly warm, intimate. She enjoyed the musky male smell of the man she was tending. Johnny reached for his shirt, pulled his tobacco pouch from a pocket, then built a cigarette while Sheila cleaned the wound.

He lit the cigarette and blew smoke out with a soft sound.

Sheila looked up at him, hesitating, not sure she should say what she wanted to say, then went ahead. It had been on her mind for a while now. "Tell me about her."

Johnny turned to Sheila, scowling. "Who?"

"Your wife."

Frowning, Johnny took a drag from the quirley, then blew the smoke toward the back wall again. He shook his head. "No."

Instantly, she regretted asking. She supposed he'd tortured himself long enough, thinking of his dead wife. Sheila was curious about their boy, as well, but since his wife was off-limits, she supposed their son was, as well.

They sat in silence, her working quietly, gently, him smoking and staring off at a hide of some kind hanging on the cabin's back wall. The rain tapped on the windows, forming miniature, winding rivers along the glass.

When she'd cleaned the wound sufficiently, she rose from the bed, walked over to an open carpetbag on the table, and returned to the bed with a small, stoppered bottle of Labbaraque's Solution of Sodium Hypochlorite and a roll of felt.

"You come prepared," he observed.

"Of course."

She poured some of the sodium hypochlorite onto a folded piece of flannel and said, "This is going to burn."

He lifted his cigarette to his lips and took another puff.

She pressed the flannel to the ragged-edged wound. She looked up at his face as he stared at the wall. He didn't flinch or wince. If he did anything at all, he might have smiled however briefly, thinly, as though he enjoyed the pain. As though he welcomed physical discomfort of any kind.

Why?

To help cover the mental misery that she sensed was assaulting him constantly, following him moment to moment, like a rabid wolf that had found its way into his home and followed him from room to room, snarling.

Guilt.

Self-recrimination.

Sheila sensed that he hated himself immensely and wanted to die. That was why he'd had that glint in his eyes when he'd thundered down that mountain slope, heading straight for Sheila's armed attackers. He'd maybe thought, even hoped, that they would kill him and put him out of his misery. After all, he no longer had the alcohol to assuage that agony. He'd decided the alcohol was a luxury he didn't deserve. He'd decided that his penance was suffering. His only escape from suffering was death.

"Why're you crying?" he asked.

The question surprised her. She hadn't realized she'd sobbed. She was leaning very close to him, wrapping the long strip of flannel around his waist, over the wound. She saw that one of her tears had dropped onto his belly, just above his belly button.

She swiped up the tear with her finger. "I'm sorry . . . I didn't . . ." She shook her head, sniffed, and tied off the flannel, forming a neat, clean pad over the wound. "Never mind."

Johnny placed his hands on her arms. "What's the matter?"

She convulsed with another, deeper sob. More tears dribbled down her cheeks. She was embarrassed and frustrated. "No . . ."

Johnny shook her gently. "Tell me."

He held her fast before him. He wouldn't let her go. Those hawkish eyes bored into hers. She couldn't meet them head-on. She had to look away.

She shook her head, willing the tears to stop, but they wouldn't.

He released one of her shoulders and turned her head toward his, two fingers on her chin. "Tell me."

"I don't want you to die, Johnny!"

His lower jaw sagged slightly. He frowned at her, dumbfounded, surprised that she'd probed him so deeply that she'd uncovered a secret he'd obviously thought he'd stashed so far within himself that no one would ever know.

But she'd found him out.

"I know you ache," Sheila said, placing her hand on his cheek. "But I don't want you to die." She stopped, looked down. She knew she shouldn't say this other thing she had to say, but there was no going back now.

She looked up at him, stared into his eyes. "I love you, Johnny."

She drew a breath. It was like a gasp. He shook his head slowly. "No . . ."

"Yes."

"No."

"Yes!"

She threw herself against him, closing her mouth over his. He tried to push her away, but this time she would not be denied.

CHAPTER 31

Johnny heard a sound and instantly he was awake, sitting up on the bed and reaching for one of the Twins leaning to his right. The cabin door had been kicked open, and Harry Seville bounded through it, swinging his Colt's revolving rifle toward the bed, his slitted demon eyes bright with laughter.

Johnny took the Twin in both hands, thumbed both hammers back at the same time, tripped both triggers. The explosion rolled around the room, bouncing off the walls like boulders bounding down a canyon.

Sheila lurched to a sitting position to his left, gasping, pulling the blanket they'd been sharing up over her bosom.

Johnny tossed the empty shotgun down and reached for the other one, clicking both hammers back, resting his right index finger against a trigger, his heart racing as he waited for another man to bound through the open door that glinted faintly umber in the light from the dying fire. It turned blue and white when lightning flashed, glistening silver as the rain pelted it through the opening.

Lightning flooded the windows, lighting up the entire room briefly.

Johnny frowned as he stared at the door.

Sheila turned to him and said, "No one there, Johnny."

"Wait here." Johnny kicked the blanket off his legs, dropped his feet to the floor, and walked quickly over to where the door hung open, leaning back against the cabin's front wall. The ten-gauge's double barrels had blasted a pumpkin-sized hole through it.

Harry Seville was not sprawled on the floor, as Johnny had suspected he would be. He peered out the door and into the stormy, rainy night, the rain hammering down at a slant—billowing curtains of silver downpour. Broken streams of water tumbled from the cabin roof's overhang. Johnny poked his head out and looked around carefully, the frequent bursts of blue-white lightning illuminating the yard fronting the cabin.

No one was out there but the rain.

No one inside. No one outside.

The door must have a bad latch. A wind gust had blown it open, and in his half-sleep, Johnny had dreamed that Seville was bounding through it. Those two grinning demon eyes still burned just behind Johnny's eyelids.

"Come back in," Sheila said softly behind him.

He lowered the shotgun, stepped back, and turned to her. She closed the door, though the rain continued to slither through the hole he'd blown through it. Sheila had only a blanket draped around her shoulders. She opened it, stepped up to him, wrapped it around them both, holding him tightly.

"We're alone here, Johnny," she said, pressing her moist lips to his chest. "They won't hunt us in the rain." She kissed him again, looked up at him, shivering. "Come back to bed. It's cold."

She hooked an arm around his and led him back to the bed. She tossed a couple of dry logs on the fire, then crawled into bed. He leaned the loaded Twin against the bed then lay down beside her. She pulled the blanket over them both and curled against him, shivering for a time before his warmth seeped into her, hers into him.

He lay staring up at the ceiling where the umber light from the flames danced, pushing a welcoming heat against him. The smell of the burning pine and aspen pushed a sweet minty aroma through the cabin.

"Her name was Lisa," he said after a time.

Sheila had been lying with her face against his chest. Now she lifted her chin slightly to gaze up into his eyes. "Your wife."

"Yes."

"My boy's name was David."

"How old?"

"Seven when he died." Johnny drew a deep breath as he lay staring up at the flames shunting shadows across the herringbone-patterned ceiling, glistening in the spiderwebs clinging to the corners between the ceiling and the log wall. "I met Lisa when Joe was raising me on his ranch near Reno. She was the mercantiler's daughter. After I saw the beautiful, snooty blond girl about my age workin' in her father's store, I volunteered for all the supply runs to Reno."

He smiled at that. Sheila chuckled softly, stretching her lips back from her perfect white teeth.

"A real looker, Lisa McNamara. At first, she gave me the cold shoulder. I had a wild streak, and it was widely known."

"How surprising," Sheila said with gentle sarcasm.

"Anyway, Lisa didn't want nothin' to do with old Joe Greenway's adopted, half-wild Basque son—old Joe had quite the reputation himself around Reno, as did most of the men on Joe's roll. But then I ordered a nice dress out of the Montgomery Ward catalog. Peach gingham with fancy white lace. Lisa helped me order it. I told her it was for a girl about her size, the purtiest girl I'd ever laid eyes on, that I was pie-eyed for her, and I really wanted to make a good impression on her." He paused to give a delighted chuckle at the memory, then fingered a tear from the corner of his eye. "Cost a purty penny, too. A whole two dollars and fifty cents."

Sheila whistled.

"That made her jealous, I could tell," Johnny said, smiling as he spoke. "The dress took a while to come in. Meanwhile, I stopped pestering Miss McNamara when I rode to town for supplies. Stopped sparking her. I decided I could play just as cool a hand as she could."

"What happened when the dress came in?"

"She handed it over to me and said in a real sneering sort of way, 'Here's that dress for the purtiest girl in the world, Johnny Greenway. I hope you an' her both enjoy it.'"

"'Why, thank you, kindly, Miss Lisa,' I said with the most winning smile I could muster." I held the package across the counter to her and said, "'I hope when you wear it, you'll think of me. And, oh, by the way, there's a dance out at Mill's Creek Hall this Saturday night. Maybe see you there, if you're of a mind to mix with us unwashed country folks . . .'

"I pinched my hat brim to her and left the store. I could see her reflection in the glass—just starin' at me with her jaw hangin'." Johnny laughed.

"This story's gonna make me cry, Johnny," Sheila said in a voice thick with emotion. "If it turns out how I think it is . . ."

"If you're thinkin' she showed up in that dress to the dance that Saturday night, you'd be right."

"Oh!" Sheila chortled, tears of unabashed delight at the sugary sentiment running down her cheeks.

"We were married three months later out at the Maggie Creek Ranch. Old Joe had a cancer growin' in him. Died the next year. His segundo, Marcel, was soon to follow. Those two were like an old married couple. One couldn't live without the other, I reckon. Lisa and I lived out there for a time. I tried to run things, Joe not having any other kids. Only, when Joe died, the lawyers told me how much debt he was in. I had to sell the ranch to pay off his creditors. I wasn't much of a rancher, anyways. Hell, I'd been raised with sheep. Lisa and I went to Reno, and I became a deputy town marshal. Rode shotgun for a stage line. Went from one law job to another, got a deputy U.S. marshal's commission. Those were good years—Lisa an' me in our little frame house in Reno. When David came along, things got even better. At least, for a time . . ."

He paused, shook his head, sighed with regret. "I don't know what happened. The wild Basque blood, I reckon. I got restless. Met a woman. An actress from Leadville who came to Reno to perform at the opera house. I met her when a jealous suitor threatened to kill her. One thing led to another . . . and . . . I shouldn't have done it, but I did. I should have stopped it, but I couldn't. I loved Lisa . . . little David . . . but so help me, I couldn't stop. And then Lisa found out. We were arguing that night I came home late with whiskey on my breath and the smell of Allondia Cascade's perfume on my shirt. I was distracted . . . hadn't heard the horses pull up. In my drunkenness, I'd forgotten to lock the door."

Johnny's voice pinched off in a howling wail. He thrust his arm across his eyes, trying not to cry but with no success.

Sheila wrapped her arms around his neck and held him close against her bosom while he sobbed. The storm hammered the cabin, echoing Shotgun Johnny's grief.

They left the cabin very early the next morning.

Johnny knew what he would do if he had as many men riding for him as Seville did—he would send them out by twos and threes, like the spokes on a wheel, to scout the area for their quarry. Once that quarry was spotted, the others would be signaled, and all of those spokes would converge, and they would come as one small army. Seville was savage, not stupid. He would likely employ a similar tactic.

Johnny wanted to make sure he was well ahead of those scouts when they came, for soon one or two would find the cabin, and they would know that Johnny and Sheila had been there. The blasted-out door would tell them that if nothing else would. And because of the recent rain, Seville's quarry would be easy to track.

Johnny knew they would come. One, after what Johnny had done to them, turning the tables on them, they would want revenge for their own pride if for no other reason, but they were likely as mad as old wet hens, as well. Also, Johnny and Sheila were the only two people alive who had seen Seville's gang's faces and knew who the gold robbers were. They would have a much easier time making it to Mexico if their identities weren't known. If lawmen and bounty hunters knew who the robbers were, Seville would have to stick to the backcountry, avoiding towns and other people as much as possible.

That would make it hard to acquire supplies. It would also mean they would have to stay in Mexico for a good long time, for they'd be wanted north of the border for the rest of their lives.

Johnny wanted to get Sheila down out of the mountains, to Hallelujah Junction. Then he would return to the mountains alone, on a fresh horse and with fresh ammunition and trail supplies, to pull a turnabout and hunt the hunters. He wanted to kill Seville, at least. He thought he'd probably already killed Louis Raised-By-Wolves, but the big Indian might also still be alive though likely in very poor health.

Double-ought buckshot can do terrible things to a man's face, and that's where Johnny thought he'd hit Raised-By-Wolves. The thought made him smile, so he tried to think of it often. He had a feeling Raised-By-Wolves was the cutthroat who'd driven Bear's own bowie knife into the poor old mountain man's belly. If so, Johnny hoped he was still alive so that Johnny could exact even more revenge on the wounded savage.

Johnny thought that he and Sheila were probably still a good two days' ride from town. That dash to Bear's old cabin had set them back an extra day. Now they had to ride around Sheep's Head Mountain and take the valley of the Avalanche River back to Hallelujah Junction. The way the ridges in this part of the Sierras were laid out, that meant they had to ride north before they could turn back east and south.

Once they'd left the cabin, Johnny and Sheila rode hard, angling north along the river valley, dropping gradually from the high alpine reaches of the mountains, where the terrain was stark and severe and the weather was always formidable late in the day, to the more moderate, lusher elevations, where the late wildflowers and changing aspens painted the meadows and forested mountainsides with the deep yellows and cool browns of mid-fall, and trout streams chuckled through piney glens echoing the bugling cries of rutting elk.

They camped that night in a nest of rocks by a quiet stream. Johnny caught several red-throated trout using line and a hook he'd packed with his old trail gear, and some chubs he found under a rock. Sheila cooked the fish with bacon and wild onions, burning the hell out of them, but he told her they were delicious, smiling as he imagined Bear sitting across the fire from him, winking his delight at the young woman's poor cooking skills.

Ah, Bear . . .

Johnny slept maybe a total of a half hour that night. While Sheila slumbered in her soogan, he sat up by the fire he'd allowed to burn down to barely glowing coals, knowing that by now Seville was aware that Johnny and Sheila had spent the previous night in the cabin and that the entire gang was on their trail. They would be hard after them now.

His suspicions were confirmed around noon of the next day, when he scrutinized their back trail through his field glasses from the top of a rocky outcropping pocked with autumn-red shrubs. He cursed, lowered the glasses, and scrambled down from his rocky perch.

"What is it?" Sheila said, standing with the horses, seeing the anxiety on his face.

Johnny dropped the glasses back into his saddlebags and picked up his reins. "Change of plans. We're gonna split up. I'm going to lead them up into the high country and kill the lot of the sons of bucks once an' for all!"

CHAPTER 32

"No!" Sheila's voice was pinched with anxiety. "No splitting up!"

"I'm gonna hide you here and take your horse," Johnny said, ignoring her protest. "They'll think you're with me. If I don't make it back, there's plenty of prospectors around who'll—!"

"No!" Sheila stood before him, ramming the backs of her fists against his broad chest. "You're the only man I've ever loved, Johnny! Yes—I said it. I love you. And I know you feel something for me. No man could make love the way you did two nights ago without feeling something. I won't cower here in the bushes while you're fighting my fight for me."

Johnny squeezed her right wrist in his left hand. "It's no longer your fight. When they killed Bear, it became my fight alone."

Sheila bunched her lips and shook her head in defiance. "We go together." She paused, then, trying to appeal to another side of him, added sternly, "That's an order, Mister Greenway."

Something sizzled past Johnny's left ear. It plunked into the ground near the filly. The young horse squealed and bucked as the rifle's flat belching report made it to Johnny's ears. He glanced quickly along their backtrail to see a man levering a rifle in a nest of rocks atop a scarp bristling with small pines.

He cursed loudly, grabbed Sheila around the waist, and hurled her onto the back of her pitching, anxious horse. "Now, you've done it, *Miss Bonner*!"

Another bullet caromed toward them.

"Oh!" Sheila cried, swiping a gloved hand to her right cheek. A thin line of blood shone. The bullet had grazed her.

"See?" Johnny bellowed at her, swinging up onto Ghost's back. "Damn fool woman! Come on if you're coming!"

Johnny swung his own anxious horse up trail and ground his heels into the gelding's loins. Ghost lunged into a rocking lope, and Johnny glanced behind to see the filly hot on his heels, Sheila crouching low in the saddle, the wind blowing her rich chestnut hair back behind her shoulders. The graze was thin; the bullet had barely skimmed her cheek. Still, she was lucky. If she'd only listened to him, she'd be safe right now.

Instead, because of the time they'd wasted arguing, she'd likely be dead in minutes.

She must have spied the silent scolding in his eyes, for she returned his look with a hard, insolent one of her own. Beneath his anger, he couldn't help admiring her pluck.

Beneath the clattering of their own mounts' hooves, Johnny heard the distant thunder of other riders coming fast. He glanced behind. Several riders were just then rounding a bend behind him and Sheila. He recognized Seville at the front of the pack.

The Indian, Raised-By-Wolves, was in stride beside him. The half-breed had a bandanna wrapped at an angle across his forehead, below his black, bullet-crowned hat and over his left eye.

Despite the direness of the situation, Johnny couldn't help curling his upper lip in satisfaction at the damage his Twin had done to the big savage who'd likely tortured Bear. They were coming fast, though—damn it to hell.

He swung off the trail's right side, shouting back at Sheila, "This way!"

Several prospectors' cabins, their shake-shingled roofs mottled green with moss, crouched under pines off the left side of this secondary trail Johnny and Sheila were now following. The Avalanche River flashed through the trees on the right, like a large, yellow-skinned snake. A woman came out of the trees with a bucket of water she must have fetched from the river—an old, raisin-faced, little bird of a woman in a gingham dress, poke bonnet, and a soiled apron. She paused in the trees to scowl at the horseback riders. A short-haired mongrel stood beside her, snarling at the strangers. As Johnny and Sheila whipped past the woman, the dog ran a short way after them, barking.

A steep, forested ridge rose ahead of Johnny, blocking the way.

"Dammit!" He hauled sharply back on Ghost's reins.

"What is it?" Sheila said, stopping the filly beside him.

"We're not where I thought we were!"

"Where did you think we were?"

He didn't have time to explain that he thought

they were in Crow Wing Gulch, at the end of which he thought he could lose their pursuers up a high trail that twisted through rocks and boulders. He wasn't sure where he was now. He did know that the river rolling through the gorge on their right was the Avalanche River, so maybe this was Sourdough or Hell's Canyon. There were no other rivers in this neck of the Sierras as large as the Avalanche—only creeks and streams.

That body of water down the hill and through the trees was definitely the Avalanche.

Johnny glanced behind him. The gang was just then galloping past the old lady, who remained where she'd been before, holding her water bucket and turning her head slowly to regard the howling gang of cutthroats thundering past her, the dog just then nipping at the hocks of one of the gang's horses.

"This way!" Johnny said, and booted Ghost straight down the steep slope through brush and around trees.

"Where are we going?" Sheila called behind him as the rattling of the cutthroat gang's pistols and rifles put Johnny's nerves on an even sharper edge than before.

"I got no idea! Just keep your head down and follow me!"

"You have no reason to be so angry at me, Johnny!" she fairly screamed at him as the filly lunged down the steep slope behind him and Ghost. "I told you that I love you, you stubborn damn fool!"

"Oh, hell!" Now was not the time for a lovers' quarrel. "Get out of the damn way!" he bellowed at her when, reining his horse back around to face the slope, he found her between him and the ridge.

She jerked the filly away sharply. Johnny pulled one of the Twins and thumbed back both triggers. The gang had just started down the slope. They needed a little discouragement.

Johnny held the Twin straight out before him and sent one wad of buckshot up into the trees. A second later, he sent the other wad caroming up the slope a little left of the first wad, evoking several curses and shrill yelps, the riders yanking back on their horses' reins.

"Come on!" he yelled again, turning Ghost to gallop downstream, which was about a hundred yards wide at this point.

Several miners were panning for gold out in the knee-deep water while others worked with picks and shovels along both banks. They stopped working to stare incredulously at the man and woman galloping downstream, following the river's gentle curve to the left.

Johnny had ridden maybe a hundred yards when he spied a wooden raft drawn up along the relatively flat, gravelly shore. It rested beside a dead, sun-bleached blowdown angling out into the stream. The raft was tied by a rope to a short, spindle-like branch of the dead tree. There were some picks and shovels and a couple of sluice boxes on the raft. It probably belonged to the two men working up on the bank above and a little farther downstream of the dead tree.

Johnny checked Ghost down sharply. As Sheila galloped up behind him, Johnny quickly untied the raft from the branch, casting an anxious glance upstream. A thumb of forested land separated him and

Sheila from the oncoming riders, whom he could hear shouting and hollering and triggering lead beneath the constant rush of the river.

"Climb down!" Johnny ordered Sheila. With a deep grunt, he shoved the raft, which was about eight feet long by eight feet wide, with a wooden, long-handled rudder attached to the rear, out into the stream. The rudder doubled as a paddle.

"What on earth are you doing?" Sheila said, standing on the sandy shore, regarding him as though she had just realized she was in the company of a madman.

"We're going for a ride." Johnny steadied the raft about five feet from shore. He extended a hand to her. "Hurry!"

"You're crazy! We'll never make it!"

Johnny kicked the sluice boxes, picks, and shovels off the raft and into the stream. "We'll never make it if you keep arguing with me!"

Sheila gave a groan of exasperation then stepped out into the river, throwing her hand out to Johnny, who grabbed it and guided her aboard the raft.

"Hey!" yelled one of the men working on the bank above and beyond them. They both scowled at Johnny and Sheila. They were both bearded—one tall, the other of average height and wearing an eyepatch and a coonskin cap.

"Need to borrow your raft!" Johnny shouted, nudging Sheila and the raft out into the stream.

When the raft started bobbing in the current stitched with the foam of water licking up over half-submerged rocks, Johnny rammed it between a driftwood snag and a large rock then ran back onto shore.

"Johnny!" Sheila cried, glancing around nervously

at the river. "Where are you going?" She was down on one knee, throwing her arms out for balance.

"Be right there!"

Johnny ran upstream a few feet until he could see Seville's bunch galloping toward him around the thumb of forested land. He drew his loaded Twin and cocked it. Seville and Raised-By-Wolves were still in the lead. Seville's eyes widened when he saw Shotgun Johnny bearing down on him with the single Twin. He drew back sharply on his horse's reins and, wheeling the horse toward the shoreward side of the river, shouted, "Pull back! Pull back!"

Johnny cut loose with the ten-gauge, sending both barrels of double-ought buck into the pack that was maybe thirty yards behind him. Horses whinnied and men screamed as the gang dispersed like a flock of chickens fleeing the wheels of a runaway farm wagon. Johnny wheeled and ran back around the bend to where his horse and the filly stood regarding him skeptically. The two miners had started toward him, but they stood a little farther down on the slope than where they'd been before, warily regarding the big, black-clad man with the two shotguns.

Johnny shucked his Winchester from the saddle boot. He pulled an old, war-era cartridge pouch with a canvas lanyard from a saddlebag pouch. He looped the lanyard over his head and right shoulder. He patted the cream's wither and said, "Follow me, boy. Follow me!"

He ran out into the stream. Sheila regarded him nervously, her face pale. The blood on her grazed cheek had dried into a crusted, dark-red line she'd smudged with her hand.

"I really hope you know what you're doing, Johnny," she said.

"So do I." Johnny gave the raft a shove out into the current then hopped aboard. He dropped to a knee. Seville's men were firing now from the far side of the bend. Johnny could see them from this vantage from the stream. Most of the cutthroats were down on a knee while some were still mounted and milling around, still distressed after taking four more barrels of buckshot. Three men were down, apparently wounded. The big Indian, Raised-By-Wolves, was running downriver along the shore, cocking a Henry rifle and shouting angrily though Johnny couldn't hear what the man was saying above the river's rush and the clattering of the other men's pistols and rifles.

Probably something about that eye Johnny had apparently turned to cherry jelly.

Or maybe about Wolves' sister, whom Sheila must have taken out of action for good, for she wasn't in sight.

Johnny sent two rounds caroming toward Raised-By-Wolves, both shots pluming gravel behind the big, copper-skinned, long-haired man. The raft was bouncing around on the uneven current too violently for accurate shooting. That wasn't all bad, for it made Johnny and Sheila hard-to-hit targets, as well.

The bullets of the Indian and the others tore into the water to both sides of the raft or spanged off rocks poking up out of the river or made devilish whirring sounds as they sailed over and beyond their targets. Soon, the raft was far enough downstream that the men on shore were little larger than stick figures, nearly out of rifle range though they continued firing, smoke puffing around their rifle maws.

Ghost was galloping along the shore, whinnying and laying his ears back against his head, trying to keep up with the raft. Sheila's filly was following the big gelding, both mounts trailing their reins, their eyes wide and white-ringed, upset over the commotion as well as by the inexplicable desertion by their riders.

Johnny set the Winchester down and quickly reloaded each Twin in turn.

Sheila sat on the raft with one leg curled beneath the other. She looked from Seville's men to Johnny.

"What's the plan?" she asked, her voice brittle.

"Plan?" Johnny laughed without mirth. "Hell, I don't have a plan. I just know they would have caught up to us on shore or run us to ground and starved us out or waited till I'd snapped through all my ammunition. I reckon if I had a plan, it was to buy us some time . . ."

He let his voice trail off as he stared downstream and saw that the river split into two separate directions maybe a hundred yards ahead. Between the tines was a narrow strip of rocky, driftwood-littered land that widened farther downstream and was bristling with tall, old firs and spruces.

Johnny looked behind and shoreward. Seville's men were mounting their horses again and were starting to gallop downstream, pursuing the raft.

Johnny turned to the split in the river again. If he swung the raft onto the right tine, he might be able to buy him and Sheila even more time, for that right tine was even farther from the river's left side, where Seville's men were riding hard now, leaping obstacles along the waterline.

The only problem was, between the raft and that right tine was a gnarly-looking rapids. If they didn't swamp, they'd be all right. If they swamped, they were doomed.

"Hold on," Johnny urged, grabbing the rudder's long, wooden handle. "This could get a little hairy."

"What are you talking about?" Sheila said half to herself. "It's *been* hairy since we left Hallelujah Junction."

CHAPTER 33

Johnny pulled the rudder from its lock and stood on the raft's left side. He used the rudder like a paddle as well as a boat pole, churning the water back behind him and ramming the end of the rudder against the river bottom, thrusting the raft out to the right, heading them for the river's right fork.

The water was rough where the river split in two, curling and rooster-tailing around and over large rocks. Kneeling beside him, Sheila placed her hands flat against the raft's halved logs, holding on and trying to maintain her balance. The water splashed up along the raft's right front corner, pooling in the gaps between the logs. Sheila shivered as the spray washed over her.

As Johnny fought the raft farther and farther to the right, the craft bobbing wildly beneath him and Sheila, the woman glanced up at him skeptically. "Have, uh . . . have you ever done this before? Pilot a raft . . ."

Johnny glanced at her and laughed. "Hell, no!"

"That's what I was afraid you were going to say."

Finally, Johnny had them beyond the rapids where

the river split. He narrowly avoided a run-in with a couple of large boulders, and then the current of the right fork grabbed hold of the raft and swept it on past the right side of the narrow strip of land that must be an island though Johnny couldn't see beyond it just yet.

All he knew was that now the cutthroats were nowhere in sight.

At the moment, that was just fine with him. He knew they were galloping downstream, hoping to meet up with their quarry again soon. And they would likely do just that. Johnny and Sheila were in a tough spot, but it had been a lot tougher just before he'd spotted the raft. If he and the woman had stuck with the horses, with Seville dogging them so closely, they'd likely be crowbait by now.

The raft bobbed and pitched. Water sprayed over the front end, giving Johnny and Sheila sporadic cold showers. Johnny glanced over the side to see gravelly stretches of river bottom between submerged boulders maybe five feet below the raft. The water wasn't deep, but the rocks and occasional driftwood snags made it treacherous.

As they drifted along, Johnny having to paddle only occasionally, mainly to steer around obstacles, the far end of the land to their left came into view. The land strip was an island, all right. The downstream end was coming up fast. As the raft continued wobbling along the current, occasionally nudging hidden rocks, it drifted on past the island.

Johnny cast his gaze to the left shore, his blood quickening.

He squeezed the end of the rudder with his left

hand and lowered his right hand to the rear stock of his right-holstered Twin. "Get ready."

Sheila shunted her weary gaze toward the far shore.

Johnny's heart eased when he saw no riders over there. Thick woods—dark-green pines and white-stemmed aspens and birches pushed thick and close to the edge of the water. The bank was around six to ten feet high, and rocky. Riders couldn't make it through there.

"So far so good," Johnny thought, optimism rising in him.

Maybe they'd flee the gang, after all, and he could still get Sheila back to Hallelujah Junction in one piece.

Sheila glanced up at him. He looked down at her. She was feeling the same relief he was. Her bullet-grazed cheek rose in a slight smile. Johnny felt even better when two sheer stone walls, maybe two hundred feet high, rose just ahead of the raft.

The cliffs towered over both sides of the stream. They were so sheer that not even a bighorn sheep could negotiate their streamside faces, and there was no room between them and the water for either a horse or a man. The formations blocked the sunlight so that the river ahead appeared nearly as dark as a tunnel.

So far, so good.

The raft drifted into the shadows of the steep cliffs.

The water was a little shallower and a little rougher here, but Johnny, using the paddle and occasionally switching from one side of the raft to the other, negotiated the competing currents around rocks poking their gray heads above the water. He kept glancing along the shore to his left, half-expecting to see the gang, possibly having found a crack through the cliff wall, heading toward them.

So far, so good.

Ahead, the cliff walls lowered and grew less sheer, strewn with slide-rock and boulders that had probably tumbled down from the higher reaches during ancient earthquakes or the erosions of time and weather. The river narrowed and made a broad turn to the right, then back to the left before stretching out straight and wide again between banks that were craggy but only fifty to a hundred feet high. Beyond them, Johnny could see no sign of the trail. Better yet, no sign of the gang he knew was still stalking them, no doubt looking desperately for a route back to the river.

They'd followed him and Sheila this far. They wouldn't give up so easily. Not when they had maybe a quarter of a million dollars in gold stashed away somewhere and needed time to pack it and get it down the mountains and across the Mojave Desert to Mexico. They needed time for all that. They didn't need lawmen or bounty hunters stalking them, and that's what they figured would happen if they let their prey make it back to relative civilization—if you could call Hallelujah Junction civilization.

A placid, slower stretch of river drew up around the raft. The water was dark-green, lens-clear, and very deep. They must be over a submerged gorge. Johnny took a break from paddling. He housed the paddle in its rudder fitting then took a knee over his rifle, looking around, taking a minute to enjoy the beauty of this remote stretch of the Avalanche, a river

he'd once known well when he was a very young boy
and he and his birth father were shepherding a herd
of sheep through these valleys during the short
mountain summers.

Of course, he didn't remember details of the
stream, or the places they'd camped back then in
those short, fleeting days of his young boyhood
before a cattle rancher had hired regulators to
murder his family—killers who'd never been brought
to justice, he needed no reminding.

Still, the river looked familiar. Everything he
saw—that boulder balanced precariously atop another one way up high on that craggy cliff, that
eagle's nest at the top of an ancient fir on the bank
to his right, that little bay on whose shore was littered
the remains of a beaver dam that had likely given way
during a heavy spring runoff—he felt . . . knew . . .
he'd seen before during a more innocent time,
when he was young and the world hadn't yet pum-
meled him into a shadow of himself.

"What're you thinking about?" Sheila asked him as
they drifted along, the river strangely hushed except
for the quiet lapping of the water licking up against
the raft.

"Joseba Ramon Beristain. My father. He introduced me to this country when I was just a little
shaver. He and my mother, Yolanda; my brother,
Arnauld. Arnie for short."

She frowned. "They're all dead?"

Johnny nodded. He didn't want to think about
those times. Not now in a relative time of peace
before the next storm he knew was coming, but he
couldn't help remembering—feeling the sadness,

the anger of having been cheated out of his natural family for so many years.

"Murdered."

"By who?"

"Assassins hired by a rancher who hadn't wanted sheep on his land nor the funny, dark people who tended the flocks. There was no investigation, of course. My folks died too remote, and no one cared about we funny foreign people. I was off tending a flock while my father had returned to our base camp for supplies. He said he'd be gone only a few hours. That stretched into two days. I started home but was intercepted by some friendly cowpunchers who knew my father. They'd found my family. They wouldn't let me see them. No matter how hard I tried to get to the bodies, those men wouldn't let me see them. Then they were buried and gone, and I have only memories now."

"You mean . . . no one was brought to justice for such a crime?"

Johnny chuckled at her naïveté. "We were brown-skinned people. Talked funny. Dressed in strange clothes. We herded sheep in cattle country. It was open range, but the ranchers saw the range as theirs. We weren't wanted anywhere we went. They said our sheep killed the grass, but that wasn't true. We tended them well, tended the range well—better, even—than the cattle ranchers did. We stayed with our flocks night and day, all year long. When they cropped the grass to a certain length, or threatened a watercourse, we shepherded them on to another watershed. Few cattlemen managed their stock as well as we did."

"Do you know who did that horrible thing?"

"Not the regulators who did the actual killing. They likely drifted on. Might be old men by now. But, old Joe . . ." Johnny smiled, wistful, as he rolled a smoke.

"What?" Sheila asked. "Tell me."

"Old Joe found out who the rancher was who hired the killers. He didn't know who they all were, but he knew who one was. Burt Pfeiffer. Territorial senator who owned a spread out here. He was bragging about the deed in a Reno parlor house, and Joe hired a man to cut his throat. Joe confessed it to me on his deathbed. He couldn't help himself, old Joe couldn't. Not when he heard Pfeiffer bragging about it so openly and proudly. Joe hired a seedy killer to do the dirty deed, and Burt Pfeiffer died in a whore's crib, drowning on his own blood."

Johnny chuckled as he lit the quirley, blowing smoke out his mouth and nostrils. "God, how I loved that old man. Damn near as much as my own father and mother. He was stubborn and irascible, often a drunk and a whoremonger. But he was just and fair and he didn't hold a man's skin color or language against him . . . and he sure as hell loved me and took the time and sweat to gentle the young stallion I was when no one else would have."

"I'm glad you had a good father, Johnny. Two good ones. I had a good one, too." Sheila looked away, her eyes cast with sadness. "I miss him terribly. He died from a weak heart, but it was Harry Seville and that Raised-By-Wolves creature who killed him. Just as surely as if they'd shot him with a gun."

"Well," Johnny said, "we might just get a chance to talk to Seville about that."

Sheila swung her head to him sharply. "What are you talking about?"

Johnny was staring at the low, crumbling stone ridge on the bank to his left. He'd just seen two riders pass behind a gap in the low jog of rocky hills.

"What did you see?"

"Trouble." A low rumbling sounded ahead, tearing Johnny's gaze from shore. He stared ahead along the broad, dark, slow-moving water. "Oh, hell . . ."

Sheila looked at him again and followed his gaze out ahead of the raft. "What . . . ? Oh, no!"

She'd just seen it, too. About a hundred yards beyond them, the river dropped over a ridge. As the raft slid closer and closer to the ridge, the rumbling of the water falling over the ridge and down the other side grew louder.

Sheila turned back to Johnny, her eyes wide with anxiety. "Is that what I think it is?"

Johnny nodded. "Coyote Falls. Plumb forgot . . ."

"Oh, my God," Sheila said. "Can we make it?"

"I don't know." Johnny couldn't remember how steep the falls was. He remembered the name, for there was a relatively flat area along the eastern bank that made a good camping spot.

It was likely a good place to fire rifles toward the river, too . . .

Johnny's pulse picked up as he stared ahead toward that ridge where the serene water dropped like a downward curving tongue, over which he and Sheila were destined to plunge. He quickly looked to each side.

To his right was another sheer stone wall. There'd be no escaping the river on that side. To his left, more horseback riders galloped through rocks and pines, approaching the river from the forest beyond the shoreline. Johnny's spine tingled at the chilling metallic rasp of rifles being cocked.

There'd be no escaping the river on that side, either. Unless he and Sheila wanted to escape into a hail of hot lead . . .

As though to validate his assumption, a bullet skipped off the top of the raft between Johnny and Sheila, nearly missing Johnny's rifle lying there and leaving a gouge in the wood of one of the halved logs. The whine of the bullet was followed a half-second later by the hiccupping report of the rifle vaulting out over the river.

"Johnny!" Sheila cried, staring in shock at the bullet-scarred wood. "What're we gonna do?"

"Hold on!" Johnny raised the Winchester, rammed a cartridge into the action, and began firing toward shore—three quick shots, the cartridge casings arcing out over his right shoulder and into the stream behind him.

"Johnny!" Sheila cried again.

As the cutthroats began shooting at the raft, smoke puffing along the shoreline, Johnny turned forward. He cursed. He rose from his knee, straightening, his stomach lurching into his throat as the nose of the raft dropped over the falls.

Sheila screamed.

The scream was quickly drowned by the roar of the tumbling water.

Chapter 34

"Jump clear of the raft!" Johnny shouted to Sheila as the raft plunged downward.

He didn't know if she heard him or knew instinctively what to do, but she jumped off the raft as the front dropped away below her. She leaned to the right so the raft had less chance of striking her as it plunged toward the bottom of the falls, which was maybe a fifty-foot drop—a rolling cascade of water crashing off rocks as it dropped toward a relatively sedate pool below.

As the raft plunged down and away from Johnny, he saw to his left several of the gang members standing on rocks a few dozen feet out from shore, aiming rifles toward him and Sheila. There was a large boulder just down from the top of the falls, to Johnny's left. Without thinking but more or less reacting to the situation, as his experience as a deputy U.S. marshal had trained him to do, he leaped onto the top of that boulder.

It was a ten-foot drop. He planted his feet atop the boulder over which and around the tumbling water swirled, threatening to rip him off the boulder and take him on down the falls.

He resisted the water's force by dropping to his hands and knees, grinding them into the boulder, maintaining a precarious purchase as the roiling river churned all around him and against him, instantly soaking him. The crash of the rifles to his left braced him, as did the whir of bullets around him.

Johnny heaved himself to his feet, clawing both of the Twins from their holsters and raising them, brushing back the heavy hammers with his muscular thumbs and detonating a barrel of each ten-gauge at the same time. The buckshot blew two cutthroats from their respective rocks, screaming and plunging straight back into the water, throwing their rifles out away from them, hats flying.

Fighting against the water trying to sweep his ankles out from beneath him, Johnny hastily aimed his left shotgun. He'd caught flat-footed a man on a rock fifteen feet away from him and nearly straight to his left, just then ejecting a spent cartridge from his rifle's breech.

Seeing the big maw yawning at him, the man dropped his rifle, opened his mouth wide in protest, and raised his arms in front of his face as if to shield himself from the double-ought buck.

They did no such thing.

The buckshot shredded his hands and wrists and hurled him backward and down. He struck his head on a rock behind him with an audible cracking sound and disappeared into a funnel of water churning between the half-submerged boulders.

Johnny emptied the right-hand Twin's second barrel into another man whom he vaguely and absently recognized as Homer Granger, a former deputy sheriff from Winnemucca—a deputy sheriff turned outlaw, apparently.

Granger triggered his rifle at Johnny. The bullet nipped the outside of Johnny's left thigh just before the blast took Granger in the belly and hurled him shrieking into the river, instantly turning the white foam he'd disappeared into red with blood and viscera.

Seeing more men blasting away at him from shore, Johnny quickly holstered the Twins, snapping the keeper thongs over the hammers. He saw the pool of dark-blue water beneath him, at the bottom of the falls. He leaned forward, threw his arms up, and leaped off his heels. As a bullet sliced a burning line across his left calf, he plunged downward through the spray of the hammering falls.

He hit the water like a knife with his outstretched hands, and his momentum drove him deep until his fingers brushed the pool's slick, polished stone bottom. He pushed off the bottom, lifting his head and arms. He swam toward the surface, his head breaking free of the water a moment later.

The current had ahold of him and was pulling and pushing him down, down the sloping stream between large, black granite rocks. Whitewater churned around him. Between the rocks on his left, he saw Seville and several others running downstream along the shore, triggering lead at him, yelling back and forth to one another.

A bullet spanged off a rock near Johnny. He flinched, cursed, and continued on down the falls, looking wildly around for Sheila but seeing no sign of her. The falls was leveling out, the whitewater pulling away behind him. Finally, he was on level water—deeper, slower moving water. The rocks fell back on his left. Seville's bunch was running along beside Johnny, still hurling occasional shots at him, yelling, wanting to get closer for more-certain shooting.

The problem for them was that the river was wider here, and deeper, and there were no rocks on which they could hopscotch out into the stream. The problem for Johnny, he saw now as he stared straight ahead along the darkly sliding water, was that what appeared a rocky ford lay dead ahead of him, maybe a hundred yards away.

When he reached that ford, Seville's men would swarm him, and it would all be over.

He looked around again for Sheila.

As he did, she called his name.

He followed the disembodied voice ahead and to the right. She was clinging to a rock near the far-right shore, which was abutted by a steep rock wall. The young woman was partly hidden by the shade of a short, stocky, lightning-topped spruce growing up out of a wide crack in the rocky shore, angling out over the water.

Hugging the rock, she stared toward Johnny, and called to him again. As he swam toward her, several more bullets plunked into the water around him.

"Are you all right?" he asked as he approached her, flinging his arms at the water, flinching as yet another bullet curled the air near his left ear and made a chilling tinkling sound as it hit the stream only a foot away.

She was shivering. The water was cold and deep.

She nodded. "Bruised is all. Cold. Tired." She glanced toward Seville's men running in a loose group, some standing on the shore directly across the river from Johnny and Sheila, aiming rifles. "What're we gonna do, Johnny?"

Johnny pulled Sheila back behind the rock for better cover, pressing his body up against hers, protecting her. He looked around. The shore behind them was their only hope of escape. The problem was the ridge looming over it looked sheer and solid. No way up and no way through.

No, wait.

His heart beat with guarded hope.

He glanced around his covering rock toward Seville's men. They were all yelling like jackals now. They'd seen the ford and were running toward it—wolves on the blood scent.

Johnny squeezed Sheila's shoulder. "Follow me. Stay close."

Shivering, her voice small with fear and exhaustion, she said, "Where are we going?"

"Not sure yet, but we can't stay here."

He turned and swam toward the shore, which was about thirty yards away. He swam between small rocks reaching out from the shoreline then began climbing the rocky bank, turning to take Sheila's hand and to pull her up behind him. He glanced downstream.

The killers were running across the rocky ford, splashing like playful children, only these children ran with rifles or pistols in their hands. A quick count gave Johnny the rough estimate of twelve remaining in their pack. Better than twenty-plus, but he was still badly outnumbered.

And he'd lost his rifle in the river. He had only the Twins. As wet as they were, the wads doubtless being fouled by the water, they were useless. He had fresh, dry loads in the canvas knapsack that was still hanging from his neck and shoulder—he'd made sure not to lose it in the river—but at the moment he had no time to reload. Besides, even if he could recharge the shotguns, they were likely still wet, and the wet steel might foul the new loads.

"Come on," he said when Sheila had gained the rocky bank of the stream, water tumbling off both of them, splashing on the rocks and gravel at their feet.

He started jogging ahead, but when Sheila groaned, he turned to see her dropping to her knees, breathing hard, her soaked hair hanging down both sides of her face. "Oh, God, Johnny—I'm so tired!"

Their time in the river had fatigued her. He felt it himself—a heavy weight of exhaustion pushing down hard against his shoulders. They both had to resist it.

"No time to rest," Johnny said, grabbing her wrist and pulling her to her feet, jerking her along behind him. He glanced at the killers, the first ones—Seville and then the Indian, Raised-By-Wolves—just then gaining the same shore that Johnny and Sheila were on, maybe a hundred yards behind them. "They're close and they're getting closer!"

"We're not going to escape them, Johnny," Sheila moaned as she ran along behind him, her knees nearly buckling. "We might as well face it!"

"There's a chance." Staring straight ahead as he ran, tugging Sheila by her wrist grasped firmly in his left hand, he saw an opening in the cliff wall ahead of him. As they approached, hope grew in him. Could they have stumbled onto a canyon running perpendicular to the main one?

A possible escape route?

As he and Sheila approached the gap opening on their left, Johnny paused, breathing hard, to stare into what he'd hoped was an intersecting canyon. Disappointment was a cold stone dropping in his belly. He was staring into a canyon, all right—a *box canyon*. It appeared to dead-end at another steep slope maybe a hundred yards beyond the mouth.

Johnny looked upstream. There didn't appear to be another escape route in that direction. Hearing the shouts of their blood-hungry pursuers from downstream, Johnny took Sheila's hand and pulled her into the intersecting canyon, breaking into another run, half-dragging the poor girl along behind him.

The canyon curved to the right, then to the left. It wasn't very wide—maybe fifty yards at its widest, and strewn with boulders. Brush and a few trees grew along the edges. Down the middle of the cut was a dry, sand-bottomed creek bed littered with sun-bleached bits of driftwood and other debris.

As Johnny and Sheila reached the far end of the canyon, at the canyon's back wall, Johnny stared up at the slope before him. It wasn't as steep as the walls of the main canyon, nor as steep as those to each side of him now. Scattered rocks and clumps of dry brush offered hand- and footholds as well as cover from shooters below.

It could be climbed. In such a situation, it would *have to* be climbed. It was their only chance.

Shouting rose behind them. It must have taken

Seville's bunch a few minutes to figure out that their prey had disappeared into the side canyon, but they were coming now. Johnny couldn't see them, but he could hear their coyote-like yips and taunting yowls issuing from behind a bend in the side canyon's wall.

Johnny climbed onto a small boulder and stepped onto a larger one just up from the first. He turned to offer his hand to Sheila. "Come on!"

She was fading fast, breathless, her face a mask of bitter anguish. "Wh-where . . . what are you . . . ?"

"Take my hand, dammit!"

With another weary, breathless groan, Sheila tossed her hand to him. He closed his own hand around her wrist and pulled her up behind him. He climbed onto another boulder, pulled Sheila up behind him, her soft grunts and shrill groans biting him deep.

He came to a clear stretch of slope and traversed it quickly, knowing he was open to the shooters approaching below. Quickly, he climbed up and around a finger of rock jutting out from the slope's steep face. As he pulled Sheila behind the shelter, a bullet hammered the face of the finger, spraying rock shards in all directions.

She gasped, fell against him, her knees buckling.

"Johnny!" she cried. "I can't . . . I'm sorry . . . I *can't* . . . !"

Johnny glanced down at the dozen men closing on the base of the slope he and Sheila were on. His heart lurched in his chest. They'd be on top of him soon.

"You have to! You have to try, dammit!" Johnny grabbed her arms and shook her violently. Her drying, dusty hair flopped around her face. "Do you understand me? You have to! I'm not going to let you die!" From where the next several words came, he had no idea, but they leaped from his lips, sounding as true and resolute as anything he'd ever said before. "*I love you, confound it!*"

CHAPTER 35

Johnny's words were a sharp slap across her face.

Sheila raised her drooping eyelids and gazed back at him for a full second through the mussed screen of her hair, staring into his own eyes, startled. She nodded forlornly. "Okay," she wheezed out, trying to smile but managing only a pronounced wince. "Okay . . ."

Guns crashed below as Seville's wolves began climbing the slope, triggering lead. Johnny grabbed Sheila's hand and continued climbing the ridge. He scrambled up the slope, keeping her wrist taut in his right hand, pulling her up behind him. Sometimes she was a deadweight, and he literally dragged her. Sometimes, sobbing, she managed to half crawl and help him pull her up the slope.

Meanwhile, the killers were laughing as they closed on their prey. They were no longer shooting. They knew they needed to waste no more ammunition. They were close, and their prey was defenseless.

Johnny climbed, tearing his fingers on handholds, ripping out the knees of his whipcord trousers, badly scuffing his boots. When his right arm weakened so that he could no longer pull Sheila with it, he switched to his left hand and continued, gritting his teeth, breathing hard, something inside him unwilling to accept the bloody fate that deep down he knew was likely his and hers . . .

Someone was wheezing crazily behind him. At first, Johnny thought it was Sheila. He indulged in a backward glance.

No, it wasn't the woman. A man was closing on them quickly, scrambling on hands and knees, laughing through his teeth.

He was ten feet behind Sheila and closing . . .

Johnny threw Sheila to the ground to his right and picked up a rock. He hurled it at the man approaching ahead of the others, who were scrambling up the slope behind him and to both sides, fanned out across the rock- and boulder-strewn incline.

The man ducked. Johnny's rock sailed over the man's head.

The man straightened, his smile broadening, his lewdly glinting eyes going to the woman groaning on the slope to Johnny's right.

Another stone was in Johnny's hand. He hurled it. The man had just slid his eyes back to Johnny from the woman. The lewd glint went dark when the man saw the rock flying toward him a quarter of an eye wink before it smashed soundly against the bridge of his nose.

"Oh!" the man cried, clamping both hands to his face as he stumbled backward and sideways against a large rock. His hat tumbled off his shoulder.

Johnny scrambled sideways down to the man, nearly losing his footing. He grabbed one of the man's six-shooters from a holster on the man's waist.

Gritting his teeth, Johnny raised the Colt .45, clicked back the hammer, and shot the man point-blank with it, drilling a quarter-sized hole in his forehead, just beneath the pale line left by his hat. The man slumped back and down, exposing another man running up behind him.

"Whoa!" the man cried, raising both his own empty hands when he saw Johnny narrowing his right eye as he aimed down the barrel of the cocked Colt. *"Wait!"*

Johnny blew a .45 round through the man's heart. He flung lead to his left and then his right, killing two more men closing on him from ten feet away. He killed another and another and wounded one more before he tossed away the empty pistol, grabbed another Colt from the cartridge belt of the dead man before him, stuffed the gun down behind the waistband of his pants, and scrambled up the slope. He grabbed Sheila and began climbing again, hearing the angry howls and wails and shrill curses of the killers behind him.

His sudden, turnabout attack had taken them flat-footed, and they were cowering now like chicken-killing dogs. As Johnny ran up the slope, weaving around covering boulders, the killers began firing on him again, hammering the slope and rocks around him with an angry barrage of lead.

"Ow!" Sheila cried as a bullet hammered a rock ahead of her.

Johnny shoved her into a cleft down and between two boulders—one about five feet tall and chair-shaped, the other shaped like a stock trough. He bellied down beside Sheila. A low hump of ground and a small, twisted shrub before them now offered a modicum of cover from the downslope.

"You all right?" Johnny asked Sheila as he grabbed the canvas knapsack hanging round his neck.

Sheila winced as she kept her chin low to the ground, and nodded. "Just a burn, as you call them. On my calf. I'll live . . . for the moment."

Johnny peered down the rocky slope. Several of the curly wolves were scrambling toward them. He saw Seville about thirty yards down and slightly right, scrambling off his hands and feet, occasionally off his knees, a pistol in one hand, a grimace on his sandy-bearded face with its slitted, devil's, perpetually leering eyes. The big, lumbering Raised-By-Wolves ran beside him, also shoving off his hands and knees. The Indian held a rifle.

Johnny raised the second Colt he'd taken off the dead man. Staying low, resting the Colt's barrel on the hump of ground before him, he narrowed an eye as he aimed at Seville. The outlaw saw him aiming the pistol, and dove behind a rock just as Johnny squeezed the Colt's trigger.

The bullet blew rock dust from the face of the man's cover.

Johnny had missed his target, but the shot had caused the others to go to ground, buying him and Sheila some time.

Seville gave a chortling laugh as he peered around the side of his rock. "You're done for, Shotgun Johnny! The girl's ours! The girl an' the gold! Step on out here and we'll kill you fast! Otherwise I'm gonna turn my pard Raised-By-Wolves loose on you, let him give ya what that fat old mountain man got! Oh, he died howlin', I tell you—didn't he, Wolves?"

Louis Raised-By-Wolves peered out from between two covering rocks. A red bandanna angled down over his left eye socket. He grinned and licked his lips then lifted his head and gave a wolflike howl.

Beside Johnny, Sheila shuddered.

"Come on out, Johnny!" Seville shouted again. "Them loads in that Greener are wet and no good, an' you know it! You're defenseless! That Colt ain't gonna hold us off for long!"

"When I'm out of forty-five shells," Johnny yelled, "I'll throw rocks!"

Several of the men, including Seville, laughed.

A couple triggered shots that plumed dust from the covering hump before Johnny and Sheila, blowing grit onto their hatless heads.

Johnny gave Sheila the Colt. "Trigger a shot down there, will ya? We gotta keep those wolves at bay for another minute or two."

Keeping her head low, Sheila snaked the Colt up over the lip of the hump, narrowed an eye, and fired.

"What're you doing?" she asked Johnny, then fired another round.

He'd pulled a square metal box from his knapsack. He flipped a clasp and opened the box. It was lined with paraffin, even the underside of the lid. Inside were ten shotgun wads, five on five.

"Backup ammunition for the Twins," Johnny said. "This is a watertight box. I've never had the chance to test it before, but it looks dry, all right."

"Ohhh," Sheila sang softly with approval. "Still, Johnny," she quickly added, "you're only one man against a dozen or so."

"Yeah, but we got the upper hand."

"If you mean the high ground . . ."

"No, I don't mean that." Johnny plucked out the spent wads from the left Twin, and replaced them with fresh, dry wads from the box. He snapped the left Twin closed and set it aside as Sheila triggered another shot down the slope, evoking an indignant curse from one of the wolves. "I mean," Johnny continued as he reloaded the right Twin, "that our situation is more desperate than theirs. You know what they say—the most desperate of prey are the ones to fear the most."

He picked up the right one.

"No, I didn't know they said that," Sheila said, squinting as she triggered two more rounds down the slope. "But now I do."

CHAPTER 36

"Pull back," Johnny told Sheila, placing his hand over the Colt in her right hand. He gave her a grave look. When she'd slid back and pulled her head down behind the hummock of covering ground, between the rocks, he said, "You'd best keep one pill in the wheel."

"Why's that?"

"In case I don't make it, you're gonna want one for yourself."

She blanched as she stared back at him, gave a slow, knowing nod. "Right."

"Keep your head down."

Johnny started to rise. Sheila grabbed his right arm. "Johnny . . ."

She stared at him.

He smiled.

"Hey," he said, letting the smile grow a little, reassuringly. "It's almost over."

"Yes," she said, wearily. "One way or another . . ."

Johnny scrambled to his feet and stepped out from between the rocks, holding the Twins outstretched in both hands, aiming down the slope. *"Come and get me, you stinky, ugly, hydrophobic curs!"*

One man had been scrambling up the slope to his left, crouching low, pressing a tongue to his lower lip as he climbed with stealth. Now he stopped and extended both pistols in his hands. Johnny's left-hand Twin cut him nearly in two and threw his mangled carcass wildly down the slope.

Another man appeared near where the first one had fallen, and Johnny blew the man's head off.

Quickly, he holstered the left-hand Twin, took the right one in both hands, dropped down the slope a few steps, and emptied the right-hand Twin into four men scrambling toward him on his right, triggering Winchesters. Several bullets whirred through the air around Johnny's head, one kissing the nap of his left shirtsleeve.

Ka-boom!

The shooters screamed as the two barrels of double-ought buck cut through them, shredding their upper chests and faces and throwing them down the slope, wailing.

Bullets came from both right and left and directly below now. Johnny threw himself forward and right down the slope. He hit the ground and rolled behind a small boulder, instantly breaking the right Twin and shaking out the spent wads. He'd stuffed the spare shells from the airtight box into his coat pockets.

Now he plucked out two and shoved them into the right Twin just in time to make a tall, dark-haired string bean wish he hadn't come up on Johnny's right side so fast, howling like a gut-shot coyote.

He was gut-shot, all right. A good bit of his buckshot-ruined belly plopped onto the ground at his feet just before he triggered his Henry rifle into his own left boot and rolled wildly back down the slope, tripping a man who'd been running up behind him.

"Oh, no!" the next man cried from hands and knees when he looked up see Johnny aiming the right Twin at him, the man's eyes snapping wide in horror.

The right Twin's second barrel ripped his head off his shoulders.

Johnny dropped flat on his back, head leaning up against the side of his covering boulder. Automatically, he reloaded the right Twin, looking around him desperately, expecting to see other wolves running toward him, shooting. He reloaded the left Twin. The right Twin lay on the ground to his right. He held the left Twin in both hands straight up and down before him, ready to draw more blood.

He glanced up the slope. Sheila gazed out from between the two rocks at him, eyes round and bright with fear. She jerked her chin up suddenly, scrunching up her eyes and screaming, *"Johnny!"*

Following the woman's fear-bright gaze, Johnny rose onto his butt, twisting around and extending the Twin in his hands. Two men were within three and five feet of his rock, both crouched low and wielding a Winchester and Spencer repeater respectively. They'd been about to shoot Johnny from over the top of his rock.

Now they went howling and kicking up dust and gravel in their own wild backward plunge down the slope as the rocketing report of Johnny's Twin vaulted out over the slope and the canyon below.

"Johnny!" Sheila screamed again.

He whipped around in time to see her stretch the Colt out to her left and trigger a shot down the slope. She hit none other than Louis Raised-By-Wolves his own nasty self, as the man had tried to steal around on Johnny's left.

Now the big Indian grunted and cursed, grabbing his left leg as he dropped stiffly down behind a rock maybe fifteen feet away from where Johnny crouched behind his own covering boulder.

"The other side!" Sheila warned.

Johnny whipped around, dropping the empty Twin and raising the charged one. Three men stormed toward him as another man shouted from cover, "Take him, boys! Take him!"

They fired rifles and pistols. One slammed into Johnny's left arm. It felt like a sledgehammer blow. Another bullet sliced across his right ear. He tripped one of the Twin's triggers, and the nearest attacker dropped to his knees, firing his pistol into the ground, cursing.

Johnny raised the Twin a little higher and slid it slightly left.

Ka-boom!

That crumpled the other two, one dropping his rifle and clawing at his tomato-red face before he went down, also howling and writhing.

Johnny faced across the slope to the south. He spied movement to his left and wheeled.

Sheila must have seen Seville at the same time, for again she screamed.

"Uh-uh." Harry Seville stood seven feet down slope from Johnny, aiming down the barrel of his cocked Colt's revolving rifle at Johnny's head. He grinned his devil's grin, green eyes glinting menacingly between slitted lids. "You're out, Shotgun Johnny. I was countin' your loads. You done killed most of my men . . . an' I thank you for that. More gold for me . . . once I finish off ole Poindexter. But you're bone-dry"—he widened his grin—"and about to die . . ."

"Johnny!" Sheila screamed, now standing up the slope behind him and on his left, the empty Colt hanging low by her side. One hand covered her mouth in horror.

Johnny grimaced against the pain of the bullet in his arm. The wound bit him deep. He could feel it all the way down to his toes. "P-Poindexter?" he asked, frowning. "He was your inside man . . ."

"Sure. Every good outlaw needs an insider. Ole Poindexter was ours. You know, I believe the damn fool actually believed we were gonna share that gold with him, and he was gonna ride off into the sunset a very rich man heading for a very comfortable retirement overseas somewheres."

"One's born every day."

"Shoulda stayed a drunk, Johnny," the outlaw said with a snorting laugh. "You'd have lived longer."

Seville steadied the Colt's barrel at Johnny's forehead. Johnny held his breath, awaiting the bullet.

Harry drew a breath and held it. He squeezed the trigger. Johnny watched the movement. It was like watching the executioner swing the lever that would drop the gallows door out from beneath your boots.

Only, the door didn't open. The rifle clicked on an empty chamber.

"What the . . . ?" Seville lowered the rifle and stared down at it, his jaw hanging in shock.

"Empty," Johnny said, smiling. The fool might have counted Johnny's shots, but he hadn't counted his own.

Seville looked at him, his eyes wide now in exasperation. He dropped the rifle like a hot potato and reached for the two Colt pistols bristling on his hips. Suppressing the pain in his wounded arm, Johnny lunged toward the man and swung the butt of his Twin against Seville's right temple. Harry fell, dropping both pistols he'd just pulled free of their leathers. He fell and rolled down the slope.

Johnny followed him down. Seville rolled up against a rock, on his back, and lifted his head and his dusty beard, glaring up at Johnny moving toward him carefully, staggering a little from pain and blood loss. He moved sideways down the slope, plowing rocks and gravel before him.

He stopped before Seville. Blood oozed from the nasty gash on the killer's temple.

"You devil," Johnny said, remembering how the man had flanked him and shot him and left him for dead while Raised-By-Wolves had tortured and killed Bear Musgrave. "You're finished."

Seville pushed up on his elbows. Once again, his eyes slitted devilishly, and his bearded face swelled with rage as he shouted hoarsely, "Get on with it, then, you son of Satan!"

"Be happy to."

Johnny bashed the butt of the Twin against Seville's right temple once more. It was a solid blow made even more gratifying by the cracking sound it evoked from the killer's shattered skull. Seville's head whipped sharply left and down, and the outlaw lay writhing a little as he died, blood welling up through his mouth to dribble down his bearded chin.

He grunted, groaned, blinked his eyes rapidly, then lay still with a long, ragged, final sigh.

Johnny blew out his own relieved breath.

A large shadow slid across the ground beside him.

Sheila screamed.

Johnny whipped to his left as Louis Raised-By-Wolves threw his hulking, broad-shouldered body toward Johnny. Johnny dropped the Twin and reached up with both hands to grab the right wrist of Raised-By-Wolves, who wielded a big, savage bowie knife in that hand. The hooked tip angled down toward Johnny's right eye, threatening to carve it out like Johnny had carved out the Indian's left eye with buckshot.

Johnny grunted as the big man's powerful body bulled him straight backward. He struck the slope hard, his breath punched violently from his lungs. Instantly, he weakened. Raised-By-Wolves had no trouble wrenching his own wrist free of Johnny's grip.

He grinned as he straddled Johnny, his lone, molasses dark eye flashing in the sunlight. He raised the bowie up in front of Johnny's face, then repositioned himself slightly on Johnny's prone body. Johnny tried to fight, but he had no fight left in him. He felt as ragged as an empty burlap sack.

He was finished.

"Now," Wolves said, smiling, his sour breath blowing against Johnny's face, "you're gonna die just like that old man did. Slow!"

Laughing, Wolves lowered his right hand and started to thrust the Bowie's razor-edged tip toward Johnny's right side, angling it toward the soft flesh below the ribs. Johnny stared up at the one-eyed man. He tried to sit up, but it was no good.

Wolves chuckled knowingly, enjoying himself. His expression changed, however, as blood sprayed from the savage's right ear, warm droplets grazing Johnny's left cheek.

"*Ach!*" Wolves dropped his knife and swiped at his ear with his right hand. He looked at his bloody hand, and then he frowned down at Johnny as though Johnny had said something the big Indian couldn't understand.

Johnny saw that the man's ear was no longer where it should be. It lay in shreds on the gravel beside them both.

Wolves sagged off Johnny and rolled onto his back, cupping his right hand over the bloody ear—or what was left of it.

Johnny stared straight up to see another figure move toward him.

Sheila stopped on the slope over Raised-By-Wolves. Her eyes were hard. Her hair was a messy, dusty, chestnut cascade around her face and over her shoulders. She held a smoking Remington revolver in her right hand.

Wolves stared up at her. He gave an enraged, bellowing wail. It was the exclamation of an exasperated bear. He thrashed his legs out, trying to kick her, but she was on the upslope from him, glaring coldly down at him. He reached for a pistol on his cartridge belt but stayed the movement when Sheila raised the Remington, clicking back the hammer.

Wolves froze, staring up at her in silent fury and horror.

"This is for my father, you savage dog," Sheila said tautly, quietly. "This is for Mister Musgrave."

The Remington roared.

Wolves's head jerked back against the ground with a thud. He lay squirming like a bug on a pin as his life bled out through the hole between his eyes.

Sheila knelt beside Johnny, staring down at him, her eyes raking his bloody, battered, and beaten, six-and-a-half-foot frame.

Her gaze met his. Johnny drew a breath, licked his lips, winced against the pain. Dryly, he said, "I told you to save one for yourself."

She pressed a lock of his hair back from his sweaty, dirty forehead, and placed her hand against his cheek. "Hey," she said, fighting back an onslaught of exhausted tears. "Who's the boss here?"

CHAPTER 37

It wasn't until a week later that Johnny and Sheila rode down out of the mountains and into the outskirts of Hallelujah Junction, trailing the two gold-bearing pack mules they'd confiscated back from the dead Seville and Raised-By-Wolves bunch.

They'd both needed a week to recuperate from their injuries.

Fortunately, they'd been assisted on their road to recovery by the Russian widow of an old prospector who served as a midwife to many women around that neck of the mountains, along the Avalanche River, and knew her way around a bullet wound or two, as well. Johnny and Sheila had holed up for several days in the stout old pipe-smoking woman's cabin, being tended like a king and queen while the woman herself, Marina Akhmatova, bustled about her tidy little hovel, smoking, swigging tea, humming jovial Old World dance songs, and cooking and cleaning while her old dog and cats napped on colorful rugs in the sunshine angling through the cabin's scrubbed windows.

Mrs. Akhmatova had applied fresh poultices every

day for three days to Johnny's arm, after she'd dug out the bullet. By now, while the wound was painful, it felt on the same road to recovery as the rest of him did. He rode with it now in the sling Mrs. Akhmatova had fashioned out of a clean cotton sheet, glancing around at the town partly hidden by the late-day shadows drawing out from the business buildings lining both sides of Paiute Street.

Johnny glanced at Sheila riding on his right atop her filly, which, along with Ghost, had followed their riders on their wending way down the Avalanche. Sheila had spied the loyal mounts after she'd helped Johnny out of that intersecting canyon and onto the bank of the river, which is where Marina Akhmatova had soon found them while she'd been out checking her fish traps with her dog at her heels.

"Feel good to be home?" Johnny asked the beautifully tanned young woman who was looking around with a wistful expression on her heart-shaped, brown-eyed face, her thick chestnut hair pulled back in a loose mare's tail that trailed down her slender back, over the light coat she wore.

She turned to Johnny, gazed at him for a moment, pondering her answer, then seemed surprised to say, "Yes. Yes, I do, in fact. And"—she gazed around again at her rustic surroundings cloaked in the fragrant smoke of early supper fires—"it *is* starting to feel like home."

As they approached the bank on the right, Johnny checked Ghost down to a stop and Sheila followed suit beside him. They both stared ahead at where George Poindexter was just then stepping out of the bank and pausing to lock the door behind him.

The stout man in his sixties was dressed in a long,

black wool coat against the pronounced chill that had entered the air now as fall had descended the lower elevations. A black beaver hat was snugged down on his gray, round-faced, bespectacled head.

"Oh, George," Sheila said tightly, mostly to herself, beside Johnny. She stared hard at the man, narrowing her eyes with a long-simmering wrath, filling up her lungs with a tense breath.

She was reflecting on the man's betrayal of her father, Johnny knew.

"Oh, George," she said again, her voice as taut as razor wire.

"Yeah," Johnny said, staring at the man, as well. "Oh, George."

Poindexter had just turned from the door to his horse and buggy parked in front of the bank, facing in the opposite direction of Johnny and Sheila. The Bank & Trust's vice-president stopped suddenly and turned toward them sitting their horses fifty yards beyond. He froze, lifting his head slightly, staring. Even from this distance, Johnny could see the dark surprise entering the man's gaze, behind his glinting round spectacles.

Johnny and Sheila were the last two people he'd expected to see riding down out of those mountains. He'd likely been impatiently awaiting word from Seville that Johnny and Sheila were dead, that the last load of bullion was secure in the outlaws' hands, and that they were ready to split up the plunder and go their own separate ways.

Sheila put her filly forward. "Hold up, George," she called. "We'd like a word."

Johnny nudged Ghost ahead, as well.

Poindexter lurched forward, throwing the valise

he was carrying into his covered buggy. He grabbed something off the buggy floor and swung around, raising a silver-chased pistol in both his black-gloved hands. Johnny heard the hammer click back.

"Sheila!" He booted Ghost up fast and hard, ramming the cream into the side of Sheila's filly.

Poindexter fired three quick shots, gritting his teeth and cursing. The revolver's cracks cut angrily through the late-afternoon quiet of the nearly deserted street. "Damn you!" he bellowed.

The bullets screeched around where Johnny leaned toward the filly, shielding Sheila's body with his own torso. The lead shattered glass behind him, and thudded into awning support posts. Poindexter cursed again, then leaped clumsily, heavily into the buggy's right side, the wheeled contraption jouncing with his weight.

Johnny turned to Sheila crouched over her saddle horn, and said, "Are you hit?"

Sheila looked at him, red-faced. She shook her head. "No." She saw one of the ten-gauges in Johnny's right hand, and said, "Try not to kill him, Johnny! I want him to answer for what he's done!"

Johnny turned to stare up the street down which Poindexter was breaking away in the covered buggy, whipping his reins against the back of the horse in the traces and yelling, "Hi-yahhh! Hi-yahhh, there—*go, horse!*"

Johnny holstered the Twin and turned back to Sheila. "You stay here!"

He took Ghost's reins in his right hand and, his left arm angled across his belly, secured by its sling, booted the cream on down the street and into the dust of the fleeing banker. He was within a few yards of the buggy when Poindexter was at the edge of town and following the stage road along the north bank of the Paiute River, between rows of golden aspens.

Johnny pulled up to the wagon's left rear wheel and shouted, "Check it down, Poindexter. It's over. You can't outrun my horse, you fool!"

The beefy, bespectacled man poked his head out the buggy's left side and shouted, "Leave me alone or I'll shoot you. I swear I will!!" He was half-crazed with anxiety, his craggy face flushed and swollen. The thought of hanging had him in a full panic.

He snaked the pistol, clutched in his right hand, out of the buggy and back across his left shoulder. The maw lapped smoke and flames. Johnny ducked as the bullet caromed past his left cheek. Poindexter fired again, and again, then cursed and threw the empty pistol out of the buggy and turned his head forward, again shaking the reins over the horse's back and bellowing.

Johnny took Ghost's reins in his teeth and drew his right Twin from its holster. Riding up fast off the buggy's rear corner, he aimed down at the left rear wheel and triggered the left barrel. The buckshot chewed into the wheel's felloe, tearing out several spokes. The wheel wobbled dangerously then broke away, the buggy lurching down onto the left side of its rear axle.

Poindexter screamed just as the horse gave a frightened whinny. The banker came hurtling out of the buggy and onto the trail, rolling, while the horse dragged the buggy off down the trace, following a slow right curve along the river. Dust wafted around the banker, who lay crumpled now in the brush along the trail, in a patch of aspen shade.

As Johnny checked Ghost down and leaped out of the saddle, the banker rolled onto his back, grabbing his left knee with both hands. "My ankle!" Poindexter cried. "Oh, it's my ankle. It's broken!"

Johnny strode up to the dusty, bedraggled man, whose glasses hung from his right ear, one lens cracked. He'd lost his hat, and his thin gray hair was mussed around the nearly bald crown of his skull. His gray mustache and goatee were caked with dust.

"Oh, God! Oh, God!" the banker cried, his face a swollen red mask of misery.

Hoof thuds rose behind Johnny. He glanced over his shoulder. Sheila was galloping up behind him. As she drew rein several feet away, Johnny turned back to the howling banker.

"Where is it?" he asked.

"My ankle! I need the doctor! Oh, please fetch the doctor! It hurts miserably!"

Sheila dismounted and walked over to stand beside Johnny. "George," she said, shaking her head slowly. "I didn't want to believe it. I *didn't* believe it until I heard it from Seville himself."

Poindexter looked at her with feigned incredulity. "Heard *what* from Seville?"

"That you were his inside man," Johnny said.

Poindexter glared at the tall man standing over him. "Go to hell! You're nothin' but a drunken Basque!"

"Don't make it any worse for yourself, George," Sheila said, dropping to a knee beside him, staring down at him in mute rage and befuddlement. "How could you do that to my father? You were friends. For a long time . . . you were friends!"

"Look!" the banker yelled hoarsely. "Your father was not a good operator. He was losing his memory, and he was making bad investments. I tried to tell him, but he wouldn't listen. Even when he did listen, by the next day he'd forgotten our conversation!"

"So you thought you'd help him along on the road to *ruin*?" Sheila asked disbelievingly.

Poindexter gazed at her with a helpless expression. He turned away, sheepish. "You don't understand. Claudia's medical bills . . . God, I'd lost practically everything. I was desperate, you see! *Desperate!*"

"Desperate enough to double-cross a man who made you what you are," Sheila said. It wasn't a question. It was a statement of fact that she was trying to wrap her mind around. She, too, had been so thoroughly fooled by the fatherly old man, George Poindexter.

"Please," the banker cried. "My ankle is broken terribly. You must fetch the doctor for me!"

"Only after you've told us where the rest of the gold is." Johnny stepped up, sliding his shadow menacingly over the sobbing man, who lay back against the ground now, breathing hard and sweating.

A mulish defiance swept over Poindexter's features. He hardened his jaws as he glared up at Johnny and said, "*No!* Go to hell! You'll make sure I hang! I'll be *damned* if I'll tell you where it is!"

Johnny sighed. He took another step forward and dropped to a knee near the banker's already-swollen ankle. "Let me take a look there."

"Oh, Johnny," Sheila said. "Please don't . . ."

But all Johnny had to do was wrap his hand

around the banker's ankle and begin to squeeze before the cowardly Poindexter spilled everything— the exact location of the vacant mine shaft only three miles from Hallelujah Junction in which Seville's bunch had stowed away the looted gold behind a heavy padlocked timber door. Poindexter had one of two keys to the padlock; he wore it on a chain around his neck, under his shirt.

More hoof thuds rose from the direction of town.

Johnny and Sheila rose and turned to see a man galloping toward them on a bay horse. A five-pointed star winked on the man's brown leather vest. Marshal Jonah Flagg reined the mount up near Sheila's filly and stared curiously down at Johnny, Sheila, and the moaning and groaning banker.

He shot a nasty glare at Johnny and said, "You again!"

Johnny poked his hat back off his forehead and hooked an ironic half-grin. "Me again."

Flagg glanced at Sheila, and the lawman flushed a little, then pinched his hat brim to the woman. "Miss Sheila. I was worried about you . . ."

"Why, thank you, Marshal. I'm fine. I believe Johnny . . . er, I mean *Mister Greenway* and I have solved the mystery of the mine's stolen gold." She glanced at Johnny, blushing a little.

"Mister Greenway, eh?" Flagg said, silently scoffing and firing another accusatory glare at the tall, dark man with his left arm in a sling. Then turning back to Sheila, frowning skeptically, the marshal said, "You *have*?"

"We'll explain in good time," Sheila assured the man. "In the meantime, Mister Poindexter has had an accident. Would you please fetch the doctor and his buckboard?"

Flagg gave an offended chuff. "What am I? Just an *errand boy?*"

He looked from Sheila to Johnny and back again. Neither said anything.

Finally, Flagg said, *"Bahh!"* then neck-reined the bay around and galloped back in the direction of town.

Johnny looked around, then turned to Sheila. "Hey, where are the mules?"

Sheila shrugged. "Where you left them when you went after Mister Poindexter, I suppose. They should be safe for now." She stepped up to Johnny, wrapped her arms around his waist, and smiled up at him. "If not, I know a man who can run them down."

Johnny brushed his thumb playfully across her nose. "As I remember, I told you to stay put."

"Hey!" Sheila pulled his hat brim down over his eyes. "Who's the boss here?"

TURN THE PAGE FOR AN EXCITING PREVIEW!

JOHNSTONE COUNTRY.
WITH A DETOUR THROUGH HELL.

**Legendary gunfighter Perley Gates always fights
on the side of the angels. But in the East Texas
county of Angelina, the war is half over—
and the devils are winning . . .**

In spite of his holy-sounding name, Perley Gates is
not his brother's keeper. Even so, he can't refuse a
simple request by his elder brother, Rubin. Rubin is
starting his own cattle ranch, and he wants Perley to
deliver the contract for it—through a lawless stretch
of land called Angelina County. Perley can't blame his
brother for wanting a piece of the American Dream.
But for the famed gunslinger, it means a nightmare
journey through hell itself . . .

The trouble starts when Perley and his men meet
some damsels in distress—a lovely group of saloon girls
with a broken wagon wheel. Being a Good Samaritan,
Perley feels honor bound to help them. But when the
travelers cross paths with an ornery gang of vicious
outlaws, things turn deadly—and fast. It only gets
worse from there. Angelina County is infested with
a special breed of vermin known as the Tarpley family.
And this corrupt clan has a gunslinger of their own—
who'd love nothing more than to take down a living
legend like Perley Gates . . .

**National Bestselling Authors
William W. Johnstone and J.A. Johnstone**

**THE LONESOME GUN
A Perley Gates Western**

On sale now wherever Pinnacle Books are sold.

Live Free. Read Hard.
www.williamjohnstone.net

Visit us at www.kensingtonbooks.com

CHAPTER 1

"Becky, another hungry customer just walked in," Lucy Tate said. "I'm getting some more coffee for my tables. Can you wait on him? He looks like trouble." She looked at Beulah Walsh and winked, so Beulah knew she was up to some mischief.

"I was just fixing to wash up some more cups," Becky said. "We're about to run out of clean ones. Can he wait a minute?"

"I don't know," Lucy answered. "He looks like he's the impatient kind. He might make a big scene if somebody doesn't wait on him pretty quick."

"I don't want to make a customer mad," Beulah said as she aimed a mischievous grin in Lucy's direction. "Maybe I can go get him seated."

"Oh, my goodness, no," Becky said. "I'll go take care of him." She was sure there was no reason why Lucy couldn't have taken care of a new customer, instead of causing Beulah to do it. Beulah was busy enough as cook and owner. She dried her hands on a dishtowel and hurried out into the hotel dining room. Lucy and Beulah hurried right after her as far as the door, where they stopped to watch Becky's reaction.

"Perley!" Becky exclaimed joyfully, and ran to meet him. Surprised by her exuberance, he staggered a couple of steps when she locked her arms around his neck. "I thought you were never coming home," she said. "You didn't say you were gonna be gone so long."

"I didn't think I would be," Perley said. "We were just supposed to deliver a small herd of horses to a ranch near Texarkana, but we ran into some things we hadn't counted on, and that held us up pretty much. I got back as quick as I could. Sonny Rice went with Possum and me, and he ain't back yet." She started to ask why, but he said, "I'll tell you all about it, if you'll get me something to eat."

"Sit down, sweetie," she said, "and I'll go get you started." He looked around quickly to see if anyone had heard what she called him, but it was too late. He saw Lucy and Beulah grinning at him from the kitchen door. Becky led him to a table right outside the kitchen door and sat him down while she went to get his coffee. "I was just washing up some cups when you came in. I must have known I needed a nice clean cup for someone special."

He was both delighted and embarrassed over the attention she gave him. And he wanted to tell her he'd prefer that she didn't do it in public, but he was afraid he might hurt her feelings if he did. Unfortunately, Lucy and Beulah were not the only witnesses to Becky's show of affection for the man she had been not so secretly in love with for a couple of years.

Finding it especially entertaining, two drifters on their way to Indian Territory across the Red River spoke up when Becky came back with Perley's coffee.

"Hey, darlin'," Rafer Samson called out, "bring that coffeepot out here. Sweetie ain't the only one that wants coffee. You'd share some of that coffee, wouldn't you, Sweetie?"

"Dang, Rafer," his partner joined in. "You'd best watch what you're sayin'. Ol' Sweetie might not like you callin' him that. He might send that waitress over here to take care of you."

That was as far as they got before Lucy stepped in to put a stop to it. "Listen, fellows, why don't you give it a rest? Don't you like the way I've been taking care of you? We've got a fresh pot of coffee brewing on the stove right now. I'll make sure you get the first cups poured out of it, all right?"

"I swear," Rafer said. "Does he always let you women do the talkin' for him?"

"Listen, you two boneheads," Lucy warned, "I'm trying to save you from going too far with what you might think is fun. Don't force Perley Gates into something that you don't wanna be any part of."

"Ha!" Rafer barked. "Who'd you say? Pearly somethin'?"

"It doesn't matter," Lucy said, realizing she shouldn't have spoken Perley's name. "You two look old enough to know how to behave. Don't start any trouble. Just eat your dinner, and I'll see that you get fresh coffee as soon as it's ready."

But Rafer was sure he had touched a sensitive spot the women in the dining room held for the mild-looking young man. "What did she call him, Deke? Pearly somethin'?"

"Sounded like she said Pearly Gates," Deke answered. "I swear it did."

"Pearly Gates!" Rafer blurted loud enough for everyone in the dining room to hear. "His mama named him Pearly Gates!"

Lucy made one more try. "All right, you've had your fun. He's got an unusual name. How about dropping it now, outta respect for the rest of the folks eating their dinner in here?"

"To hell with the rest of the folks in here," he responded, seeming to take offense. "I'll say what I damn-well please. It ain't up to you, no how. If he don't like it, he knows where I'm settin'."

Lucy could see she was getting nowhere. "You keep it up, and you're liable to find out a secret that only the folks in Paris, Texas, know. And you ain't gonna like it."

"Thanks for the warnin', darlin'. I surely don't want to learn his secret. Now go get us some more coffee." As soon as she walked away, he called out, "Hey, tater, is your name Pearly Gates?"

Knowing he could ignore the two no longer, Perley answered. "That's right," he said. "I was named after my grandpa. Perley was his name. It sounds like the Pearly Gates up in Heaven, but it ain't spelt the same."

"Well, you gotta be some kinda sweet little girlie-boy to walk around with a name like that," Rafer declared. "Ain't that right, Deke?"

"That's right, Rafer," Deke responded like a puppet. "A real man wouldn't have a name like that."

"I know you fellows are just havin' a little fun with

my name, but I'd appreciate it if you'd stop now. I don't mind it all that much, but I think it upsets my fiancée."

Perley's request caused both his antagonists to pause for a moment. "It upsets his what?" Deke asked.

"I don't know," Rafer answered, "his fi-ant-cee, whatever that is. Maybe it's a fancy French word for his behind. We upset his behind." He turned to look at the few other customers in the dining room, none of whom would meet his eye. "We upset his fancy behind."

"I'm sorry, Becky," Perley said. "I sure didn't mean to cause all this trouble. Tell Beulah I'll leave, and they oughta calm down after I'm gone."

Beulah was standing just inside the kitchen door, about ready to put an end to the disturbance, and she heard what Perley said. "You'll do no such thing," she told him. "Lucy shouldn't have told 'em your name. You sit right there and let Becky get your dinner." She walked out of the kitchen then and went to the table by the front door where the customers deposited their firearms while they ate. She picked up the two gun belts that Rafer and Deke had left there, took them outside, and dropped them on the steps. When she came back inside, she went directly to their table and informed them. "I'm gonna have to ask you to leave now, since your mamas didn't teach you how to behave in public. I put your firearms outside the door. There won't be any charge for what you ate if you get up and go right now."

"The hell you say," Rafer replied. "We'll leave when we're good and ready."

"I can't have you upsettin' my other customers," Beulah said. "So do us all the courtesy of leaving

peacefully, and like I said, I won't charge you nothin
for what you ate."

"You threw our guns out the door?" Deke re
sponded in disbelief. He thought about what she sai
for only a brief moment, then grabbed his fork an
started shoveling huge forkfuls of food in his mout
as fast as he could. He washed it all down with th
remainder of his coffee, wiped his mouth with hi
sleeve, and belched loudly. "Let's go, Rafer."

"I ain't goin' nowhere till I'm ready, and I ain
ready right now," Rafer said, and remained seated a
the table. "If you're through, go out there and ge
our guns offa them steps."

"Lucy," Beulah said, "Step in the hotel lobby an
tell David we need the sheriff."

"Why, you ol' witch!" Rafer spat. "I oughta give yo
somethin' to call the sheriff about!" He stood up an
pushed his chair back, knocking it over in the proces

That was as far as Perley could permit it to go. H
got up and walked over to face Rafer. "You heard th
lady," he said. "This is her place of business, an
she don't want you and your friend in here. So wh
don't you two just go on out like she said, and ther
won't be any need to call the sheriff up here."

Rafer looked at him in total disbelief. Then a s
smile spread slowly across his face. "Why don't you g
outside with me?"

"What for?" Perley asked, even though he kne
full well the reason for the invitation.

"Oh, I don't know. Just to see what happens,
reckon." Finding a game that amused him now, h
continued. "Do you wear a gun, Perley?"

"I've got a gun on the table with the others,
Perley answered. "I don't wear it in here."

"Are you fast with that gun?" When Perley reacted as if he didn't understand, Rafer said, "When you draw it outta your holster, can you draw it real fast?" Because of Perley's general air of innocence, Rafer assumed he was slow of wit as well.

"Yes," Perley answered honestly, "but I would only do so in an emergency."

"That's good," Rafer said, "because this is an emergency. You wanna know what the emergency is? When I step outside and strap my gun on, if you ain't outside with me, I'm gonna come back inside and shoot this place to pieces. That's the emergency. You see, I don't cotton to nobody tellin' me to get outta here."

"All right," Perley said. "I understand why you're upset. I'll come outside with you, and we'll talk about this like reasonable men should."

"Two minutes!" Rafer blurted. "Then if you ain't outside, I'm comin' in after you." He walked out the door with Deke right behind him.

Becky rushed to Perley's side as he went to the table to get his gun belt. "Perley, don't go out there. You're not going to let that monster draw you into a gunfight, are you?"

"I really hope not," Perley told her. "I think maybe I can talk some sense into him and his friend. But I had to get him out of here. He was gettin' too abusive. Don't worry, I'll be all right. He oughta be easier to talk to when he doesn't have an audience."

He strapped his Colt .44 on and walked outside to find Rafer and Deke waiting. Seeing the expressions of gleeful anticipation on both faces, Perley could not help a feeling of uncertainty. If he had looked behind him, he would have seen everyone in the dining room gathered at the two windows on that side of the building, that is, everyone except Becky and Beulah. All of the spectators were confident of the unassuming young man's gift of speed with a hand-gun. As far as Perley was concerned, his lightning-fast reactions were just that, a gift. For he never practiced with a weapon, and he honestly had no idea why his brain and body just reacted with no conscious direction from himself. Because of that, he was of the opinion that it could just as easily leave him with no warning. And that was one reason why he always tried to avoid pistol duels whenever possible. He took a deep breath and hoped for the best.

"I gotta admit, I had my doubts if you had the guts to walk out that door," Rafer said when Perley came toward them. Aside to Deke, he said, "If this sucker beats me, shoot him." Deke nodded.

"Why do you wanna shoot me?" Perley asked him. "You've never seen me before today. I've done you no wrong. It doesn't make any sense for you and me to try to kill each other."

"The hell you ain't done me no wrong," Rafer responded. "You walked up to my table and told me to get outta there. I don't take that from any man."

"If you're honest with yourself, you have to admit that you started all the trouble when you started makin' fun of my name. I was willin' to call that just some innocent fun, and I still am. So, we could just forget this whole idea to shoot each other and get on with the things that matter. And that's just to get along with strangers on a courteous basis. I'm willing to forget the whole trouble if you are. Whaddaya say? It's not worth shootin' somebody over."

"I swear, the more I hear comin' outta your mouth, the more I feel like I gotta puke. I think I'll shoot you just like I'd shoot a dog that's gone crazy. One thing I can't stand is a man too yellow to stand up for himself. I'm gonna count to three, and you'd better be ready to draw your weapon when I say three 'cause I'm gonna cut you down."

"This doesn't make any sense at all," Perley said. "I don't have any reason to kill you."

"One!" Rafer counted.

"Don't do this," Perley pleaded, and turned to walk away.

"Two!" Rafer counted.

"I'm warnin' you, don't say three."

"Three!" Rafer exclaimed defiantly, his six-gun already halfway out when he said it, and he staggered backward from the impact of the bullet in his chest. Deke, shocked by Perley's instant response, was a second slow in reacting and dropped his weapon when Perley's second shot caught him in his right shoulder. He stood, helplessly waiting for Perley's fatal shot, and almost sinking to his knees when Perley released the hammer and returned his pistol to his holster.

"There wasn't any sense to that," Perley said. "Your friend is dead because of that foolishness, and you better go see Bill Simmons about your shoulder. He's the barber, but he also does some doctorin'. We ain't got a doctor in town yet. You'd best just stand there for a minute, though, 'cause I see the sheriff runnin' this way." Deke remained where he was, his eyes still glazed with the shock of seeing Rafer cut down so swiftly. Perley walked over and picked up

Deke's gun, broke the cylinder open, and extracted all the cartridges. Then he dropped it into Deke's holster.

"Perley," Paul McQueen called out as he approached. "What's the trouble? Who's that?" he asked, pointing to the body on the ground, before giving Perley time to answer his first question.

"I think I heard his friend call him Rafer," Perley said. "Is that right?" he asked Deke.

Deke nodded, then said, "Rafer Samson."

"Rafer Samson," McQueen repeated. "I'll see if I've got any paper on him, but I expect you could save me the trouble," he said to Deke. "What's your name?"

"Deke Johnson," he replied. "You ain't got no paper on me. Me and Rafer was just passin' through on the way to the Red."

"I don't expect I do," McQueen said, "at least by that name, anyway. You were just passin' through, and figured you might as well cause a little trouble while you were at it, right?" He knew without having to ask that Perley didn't cause the trouble. "How bad's that shoulder?"

Deke nodded toward Perley. "He put a bullet in it."

"You musta gone to a helluva lot of trouble to get him to do that," the sheriff remarked. "Perley, you wanna file any charges on him?" Perley said that he did not. "All right," McQueen continued. "I won't lock you up, and we can go see Bill Simmons about that shoulder. Bill's a barber, but he also does some doctorin', and he's our undertaker, too. He's doctored a lotta gunshots, so he'll fix you up so you can ride. Then I want you out of town. Is that understood?"

"Yessir," Deke replied humbly.

"Perley, you gonna be in town a little while?" Mc-Queen asked. When Perley said that he was, McQueen told him he'd like to hear the whole story of the incident. "I'll tell Bill to send Bill Jr. to pick up Mr. Samson." He looked around him as several spectators from down the street started coming to gawk at the body. "You mind stayin' here a while to watch that body till Bill Jr. gets here with his cart?"

"Reckon not," Perley said.

Bill Jr. responded pretty quickly, so it was only a few minutes before Perley saw him come out of the alley beside the barbershop, pushing his hand cart. Perley helped him lift Rafer's body up on the cart. "Sheriff said he called you out," Bill Jr. said. "They don't never learn, do they?" Perley wasn't sure how to answer that, so he didn't.

Visit our website at
KensingtonBooks.com
to sign up for our newsletters, read
more from your favorite authors, see
books by series, view reading group
guides, and more!

BOOK   CLUB
BETWEEN THE CHAPTERS

Become a Part of Our
Between the Chapters Book Club
Community and Join the Conversation

Betweenthechapters.net